FLAMES OF ARTSAKH

ISBN 1-878696-2-5

Printed in the United States of America

FLAMES OF ARTSAKH

Peter Khanbegian

Wright Publishing House
Goff Falls Road, Box 243, Manchester, NH 03108

WRIGHT PUBLISHING HOUSE
BOX 243
WINDHAM, N.H.
03087

To all the Armenian women
who fought for their families,
homes and values with unswerving
heroism and courage—yesterday,
today and in future.

PART ONE

BOSTON-WASHINGTON

1

"Shall we know once more your glorious past
meadowlands and mountains rising
Artsakh—ancient Motherland . . ."
—Songs of the Homeland—

An east wind blowing in from the Charles River chilled the morning air
air as it swept along the concrete corridors of Boston. The skyline stood
somberly grey, before sunlight broke through the overcast, suddenly
drenching the city with warm light. Along the esplanade, two people
jogging in easy rhythm glanced occasionally at each other and smiled.
Lance Bagdasarian was thoughtful as he quickly caught a side glimpse
of his wife, Karamine, who kept pace with him, after a full mile. Has it
really been fifteen years since we were married, he thought; it seems like
only yesterday we were both in college, and had just met at the Armenian Cultural Club.

"Why are you smiling?" Karamine asked, her breath coming in
short gasps, "you think I can't keep up with you, huh?"

"You kidding? You can probably outpace me," Lance quipped with
a good natured laugh. "I was just thinking how long it's been since we
met at the university and what a couple of hot-headed idealists we were
then." He laughed again. "Hey . . . here's a bench, let's take a break, and
enjoy the view of the river."

"Well I wouldn't go so far as to call us hot-heads, Lance," Karamine
commented, dropping to the bench beside him. "Besides, we haven't exactly lost our ideals for the future of our Armenian people, have we?"

"You know I didn't mean that, Karamine. I was thinking more of
you and me, and of what seemed to be such irreconcilable differences

3

between us at that time . . . have you forgotten? You didn't even think I was Armenian . . . an *odar* (other nationality) in the wrong place." Lance laughed again and touched her hand affectionately. "I guess I fell in love with you that first moment, but was too blind and headstrong to admit it. I certainly never thought we could resolve our differences . . . me the given radical and revolutionary, and you with your doctrine of love and forgiveness."

A soft smile traced Karamine's features. "I often think of that night we met, Lance, and wonder what would have happened had you not come to the meeting. Just think . . . we may never have met . . . no . . . no," she added, decidedly shaking her head, "we would have met, somehow, somewhere . . . I just know it."

"Predestination, right?" Lance teased.

"Why not? There is such a thing, you know. Aren't you even mildly interested in the possibility?"

"No, not really. I'll deal with each possibility as it comes along and let God decide the future. I don't want to know what's in store for me, since I'm not able to change it anyway."

"Well, I still think we were meant to meet and it was one chance in a million we did. Our lives have certainly been better for it . . . these last years have been terrific . . . you've got your radio program, and I've got my work at the children's hospital, which is almost completely fulfilling." Karamine paused a moment, then, distractedly bent down to retie her shoelace.

"Almost? What do you mean almost, Karamine?" I thought you were completely happy over there in pediatrics."

"You know I am, Lance," Karamine interrupted quickly. "It's just that I've never been able to completely release that old longing and frustration to have a child of my own, that's all. I know, I know . . . we've been over it a hundred times and it's difficult for you to understand why it should still bother me, but it does, Lance, it does. I just keep asking why and wondering. God knows we've tried enough approaches and remedies. I was so positive that my change of careers from business to medicine, especially becoming a children's doctor was the answer. But, it's not, and there are still times when I have to admit I feel cheated and barren." She bit her lip slightly to control the flood of emotion the subject always evoked.

Lance took her hand. "Look, Karamine," he said gently, "there's still the option of adopting one of those Armenian orphans; I haven't brought it up lately because it always upsets you. Besides, I thought you were contented now that you have your work with the children."

Karamine shook her head. "No . . . it's not quite enough. I want our own child, Lance, yours and mine . . . ours. I want to feel my own child within me, hold it, watch it develop and grow up. Is that asking too much? I know my work compensates for much of the emptiness, but every once in awhile that old need within me resurfaces; it reminds me . . . well . . . that I'm not totally fulfilled. That's all I'm saying, Lance."

Lance put his arm around her but remained silent. He always felt that same sense of helplessness whenever the subject of their inability to conceive a child came up. His disappointment had never been as keen as hers, however. With wholehearted support, he'd encouraged her decision to enter medical school, and until today, he'd always assumed the intense desire to have her own child had been assuaged by her involvement with the Children's Hospital.

"How's the new format for the radio show coming along?" Karamine asked, deliberately changing the subject.

"Great! More than I'd ever expected. I think it was an absolute stroke of genius on John's part to come up with the idea of discussing political issues with representatives from both sides . . . left and right. Seems to stimulate the audience into thinking, and, as I've always said, if the public is honestly presented with both sides of a question, no slanted propaganda or distortion, people will usually make correct decisions." Lance glanced at his watch. "Hey . . . we'd better get movin' it's 7.20 already." They continued their run down the esplanade in silence, preoccupied and absorbed by their own thoughts.

In the years since Karamine and Lance had graduated college, both had come a long way in achieving their goals. Lance's radio talk-show which he named *ON TARGET* had been a fall-out from his days in college, where his razor-sharp wit and insouciant charm had made him a natural moderator for the debating team.

John Dixon, a local entrepreneur, observing Lance's skill in maintaining control over debaters and audience, had been deeply impressed, and had offered Lance the opportunity to host a political talk show. Dixon, a burly, brisk man in his early fifties, had acquired a radio station for the sole purpose of balancing the public's perceptions and views of current politics and politicians; according to Dixon, many politicians promoted their own agendas through an unchallenged and sometimes biased media. Dixon had pledged himself to even up the odds. At first the program began with local audiences, but eventually had expanded to national level.

Lance's keen perception and background in political science gave him an easy style and genuine manner; his guests responded with freedom and informality. Lance handled the most hostile telephone calls with such acuity and tact, he disarmed his opponent and increased his listening audience. Current events in every field were probed—politics, science, theology. By exploring all subjects, Lance felt the driving impetus of life, interweaving, shaping and molding the ever-changing image of civilization and modern society. He loved the challenge of his work and tackled the most perplexing problems and issues of the day with powerful energy.

Karamine found her career as a medical doctor specializing in pediatrics, equally challenging. Responding to some deep inner need, she'd made the switch initially to help her Armenian people. Since she'd always been a person of certitudes and deep caring, her decision had come as no great surprise to Lance, even when she'd volunteered three months of the year to travel and work in Armenia. The experience had touched her deeply, giving her new strengths and resiliency that seemed somehow to betray her vulnerability and tenderness of heart. To Lance, she was more beautiful now than the first time he'd taken her out. He remembered how she'd looked that day when they'd stood on the rocky shore at Gloucester and high winds wildly blew her long, dark hair about her. Her hair was short now, and professionally trimmed, but her face still glowed with olive tints, and her eyes flashed with the same piercing intensity behind the fashionable glasses.

Arriving at their apartment building, conveniently located just off the esplanade, they took an elevator to the fourth floor. Walking down a small corridor, Lance opened the door to their spacious apartment, its wide windows overlooking the Charles River. They both loved this view with its changing moods, bright sailboats and grey, soaring seagulls; they appreciated the relaxing effect it offered them, especially after difficult or stressful days at work. Both felt it well worth its high cost of rental.

"Take your shower first, Karamine, and I'll make the coffee," said Lance, walking directly to his desk and picking up a batch of papers from his desk. He shuffled through them rapidly, studying the format for the evening's talk show. Replacing the papers, his eyes rested momentarily on the framed double photos of his grandparents, Sahag and Raisscia, which he always kept on his desk. A faint smile flickered across his face as he picked up the pictures and felt the warm rush of emotion he always experienced whenever he thought about them; his grandfather's voice thundered in his ears once more, voicing the tales of his people, *my* people, Lance thought passionately. He closed his eyes briefly, recalling again long summer days on his grandfather's farm, where deep bonds were forged and identities cast; the restful nights when opiate silence invaded his sleep and liberated his dreams. He smiled inwardly, remembering—the summer his grandfather taught him to swim and to ride a horse; the wild demonstration to impress his dad, Antranig, who'd stood by watching, ashen-faced and furious, as his son, Lance brandishing a home-made wooden sabre galloped by at top speed shouting, '*death to the Turks!*'. From that day on his trips to the farm had been curtailed. Shaken and worried his only son was being too influenced or brain-washed by his grandfather in the old country ways, Lance's father had made other arrangements for his son's summer vacations. Yes, Dad, you sure were determined to make me into an "American," Lance thought with amusement. I'll never forget you hammering that fact into my head—"the past is gone, Lance, gone forever. We live here now, in America, and . . . *you're an American.!*"

"*Meidz-hyrig, meidz-myrig*" (grandfather, grandmother) I miss you both. Why do the people we love and care for have to leave us, he wondered with sigh, as he replaced the photographs on his desk.

For a long time after his grandparent's death, Lance had blocked out the pain by refusing to think or even speak about them. He'd shed no tears at his grandfather's funeral, remaining stoic and expressionless, as though his grief was entombed in an icy vacuum, from which no utterance was possible. But the great release of tears exploded within him one day, when he had driven back to the farm to check out some legal matters concerning his grandfather's estate. As though drawn by hypnotic force, Lance had walked alone to the hill where Avedis, Raisscia, and now Sahag slept peacefully. His grandfather's presence still charged the atmosphere. How can things change so much, yet still remain the same, Lance had wondered heavily, his eyes racing over the untilled fields, the unpainted barn, the rusting equipment. When his grandmother, Raisscia, had died unexpectedly, Sahag had simply lost his spirit, and without her, life had become meaningless for him. Through the numbing pain of Sahag's funeral, the sole sustaining thought for Lance had been the certitude and unshakable belief that Sahag and Raisscia were now together. All else had faded, had blocked out like a picture on a screen.

Only on his first return to his grandfather's farm, did awareness of that day surface, stirring memories anew. He recalled again in accurate detail, the burial service, the presence of his parents; his father, Antranig, struggling to suppress his emotions, older and thinner now, but handsome still with his strong cleft chin and silver-grey hair that softened his countenance. Kate, his mother, the Canadian nurse who'd fallen in love with his father from the first time she'd set eyes on his dark, good looks. His mother had taken care of Antranig when he'd been in a coma, critically wounded from a battle during World War II. She'd often told Lance the story of their meeting and falling in love, how she'd come to the United States not knowing she was pregnant with him. He'd remembered her the day of the funeral, wearing a black dress and lace shawl that loosely covered her hair and shoulders when she'd stood calm and poised by his father's side. Then there was Karamine, who'd held his hand tightly, shared his pain and understood. But, most of all, Lance remembered his grandfather—that towering giant of a man who'd always seemed larger than life to him—his grandfather's words echoed once more through his heart and memory that day, and seemed to release the inner coil that bound his energies. "*Armenians are a proud and noble race, my boy; our enemy, those savage butchering Turks, have stolen our holy motherland . . . our people have become exiles. But they can never steal from us our honor, our history or pride. Remember, Lance, Armenian blood flows in your veins, and Armenians prefer death to compromise.*"

The maple trees along the edge of the clearing had stirred restlessly, as though suddenly charged by a quickening breeze; lambent light flickered briefly over the landscape then disappeared; only silence and crushing emptiness remained.

Lance had wept then, freely and without restraint. He leaned heavily against the rough texture of the oak tree that had grown massively since his youth, and abandoned himself to the flood of loneliness and grief. "*Meidz-hyrig, Meidz-hyrig,*" he'd cried aloud, "I miss you so much. How many times have I faltered and failed, but your words of strength and encouragement have always seen me through. You really let me know who I am, and you were the one who gave me my great sense of pride in that. It was your guidance—I know that now, especially your teaching me to stand up for what I truly believe in; This has helped strengthen my resolve to pursue truth and justice. Grandpa, you've given me so much. How I longed to be able to share with you the joy and truth of the life I'd found—I tried that day I came back from New York with Karamine and Nevart, but your bitterness was hard to break through. I'll never forget, *meidz-hyrig* . . . we knelt together, right here by Avedis' grave . . . we asked for forgiveness. I still don't know whether you did it just for my sake, or whether you actually felt it within you. In many of our conversations later, you seemed to understand, but then at other times, the bitter past still overshadowed everything.

As tears gradually subsided, Lance had remained in motionless silence for a long time. Fleeting shafts of gusty light touched the windows of the farmhouse creating movement and shadow images, but no voice or sound came forth; Lance's heart felt heavy as stone. "Just be free, grandpa . . . free and at peace, that's all I ask and pray for you." He'd shivered suddenly when a raw-edged wind piled fallen oak leaves in small mounds about his feet.

A shrill ring of the telephone brought him sharply back to the present. "Hello . . . yeh . . . Lance . . . Hi John, what's on your mind so early this morning? Tonight? Well, I don't know, John, I'll have to check with Karamine and get back to you on it; Why is it so important? Okay . . . I'll call you right back."

"Who was on the phone, Lance?" Karamine called, walking from the bathroom shaking her hair with a dryer.

"John. He wants us to come to dinner tonight. He sounded a bit enthused . . . and . . . kind of mysterious . . . said there would be another couple there too, but wouldn't say who it was."

"Kind of short notice isn't it?"

"Well you know John, he does everything spur of the moment. I wonder what he wants."

"I'm okay for tonight, Lance, nothing scheduled," said Karamine, studying a pad on her desk. "What time?"

"Well, I've got the show at six, it would have to be after that. . . . "

"It will have to be a late dinner, then. You're not through at the studio till after seven, and by the time we get there it will be after eight.

"Well, there's nothing much we can do about that. I'll call John and tell him we'll be there, but it will be after eight."

Lance picked up the telephone and carefully dialed John's number. "John? Karamine's free, so I guess it's all set for tonight," he said, after a few minutes pause. "But don't forget . . . I have the show tonight, so it will have to be after that, probably sometime after eight, okay? Good. See you then."

He hung up the phone and looked quizzically at Karamine. "Humm! What's going on with John, I wonder . . . and who are the other couple?"

"Must be something important. We'll find out tonight. Lance put his arms around Karamine and kissed her firmly on the mouth. "Hey . . . you look sexy and inviting . . . let's call everything off this morning and stay home and have some fun. Good idea, huh?"

Karamine laughed as she put her arms around Lance's neck, responding to his kiss, before gently pushing him toward the bathroom. "Take a shower and cool off, Romeo. We've got lots to do this morning."

"Now look what you've done. You've just killed a beautiful moment," said Lance, responding with a short laugh before heading to the bathroom.

2

"**F**our . . . three . . . two . . . one, you're on the air," Lance heard through his earphones.

"Good evening, ladies and gentlemen, this is Lance Bagdasarian bringing you another informative and enlightening evening in the series ON TARGET. Tonight, our targeted guest is Senator Jason Crawford from our own great state of Massachusetts. Senator Crawford has been duly elected to the Senate for the last four terms, and he is a major whip of the Democratic party. Through his efforts and experience, he has guided many programs and environmental issues through the senate. He has been active in the field of education, welfare, civil rights and gun control. He's been the great champion of the poor and oppressed, minorities, and, through his forceful legislation, has also been the instrument of many changes in the attitudes and infrastructure of our country.

Senator Crawford was a man in his late fifties. Years of working at his desk had slightly stooped his six foot frame. At first meeting, he gave the impression of a deeply sympathetic and benevolent man, paternal and kind to the utmost; only his eyes betrayed the charming smile— glacial, pale, ever watchful, as though measuring all situations and persons to his own design and purpose. His glance was scrutinizing and quick, full of condescension or disdain, whenever he was challenged on an issue he heatedly opposed; his jowls hung loosely about his jaw, evidence of high living and many parties on the Washington scene, but his voice was authoritative and commanding, with an unmistakable ring of power to it. Armed with awareness of his effective rhetoric, he used it constantly, with persuasion and influence especially on the senate floor. Now, facing Lance, he gazed at him with cool self assurance, confident in his own ability to match wits with this conservative upstart, to earn further honors and distinction for his own political agenda as well as for himself personally. His advisors had warned him not to do the show, and also had well informed him of the pointed questions Lance and his audience would ask. Senator Crawford however, was not a man to turn down any opportunity to bask in the limelight, and rarely refused an occasion to press his point.

"Senator Crawford," Lance began after the usual opening remarks, "how do you justify the unconscionable raise in salary the congress have taken for themselves. Both the senate and house of representatives have voted overwhelmingly for it despite the fact that eighty percent of the American people were against it. Liberals and conservatives, are both guilty here of overriding the people's will, and I understand it was passed in the middle of the night."

The senator narrowed his eyes and stared at Lance. "I'm glad you mentioned that it was non-partisan, and that both sides of the aisle were instrumental in the bill's passage. The pay raise has been long overdue, and the amount is cumulative to the years we have lagged behind in its enactment. The congress works hard, many times late into the night, which many people may not be aware of, but the main point is if you want to attract good people to government, the salary must be equal to the caliber of the person you want."

"You missed the point, senator, the people felt you did not deserve a raise. How can you say you deserve it when the ordinary citizen can't vote himself a raise, even when he feels it is due him. Some people would consider this action the height of arrogance, and one that certainly proves the congress is out of touch with the voting public."

"Oh . . . the phone light is on . . . let's see what the voters have to say about it, senator . . . hello, L.A. California, you're on the air . . . "

"Senator" . . . the caller began . . . "you justify this huge pay raise as something due you because you say you haven't had one in a long time. I get a review every year and the raises I get amount to about two or three percent of my gross salary. These raises just about stay within the inflation rate. During Carter's time with inflation running at double digit, I fell behind in my buying capacity. How can you sit there and say the congress deserves this, especially when congress has not balanced a budget in over thirty years, and has increased the national debt to staggering proportions?"

An icy ray flashed from the senator's eyes, but his response was immediate.

"First of all, you must understand, that the national debt is due to the presidents who do not give us a balanced budget. Furthermore, our work load has increased two-fold, forcing us to increase our staff. The raises were necessary and timely for operation today on Capital Hill."

"I disagree, senator," the caller insisted. You and I both know, and I'm sure every thinking American knows, that congress is the one who spends all the money . . . the executive branch can't spend a single dime unless the congress says so. No, I say what congress should be getting is a cut in salary, not a raise, until they learn to balance the budget and reduce the debt. Furthermore, why not give the president a line veto, like forty governors of our nation have. That would go a long way in curbing some of this excessive spending."

"Line veto! Senator Crawford exploded. "Impossible!" That would simply give the president too much power."

"But senator . . . " Lance interrupted persuasively. "Just think . . . all of those pork barrel plums could then be vetoed out of the budget without congress taking the blame. This would save billions and billions of dollars, monies that could be put into other channels or simply used to lower the debt. Anyway, there are quite a number of constitutional lawyers and judges who say that the president does have the line veto. Since congress passes each bill individually, the president also has the right to veto each bill in front of him. The president could do this, then let congress take it to the Supreme Court for its constitutionality."

"No . . . never . . . " the senator broke in vehemently. "That's the only way we are able to control the executive and keep them in line . . . " The senator cut off his remarks abruptly, realizing that this was a statement he had not wished to make.

"Senator," Lance continued gently but firmly "there has been a 70% pay raise since 1987 . . . isn't that somewhat of a travesty? In 1789, James Madison warned the people quote, *"Leaving any set of means without control of congress is to put their hands into the public coffers, taking money to put into their own pockets."* But, let's go to another caller . . . hello . . . Mesa, Arizona . . . "

"Senator . . . I understand from all the media reports, that you are in favor of making Washington D.C. the first city state in the union. This would give them two senate seats and several house chairs, isn't this true?"

"Yes, I believe this would be an ideal situation where we in congress would show that we care for the minorities in our great city of Washington, and they in turn would be an asset to congress, focusing on the many minority problems we have nationwide in the field of quotas, affirmative action and social justice. Yes, I'm committed to this, and will fight hard to push it through the congress with all the power and means at my disposal."

"Senator," the caller continued, "how can you honestly say the minorities in Washington will be an asset to congress, when everyone knows that Washington has more crime, corruption, drugs and poor government that anywhere else. In good conscience, how can you say that those sent to congress would be representative of the best minorities of the community?"

"I feel," the senator hummed on persuasively, "that the people will vote the brightest and most qualified people for the enrichment of congress . . . they will bring in new and fresh ideas in the field of social justice, and we democrats will do our best to further efforts in this field, especially regarding some of the ideals of Martin Luther King. We must push congress and the executive branch for much needed legislation in the field of affirmative action, quotas and other civil rights issues."

"We have a call from Virginia . . . go ahead Virginia . . . " Lance prompted.

"Yes, senator . . . You're obviously not acquainted with the staggering problems in Washington. May I remind you that Washington is considered the crime capital of America . . . the streets are unsafe; the police are disarmed by restrictive laws governing the pursuit of criminals, the judiciary releases habitual criminals by the thousands, there's a corrosive welfare system employed that's literally destroying family life among the lower income and minority classes. Can you please explain to me how statehood will alter or change these problems?"

"Well obviously statehood would bring in more money to operate the communities; police would do their jobs better, schools would be refurbished, and the general infrastructure repaired."

"So your answer to all the problems in Washington is more money and statehood;" the caller argued with a short ironic laugh. "I'm sorry, senator, but with all the crime and corruption there I doubt if those ideas will do much to change anything in a positive way." Thanks.

"Senator Crawford," Lance interjected, "isn't there a constitutional requirement stating that Washington shall always be a Federal city?"

"It's what we, the majority of congress decide it to be," Senator Crawford stated imperiously, "we have the votes."

"Yes . . . you're on the air New York . . . "

"Senator, as you know it is virtually impossible to defeat an incumbent. Don't you think with all the perks and privileges the congressmen have, there should be a two term limit just like the presidency? This would prevent the congress from becoming career politicians, stagnating on the job, and make them more receptive to the people?"

"Look," the senator replied, gesturing with his hands, "if you have good representatives there and the people continue to put them in office why shouldn't they continue? It's the people's choice."

"Don't you feel, senator," Lance cut in, "that the longer an incumbent stays in office, the easier it becomes to lose touch with his constituents, and perhaps to lose touch also with that which he perceives as the will of the people? As the caller has indicated, it's almost impossible to defeat an entrenched incumbent; most congressmen and senators have continual exposure in the media, which a candidate very seldom has access to."

"That's the problem of the candidate, not ours. We in the business of government simply do not have time for campaigning. We need these so-called perks in order to return to congress to do our job."

"Hello . . . you're on the air, Florida . . . "

"We have quite a few states passing the two term limit, senator," the caller began, and the number will increase, whether our government representatives like it or not."

"Well, that's indeed regretful," Senator Crawford replied, "and will only serve to reduce the quality of congressmen serving our country. I'm against it, and will fight any such legislation I see fit, to the limit of the law."

"You're on the air, Tampa Florida, what's your question?"

"Good evening, Senator Crawford, you're doing a great job, and I hope you stay in the senate permanently; well, to begin with I would like to comment on the budget . . . it seems as though every time the taxes are raised one dollar, the congress spends fifty. Isn't this what brought the deficit up to three trillion dollars in the first place? Aren't those folks up there on Capital Hill inclined to overspend?"

"Excellent question. You must understand that the needs of our people in the lower strata, below the poverty line as the media refers to it, must be met. There is also the problem of the defense industrial complex which further drains the economy. These people get billions of dollars in contracts and the corruption there is tremendous."

"I agree, senator, yet this industrial complex as you call it, creates jobs, and these jobs create tax revenues, while welfare only creates limousine bureaucrats who sap the system of its effectiveness in helping the needy." I also feel we should do away with the IRS thereby saving billions of dollars per year and replace it with a flat tax across the board with no deductions. For the lower income people we could have a cut off point at let's say $20,000 or wherever the proper point should be."

Senator Crawford shook his head emphatically, "too simplistic, unreal and . . . much too simplistic," he repeated.

The caller has a point, Senator, don't you think? Lance commented, or . . . we could collect tax revenues through a use or surtax. This way we could abolish the income tax which everyone detests. I see the light is on again . . .

"Hello, you're on the air, San Diego. . . . "

"Yes, thank you, finally got on . . . Let me say first Senator Crawford that it is a real privilege to speak to you. I think you have done an outstanding job in the field of health care, equal opportunities and welfare. You've shown real concern for the poor and needy, not like some of the republicans . . . "

"Do you have a question for the senator?" Lance interrupted flatly.

"Yes. I want to know if there's a possibility of having everyone under healthcare this session of congress?"

"Senator Crawford cleared his throat. "The problem is, the party across the aisle will not cooperate to push through such a bill. We democrats are doing our best and have a program all set to go, but can't get it through the congress. The opposition is adamant against its passing. We've done all we can do to have this bill passed, but at the present time it's in limbo."

"Senator," Lance broke in, "you know that is not exactly true. Your party outnumbers the republican party two to one in the congress, and your real problem is, your own members. Luckily, those same members understand the pitfalls that this bill creates for business throughout the country. The cost of such high premiums to the smaller companies employing fewer people would be devastating. These companies would soon be out of business and millions of workers consequently unemployed; and another thing Senator . . . you know the backbone of this country's economy has always been the small business'."

"South Carolina, you're on the air . . . "

"Yes, I have a couple of questions, Senator . . . First of all, do you belong or are you by any chance a member of a group or organization known as The Trilateral . . . are they part of another group known as The Council of Foreign Relations? If so, what exactly are their aims and aspirations, and also, who are the members?"

There was an awkward pause while Senator Crawford pondered his response to the penetrating question. "Yes, . . . ah well, first of all . . . although the Trilateral and the Council are similar in their goals, the membership is different. As you may be aware, the Tr ilateral is one of the finest humanitarian organizations in existence today, and yes, I am indeed a member. The members are comprised of the best the world has to offer . . . in all fields . . . industry, international banking, economy, and academia. As for goals . . . both groups champion only the most ethical and high principled precepts, through which we hope to create a new and brighter world order, free of the curse of war, strife and intolerance. By abolishing national boundaries, and striving for equitable monetary systems, we hope to change obsolete moral, spiritual and social values, which will enable us to go forward with a new world peace and harmony."

"Wasn't the Council of Foreign Relations the brain child of John Ruskin and his protégé Cecil Rhodes of the gold and silver mines of

Africa fame? I believe Rhodesia was named in his honor, Senator," Lance queried.

Senator Crawford eyed Lance, his narrowed gaze clouded with scrutiny. "As a matter of fact, yes, and I might also add that his money has created scholarships for bright, intelligent students around the world to advance their careers. I believe everyone is aware of the enormous contributions made by these Rhodes scholars. Through world politics, great steps and changes have been made, especially in the social, moral and spiritual fields, where arcane and obsolete formats no longer have relevance or value. Yes, . . . we owe a lot to these pioneers of the new world order."

Lance looked intently at Senator Crawford, then smiled with cool self-assurance. "The last time I remember of anyone saying something like that was Thule Gesell Schoft of Germany's national socialist party; I believe if I recall correctly, it was way back there in the early thirties. They called it the New Age."

Senator Crawford's face reddened. "Are you calling me a Nazi?" he replied angrily.

"No, just giving you some basic facts I came across during my studies of political science in university days."

"Why should that interest you . . . even in those days, Mr. Bagdasarian?"

"Well . . . at that time I was interested in Woodrow Wilson and the League of Nations, and wanted to get more input in the formation of the Armenian Republic after World War I. Wilson was a major influence, and naturally, being of Armenian heritage I wanted to know more about this man who was so revered by our Armenian people. When I got deeper into the research, a shadowy figure emerged. His name was Colonel House . . . full name Colonel Edward Mandell House, and he was Wilson's aide at that time. Way back then he referred to the new world order of peace and security; then, Walter Millis in his book, ROAD TO WAR, also spoke of it. According to Millis, Wilson never did or said anything without clearing it through Colonel House first. In fact, some historians claim that Colonel House was the real president . . . and he was also a member of the Trilateral."

"So, what's wrong with that?" slammed the senator.

"Senator," Lance replied assertively, "this so called new world order you subscribe to, as I understand it, would be a renunciation of our United States of America in an allegiance to a sovereign new world order or new age order or whatever you want to call it. This would mean the prosecution of American citizens in a world court completely alien to our Constitution and Bill Of Rights. For myself, and for many Americans, the Constitution and the Bill of Rights are the most important documents ever created since the Magna Carter. I seriously doubt any intelligent American citizen would knowingly wish to relinquish the rights and privileges we now enjoy under their protection to some new alien philosophy."

"That's pure isolationism, and America is too great a country to indulge herself along those narrow lines. If we are to survive as a human race in this global village, we've got to put an end to wars, end human suffering, and make the world secure for our children and grandchildren. Isn't it worth it for world peace . . . we could have a thousand years of peace . . . "

"Or tyranny" . . . Lance rebutted, "I would never trust the lives and aspirations of the American people to who knows what . . . the U.N. with all those banana republics or third world countries? Will we also have a new world elite in charge . . . completely unelected by the people as well as a social order where all private property would be confiscated in the name of humanity and social equality? Wouldn't that be a socialist state?"

"You have a great sense of exaggeration, Mr. Bagdasarian. I don't know where you get your information."

"I get my facts from the books I've read, it's available in libraries for anyone who cares to research it . . . Senator, I see we are out of time, but I hope you'll come back and visit us again when we can discuss this new world order in further depth. Thank you very much, Senator Jason Crawford, for joining us here this evening ON TARGET."

The red light blinked, indicating they were off the air. Both men stood up and stretched. Lance walked around his desk and shook the senator's hand firmly. "I want to thank you again, Senator Crawford for coming on the show. It was quite an interesting and illuminating session I must say."

"To say the least. Where do you get all your information Mr. Bagdasarian? You are unusually well informed. How about quitting this job and working for me. You can run my staff, do research and write my speeches. You could do well and go far . . . "

Lance laughed, pausing to wave at Karamine through the glass partition as she entered the studio. "Thanks, senator, but I enjoy working at my program. It's a constant challenge to keep it interesting and informative for my audience. You'll have to excuse me now senator, as I see my wife has just arrived, and we have a dinner engagement. As I said, thanks and let's do it again, soon."

"Certainly, I'd be pleased to do it again," said Senator Crawford, looking past Lance to appraise Karamine.

They walked toward Karamine who smiled greetings. Chic and striking in a red and black wool dress she extended her hand toward

Senator Crawford, as Lance introduced them. "I understand now what drives and inspires this husband of yours," he said smoothly, holding her hand tightly, while his eyes enfolded her.

"Hurry, Lance," Karamine said with a nervous little laugh, as she tried to withdraw her hand, "I've got a cab waiting."

"I'll be right with you," Lance replied, walking toward his office. When he returned he noted Senator Crawford had already departed. Taking Karamine by the arm, he led her quickly to the elevator.

On Beacon street, the taxicab pulled up in front of a three-story brownstone building. The dull red brick exterior with its sculptured trim around doorways and windows was typical of most architecture in the area built at the turn of the century. Leaving the cab, Lance and Karamine walked up the front steps and quickly stepped through the glass-paneled doorway into a small foyer. Lifting an ornate brass knocker, Lance rapped twice, then waited. Almost immediately, the heavy mahogany door swung open and Edna, the Dixon's housekeeper greeted them pleasantly.

"Mr. and Mrs. Bagdasarian . . . please come in. How are you both this evening?"

"Very well, Edna. I see you've gotten rid of that cold you had the last time we were here. Hope we're not too late. I'd hate to hold up your fine dinner," Lance replied warmly. The housekeeper smiled broadly. "Oh no, we understand you'd be coming after your show, and made allowances for a late dinner."

She led them through a corridor attractively lit from reflected lights which were sharply focused on a series of landscape paintings lining the walls. They paused momentarily while Edna opened the large sliding doors to the drawing room. As often as they had been there, Karamine was always struck by the elegance and taste of the Dixon's spacious drawing room—a skillful blend of old world charm and contemporary style. Built for ease and comfort, the sofas and chairs were of soft spanish leather in a simple design and mellow shades of beige that set off the bold striking colors and patterns of the oriental rugs. A crystal chandelier flung incandescent lights on the pale-tinted ceiling and dark wainscoated walls, giving the room an aura of luxury and ease. Above the spanish-tiled fireplace, a large painting of the sea commanded the immediate attention of everyone who entered. A favorite of their collection, John and Miriam loved to explain how they had fallen in love with it while visiting Bar Harbor, Maine. "We simply felt we couldn't live without it," Miriam had always pointed out to her guests, "especially after meeting the artist, and up an coming young woman painter who interpreted her feelings about it to us, and explained why she felt inspired to paint it."

"I don't believe you've met before," Miriam commented, glancing toward another couple, after her initial greetings to Karamine and Lance.

"Lance, this is Richard Blair, the chairman of the Republican party in our state," John Dixon said, quickly stepping forward to introduce the other couple. As I'm sure you've heard, Richard's been doing a great job of recruiting young blood and fresh new ideas for the party. You know . . . the opposition feels they've tied up this state, and no one has a chance to reclaim it, but, with men like Richard and programs like ON TARGET, we may still have a chance to inform and enlighten people on free thought enterprise.

Lance smiled amicably as he extended his hand toward Richard Blair. "Yes, I've read a lot about Mr. Blair, and find myself in complete agreement with many of his ideas. Too bad your candidate lost the last governor's seat. On my program I tried, subtly of course, to point out the differences between the two candidates, but I guess we failed to convince the majority."

Richard Blair studied Lance's face intently before answering. "Well the votes were the closest we've seen in years, and I attribute a lot of credit to your program and the way you hammered at the issues, which were never discussed during a campaign, by the way." he added pointedly.

"John! You haven't introduced Richard's wife," Miriam said, suddenly breaking into the conversation. "Alice, let me introduce you to two of our brightest young friends, Karamine and Lance Bagdasarian."

Alice Blair smiled cordially and extended her hand toward Lance and Karamine. Two slight dimples on each side of her mouth enhanced her expression, giving her the illusion of being much younger than her actual forty-six years. Her brown eyes sparkled with interest as she spoke; Karamine and Lance liked her immediately.

"I've heard so much about you both," she said, taking Karamine's hand. "I can't imagine how you manage all of your activities . . . your medical career and traveling half-way around the world three months of the year to help your people. It's quite remarkable, really. And your program ON TARGET" she continued, turning to Lance, "is the most through provoking riveting show around. I understand it is now on many networks?"

Lance laughed softly and shook his head affirmatively. "Yes, although I don't really know how many outlets we have, but I do know we're in every major city in the country."

"Well, now that we all know each other," John Dixon interjected, "How about something to drink?" He nodded toward Edna who competently took each order, then quietly left the room.

"By the way, that was a great show tonight, Lance. I was amazed our senior senator would consider doing it."

Lance smiled and nodded his head thoughtfully. "I really didn't expect him to accept our invitation when we first approached him, but, he called back the next day and said he'd be delighted to come. I'm reasonably sure he'd been advised by his staff that I'd probably be hostile . . . I wouldn't call it hostile, would you?" he queried, glancing from John to Richard.

"Hell, no!" Richard replied before John could utter a word. "All you did was refer to his record, and what he stood for. If a person can't stand for his voting record and what he believes in, then he certainly has no business being in Washington, especially in the senate. Personally, I thought you did a great job of drawing him out, so people can see where's he's coming from."

"I agree," John added, "what you're doing is something that should have been done a long time ago in this state . . . maybe then we wouldn't have had so many one-sided elections. I for one believe that allowing one party . . . Democratic or Republican, to stay in power beyond two terms is to invite corruption and elitism. God! Where are the days when a new party came in, fired all the bureaucrats and replaced them with fresh thinking people?" John Dixon lifted a drink from the tray Edna offered.

"Mr. Harry Truman took care of that the last month he was in office," Lance commented with a disgruntled expression. "He made all the government agencies civil service before he left, so there's just no way of getting those career bureaucrats out, short of an act of congress. Gone are the days of the "broom" when a new administration coming in swept clean all the former departments. On top of that, now we have civil service unions to contend with . . . plus the media who are always suspicious of change. I call it THE TROIKA . . . bureaucrats, unions and media." He laughed derisively.

John Dixon placed a supportive arm around Lance's shoulder. "There, you see, Richard, here's a man who's got his facts straight, and is not afraid to speak out. This is exactly the caliber of candidate we need to run for office . . . someone honest and straightforward . . . someone who doesn't test the air to see which way the wind is blowing, then change his position on issues to suit his purpose. No, we need candidates with specific goals that voters can relate to; someone who won't compromise in achieving them." John studied Richard Blair's face closely for a reaction, before walking to the fireplace and carefully picking up fire tongs to reposition a log. Replacing the tongs, he eyed Richard closely. "Well, what do you think, Richard?" Dare we ask him now, or shall we let it go till after dinner?"

"My God, John, they just got here!" Miriam exclaimed. "Can't you at least wait until we've had our drinks and socialized a bit? I want them to get to know each other a little, before you say anything."''

"What are these men up to anyway, Miriam?" Karamine asked, scrutinizing her keenly for some hint of what was taking place. "I'm really curious now . . . and a bit apprehensive. The quick invitation, the chairman of the Republican party, the late hour." She smiled, glancing inquisitively from one to the other. "What are you all up to anyway? I believe there's some sort of conspiracy going on here, Lance."

"Conspiracy? Well now, I wouldn't go so far as to call it a conspiracy . . . would you Richard?" John Dixon winked and assumed a mysterious air. Richard remained noncommittal.

"Come on," Karamine coaxed persuasively, "you're up to something . . . "

"Yeah, come on . . . " Lance added with an amused smile. "What's going on?"

"John!" Alice exclaimed impatiently, "Will you and Richard quit playing games; tell them what this is all about, and what's on your minds . . . "

John hesitated and scratched his head nervously. "Well, we really wanted to wait till after dinner, but somehow the conversation got ahead of us rather quickly. Since the cat seems to be out of the bag anyway . . . "

"John! Will you please get to the point," Alice interrupted impatiently.

"Right," said John, setting down his drink and raising his hand defensively. "Lance, what we're going to ask you is not something we've just dreamed up. In short, and to the point, we want you to run on the Republican ticket this fall, for the senate seat . . . "

There was silence in the room as Karamine and Lance absorbed John Dixon's statement with its profound implications.

"Are you saying you want me to run against Senator Crawford, John? You can't be serious! To begin with, I'd never have a chance in this state." He looked quickly at Karamine who remained silent, a fixed smile on her face.

"Yes, Lance, we do want you to run against Senator Crawford, and we have full confidence you can do it or I would not have agreed with John. You could rip him apart in a debate, and I'm quite optimistic of the final outcome," Richard Blair said seriously.

"Run against Senator Crawford here in Massachusetts?" Lance repeated, shaking his head in disbelief.

"Exactly. Richard's right, you could cream him," John echoed enthusiastically.

"You're the ideal one for the job, Lance, and we make no bones about this," said Alice, stepping forward to grasp Lance's wrist. "You'd appeal to the young voters, and I believe you could finally break the grip of the opposition, which has had a hold on this state for decades . . . you're the only one who could do it."

Lance took a deep breath, and threw Karamine a piercing glance. "What do you think, Karamine . . . is it madness to even consider their proposal?"

Karamine gently placed her wine glass on the table. "I really don't know, Lance, . . . I'd have to think about it."

"Look, don't say anything just now," John broke in, "we want you to think about it, and discuss it together. I know it's a bit of a shock . . . and a big step to consider, but we all feel it would be the right decision for our party."

"Yes, Lance, think about it," Richard chimed in, "but just know you have our full confidence and support."

"Dinner is ready to serve," Edna announced quietly, entering the room.

"Ah yes, and not a moment too soon," said Miriam, linking an arm through Lance's, to lead the way to the dining room. "You all must be starving."

During dinner, the conversation was light. Most of it centered on the appetizing main course, a specialty of Edna's consisting of poached halibut steaks Bostonian, served with red potatoes and tiny peas. A rich rum pudding followed, along with freshly ground Kona coffee, imported from Hawaii.

"Edna is a god-sent gift to you, Miriam, you are so lucky to have her," Karamine remarked later, settling once again into a comfortable chair in the drawing room.

"She is indeed," Miriam agreed, "she's part of our family. We take her everywhere we go and we treasure her dearly. By the way, feel free to smoke, if anyone cares to . . . John and I quit some time ago, but Richard, please go ahead if you wish. I know Lance and Karamine are non-smokers."

Richard gave a short laugh. "No, it's all right, Miriam. I can suppress my desire to smoke in the presence of non-smokers. But thanks for asking." He settled into his chair and turned to Lance. "Please think over our proposal, Lance, and look at it from all sides before you decide. I know it's a big decision, but . . . if you could give us your answer let's say ah . . . in about a week . . . and you decide to run, it would give us plenty of time to orchestrate a formidable campaign. Don't let it scare you, Karamine," he said, turning to her, "we'd be with you from beginning to end, no matter what happens. Just make sure your background is clear of anything . . . ANYTHING that they could use against you, because believe me, they'll look for the tiniest detail and blow it up into a full-scale scandal to discredit you."

"Yes," Alice explained, throwing a concerned glance toward Karamine, "make sure you understand, Karamine . . . Richard is only talking about Lance, but if he runs, you'll be losing all your privacy as well, and not only you but your whole family. They'll put you under a microscope, they'll search and probe for any small thing they can use against you. You'll have to be ready to subject yourselves to this kind of scrutiny."

"Oh yes, our great newspaper, The Daily Examiner," John said with exasperation, "who claims to speak for the people of Massachusetts will try everything in its power to destroy you. They'll use innuendo, and may even try to fabricate something out of nothing . . . they've done it before and I'm damn sure they'll do it again."

"Wouldn't that be libelous? They could be taken to court for damages," Karamine asserted.

"Yes, how could they get away with something like that?" Miriam questioned.

"Huh!" Alice snorted angrily, "you should have seen what they accused my husband of . . . running around with some young chippy! Can you imagine it? After he was defeated for congress, they printed a retraction and apologized. We went to our lawyer to see if we could take them to court for their false accusations, but our lawyer discouraged us and told us to forget it . . . he said we'd have to prove 'malicious intent' on the part of the newspaper . . . which is virtually impossible. I know, because others have tried to no avail."

"Yes," Richard continued with a an ironic smile, "they all came to me to say they were really sorry about printing the articles, but the damage was done, and it served their purpose. All their retractions and apologies didn't change the fact the elections were over, and I had lost. This is an old tactic, and one they've used many times with the same success.

"How can they get away with something like that?" Miriam asked, searching for answers.

"It's a Supreme Court's decision . . . malicious intent is vague and difficult to prove, and you, the accused, must prove that the media had done the libelous act or made the statement with malicious intent. It's a hell of a thing to prove, believe me. I'm just warning you that when you run against an incumbent in this state, you have to be ready for anything, that's all."

"So why would anyone want to run for office, I wonder," Lance stated, noting Karamine's troubled expression. "Well . . . that's another point Karamine and I will have to think about and consider."

"Yes," Karamine added weakly, suddenly feeling tired and drained from some inexplicable sense of foreboding.

"Look, John, it's late, and we've had a long day. We will consider your proposition and let you know of our decision in plenty of time. Meanwhile, I want to thank you both for a wonderful dinner. It's been a most enlightening evening. Great meeting both of you also," Lance added, turning to the Blairs with a cordial smile and shaking their hands.

Karamine and Lance were silent as the cab wound its way through the dark city streets, empty now of surging crowds and deserted, except for an occasional taxi or city bus. It began to rain lightly; a damp mist floating up from the river transformed the trees along the esplanade into shadowy images; headlights from passing cars glimmered dimly as they splashed along the wet pavement. Both were deeply absorbed in their own thoughts and the unexpected turn of events. Do we really need the hype, the loss of privacy, that horde of probing reporters, who'd twist and misquote my every word, Lance wondered silently. And what about those investigations? He shifted uneasily and looked at Karamine who'd leaned her head lightly against his shoulders. Studying her dark head with its smart hairstyle, he noted the lines of strain about her mouth, and he felt a sudden tenderness.

"Tired, Honey?" he asked gently, reaching for her hand.

Karamine forced a smile. "A little. It's been quite a day." She was tired and disinclined at the moment to sort out or attempt to analyze the complexities of her feelings regarding this new development. In a vague sort of way she sensed it meant change, drastic change, and her immediate response was to block it out, beat it back, to concentrate on something—anything that might distract or move away from the inevitable chain of events that seemed to be moving in and taking shape around her. A thousand unanswered questions ran through her mind; how will these new intrusions change the way we live, affect our current careers? The thought troubled her. Lance would be a formidable candidate, true, and he could be exceedingly persuasive when speaking to the voters— yet, why does he need it? He seems totally fulfilled with his talk show, especially now that it is broadcast nationwide. He's in a position to get his point of view across and he's able to convert many of his listeners. 'Strive for excellence' he's always claimed, 'I alone am responsible for my actions, not the government, not society or the environment. I never make excuses for my shortcomings or failures, and I'm willing to pay for my actions.' But what about me? My work? What's going to happen to my work if Lance runs and is elected? I can't leave my practice and the hospital to live in Washington, and I certainly won't abandon the new hospital procedures I've been setting up in Armenia—those people depend on me, I've got promises to keep 'the media will put you under a microscope, not just Lance, but his whole family.' Alice Blair's words resonated in her ears and disturbed her deeply. Are we really up to the scrutiny? That whole New York episode—the press would have a field day with that, young and idealistic though Lance was at the time—innocent too. She closed her eyes and was suddenly aware her head ached slightly. I simply can't deal with it all tonight, she thought wearily.

The cab came to a quick stop in front of their apartment. Assisting Karamine out of the car, Lance turned to the driver and reached for his wallet.

"It's all been taken care of by the Dixons, even the tip," the cab driver informed Lance, before waving cheerfully and driving off.

Lance and Karamine walked to the front door of the building, and nodded to the security guard. In the elevator, he pushed the fourth floor button, then looked sharply at Karamine who still hadn't said a word.

"Sort of took us by surprise," he said with an awkward laugh. "You haven't had much to say about it, Karamine. You've been mighty quiet since we left the Dixons.

Inside the apartment, Lance took off his jacket and loosened his tie. He dropped down to a comfortable chair and let his gaze wander slowly over the view of the Charles River, where shore lights and anchored sailboats merged and shifted through the heavy mist.

"Can we relax a few minutes before going to bed . . . how about a nightcap," he called to Karamine who was kicking her shoes off in the bedroom.

"Sounds great, Lance, B & B would be fine, I'll be out in a minute, soon as I change to a robe."

Karamine joined Lance a few minutes later, and picked up the small stemmed glass of B & B from the coffee table. She sipped her drink slowly, allowing its mellow warmth to taper down the nervous jumble of anxious thoughts. She fixed her glance on the flashing headlights of cars moving with high speed along the esplanade, and she wondered vaguely who they were and where they were going.

"I love this view," she said after a few minutes, "somehow from this perspective we seem still to have control of our lives . . . nothing can touch us here. I don't want that to change, Lance."

Lance regarded her silently for a moment before answering. "I know . . . we do have a comfortable and pleasant life here, and at times like this, it seems so easy to say the hell with everything . . . lets continue as we are and let someone else do the battle out there. We're doing our jobs, worthwhile jobs, too . . . we're involved, we're committed . . . " he hesitated briefly "but it's because we have so much, I wonder if perhaps we don't have a greater responsibility? God knows I don't want to change the peace and serenity of our lives for the frantic pace of a political campaign." He shook his head as though to dislodge the idea completely. "What advice would *meidz-hyrig* give me if he was here to talk to me now," he said with a half smile, "I think I know . . . 'my boy . . . if everyone were content to simply live the secure life with no hassles or fights for what is right or what we believe in, what would eventually happen to justice and truth? Where would this country be? And who would do the work, take the risks that have to be taken?'" Lance sighed deeply and took a sip from his glass. "Yes, he'd go on to inform me that if we don't take the risks and do the work, it would be left to mediocre and corrupt politicians and as always, he'd be right. Isn't that what's happening right now in Washington? We've allowed these same people who can't even balance a checkbook to run our country into a trillion dollar hole. We desperately need people of good fiscal integrity and moral character, people who are not afraid to challenge the senate and the house."

"Lance! You're not seriously thinking of running, are you?" Karamine cried with sudden panic.

Lance stared into Karamine's dark eyes, his jaw tensing like hard granite. "No . . . I haven't decided yet, Karamine, but . . . I'm giving it some consideration. I want to look at the pros and cons. We've been so blessed, you and I, our love for each other, sometimes it seems like a dream. Don't you think one has to give back a little for being so lucky?"

Karamine ran her fingers nervously through her hair. "I don't know, Lance . . . I guess the whole idea sort of frightens me. These campaigns are so . . . well . . . so ugly now, nothing is sacred. I'm worried about us, and what it might do to you. I need to think it through, come to grips with the sacrifices required for such a step."

"Look, Karamine, we don't have to make any decisions tonight. We'll think about it, talk it over and come to some sound conclusion . . . whatever we decide, it will be our decision together, yours and mine, just as its always been."

"We also have to consider our parents, Lance . . . this decision, if you decide to run, will affect everyone in both of our families."

"Yeah, right . . . I'll call my parents first thing in the morning, or, we could drop in on them and just tell them. We haven't been there in a few weeks. This will be a good chance to get some input and kick the idea around. I wonder how Dad will react . . . his son running for the senate seat against Jason Crawford." Lance laughed a little. "Come to think of it, I believe the senator belongs to the same yacht club in Marl-boro as Dad."

"Humm . . . I think you're right . . . I seem to recall . . . yes we did meet him at one of the yacht club functions. It seems to me also, if I re-member correctly, your father thinks he's doing a great job, especially in the field of social justice," she said with some uneasiness.

"The trouble with dad is, he's on a guilt trip about his success . . . like so many achievers of his generation, he's swallowed all that media propaganda where success is portrayed as greed, or selfishness." Lance stopped short, noting that Karamine was barely listening." Look, honey, I'll call my parents and see if we can get together with them this week-end, okay? Let's hit the sack, I know you're tired, and so am I."

"Good. I'll see my parents tomorrow after work and talk to them. I'm sure they'll approve of anything we decide to do," Karamine answered.

Lance's blue eyes suddenly became reflective. "Have they had any news of your brother, Vasken?"

"No, even those few postcards stopped coming," Karamine replied in a low voice. "The last I heard he was in Central America."

"Yeah, probably down there fomenting revolution with the San-danistas. I'm sure he still thinks I'm a coward, but that's his problem, not mine." Lance said coldly.

"Lance, please! Can't you forget all that. It was so long ago. Vasken knows you didn't talk when they picked you up in New York, even though the group broke up in a hurry after that. I worry about him. Af-ter all . . . he's still my brother and I love him. I've heard you call the whole episode a learning experience so many times. Can't you just let it go at that?"

"Learning experience? He beat the living hell out of me the night before New York, and that will never happen to me again, I can promise you," Lance replied bitterly.

"Is that why you've been so intent on getting your black belt in karate? You want to GET him, is that it? And where do I stand in this vendetta . . . or do I stand at all?" Karamine hurled accusingly, her voice rising sharply.

"Hey, come on now, Karamine, you know better than that . . . the classes relax me. I'd never want to use that power against anyone, es-pecially your brother. Don't you think I know what it would do to you . . . to us?"

"That's another thing, Lance . . . what if all that stuff comes out dur-ing the campaign . . . the media would have a field day with it. It makes my head spin to think of how fast they'd use it . . . and how they'd dis-tort the facts."

Lance was silent for a moment, his face suddenly grave. "Well, this is something we have to think about and discuss with our parents. I certainly don't want anyone embarrassed or upset because of me. God . . . that's the last thing I'd want! One thing I know for sure . . . I've got to tell the whole story to John and Richard before deciding anything." He got up from his seat and paced a little. "Yes . . . I have to tell them before I decide anything or get into this campaign."

Karamine looked directly into Lance's face, her eyes flickering with impatience. "Then you've already decided to run, haven't you? You're already into the campaign and making plans."

He laughed without amusement. "Look, Karamine, I'm just mulling over the considerations for everyone involved in a political campaign, that's all. It's a tough decision to make, and if I do decide to run, I want everything open and above board right from the start. Anyway, we're both tired. Let's forget the whole thing for now and get some sleep."

Karamine managed to smile weakly. "Right. It has been a long day, and I guess I'm a bit tired and . . . and a bit edgy. She picked up the two glasses from the coffee table and took them to the kitchen sink, then followed Lance to the bedroom.

3

The door of the two car garage was open as Lance turned into the driveway of his parents home in Newton. He smiled slightly as he caught sight of his old red MG, its chrome headlights reflecting the noonday sun. A lot of memories wrapped up in that little car he thought briefly, remembering his first date with Karamine, and the long drive they took along the coast of Rockport and Gloucester. Now, he kept the car here in his father's garage rather than bringing it into the city where congested traffic and unpredictable parking was a constant problem. Besides, the car was a classic and was now a collectors item, although Lance appreciated its sentimental value much more than its commercial worth.

"Hey-look at our little red car," he commented, turning to Karamine, "looks pretty good, huh? Remember how it took us all over Cape Ann and Gloucester?"

"And our honeymoon to Cape Breton to visit your grandparents," Karamine added warmly.

"Yeah it sure got me everywhere I needed to go, even though it was a compromise over the motorcycle I wanted," he added with a laugh. "I really got to love driving that little bomb." "I think Dad loves driving it, too. I notice he's been using it a lot lately since he's retired. He takes it down to the Club at Marblehead, even when he's not sailing."

Lance hopped out of the car and opened the door on Karamine's side. As they walked from the driveway, the front door opened and Kate, Lance's mother, greeted them warmly.

"Hi! What a great surprise to see you both! We've been waiting ever since you called and said you were coming . . . how are you Karamine,

29

you're looking wonderfully well," Kate said with much enthusiasm, embracing her son and daughter-in-law. "Come in."

Antranig, Lance's father, met them as they entered the hallway, an affectionate smile on his deeply-tanned face.

"Well . . . quite an occasion having you both over on a Sunday afternoon, especially knowing your schedule," he said, laughingly, gently shaking his son while embracing him. "Karamine, pretty as ever," he added, turning and kissing her lightly on the cheek."

"C'mon, Dad. You know we always make time for you and Mom in our schedule," Lance said good-naturedly, noting how well his parents looked, especially now that his father had sold his engineering firm, and had retired from business. Except for a few consulting jobs, Antranig spent most of his spare time following his first love, sailing. He had purchased a handsome schooner and christened it THE VICTOR, then spent many days and weeks sailing along the Northeast Coast from Marblehead to Nova Scotia. Sun and sea air had deepened his skin color to a tawny red, emphasizing the steel-silver tones in hair; his dark eyes however had not lost their blazing quality of youth and passion over the years, but seemed intensified and more high-powered now by the striking contrasts of his features.

"Sit down everyone and be comfortable, I'll get the tea," said Kate in her matter of fact way that always put everyone instantly at ease.

"Canadian tea, Mom?" Lance teased, knowing his mother's fondness for the Canadian blend she always brought home whenever she traveled across the border.

"Naturally, is there anything else?" she called from the kitchen.

When Karamine got up and joined Kate in the kitchen, Lance settled easily into a comfortable chair and looked intently at his father.

"How's retirement going, Dad, you still entering the races with Jim Travis? The two of you make a formidable team."

Antranig chuckled. "Yep, I'd say we give those younger members a pretty good run for their money. Of course, it's all timing and understanding the wind, not to mention skill and experience. But, changing the subject, I listened to your last week's program targeting Jason Crawford. You did a damn thorough job, I must say, Lance. Your audience really surprises me with some of the questions they come up with. How do you manage to keep ahead of them," he queried.

Lance gave a short laugh. Lots of reading, Dad, not just the newspapers, but periodicals, journals, newsletters, you name it. Just constant research, then analyzing, comparing, checking—like your understanding of the winds, I have to inform myself of the winds of government, and change, be alert to the signals, in short, keep one step ahead of my listeners." He laughed again. "But that's not what I came over to talk about, Dad. I want your input, yours and Moms, on another matter."

Kate entered with a tray of oatcakes, a teapot and cups and saucers. Karamine followed closely behind, then sat next to Lance on the sofa, facing Antranig.

"Karamine says you have some exciting news for us," Kate said, as she poured the tea and passed the cups around.

"Yes, we do, Mom, and I'm anxious to know what you think of it."

Antranig and Kate watched their son with interest, as they settled comfortably into their chairs.

"Well, it all began when the Dixons . . . you remember my mentioning them don't you? They're the owners of the radio and TV stations I work for. Anyway, they suddenly invited us for dinner the other night. When we arrived, the Chairman of the Republican party, Richard Blair and his wife, Alice were also guests. I should have suspected what was up when we were invited on such short notice, but the upshot of the event is they want me to run for the senate this Fall against the machinery of the Liberal establishment in the State . . . "

"Not Jason Crawford," Antranig interrupted suddenly, placing his cup on the table before him, "you can't be serious, Lance, no one has ever been able to unseat him."

"You're right, Dad, it would be a tough fight, all the way. Crawford has the media, and he's Chairman of so many committees, he'd have strong support everywhere. Still . . . someone has to run against him, challenge the political status quo here in Massachussetts. I'm sort of flattered they think I can do it, and I'm considering it very seriously."

"Dad, they think Lance would be a formidable opponent, who could and does talk about issues troubling the country." Karamine added, "Richard and John seem to think Lance is qualified to expose some of the hypocrisy and corruption here in the State. Someone has to start fighting for what we believe is just and right. Personally, I believe he'd make a wonderful Senator, don't you?" she asked proudly, smiling at both Antranig and Kate.

"Beyond a doubt, yes," both Kate and Antranig answered simultaneously, but Antranig's expression remained thoughtful.

"My son against Jason Crawford? You know he's a friend, Lance." Antranig said after a moment's pause.

"Yeah, I know, and I've thought of that, Dad, but, unfortunately whether you like it or not, he's part of the problem, a big part. But, that's why we're here this afternoon. Nothing's definite yet, and I did want to know what you both thought before committing myself."

Kate and Antranig remained silent, seemingly lost for words.

"You have to know and fully understand how this will impact all of us," Karamine interjected softly, but firmly, "Every aspect of our lives . . . our homelife, our work, our friends, everything will be scruti-nized and inspected. The media won't leave a stone unturned, and nothing whatsoever will be sacred or private to the reporters and jour-nalists. They'll be busy looking for some piece of information they can twist or turn and use against us."

"Have you spoken to your parents about this, Karamine?" Kate asked gently.

"Yes, I talked to them by phone, and they indicated they would sup-port any decision Lance and I would make. They said not to worry about them. The trouble is though, I do. This could be a strenuous or-deal for them, and for you also, especially if the New York incident should ever come out . . . " Her voice faltered slightly.

"Karamine," Kate said persuasively, "that's been so many years ago, when Lance was a mere youth filled with passion and high ideals, it shouldn't pose a problem now."

"Absolutely not," Antranig broken in quickly, "besides, that account was completely expunged from the police records, thanks to the com-petence of our aunt Nevart. None of the newspapers picked up the story either, so, I don't think you need have any undue concern there, Son."

Lance's jaw was set in determined lines. "Well, I've given it some thought and I've decided to tell John and Richard the whole story. I can't risk a media frenzy of distorted facts and exaggeration. It would be dev-astating to the Party. The last thing I'd want to be is an embarrassment to them, much less what it would do to the family."

"Look Lance, there wasn't a single word in any of the New York pa-pers about it. Your mother and Nevart scanned all of the dailys search-ing for one small line. There was nothing," Antranig said firmly.

"Hummn, that's true," said Lance, but still unconvinced.

"Anyway, the important thing is you were not guilty of anything, outside of impulsive idealism, maybe, but that's all," Antranig stated emphatically. "Look, Son, . . . you know I don't agree with a lot of your views, but if after you talk to your friends, John and Richard, you still decide to run, know you can count on your mother and me for a hun-dred percent support of your campaign."

Lance smiled, his blue eyes reflecting sudden excitement. He glanced at his parents, then to Karamine before he spoke. "Don't see how I can lose with all of you behind me. So, if John and Richard agree after I talk to them . . . I'll run."

On the drive back to Boston, Lance and Karamine spoke little. Each seemed caught up with the afternoon's events, the conversation, and new changes that seemed inevitable. The ramifications of running a campaign against an entrenched opponent like Jason Crawford seemed awesome. He had the whole political structure of the Democratic party behind him—power, money, plus the most influential newspaper in the State, The Examiner. Up to now Lance had only been enlightening his audience regarding the politics of the State and nation, but now, it would actually be a head to head confrontation. Is it worth it, he wondered silently. Is it really worth all the sacrifice of personal freedom and privacy, the upheaval to the family, the mud-slinging and hostility of a dirty campaign? Could he really make a difference? How many others had tried and failed. How was it possible to make a difference when state workers, unions and the media always back the incumbent. Could he actually convince the voters that a change was needed to make state and national government return to fiscal responsibility? They destroyed Nixon . . . whoever could imagine such a thing would be possible, but it was, even though it was Nixon's own stupidity. He never should have tried to cover up the break in. Hell," Lance reflected, "why didn't he just come out and tell the truth, and let the people know it was members of his staff who, without his knowledge, took it upon themselves to break into the Democratic Headquarters at Watergate. All they wanted was evidence that the Democratic party was getting support from Castro. He should have come directly to the people and told them the truth— they would have listened, and the truth would have saved the Presidency. He was poorly advised.

"You haven't said much since leaving the house," said Lance, suddenly aware of Karamine's quiet mood. "What's on your mind?"

Karamine shrugged a little. "Oh, I don't know . . . I guess I was just thinking how little time we have to spend with our parents these days . . . we're so busy, Lance, and now, we seem to be more involved than ever. I sensed your parents hated to see us go today."

"Yeah, I know, but, what can we do. It's the times we live in, Karamine, everything is instantaneous and speeded up. I don't know what the answer is. Just now, I was thinking of Nixon, and how quickly he was destroyed . . . and look what's happening to the Justice system. It's trial by media now, it seems, rather than by jury. Somehow they seem to think of themselves as guardians of the people's rights. If someone does not agree with their premise or ideology, they begin a probe into a person's past looking for anything to twist or distort in order to smear or destroy that opposition. The media always takes a decided point of view and invariably dismiss any information or evidence to the contrary. And God forbid you bring up this subject, then its censorship, or you're labeled a fascist. I tell you, Karamine, through selective reporting and misinformation, they hold back information voters should have. And notice, they put important information on the obituary pages for God's sake. I keep wondering if I'm doing the right thing toying with this idea of running. It seems like such a no-win non-rewarding endeavor. What makes me think I could do any better than other candidates who've tried before and failed?"

"Come on, Lance, you love it, you know you do. I can't imagine you turning away from a good political debate or fight. Since when? Especially when you can bring forth all your axioms and moral codes of government, and particularly against someone like Jason Crawford."

"I thought it was great of Dad to back me in spite of his friendship with Crawford." Lance said affectionately.

"Well, I'd expect him to," Karamine asserted. Personally, I can't see what your father sees in a friendship with him anyway."

Lance smiled a little. "Well, you know Dad—he thinks he's a good liberal, but basically he's really conservative. Only he doesn't know it. He laughed. Actually, he's against everything Crawford stands for, abortion on demand, prayer out of the classroom, and Dad is for complete reform of the welfare system. I've heard him say so many times."

"That's true. Crawford is a humanist, too," Karamine added.

"Well, he belongs to the Yacht Club, and whenever they meet, they just don't discuss politics, is the way Dad tells it."

It was some minutes before Karamine spoke. "What if you do run and by some stroke of fate were elected to the Senate, Lance. You'd have to go to the Capital, and we'd be separated. Have you thought about that?"

"Well . . . you'd come with me, wouldn't you? He took his eyes off the road momentarily to look at her sideways. "You would be coming with me, wouldn't you, Karamine?" he repeated urgently.

"Lance . . . I do have my work at the hospital you know. Also, my work in Armenia. People depend on me there. I just can't pick up and leave my practice and the work I love, to attend parties and social gatherings with politicians in Washington. I'd be lost without my work, my family and friends."

Lance's jaw tensed slightly. "Are you saying you're not coming to Washington with me if I'm elected, Karamine, is that what you're saying?"

Karamine remained silent staring straight ahead.

"You know, when you go to Armenia for months at a time, I miss you, deeply, Karamine, but I try to understand and support you, because I know how important this is to you and our people," Lance continued in an aggrieved tone. "Can't you feel this is important to me too, and give me some understanding and support as well?"

Karamine gave a short exasperated sigh. "Look Lance, let's think about one thing at a time. First tell John and Richard about the New York episode, then, if they give you the go ahead, we'll campaign hard, and I'll do my utmost to help you succeed. If you are elected, then we'll see what can be done, no sense talking about it now while everything is in limbo. No matter what, you know I love you and will always support you, but we have to think carefully and make new adjustments, that's all."

Lance and Karamine drove the rest of the way home in silence, both involved in their own thoughts regarding the rapid sequence of events shaping up ahead.

4

Karamine's office was located in the large professional building near the hospital. It was a modern structure, with huge windows and plenty of parking space. Mothers, and young, active children, filled her waiting room, which was comfortable and well stocked with toys and books to amuse the children and absorb their attention and energy.

Now in one of her more quiet moments, Karamine sat at her desk and examined some reports the nurse had left there. She was constantly astounded by the cost of prescription drugs and pharmaceuticals, yet, compared to the quality of medicines in Armenia and Karabagh, she felt somewhat less perturbed. Much as she loved traveling to Armenia, she was always reminded of their archaic procedures and primitive equipment. And, as much as she contributed and brought new equipment and medicines, she felt the soviet attitudes of complacency and dogma made it difficult for change to prevail. Still, she felt a deep and overwhelming sense of kinship with the people, and never tired of trying to awaken them to the use of new methods and procedures she had initiated. She felt fortunate to have the cooperation of an old classmate to fill in for her while she was in Armenia. Otherwise, it would have been difficult to leave her practice for two or three months at a time. Her friend Donna, also had her office in the same building, so, they were able to cover each other without too much disruption. Most of her patients were from neighboring towns, and although they hated to see Karamine leave on her annual trip to Armenia, the mothers and children had learned to trust her associate. A mother herself, Doctor Donna MacDonald had taken a few years off to raise three boys in the earlier formative years, but when they were on their own, she had resumed her career, and was happy to take over an older doctor's practice, especially in the same building as her former classmate, Karamine.

The telephone rang and as Karamine picked up the receiver Lance's voice greeted her. "Oh Lance, I was just thinking about you and wondering how your meeting with John and Richard went this morning."

"Well, I told them everything, Karamine. I even told them about Vasken."

"Why was it necessary to mention Vasken's name, Lance?" Karamine replied with a slight edge to her voice.

"Look, Karamine, I wanted to be completely honest with them and I didn't want to leave out any facts concerning that incident so they can make a valid decision."

"Well, I think you could have told them about everything without naming names, Lance. I don't want my brother to get into any trouble."

"He's not going to get into any trouble, Karamine. The conversation was strictly confidential, between John, Richard and myself. No one else was present.

"Okay, so what was their decision, how did they take it?"

"Well naturally they asked me a lot of questions, especially if I had altered my thinking beliefs since that time. I also gave them an out. I told them if they had any reservations whatsoever to discount me as a candidate, and look for someone else. They had a small meeting then, without me; Came back about a half-hour later. They asked if Aunt Nevart had all the records expunged from the New York episode. When I assured them every trace had been expunged, and that she had even managed to get the old pistol back, they were completely reassured. They made a few phone calls, then returned and said unanimously that they did not think it would present any problems if I should run. 'It's a go' they said, as far as they're concerned. They still want me, so that's the way it stands now, unless, uh," he hesitated, "you have any objections, Karamine? I told them I would check with you and call them back tonight."

"You know it's what you want to do, Lance. How could I have any objections? I understand what's involved, I've thought of little else for the past week. I realize it will be uncomfortable at times, but, I'm with you. We'll give them the best we've got, and let the chips fall wherever."

"Great! That's my girl!" Lance responded with a burst of enthusiasm. "Hey, have I told you lately that I love you?"

Karamine laughed softly, her face flushed with pleasure. "Yes, but a girl likes to hear it again . . . and again."

"Well, I'll see you at home this evening. We'll talk more about it then. Bye."

The election for the senate was running full tilt with both Republicans and Democrats doing their best to convince voters that they were the party with the greatest interest of the people. Jason Crawford used the same old rhetoric he'd always used in past campaigns—that government could do for you what you were unable to do for yourself. He expounded profusely on all he had done for the state, constantly reminding everyone of grants obtained for arts and sciences, monies spent on state projects, new buildings, work for the ship yards and all other pork barrel benefits he'd been able to muster through his chairmanship on a decisive finance committee. He repeated continually that his chairmanship was at stake, and a vote for his opponent was a vote against the economy of the state. State workers, unions and welfare recipients, as well as many in the private sector who had been rewarded by fat contracts from the government and state, had rallied around him to secure their continued source of contracts.

Senator Jason Crawford continued to travel throughout the state, seeking all the support he could muster to overwhelm his opponent. He was determined to crush this radio talk show upstart once and for all, not just by a mere win, but by an overwhelming victory. His strategy was specifically directed toward teaching a lesson to Lance or any other who dared challenge the political apparatus of the state. Lance, in the meantime had left his radio show ON TARGET to avoid a conflict of interest. However, much to his frustration, he now found that he had little opportunity of reaching voters with his unabridged message. Most of his TV interviews were stacked to his disadvantage, with a panel of liberal pundits who made personal attacks against him, ultimately forcing him to defend himself. Although he felt anger and a sharp sense of exasperation, he knew better than to lose control, or let one statement go by unchallenged. Time and time again he pressed the interviewer to restate the question asked, then, with deliberate skill, acquired from his debating days, he answered clearly and concisely. He was learning fast, and discovered the pitfalls of the campaign early. He knew the task ahead was monumental. Senator Crawford had held the seat for the past eighteen years, and had worked himself into the powerful position of chairman of the finance committee, where he had become influential in his party's internal structure. He wielded tremendous power over the senators, and those who did not support him or his wishes, were likely to become deprived of appropriations. Many young and inexperienced senators with noble aspirations soon felt the brunt of his power, and eventually capitulated to his will.

Lance had always felt that these chairmanships in the senate and house should not be captive to one person, no matter who controlled either house. Although it's true they are elected by their respective states, still, he felt the rest of the country should not be held captive to their states' elections. He felt deeply, that in order to express a true democracy, chairmanships should be limited to two terms, thus insuring that government truly reflected the will of the whole country.

However, with the support and endorsement of John and Richard and their combined strategies, all other candidates were soundly defeated in the early primaries, and Lance was now the Republican standard bearer against Jason Crawford. Karamine tried to be with him as much as possible as he toured from Boston to Springfield, Beverly, Lowell, Haverhill and Lawrence. Voters liked her, and gradually, she became more confident as a speaker, packing punch in her delivery. She reiterated Lance's message, and tried to convince the people of his sincerity in attempting to break the grip of the Massachusetts political machine. She explained in minute detail the difference between government jobs and the private sector, her theme became socialism or free enterprise.

Gradually, as they hammered their message, Lance noticed the crowds increasing. They moved to larger quarters and continued to stump. As people listened, slowly the message took root and Lance began receiving support among the taxpayers, libertarians, and conservatives of both parties. Little by little he made inroads into the moderate element of the opposition, as well as into many working minorities who had difficulty making ends meet after payroll tax deductions. As expected, the media exaggerated and embellished his views, giving it their own spin. His statement on entitlements, where he merely declared they should be examined and certain reforms undertaken to assure solvency for future social security recipients, drew a flood of letters from senior citizens. According to media reports, Lance planned to do away with social security benefits, and elders were fearful of losing their monthly checks. To avoid distortion of his message, Lance came to the conclusion he would only grant live interviews and take part in debates. He refused to give taped interviews because he couldn't control the editing or important deletions critical to his message. He also came to the conclusion that in order to win, he needed high visibility which meant he had to tour and campaign in most of the towns and cities of the state.

Lance's weighty speeches did not go unrecognized by his opponent, Senator Crawford or his political machine. Polls reflected constant erosion of support, as discontent among working people of his own party grew. The Crawford camp lost no opportunity to discredit Lance, often resorting to personal attack and innuendo, which the media seized and hyperbolized with gross exaggeration. Lance's quick temper flared at times, but he remained calm, ignoring the accusations to refocus his message. "Break the chains of bureaucratic slavery and reach for the sky—look to the best that each one of us can be, and refuse to allow government bureaucrats to lower our ideals and aspirations. You want jobs? Then let's get the government off the backs of the people and watch the economy grow. We can do it if we unite. Get out and vote—we can win."

With Lance's popularity rising in the polls, Senator Crawford in desperation, finally challenged Lance to a no holes barred debate. The Senator, assured of his own ability to get the better of Lance, soon had his aids set up the time and place. While on Lance's radio show, ON TARGET, Senator Crawford felt Lance had the advantage because he conducted the interview. In an open debate, however, with only a moderator to check the time, the roles would be reversed, he reasoned confidently; Once and for all he would demonstrate his expertise and experience in handling opposition, and he savored the taste of victory.

———————

The auditorium was filled to capacity the night of the debate. Lance felt the heat of the glaring T.V. lights as he glanced out toward the audience, then looked at Karamine for support. Each candidate had been groomed as to what questions may be asked, and each had been advised and guided away from the pitfalls to avoid at all costs. Each would have an opportunity to ask a question, the opponent would have four minutes to answer. There will also be a follow up after each question, the moderator explained.

Karamine waved and gave Lance a confident smile from her seat in the front row between John, Richard and their wives. Then, the countdown was called and the cameras closed in on the narrator.

"Good evening, ladies and gentlemen, tonight we have a debate between Senator Jason Crawford, the Democratic incumbent, and his challenger, Lance Bagdasarian. This debate is sponsored by the Committee For Fair Taxation. The rules have been agreed to by both parties and their staffs, so without further delay we will explain them. Debaters may ask questions from any area they choose; the answer time shall be limited to four minutes. There will be a two minute follow-up after each question. And now, with a toss of a coin determined before, Senator Crawford has the first question. Senator, go ahead with your question."

Senator Crawford drew a long breath, glanced first at the cameras, then focused a long penetrating gaze on Lance. "Mr. Bagdasarian" he began slowly and deliberately, "Can you tell me why it is that you Republicans are always for the interests of the rich, with no regard or compassion whatsoever for the millions of hard working people who struggle daily simply to exist and feed their children?"

Lance looked directly at Senator Crawford, and calculated his answer." Your question is one of divisiveness, Senator, always used by your party to create an atmosphere of class warfare, envy and hate. You like to give the impression that anyone who holds a good job is rich, that wealthy people have somehow obtained their money through cheating, stealing or exploiting others, which you know is not true. As a fiscal conservative first, then a Republican, I believe in as little government as possible, which then unleashes the power of our citizens to be the best they can be; it frees them to become entrepreneurs, to experience the free enterprise system creating challenging new jobs and opportunities without the restrictions of excessive government regulations. I do not believe in the redistribution of wealth as outlined in all socialist marxist countries; I don't believe in punishing with excessive taxation, those achievers who work long hours or who take on two jobs. Nor is it the purpose of government to diminish us all to the lowest denominator in order to create an equal playing field. When I speak of the workers, Senator, I refer to those men and women who produce the nuts and bolts of this fair land—those who work hard to put food on our tables each day, the ones your party has taxed to the limit. These oppressive taxes have forced the disintegration of our family units by requiring that both parents work in order to make ends meet. Yes, Senator, all your party has done for this country is to create a huge dependency class and a large bureaucracy where over fifty percent of the work force is now employed by some government agency, whether local, state or federal. The other half of the workers have to support these non-producers, pay for their sick days, holidays and pension programs, something that the private sector does not have. And who do these people vote for Senator? Your Liberal party of course. Thus they perpetuate themselves and the status quo. Compassion Senator? Have compassion for the creators and innovators of this country and quit punishing them through taxation for their achievement. Quit making profit a dirty word, and let this country be the best it can be . . . a shining light to the rest of the world."

"Your response, Senator," the narrator commented.

"I would like to inform my opponent that all of those government workers are hard-working people who get little thanks from the public. They work all hours, day and night, and my opponent and his party should be thankful to them."

"But Senator, they do not create a nut or bolt, much less a job."

A sudden applause interspersed by hissing and booing thundered throughout the auditorium. An irksome expression flashed briefly across the Senator's face as he noted the unexpected response to Lance's remark. Within seconds however, the quick charm returned, and once again Jason Crawford was calm and postured, confident of his power and the unassailable clout he wielded throughout the state.

"Please" . . . the narrator implored, "no applause, hissing or booing. We have only limited time for this debate, so we don't want to waste it. Your question, Mr. Bagdasarian."

Lance cleared his throat before addressing the Senator. "Senator, why do you refer to government spending as investment, while you degrade worker's spending as consumption?"

Senator Crawford cleared his throat before answering. "The government is like a father of a family, who looks at every aspect concerning the welfare of his children. Government has the capacity to take care of everyone—social security for example. Where would our seniors be without this pension program? Through certain laws and regulations we are able to control industry from polluting the environment, also the government sets standards for our food and drug industry through the FDA, thus ensuring a safe, and first grade food and drug supply for our people. We lead the world in this field of social achievement. This is what you so disparagingly refer to as 'bureaucracy'.

Are you against the Social Security system we have, Mr. Bagdasarian? And . . . would you have voted against the system if you were a senator at the time? Let the voters know precisely where you stand. This is what I mean when I say you represent the worst, the party of the rich who have no compassion for the poor and underprivileged. Let me tell you sir, the government is an instrument to be used to set controls for the environment, business, industry and to attend to the social needs of the people. In this manner we have opportunities available to all no matter who they are. Through laws, regulations and controls, government is able to fulfill the mandate of the people. Our government understands the needs of the masses, and should reflect it, rather than your free market philosophy, that always espouses so-called individualism otherwise known as profit and greed. Government should have the power, not the individual, this way everyone has the guarantee of a safe and secure way of life from birth till death."

There was an instantaneous burst of applause from the audience.

"Response." The narrator said, holding his hand up and looking at Lance."

"With all due respect, Sir," Lance began, "that is incorrect. You know there's nothing in the social security program but I.O.U.'s, bonds from the government who use the funds as part of the budget spending to buy votes for all their liberal programs. During Roosevelt's presidency there was another, far better program on the table in congress. It was similar to social security, but would have been run privately, where congress and politicians could not get their hands on it or use it as a political football. The idea then, as advanced by both republican and democrats bipartisanly, was that all pension and worker's retirement money would be funneled, similar to the social security, as a retirement program, to ensure the future of the workers. Workers would have been able to borrow from this fund, then pay it back with interest, ultimately increasing the total amount of the fund. By the time a worker was ready to retire, his money, drawing compound interest over the years, would have grown considerably. Naturally, the bankers didn't like it, and congress hated it, since they couldn't control it. We could still privatize social security by giving workers an immediate choice whether they wanted social security or the private plan. Ultimately then, in about ten years, social security could be phased out and the system finally privatized and out of the hands of politicians. This money in the private account would not be subject to taxes, but used only for future retirees.

As for the government thinking of the people as their children," Lance paused and shook his head, "this makes me wonder what Thomas Jefferson might have thought about it. As an architect of the constitution, he felt deeply that the role of the government should be limited. Where does the role of individual responsibility enter the picture? Today we have no fault auto insurance, no fault divorce, children are under stress because their parents are separated, hardened criminals are loose on the streets, young pregnancies and a host of other ills are all attributed to an apathetic society . . . "

The sound of a gavel interrupted Lance. "Your time is up, Mr. Bagdasarian."

"I'd like to finish, if I may."

"Use it in your summation," the narrator said curtly.

The debate continued for the specified time, with each candidate pushing his ideological persuasion. Lance promoting his premise of a free enterprise system, Jason Crawford, describing the benefits of a society protected by government intervention in every phase of its life. As the time approached for a summation from both candidates, Jason Crawford appealed directly to the listening audience. "You've just heard my worthy opponent give you all the reasons why you shouldn't vote for him. He talks without conscience about the poor and minorities of this great country, and I'd like to ask him how these people are to survive without the help of the government through welfare, jobs creation, education and other benefits the government is able to provide. Government is the primary mover of this underclass who are striving to elevate themselves to the American dream. My opponent would do away with all of these programs that we have deemed necessary for the well being of our people. The Republican party is the party of exploitation, profit and greed. Our party is for the poor and underprivileged, so don't be fooled by Mr. Bagdasarian's rhetoric of free economy and individuality, which doesn't mean a thing in the long run. Vote for the party who cares for the needs of its people, and vote the party of greed and profit, my opponent, down."

Applause filled the auditorium as Senator Crawford acknowledged his constituency nodding and raising his hand. "Thank you, thank you," he said, then sat down.

The audience quieted down as the narrator gaveled for attention, then asked Lance for his summation.

Lance held tightly to the side of the podium, and threw a glance toward Karamine, who gave him a smile of encouragement. He took a deep breath before speaking.

"The party of greed and profit is what my opponent calls us . . . the creative hard workers who put in so much time and effort to pay the taxes the Federal government uses in an unending spiral of waste and consumption. They, the congress, controlled by the liberal wing of the Democrat party, have had control for the last forty years. They have so much compassion that under President Johnson they started the war on poverty. After spending three and a half trillion dollars of your tax money, the amount of the national debt, the program is a failed one, which they refuse to acknowledge. All it has done is create a dependent class of people, whose needs have quadrupled since then. Yes, they have lots of compassion . . . with YOUR money. This is how they buy votes, and perpetuate their power. Don't be fooled by it, voters. When they talk about investment, it is taxes they mean, how to steal more money from you to perpetuate the system.

We in the Republican party only wish to give you an opportunity to be the best that you can be. Not by lowering standard in school or universities, or by quotas on the job market. We are optimists who believe in achieving high standards of excellence that everyone has an opportunity to attain. No matter who you are, don't be seduced by these so called compassionate liberals who call you inferior and unable to compete with the rest of society. It's up to you whether you wish to work hard to achieve and better yourselves. We spend more money on education than any other country in the world, yet even though they have high school diplomas, we have an illiterate underclass who still can't read. How is this possible? Through social engineering programs and progressive teaching methods, we have done away with major basics, reading writing and arithmetic. Instead, we have substituted condoms, sex education, and the dangers of profit."

A tremendous applause filled the auditorium, as the narrator appealed once more to the audience. "Please . . . let him conclude, we are running out of time."

"We can't teach them absolutes . . . right or wrong . . . because this has a moral standard which liberals can't live with. Thus the student decides for himself what is right or wrong. I could go on, but I see the narrator has indicated my time is up. So, I'll just conclude with this thought . . . let us join together to break the shackles of liberal bureaucratic bondage, once and for all. Let's crusade to throw off these career politicians who think they have the constitutional right to strip you of all your hard earned money, and let's take our state and country back. Thank you."

The majority of the audience rose to their feet and were now shouting and hailing Lance, as he bowed to them in acknowledgment of the response. Karamine, wiped her eyes under her glasses, as John Dixon and Richard Blair along with their wives applauded wildly. "I think we have a fighter and a winner this time, John," Richard shouted above the clamor and excitement.

5

Despite efforts by Senator Crawford and his contingent of support in the local media to misrepresent Lance, and the message of his party, the polls continued to climb in Lance's favor. Spurred on by the encouraging impact of the debate, he continued to tour the state, hammering out his issues—individuality, freedom and choice from government mandates, regulations and taxes. He pointed out that these factors were driving business and talented people out of the state, and in some cases corporations, who were actually leaving the country itself. Over and over he reassured people who worried about their social security and jobs should he be elected. Slowly but surely he began to win the voters confidence, as they received the message straight from Lance, and not filtered through a media bias controlled by the political machine of the state.

On the other hand, Senator Crawford's campaign had stalled. Cries of liar, bureaucrat and socialist interrupted his speeches on more than one occasion, driving his party to resort to labels and personal attack. Repeatedly, Lance admonished his people not to resort to such tactics, stating they served no purpose, and would ultimately hurt the party. "Use your power at the ballot box instead, they'll hear you loud and clear when we vote them out," he advised urgently.

With the deterioration of Senator Crawford's support and the overwhelming evidence of voter dissatisfaction, the Democrats decided unanimously to call an emergency strategy meeting to stem the tide tilting in Lance's favor. All the pundits of the Democratic party, along with top people running the Senator's campaign were invited to contribute and implement any new ideas that might revitalize their sagging ratings. Meeting in the board room of the Daily Examiner for convenience to all, the meeting began at eight PM, with everyone involved in the campaign present. The managing editor of The Examiner, Todd Driscoll, a brusk man in his early fifties was also present. Hard hitting and inclined to cynicism, Driscoll was known in the business as dedicated and single-minded. A formidable adversary, his verbal skills and delivery of brisk sound-bites made him desirable as a panel guest on many news and T.V. talk shows.

Democratic advisor and pollster, Michael Golden, dressed in his ever-present blue jeans and turtle neck, was also present. Slightly built and wiry, Mike graduated from Harvard in the top ten of his class; Sharp and confident in his appraisal of new people and situations, he was quick to grasp an opportunity to push an advantage or target an opponent. Today, however, Mike's face was unusually haggard as he shuffled through papers and made quick notes on a small pad.

Jacqueline Dustin, a tall attractive girl in her early thirties was public relations coordinator for the party. Jacqui, as she liked to be called, graduated from Wellesley College and had gone on to Brandeis for a degree in political science. Although usually quite vocal in expressing her views, tonight she seemed calmer, self-possessed, almost mysterious in her exchanged comments with her research people Tom Craven and Denise Jensen, who were seated on her right and left.

"How about a drink before we get started," Todd Driscoll suggested while walking to the highly polished cabinet that housed his private bar. "I think I need a bourbon myself." He poured himself a healthy drink from a square decanter, then filled the glass with ice from an ice machine located above a small sink. "Mike . . . What'll you have?" Bourbon?"

"You still drinkin' that Southern rot gut, Todd? No, give me a Drambui if its still there," Mike Golden answered, unceremoniously, not lifting his eyes from the paper he was studying.

"I'll have a glass of wine if there's a bottle open, otherwise, nothing," Jacqui called, "put a couple of ice cubes in it."

"Now . . . let's get to the business at hand," Mike Golden said when everyone was settled around the solid rectangular table. "As you all know, the polls are showing this talk show character gaining far too great a lead on us. We have to think of some strategy to defeat him before the whole race is lost in his favor. It's going to happen if we don't stop him now. We can't have Senator Crawford lose his chairmanship on the finance committee because of our inefficiency to influence the voters. The state just can't afford the loss, especially with new appropriations coming up next year. Massachusetts has to get its due share of the pie. So think, and fast. Give me some ideas."

"Well, every day The Examiner has been pounding away to inform the voters of what will happen if the election is lost to a newcomer," Todd Driscoll began." The loss of the chairmanship alone means a loss of all that federal money for construction, highways, navy yards, and so on. We've been showing the money loss with bars and graphs, but it's not helping. Do you think Bagdasarian is convincing the people that all of those projects are pork and in the long run it's the taxpayers who'll end up paying for it? He keeps hammering at that point all the time."

"What about another debate?" Mike Golden suggested. We could set it up with a bunch of activist reporters to do a number on Bagdasarian."

"That's a thought," Todd Driscoll added thoughtfully," Then I'll get the paper to editorialize and have feature writers blow Bagdasarian's words apart." He looked at the group for approval.

"No way, no way," Jacqui Dustin spoke up waving her hand in the air. "A live debate is no good. Look what happened last time. I don't think the Senator is up to it. Plus, the people are getting pretty wise to stacked panels. Lance has been clueing the voters on that score."

"What other choices do we have . . . what's left," said Tom Craven in a dispirited tone. "What about a set-up rape scenario. I know someone we could get to visit him in his apartment on some pretext when we're sure his wife is out. Once inside she could rip her own clothes, then run out screaming RAPE. Our cameras would catch the whole thing and . . . viola . . . it runs through the whole media. Bagdasarian is history."

"Dream on," Todd Driscoll rebutted brusquely, "That one's been tried years ago on Lee Mortimer, or was it Jack Leith who wrote Washington Confidential. Anyway, as I recall, when the girl screamed 'rape' in Mortimer's hotel room, and the cameras started to roll, his wife walks out of the bathroom asking what was going on. Made fools of everyone. No, we need something more subtle. What about getting hold of all his speeches from the archives over the last few years since he's been in the public, and scanning them for random phrases and thoughts that could be fused together. Taken out of context we could exaggerate his message and get our points across. This has worked effectively in the past, and it will work now. Plus that, it's literally undetectable. He'll be defeated by his own words."

"No, I don't believe it will work this time," Senator Crawford protested. "There are too many people in their camp who have access to those same clips and files. They'll just counter-react by showing the entire clip and then we'd be in trouble."

During most of the conversation, Jacqui Dustin sat quietly in her seat, listening intently to everyone's suggestions, but remaining unusually reticent. Since this was nothing like her typical pattern of strong suggestion and vocal confrontation Todd Driscoll wondered vaguely if she was overtired or slightly under the weather. When she excused herself for a moment to go into the outer office he was certain of it.

Jacqui however, was never more sure of herself. In the outer office she approached the secretary who had remained overtime to cover the meeting.

"Is he here yet?" she asked with anticipation.

"Yes, I put him in the small conference room."

"Good."

She returned to the meeting, with an aura of suppressed excitement about her. Settling into her chair, she studied the expression on each face before speaking, then, rising she spoke deliberately and with some obvious pleasure.

"Well . . . while you've all been casting around to find a strategy to reverse the polls, I've come up with an answer."

All eyes were riveted on Jacqui as she let the impact of her remark sink in. Mike Golden who had been totally absorbed in the papers before him removed his glasses and focused his full attention on her. Todd Driscoll beamed a slightly patronizing smile. But everyone gave Jacqui full attention, and their frank curiosity was not lost on her.

Her smile was slightly triumphant." Well gentlemen, two days ago out of the blue, a man came in to see me. He had information that will blow you away, and will certainly reverse this whole election campaign to our favor. It seems he had called our headquarters first, and wanted to speak to someone in authority. He claimed he had information detrimental to Lance Bagdasarian. They immediately gave him my phone number and he contacted our office. We set up a meeting with him and wow! The information he gave us is dynamite!"

"Why haven't you come forward with this before instead of letting us sweat out a strategy," Todd Driscoll asked in an irritable voice, "why all the mystery?"

"Yeah," Mike Golden agreed peevishly, "after all I'm supposed to be running this show."

"Let her finish," Senator Crawford broke in impatiently.

"Look . . . I had to verify this information and see if this guy was for real before saying anything. I had to be absolutely certain, so I called the New York police, and the U.N. I finally located the detective who had interrogated him. I even was able to contact the D.A. whom the detective had called when Lance's lawyer arrived on the scene. He had told the detective they had blown the case and to release him. No gentlemen . . . this man's statements are valid and authentic. Believe me you should listen to him.

"New York police, D.A. and the U.N.? What the hell do they have to do with our campaign?" Todd Driscoll exploded.

"Why don't I just bring him in and let him give you the information himself," Jacqui said calmly.

"He's here?" Senator Crawford queried, an eager light in his eye. "He's here."

"By all means then, bring him in and let's see what he has to say. Personally, I'm curious to know what he's getting out of it, and why he's doing it." Todd Driscoll said suspiciously.

"Oh he'll let you know on no uncertain terms what's in it for him," Jacqui said, as she left the room.

She was back within seconds accompanied by a tall, rather gaunt looking man; his deep-set black eyes surveyed the room with intense scrutiny as though he was someone familiar with the process of making quick judgments and sharp evaluations. His presence suggested power and a chilling indifference to the opinions or concerns of others; this was immediately evident to everyone in the room.

"Gentlemen . . . " Jacqui began, motioning toward the guest, "I'd like you to meet Mr. Vasken Casparian. He has a story to relate I'm sure you'd all like to hear. Go ahead, Mr. Casparian."

Vasken Casparian's expression of slight disdain gave way to full-blown contempt as he looked about the room, his gaze resting momentarily on Senator Crawford. So these are the self-anointed bureaucrats, he thought, clenching his teeth together. They're nothing more than a bunch of decadent capitalists—fatuous intellectuals like the days before Lenin and Trotsky—same thing. Impotent fat cats christened with the balm of benevolence. But what difference does it make? I'll use their self-serving interests to destroy that brother-in-law of mine once and for all. I gave him his lumps once, physically. But this time, I'll destroy him politically, along with all his cliché rhetoric 'you can be the best if you strive hard—everyone has the right to succeed' Who the hell does he think he's fooling with his program ON TARGET. He could always talk, but here's one he's not hoodwinking. Lance, the jackals are loose.

There was an ominous and curious silence in the room as all eyes fastened on Vasken.

"My name is Vasken Casparian," he began crisply, "and I've a story to tell regarding your opponent . . . one I think you may be able to use to win this election. But let me start at the beginning. At least sixteen years ago when Lance Bagdasarian and I were both in college. Incidentally, he just happens to be my brother-in-law, but as far as I'm concerned, that's in name only. However, that's another matter and of no value to the story.

Back in those days I was impassioned and outraged by the atrocities perpetrated on one million and a half Armenian people. Since I'm Armenian myself it struck at my very soul and I wanted to hit back, to crush those responsible for such crimes, especially the Turks. When I realized the passive indifference that existed not only in our own country but in Europe, I decided to take matters into my own hands. I formed a group of guerrillas to take the conflict right to the Turkish government, and we held regular meetings where we made plans to retaliate, and to make the statement that dedicated Armenians will never never forget the genocide of their people."

"In other words you were a group of terrorists, isn't that what you're saying?" Todd Driscoll blurted out explosively.

"Label it what you will," Vasken responded indifferently.

"Why should we take the word of a terrorist?" Todd Driscoll demanded.

Vasken's eyes narrowed. "Look . . . I'm not here to defend my actions, then or now, especially to you. And if you're not interested in hearing the story of Lance Bagdasarian's involvement with the group, then I won't waste any more of my time."

"Lance Bagdasarian was involved with an underground terrorist group?" Todd Driscoll's eyes lighted up with sudden excitement. Mike Golden leaned forward in his chair to take a better look at Vasken; the room was heavy with an ominous silence as the impact of the information sank in. "Please continue, Mr. Casparian. There will be no more interruption," Senator Crawford stated, throwing a quick glance to Todd Driscoll.

"Lance Bagdasarian came to a meeting after expressing interest in the group. He wanted to see "how an underground meeting was conducted," Vasken said with sarcasm. "Since he was dating my sister at the time, and claimed to be an Armenian with sympathies toward our cause, I took him to one of the meetings. Needless to say, he was quite impressed, and willingly agreed to attend other meetings. He was accepted, through my intervention, even though it was against the original wishes of the rest of the group. Since Lance was only half-Armenian, they somehow distrusted his motives, and felt he was more curious than dedicated. For myself, I saw through his hypocrisy immediately. This mixed-breed blonde, blue-eyed imposter may have impressed my sister, but he didn't fool me for a second, for all his talk of his Armenian heritage, and his so called dedication to our cause. I wanted to expose him, for my sister's sake, so I baited him, then waited my chance.

In the underground, we were of the belief that a state of war exists between the people of Armenia and the Turkish nation. Since we do not have an army or navy, we use the only option left to us—guerilla warfare. Any Turkish government operation or activity, whether political or military would be a target. Each one of us were willing to sacrifice ourselves, yes, even our very lives for this cause of justice, which to us meant return of our stolen lands, and recognition of the atrocities perpetuated against the Armenian people by the Turks. It's necessary you understand these details as a background for events that happened that last evening of our meetings. We had made profiles of a Turkish diplomat to the U.N. and intended to make him our first target. This is where Bagdasarian showed his true colors. After all his pretentious and high-flown speech about allegiance and dedication to the Armenian cause, he was so extremely shocked to find out we were actually planning to assassinate the Turkish ambassador. He began to argue and had the brazen gall to challenge my judgment. In fact, he even tried to persuade the others that it was not in their best interests to commit this act, and the argument heated up. After accusing him of being a hypocrite just like his father who forgets his Armenian heritage, when it gets inconvenient, and others of his relatives, who had the name of being great Armenian heroes, but never stayed on to finish the fight, it came to blows. He tried to strangle me, but, I took care of him, believe me. I knocked him unconscious, then bodily, threw him out on the street. The next thing I knew he was in New York stalking the ambassador for the purpose of killing him. Again . . . he proved himself to be the hypocrite and coward he is when he turned and ran and didn't finish the job. He was apprehended, however, and they did put him in jail."

There was an audible gasp from the group, and it was some minutes before anyone spoke.

"This is quite a serious allegation, Mr. Casparian," Todd Driscoll said at last, and again, why should we take your word on this? Is there a source we could check to validate your story?"

Vasken pursed his lips and smiled unpleasantly. "Ah yes . . . the reliable source, by all means," he said mockingly.

"Well, said Jacqui with authority, I made inquiries in New York, and the police captain and U.N. authorities verified what has been said. The reason they had to let him go was the arresting officer forgot to read him his rights, and his aunt Nevart Dederian, who practiced law here in Boston at the time got him off on the Miranda Act. She also had the records expunged because of his youth so it never got into any of the papers."

Senator Crawford shook his head. "Well, I don't know if we should use the information. Lance Bagdasarian is the son of a fellow yacht club member, and a friend. We've socialized together and it's a bit awkward."

"Are you damn crazy or just plum stupid," Todd Driscoll blasted. "This is what we've been waiting and hoping for. This is a bombshell, and it will fix Bagdasarian and his party once and for all. We've got to use it."

"Absolutely! It's a break through," Mike Golden said gleefully.

"Well . . . I don't know," Senator Crawford said haltingly. "His father is a friend."

Todd Driscoll turned toward Vasken and shook his hand. "I'd like to thank you for your cooperation in this matter. You've done us all a great service here. Uh . . . if there's anything we can do for you at any time . . . uh . . . please let us know," he said without much conviction.

"Stupid bastards, Vasken thought. They'd eat each other to grab control. I only want to get Lance, once and for all. His eyes reflected a small triumphant smile. "Thanks" he said briefly, before making a quick exit from the room.

Mike Golden walked over to Jacqui with a smile on his face and patted her shoulder enthusiastically. "You did it Jacqui, you did it kid, and now Lance Bagdasarian, you son of a bitch, we've got you!"

6

"CANDIDATE EXPOSED! NEW EVIDENCE UNCOVERS LANCE
BAGDASARIAN'S DIRECT INVOLVEMENT IN
UNDERGROUND TERRORISM!"

Like the detonation of megatons of dynamite, headlines exploded
through the pages of The Examiner, erupting in editorials and news-
rooms everywhere across the state. The sensational story took on a life
of its own, like dust caught up in a whirlwind and borne aloft, touching
down where it will. Minute details were seized upon, dissected and
probed, then served back to the public with a melodramatic spin. Lance
was stupefied and felt at times as though he were grappling with a
multi-headed monster, a beast who consumed truth then spewed it back
as allegation and fraud.

Senator Jason Crawford strategically distanced himself. He refused
to comment on anything his campaign managers or publicists said, and
cloaked his targets and real aims with benevolent statements—"There
must be a good explanation," or "I don't believe Lance Bagdasarian is
an assassin, give him a chance to explain," he'd comment with a smirk.

But the media was relentless, and played the story to the hilt, refusing to allow Lance's firm denials and statements of truth to dull the
edge of what they called a 'good story'. How did they ever uncover that
story, Lance wondered when the news first aired, now full of new ad-
ditions and commentary. At first he couldn't believe it, until he heard
Vasken's name. Now he knew, and his handsome face darkened with
rage. "Damn you, Vasken," he muttered furiously, "do you hate me so
much you could do this to your sister who's always cared for you; how
could you bring this kind of pain and grief to your parents. God, he
thought, this guy hasn't one ounce of feeling or conscience. We haven't

seen him for years and now, out of the blue, he arrives on the scene to destroy my career and bring shame to his family; what kind of man is he anyway? I want to tear him apart. I'm not that same kid he beat up years ago—this time it would be different. I'd destroy him. No, how could I? There's Karamine, and all these years she's been torn between us. I'd never hurt her like that. It would crush her, and she's suffering enough now. She's devastated by Vasken's malicious act as it is, and it's all she can do to comfort her parents. I don't think I have any choice but to step out of the race. It's useless to try and fight this thing. No one really hears what I'm saying, they're just going to believe what they want to believe. I'll have to call a meeting with Richard and John, and I'll do whatever they decide. In the long run, my main concern is for the honor and good name of my wife and family.

Lance dialed John Dixon's private number. He was relieved to hear John's confident voice on the other end.

"John . . . Lance here, look John, we've got to have an emergency meeting right away. Can you manage it?

"Absolutely, as a matter of fact, I was just going to get in touch with you to suggest the same thing. I'll get hold of Richard right away, and let's say about seven tonight? Yes, right here at the studio where we won't be interrupted."

"Great. I'll see you both then."

Back in her office in the large professional building near the hospital, Karamine picked up the telephone and slowly dialed her parents' home. She had been dreading the moment ever since the news story on Lance broke, yet she knew they waited for her now to offer some stable and logical explanation to the unexpected turn of events and the subsequent upheaval and turmoil of their private lives. Reporters and media people were everywhere, hounding both families, stalking their homes, waiting for Karamine as she arrived or left her office or hospital. Her parents had never really been told the full story of Lance's involvement in the New York episode, and since no crime had actually been committed, Karamine had thought it best at the time to forget the whole incident and put it behind them. Besides, she had reasoned, her parents would have been too deeply hurt by Vasken's involvement; In the long run, it was best to let it go, especially since no mention of it had ever appeared in any of the papers, mostly through the efforts of Nevart, Lance's lawyer and long time family friend.

Today, however, as she waited for her mother to pick up the telephone, she questioned the wisdom of that decision.

"Hello . . . *Myrig?*"

Karamine's mother, Anahid Casparian, answered, her voice edged with slight hysteria. "Karamine? What's happening? What's it all about? I just don't understand anything that's been happening . . . reporters are outside all over the place, photographers, too. It's been terrible for your father and me, just terrible . . . "

"Mom, I know," Karamine said, trying to assuage her mother's emotional state, "look is *Hyrig* there?"

"Yes, I'm on the extension," Aram Casparian answered.

"Okay. Now listen, Mom, Dad, listen carefully. Try to control yourself and listen," Karamine said calmly.

"What's this stuff about Lance's being involved in an Armenian underground, Karamine?" her father demanded sharply. "If I remember correctly, he was picked up for stalking the Turkish ambassador, but then let go when they couldn't prove it."

"Dad, he was accused of attempted murder of a Turkish ambassador at that time . . . "

"What! We were never informed it was that serious. What was the purpose of keeping this kind of information from us, Karamine, how could you do this to us?" her father accused hotly.

"Dad, please, it's difficult enough, there were so many circumstances, and it didn't serve any purpose, since Lance was innocent of the charge. Perhaps we should have talked more about it, and in that we made a mistake. I'm sorry Hyrig, there was so much going on at the time, we just wanted to put it behind us and go on.

"Vasken's involved with this too, isn't he?" Aram Casparian asked, his voice edged with bitterness and irony.

Karamine sighed deeply before answering. "Yes, Hyrig, he is."

There was loud sobbing as Karamine's mother wept openly and repeated denials. "No, no, no, he can't be . . . he's been gone a long time . . . I know he's not involved with this."

"Was Lance involved with the underground, Karamine?" her father probed intently.

"Dad, Mom, listen, Vasken was in the underground, don't you remember back in college? Anyway, he did take Lance a few times, but Lance never became a member. At the last meeting, the group talked and made plans to kill the Turkish ambassador when he came to the United Nations. Lance was absolutely opposed to that idea, and he and Vasken had a violent argument. Vasken gave him a bad beating, then threw him out bodily. The next thing we knew Lance was in New York, and they caught him outside of the U.N. with a gun. He never intended to kill the ambassador though. He told me that at the last minute he just couldn't go through with it, and was on the point of leaving when he was spotted by the police. They thought he looked suspicious, especially when Lance began to run as they tried to question him. They knocked him down, and the next thing he knew he was in jail. Of course they searched him and found the gun, a concealed weapon, so the charge was quite serious. It was an impulsive and foolish move on his part but thank God, he came to his senses. It's just too bad he was apprehended as he turned to leave."

"Yes, thank God he did come to his senses in time. Lance is no murderer and that's for sure," her mother said reflectively.

"How did they get the story after all this time?" her father asked.

Karamine hesitated before answering. "Vasken."

"Vasken!" both parents responded together. "But Vasken hasn't been around here for years. He doesn't even know what's going on, how could he know?" Karamine's father said quickly.

"I don't believe Vasken would do this to us, I know he didn't like Lance, but he wouldn't do it to us, his parents, and you, Karamine . . . Vasken always loved you," Anahid Casparian insisted emotionally.

"I don't understand it either Mom. I'm heart-broken. But, Vasken is back in Boston and he's made all this trouble for us. He gave the story to The Examiner for the express purpose of destroying Lance. I just can't believe he hates Lance so much, or that he loves me so little. I don't understand him."

"Well I do!" Aram Casparian shouted angrily. Vasken's a damn bolshevik isn't he? All these years you've both been covering for him, covering his hostility, covering his actions, making excuses and hiding things from me. It was easier not to face facts, I guess, but now we have to face them and the facts are that Vasken is a bolshevik, an out and out bolshevik who doesn't give a damn about anyone or anything."

"No, Aram, don't say that," Karamine's mother pleaded. "It's not true. He needs understanding and . . . forgiveness."

"Understanding? That's all we tried to do with him all these years, understand him," Aram Casparian exclaimed with exasperation, God, how did I ever father a son so hard and cold, so full of hostility and malice, especially toward us, his own family, who've never done anything but love him. Well, I'm through listening to any more excuses. We have to face facts now, and know him for what he is . . . a bolshevik bastard who'll sacrifice anything and everything on the altar of Lenin and Marx. Well, I'm through with him, he's no son of mine."

"Please Hyrig, don't deny your son this way. Don't do something you'll regret," Karamine said, with pain in her voce. It's too late now for recrimination. It has nothing to do with you or us, or as to the way we were both brought up. It's Vasken, he knows right from wrong, you gave us both values that can never change no matter what the circumstances. It was his decision to expose us, his family, to this turmoil, and he has to live with it. There's nothing we can do about it. In the meantime, listen . . . if anyone comes around, DON'T open the door, much less say anything to them. No matter what they say, just answer with 'no comment'. They'll say things about Lance that will make you so angry you'll want to explode and say something. Don't. They'll twist whatever you say so badly you won't even recognize you said it. Don't watch the T.V. or listen to the news broadcast because the air is filled with all sorts of distortions and lies. They're playing this to the hilt to destroy Lance, so remember, 'no comment' if anyone comes around asking questions.

"How is Lance holding up under all this pressure?" Karamine's mother questioned.

"Well naturally he's devastated. He simply feels he should step out of the race, but I want him to stay in and fight," Karamine answered firmly. "He has a meeting with John and Richard today. They're going to work out some sort of strategy to confront all this. They're meeting at seven tonight, so we should know something after that. Unfortunately, election day is so close, we don't have much time to reach the people."

"Vasken," her mother said softly, "we haven't heard from him in ages, and I'm greatly worried."

"I got a card from him about a month ago while he was still in Europe, but he's back now, he must be, since he was the only one who could have given the story to The Examiner."

"What does he do away so often and so long," her mother asked gently.

"Probably planning to overthrow the world," her father exclaimed contemptuously. "I can't understand his dedication to such a system that pits brother against brother, family against family, with cruel and disastrous results. The only way it can sustain power is by liquidation of the people. These old bolsheviks and socialists hold on forever it seems; anyway, I'm glad you called, Karamine; let Lance know we're behind him and support him all the way, and if there's anything we can do, just call."

Thanks, *Hyrig*. Just make sure the media doesn't get to you, and remember two words . . . no comment! I love you both. I'll call again as soon as I know anything."

Karamine replaced the receiver down and breathed a sigh of relief. "Thank God that's over," she murmured to herself.

7

Vasken Casparian was lean as a panther. The discipline of daily exercise brought every muscle under his will and control, an attitude compatible with his philosophy—those who lacked strong will and determination were somehow unfit, weak, and of no use or value. His black hair, now peppered with grey, was cropped short, revealing a finely shaped head, which he held arrogantly high and erect, a posture calculated to project an aura of power and authority. Without his beard and moustache, his features seemed hawklike and fierce, especially with his deep set eyes that darted swiftly from one focus to another, absorbing and appraising all persons and situations around him.

Today, his broad shoulders moved gracefully, as he walked along Beacon Street, then stopped to pick up a paper from a newstand. His lips curled in an unpleasant smile as he scanned the headlines; ASSASSIN RUNS FOR SENATE—LANCE BAGDASARIAN INVOLVED WITH TERRORIST UNDERGROUND! He was amused to read the article condemning Lance's nomination, demanding he step out of the race; he noted the liberties taken by the press with the facts he had given them, speculations and innuendo that spun the story into a soapbox melodrama. Ha! he thought with elation, the jackels are loose! He folded the paper and put it under his arm, then looked for a telephone. I must call my sister, he thought, I'd really like to know how the old boy is taking it!

Vasken Casparian had despised Lance, his brother-in-law, since his sister, Karamine first brought him home. Calling himself Armenian, he'd thought angrily at the time. Yea, sure, he speaks the language, learned it from his grandfather, the big hero who ran off and left his country; and of course that hypocritical father of his, who's more inter-

59

ested in his yacht club membership than his Armenian heritage. I've seen dozens like them, and I have only contempt for them. What do they know of the Armenian cause, and our struggle for survival—living here like fat cats basking in the luxury of profit and greed. And Lance, the worse hypocrite of them all, big talk show host with the colossal gall to run for senator! Well, he thought triumphantly, this should bring him to his knees once and for all!

He stopped by a telephone booth and looked up Karamine's telephone number in the book. Then, dialing carefully, he heard it ring and a receptionist's response.

"Doctor Karamine's office."

"Is she there?" Vasken asked curtly.

"Well, the doctor is busy with a patient at the moment, did you wish to make an appointment," the receptionist inquired politely.

"Look, this is her brother, Vasken," he said impatiently. She hasn't seen me for some time, so I'm sure she'll want to speak to me if you would be so kind as to let her know I'm on the phone."

"Oh . . . yes . . . by all means, just one moment please and I'll call her."

The receptionist went to the examining room and knocked gently on the door.

"Yes? What is it, Ann?" Karamine answered.

"I'm sorry to disturb you, doctor, but there's a man on the phone who says he's your brother . . . "

"Vasken!" Karamine gasped. It was a few seconds before she caught her breath.

"Tell him I'm busy . . . no wait . . . tell him I'll be right there."

Karamine took a deep breath. She told her patient she would return shortly, then walked to her office and picked up the telephone. "Vasken? What do you want?" she said evenly, trying to control her agitation.

"Well now, that's a fine greeting for someone you haven't seen in years. His voice had a sarcastic edge. "What I want is to talk to my sister, find out how she's doing; how are you doing, Karamine?"

"A lot you care about how I'm doing," Karamine answered hotly. "Vasken, I always knew you didn't like Lance, but I thought at least you cared about me. How could you hurt me this way? Mom and Dad, what about them and all the grief you're causing them? I remember when you used to protect me from hurt."

"Yea? Well that was before you married Lance Bagdasarian, that no good bull shooter who thinks he's going to be a senator. Well, I put a little road block in his big plans, didn't I?"

"Oh Vasken! You haven't changed at all! In all these years you haven't changed. Why are you so filled with bitterness and hate? Why do you have such hostility towards Lance? Don't you realize how much that hurts me?"

"Look, Karamine, I'm not trying to hurt you or our parents, but, you abandoned me when you married the coward who thinks he's Armenian, but who didn't have the guts to kill that Turk when he had the chance. I'll never forget or forgive him for that," Vasken responded angrily.

"Oh Vasken, Vasken" Karamine said brokenly, "why are you so hard. I pray for you each night and ask God to help you see the light, to fill you with love and forgiveness instead of this virulent poison that's consuming and destroying you."

"Don't give me that religious talk, Karamine. If there ever was a God where was He when our people were being massacred? Huh? No, if God exists, the devil must exist too, and I'll stand with the devil, because he's stronger. I'll be damned if I'll stand with the weak."

"Don't, Vasken," Karamine pleaded, "don't say such things. You don't realize what you're saying. You've never allowed me to talk to you, to help you have some understanding of love instead of hate, some hope not desperation."

"Hope? Don't make me laugh. Hope is the last refuge of ineffectual men! Weaklings who've always abbrogated personal responsibility and now believe things will somehow work out. That's not for me, Karamine. I always believed you have to take hold, and make things happen. I'll be damned if I'll sit around and hope they'll happen."

"Look, Vasken, I can see we're not communicating any better now than we ever did, so, let's just drop the subject. Do you care about Mom and Dad, and what all this upheaval is doing to them?"

"Well don't blame me for that. Blame your ambitious husband and the actions of his own dark deeds," Vasken replied bitingly.

Karamine bit her lip and tried to control her impulse to slam the receiver in his ear. "I really don't know why you're bothering to call at all, Vasken."

"I didn't call to hurt you, Karamine. I merely wondered how that husband of yours is bearing up under all the pressure of the media pack. He's getting some great publicity, and isn't that what he's always loved? Obviously, he'll have to step down. Can't see how he has any other choice now." Vasken laughed spitefully.

"Don't write him off yet, Vasken. Despite what you think, Lance is strong and forthright. He's not easily destroyed. Besides, he has lots of support, even now."

"Good! I'm glad for your sake he's bearing up."

"Are you planning to see Mom and Dad, or at least give them a call?" she asked, changing the subject.

"Are you kidding? *Hyrig* wanting to see me? Don't make me laugh. We'd only get into a fight, sure as hell. No, let well enought alone. Give *Myrig* my love and tell her I did what I had to do to further the cause."

"Cause? What cause are you talking about, Vasken, the Armenian or the bolshevik world revolution?" Karamine asked impatiently.

Vasken replied disdainfully. "My dear sister, aren't both causes the same? Sooner or later you'll understand, when we're all under a collective system, run by people who know what's good for the masses. There will be no distractions like individual rights or possession of private properties, or the so called responsibility for one's action, as your dear contumelious husband likes to preach. No, we'll inform you of your worth and just what your purpose in life will be."

"That's horrible, Vasken! Horrible! What you've just described is nothing more than a despotic oligarchy! You can get the same thing in jail or prison if that's all there is to this life," she argued hotly. "Anyway, it's pointless to continue this discussion. It only infuriates us both. What do you intend to do now? Do you have any plans to see me? Perhaps we could meet somewhere for lunch," Karamine suggested in a conciliatory tone.

"No, I don't think so, Karamine. What's the use. As you say, we only infuriate and hurt one another. Anyway, I'm leaving for Armenia in a few days. I'm involved there giving my expertise in the political field, and with the operation of their school curriculum for a better soviet state. I'll call when I'm back in town. So, as we say . . . 'minak parov' (good bye), sister." Vasken hung up, then hailed a cab to take him to his meeting.

8

Lance arrived at the apartment and immediately took a shower and made preparations for his meeting that night. He reheated some of the leftovers and ate a hurried meal alone since he knew Karamine would not be home until later. Then, scribbling a note he told her he'd give her all the particulars of the meeting when he got back.

He left the apartment and took an elevator to the street level, and walked out and hailed a cab. Getting into the cab, he settled back into the seat and tried to think. He had to come to some decision soon, regarding the avalanche of bad press now howling like a raging blizzard everywhere. He was grateful Karamine was able to reach her parents before the impact of the whole situation became full blown; the media distortions and allegations were out of control, even to the point where they connected Lance to the I.R.A. There were also insinuations from "reliable sources" of ties to other known terrorist or activist groups. Lance was shocked and dismayed at the length and limits pushed by partisan journalists who touted their own views and opinions, in preference to responsible, objective journalism; he was overwhelmed by the omnipotent power of the media to make or break a political candidate of their choice. What a charade the second ammendment has become these days, he thought dismally. You can libel anyone you wish, and when confronted, merely state you don't wish to reveal the source.

The cab stopped outside the building of the studio. Paying the driver, Lance stepped onto the curb and hurried toward the direction of the glass door entrance. He was still absorbed with the current of his thoughts as he mechanically stepped off the elevator to the fifth floor and walked briskly to the T.V. studio. Richard Blair and John Dixon were already there before him; They greeted him warmly as he entered the conference room.

"How's the family holding up under the media stress, Lance?" John Dixon queried, looking up from some newspapers he was scanning.

Lance shook his head. "It's hard. You said they were tough, and warned me, but, I guess I just didn't expect such rabid frenzy and uncontrolled hysteria without substantiating evidence. Everything they're saying is based on half truths and innuendo. It's incredible, and believe me, it's really been an eye-opener."

John's face was unsmiling. "I suppose you've heard the latest thing they're airing? They've got you connected to the I.R.A. and a few other terrorist organizations . . . this whole thing is getting out of hand, Lance. T.V. and press are loaded with all sorts of commentary, far beyond what you've told us."

Lance's jaw tensed, "Yes, I know, I've been listening to that garbage all day."

"Did you know they were over at your parents home trying to get a statement from your father? Richard commented.

"No, I didn't know that," Lance said evenly, trying to control his anger. "I didn't think they'd be there so soon. What happened?"

"Your dad was great, everything they asked him he responded with 'no comment'. He frustrated them, but, he was damn good. One actually had the gall to ask him, 'how do you feel having a terrorist for a son?' For a second, I thought your father was going to lose control, and belt him, but he kept his cool and ignored the remark."

Lance hit his fist on the table hard. "Damn! I never should have accepted the nomination. I see that now. I've ruined my personal life, my family and friends. Who needs this anyway? Who do I think I am, believing I can make a difference. Let them re-elect senator Crawford, with all his cronies, and let the country go to pot. Maybe the country deserves what it gets. All I care about right now is my family. The hell with everything else."

"Hold on, Lance, now just hold on. This is the dirty underbelly of politics, and it's your baptism of fire." John Dixon began. "First of all, we picked you for your integrity and your understanding of the political process. We see in you a standard bearer, and a return to the days when principle, honor and loyalty counted for something. I've known you for a long time, Lance, and I trust your honesty and your high moral character. You're a man of lofty ideals and substance, so let's hear no more of this defeatist rhetoric and statements of regret. Do you hear me?" He positioned his hand on Lance's shoulder with a mock punch. "This is war, and what we need right now is a strategy, a strong strategy. Let's relax now, and concentrate on that . . . just that."

"Yeah, you're right, John," said Lance with a fresh resolve. "I just lost my head for a minute, that's all."

"Well, God knows you've good reason for it. Vilification of one's character is never easy to take lying down, especially when it's unfounded and untrue. And damnit, we're not going to take it lying down."

"Well, how in hell can we deal with it?" Richard queried. We have to move fast and make a statement if the Republican party in this state is to be a viable opponent to the political machinery that's been winning here for decades. Think!" Richard Blair glanced searchingly at each one of them. "Remember Watergate? A president was toppled."

"Yeah," said Lance thoughtfully, "the trouble with Nixon was he had no faith in the American people. What he should have done was to simply come clean and tell people the truth before the media got hold of it. They would have understood an explanation stating he had nothing to do with it . . . that without his knowledge or authority, they broke into the Democratic headquarters at Watergate hoping to find a connection between Castro and the Democratic party. He could have also explained that the Justice Department would look into it, fire everyone involved, and then file criminal charges to the fullest extent of the law against them. Had he done that, he could have cleared himself, and the media shenanigans could not have changed the minds of the voters. All that hassle of stonewalling tapes could have been avoided.

"Hey . . . wait, that's it . . . " A flash of optimisim suddenly broke over Lance's features. "Yea, that's it," he repeated again, looking directly from John to Richard. "We have to get our story out to the people. I know the lines are jammed with calls from grass roots workers trying to find out what's happening . . . they deserve an answer, and by God, we're gonna give them one."

"What should we do then, take out full page ads in the newspapers? Buy some T.V. spots denouncing the accusations and false information?" John asked with concern.

"No, that's no good," Richard replied warily, rubbing his chin, "they'd overwhelm us with more false accusations and propaganda, and besides, time is so short now, we need something drastic to hit hard. Something dramatic to gain the confidence of the people.

"Forget ads, T.V. soundbites, radio. All we'd be doing here is chasing our tail, and this is exactly what they want. They've got us on the defensive, and I believe it's time to turn it around and go on the offensive," said Lance confidently.

"What are you saying, Lance? What are you getting at?" John asked in a mystified tone.

"Just this. John, you've got to make some time available on your T.V. staion, even if you have to bump a program. It's got to be in prime time, evening after dinner, around eight or even nine. Also, you've got to buy some time on the other networks, to cover the entire state in one broadcast. This way we'll tell the whole story and reach the voters of the state without interruption or commentary. Set it up as soon as possible, John,"

"Who'll tell the story?" John replied with some concern.

There was a pause as both men concentrated their attention toward Lance.

"Who else?" Lance smiled, gesturing with both hands. "All I need is half an hour, John, just half an hour without questions or interruption of any kind, especially from a panel of liberal journalists. I'll tell the story from beginning to end . . . how where, when and why. I won't leave out a thing. I'll let the voters hear the truth and let them decide once and for all, what the consequences should be. I'm not proud of what I did, but it was the action of an impulsive, idealistic youth. Thank God I came to my senses in time, and had a crash course in maturity at the same time. This way, however, the voters, not the media will judge whether or not I'm fit to serve as their senator from this state."

John and Richard exchanged glances, before responding. There was a note of confidence and excitement in John's voice as he spoke. "That's it! That's just what we've been looking for! We've got nothing to lose and anyway, it's too late in the campaign. Besides, I trust Lance and his judgement. Good thinking, Lance!"

"I like it," Richard said, nodding his head, "we've got nothing to lose, and also, we do have the best candidate for the job. Let the public hear your story, Lance. I'm with you all the way, and we'll back you to the hilt. Yeah, I like it, let's go with it. Let's go on the offensive for a change."

"I'll clear a spot on our T.V. station, Thursday, that will give you two days to get ready, and give me time to get ads in the newspapers featuring the broadcast. That's not too soon for you is it, Lance?"

"No, Thursday's fine, the sooner the better," Lance replied.

"I'll call a number of other stations to see if they'll also air the broadcast, we'll buy the time from them," said John.

"Do you think they'll carry it?" Richard queried.

"They better . . . otherwise we'll scoop them, and their ratings will go in the tank. Believe me, ratings are their primary concern. They worry more about ratings than anything else. Oh yes, they'll carry it all right," John answered, nodding his head affirmatively.

The three men stood up and shook hands. They left the office and walked to the elevator together, knowing that the stage was set.

In the space of a day, John Dixon had placed ads announcing Lance's speech to the voters in every major newspaper of the commonwealth. The ads contained statements to the effect that if anyone wanted to know the truth about candidate Bagdasarian, without bias or commentary, then tune in and listen with an open mind before casting a vote at election time. This will be the only time to hear directly from the candidate, live, the ad stated, and it should be your duty as an informed voter to decide your choice then. Some of the other television stations were hostile to the idea of a live broadcast, insisting on a panel of journalists to ask questions, as well as a moderator. John Dixon was adamant, however. "You know who the people will be watching that evening, and you also know what stations will be top in the ratings. Take it as it is or you're out, it's up to you," he told them firmly. Ultimately, they all agreed to air the broadcast of Lance's speech; however, they planned to have a commentary and discussion after the speech in order to dissect and scrutinize every word of his message.

The night of the broadcast, Karamine, Richard and Alice Blair, John Dixon and his wife Miriam, were the only personnel allowed in the studio. A tight security was set up to prevent interruption of any sort. The technicians who had often been through this before were alerted and agreeable to John's security measures.

Walking toward the set, Lance squinted and shielded his eyes from the blinding glare of the studio lights. He peered through the brightness in the direction of Karamine and his friends. Their presence, especially that of his wife, gave him a sudden surge of confidence and self-assurance, and he smiled in acknowledgement of Karamine's wave. Everything was a flurry of activity as technicians adjusted headphones and mikes, some co-ordinated lights, others positioned cameras. Lance straightened his tie and sat erect in his chair as the signal came for the count-down.

"I'll be glad when this is over," Karamine whispered nervously to Miriam Dixon.

"Lance will do fine, Karamine," Miriam assured her, "once people hear the truth for a change, they'll understand."

"Yes, I know he will. I was apprehensive at first when he told me he was going to do it; I felt they'd twist and distort the facts, but, you can never go wrong telling the truth. Lance has always been honest and forthright, and I'm grateful he has his opportunity to get the real story out before the public."

"The important thing is we have a chance to get the facts out LIVE, and without interruption," said John. "We're banking on this to turn things around before election day."

"I hear some of the stations are going to have a commentary after the broadcast," Karamine remarked.

"Yes, I'm sure most of them will. But it doesn't matter. We'll have had the opportunity to get the story out straight, without distortion, and that's what the voters will tune into first," John answered with gritty determination.

Richard smiled in complete agreement. "That's what we're banking on, Karamine, and when the broadcast is over, at least the voters will have a good yardstick to measure our candidate. John and I both see Lance as the best candidate for the office and the people have a real choice here. However, if they decide to continue with the status quo, then so be it, but quit complaining about where the country and state are going." Richard interrupted his remarks as the "ON THE AIR" light went on and the director pointed to Lance. Against objections from John, owner of the television station, and Richard, head of the Republican Party, Lance had opposed the idea of having someone introduce him to the viewers. Instead he opted to address the people directly, his premise being, that if the speech did not go well, the Republican Party could distance itself from him. Thus the whole responsibility was his alone.

Lance's expression was serious, but displayed no lack of composure and self-confidence when he stared directly into the bright lights of the first camera. He began simply. "My name is Lance Bagdasarian, and I am the Republican Party candidate, seeking the honor of serving the voters of this commonwealth in the senate of the United States. I requested this time to speak directly to you, the voters, rather than hold a press conference, in order to answer charges and allegations levelled against me over the past few days. What I intend to present to you is not mere explanation, but factual truth based on integrity. I'll hold nothing back.

I wish to begin by stating categorically, that I am not, nor have I ever been, a terrorist, a subversive, an insurgent or anarchist. I was however, and perhaps may still be, an idealist." Lance paused a moment and smiled before continuing. "I was fortunate to be brought up in a caring home by loving parents, my father is of Armenian heritage, and his parents, my grandparents, came to America around the turn of the century to escape massacres and genocide by the Turks from 1896–1915. My mother is Canadian, of Scottish descent, and although her ancestry goes back a little further, her people left Scotland for the same reasons . . . to escape persecution under English rule.

What has all this got to do with the charges? Well back in the sixties when I was in university, there was a great deal of turmoil and confusion on college campuses. A lot of it had to do with identity. The burning question then was, who am I? Where am I going? This was not a problem for me, however, I always knew who I was, thanks to my parents and especially my grandfather, Sahag Bagdasarian. I spent my childhood summers, listening to him tell and retell stories of the old country, his beloved homeland, Armenia. For many of you, Armenian history may seem obscure and far removed, unreal and strange perhaps, because it is such a distant place; for me however, it lived, vividly. I worshiped my grandfather and was filled with awe and respect for him as he described detailed scenes of plundering Turks who ravaged his village, raped Armenian women or carried them off; he told of savage Turks who massacred innocent children, then burned their homes and churches. My grandfather along with my grand-uncle Avedis, fought valiantly against them, even though they were wounded and outnumbered. They outsmarted their enemy however, and escaped, eventually making their way here to America.

Why do I talk about all of this? Simply to give you some background and perspective on why I found myself involved with an Armenian activist group many years ago when I was a university student. I was intensely interested in politics, human rights, oppressed people suffering under tyranny, and the history of the Armenian people was especially dear to my heart. One day, a notice on the bulletin board describing an Armenian Club, came to my attention. Anyone interested in the cultural aspects of Armenian history . . . music, dance, art, etc. was invited to join. The club was totally non-political; their main purpose was focused on unity in the ranks of young people, especially those whose families were divided by opposing political philosophies, but I won't go into that aspect of Armenian history now.

At that first meeting, I met my wife, Karamine, which if I may add, was the best thing that ever happened to me. Later, in her parent's home, I met Karamine's brother, Vasken, who indicated instant hostility toward me. He challenged my ethnic background, with the specious reasoning that I simply did not 'look Armenian.' He questioned my committment to the TRUE Armenian cause, and on that very first meeting dared me, DARED ME to meet some real Armenians. Real Armenians? I remember quoting him incredulously. "Yes, real Armenians," he'd replied contemptuously, "people with purpose and determination who'll fight the Turk to the end until they acknowledge the genocide and return the lands that belong to our people. Or . . . are you just another one of those phoney pietists who mouth platitudes of sacrifice and freedom but are not willing to risk a thing."

Needless to say, his words, tone and manner hit a nerve. Being somewhat of an opinioned hothead myself in those days I was outraged by his remarks. Had I not been in his parents home, and in Karamine's presence, I would have lost my temper completely and pulverized him. Instead, and against Karamine's wishes, I accepted the challenge, partly because I was curious, but mostly because I wanted to wipe that sneering smile from Vasken's face once and for all.

The next Saturday night, I sat behind him, on the back end of his motorcycle while he he drove like a maniac through dark back roads and around some never ending turns, into areas of Boston I'd never travelled before. I had no idea where he was taking me, and didn't much care. I treated it all like a huge adventure. We finally turned on a narrow street and pulled up in front of a dimly lit house. Inside, I met members of their organization, young students like myself, mostly; the conversation that night was concerned mainly with the Armenian Cause—which is briefly—recognition of genocide and the slaughter of one and a half million Armenians by the Turks, plus the return of our ancestral lands usurped by them. I remember being quite impressed at the time by their dedication and fire, and I found their arguments valid and convincing. I felt compelled to attend a few more meetings where many aspects of the fight, such as protests, debates, newspaper articles and media exposure were discussed. None of these activities prepared me, however, for the last meeting, which turned suddenly violent, and provoked wild and unthinking action on my part. The members of the organization planned to take the fight directly to the Turkish embassy at the U.N. Vasken, the group leader had the entire profile of one of the Turkish diplomats, including photos and background. To say I was stunned and shocked when it suddenly dawned on me that they were actually planning an assassination would be an understatement. I was jolted and distressed beyond reason. I tried to talk them out of it, and argued fiercely against it. I attempted to convince them it was not the way to achieve our goals, but I was denounced and discredited, shouted down by insults to my family and friends. Then Vasken stood up, and struck the most vicious blow of all . . . he insulted my grandfather and called him a coward, called my father a hypocrite, and me, a half-breed phoney who just mouthed words and pretended to feel for the Armenian cause. It was too much. I rushed towards Vasken, and literally wanted to beat him senseless, to make him apologize for his taunts and insults, especially to my family. At the time however, I was unaware that Vasken was a black-belt karate expert. The result was . . . he beat me mercilessly, then dragged me outside like a sack of potatoes and dumped me on the sidewalk. I was barely conscious but through the maze of that scene I still remember his last orders; 'keep your mouth shut; I know where your parents live;' then he made certain threats if I didn't heed the warning.

I managed to crawl to my car and struggled to get in behind the wheel. Fortunately by that time I knew the way to the meeting place and had driven there myself. Blood was everywhere, and my whole body throbbed from the beating Vasken had given me. But worst of all, dazed and bloody though I was, Vasken's words struck my heart like a hot coal. For the first time in my entire life I'd been beaten up; the thesis and premises of my whole life had exploded in my face. I saw myself in a way I never had before, and I suddenly mistrusted myself, felt doubt, felt shame. I was haunted by the memory of an argument I'd had with my dad. That same morning I'd called him a hypocrite, someone who'd merely given lip service but who never took risks for the Armenian cause, someone who simply wrote checks to soothe his conscience. I cursed myself for my bitter words to my father, because I realized and finally understood, that he at least was true to himself; he never claimed to be more than he was. My own arrogance suddenly sickened me. Whether right or wrong, I perceived myself as an empty braggart, a pretentious hypocrite. Oh yes, I was a zealot in regard to the Armenian cause all right, I was outraged and had plenty to say about the genocide and atrocities against Armenians, but when the real opportunity to strike back was presented to me I had no stomach for it. I convinced myself I was the phoney Vasken said I was, and the pain of that illusion to a young idealist was almost too much to bear. I was driven to prove to them, and most of all to myself that this was not the case.

I still don't know how I managed to drive all the way to New Hampshire to my grandfather's farm that night. Somewhere along the way I remember stopping at a service station to clean up some of the blood from my face. I knew my grandfather had always kept a pistol hidden in the basement. He had a sentimental attachment to the pistol because it had a tradition of honor, and had been used by my grand-uncle Avedis for the freedom of the Armenian people in battles against the Turks. I made up my mind to take the gun from its hiding place which I'd discovered many years ago, then with deadly intent continue on to New York.

Once I arrived in New York, I began to stalk my prey, the Turkish diplomat. I waited for an opportunity to strike, and three days passed. The cold steel of grandfather's pistol seemed to give me courage, false courage and misguided gallantry I recognized later, but, at the time it gave me a sense of heroism, and impression that I was somehow defending my grandfather's honor, as well as proving my own self worth. I was still bruised and hurting, physically, and my clothes were badly soiled. But I remember the sudden pounding of my heart when the black limousine pulled up and I came face to face with my target. I met the eyes of the Turkish diplomat in a split-second contact, and my hand closed over the pistol. But then, in that same moment, it was as though I hit an invisible wall and some powerful force held me back. I seemed paralyzed and unable to act or carry through my plan, for which I've thanked God a thousand times. Because, in that one clear-cut moment I knew, recognized, and sharply understood, that I was no murderer. I simply could not cut a man down in cold blood, and to have that kind of lucid awareness in such a moment could only have come about through the Grace of God. So . . . I turned and took the only course open to me . . . I ran.

Unfortunately, my unkempt appearance and days of loitering, did not go unnoticed. I was brought under suspicion and apprehended by two plain clothesmen. As I turned to run, they chased me and tackled me. I fell to the ground knocked unconscious by the impact of my head hitting the cement sidewalk. When I regained consciousness I found myself in a New York jail. My head was bandaged, but throbbing, and the smell nauseated me. I felt weak and dizzy. The charge was carrying a concealed weapon, and because I was spotted hanging around the U.N. I was suspected of being a member of the I.R.A. terrorist group. Allowed the usual one telephone call, I called Karamine, who is now my wife, and she in turn called my aunt, who is a lawyer. They both came to New York, and at that time, my aunt discovered that the arresting officers, in the confusion of the arrest, had failed to read me my rights. On that ground, violation of the Miranda Act, I was released into her custody, and because of my age at the time, she also had them expunge all records of my apprehension.

And this, my friends is the true account of that unfortunate episode in my life. The rash action of a gullible youth, filled with enthusiasm and high ideals, yet too immature to recognize the end does not always justify the means. I was goaded on by a false premise of justice and honor, but I thank God that He allowed me to come to my senses in time. And this, my friends has been a turning point in my life. It made me into a different person . . . a man who now thinks and looks at everything from a spiritual perspective, especially with regard to the Armenian people. Truth and absolutes are the beacons I now pursue.

Voters of the commonwealth, I came here tonight to give you all the circumstances of my actions at that time. I'm not proud of what I almost achieved, and can only excuse it by reiterating once again that I was young, impressionable and naive. I took a very bad misstep which I shall regret the rest of my life, but with all the sincerity of my heart, hope that I can make up for. I've been trying to do that ever since, and as I've stated before . . . I'm not the same person.

In conclusion, if you still feel my story is unforgivable, that I'm untrustworthy and dangerous, or you still believe the media with all their allegations, then you're right to vote for my opponent. If, however, you believe that I've told the truth here tonight, that my record these later years has been excellent and meritable, and that you have full trust in me to do my best for this commonwealth, then I ask for your vote to help tear down the political machine that has controlled this state for decades. Help with my candidacy to spearhead this change and get involved. Help me achieve this goal, with God's help. Thank you for listening.

"You have just heard Lance Bagdasarian, candidate for the Republican Party," the announcer boomed, as Lance looked out toward Karamine for a sign of approval. She nodded her head reassuringly, and the "ON AIR" light went out, clearing the studio of any transmissions. Richard and his wife were the first persons to step forward to commend Lance of his sincerity and truthful delivery. John and Miriam Dixon followed. "Excellent, Lance! Perfect presentation and great delivery! I feel very optimistic. You covered the whole area and now at least, the voters will be able to see and decide for themselves whether or not you are a man of integrity or some desperate assassin. Win or lose, Lance, you're the best we can offer to the voters of the state.

Karamine embraced Lance tightly, and kissed him on the check. "No matter what, you're the best there is," she whispered.

"Well friends, the die is cast. Let's see what kind of voters we have," John commented.

"Yeh, Richard replied, "Let's see."

9

After the broadcast, Lance and Karamine, accompanied by John, Richard and their wives left for the Copley Plaza. Entering the diningroom, a maitre d' escorted the group to a table, where they drew several glances of recognition from other diners in the room.

"I hope it's stares of approval, not condemnation we're getting," Lance commented, somewhat under his breath."

"Don't worry about it, Lance, you delivered a great speech tonight. You told the truth and now it's up to the people to understand. At least it's an alternative to all that garbage they've been getting on the media," John asserted unceremoniously.

"Exactly!" said Richard spiritedly, his eyes darting swiftly about the room, pausing briefly to take stock of a young man approaching their table.

"Mr. Bagdasarian, I just wanted to let you know, that I and many of my friends saw your broadcast tonight. We believe in you and support you," said the stranger, extending his hand to Lance.

"Thank you very much," Lance responded, returning the firm handclasp.

"We refused to listen to commentators after the broadcast. Those journalists must think the viewing and listening public are idiots who can't rely on their own understanding, and need interpreters to explain what they've heard. In any case, I just wish to say that we believe you're our only hope to get this state out of the hands of self-perpetuating politicians . . . to return to strong fiscal policies that will unburden us from these escalating taxes. We're behind you all the way. Go get 'em, and good luck!"

Lance's eyes followed him back to his table. He watched as he made some comments to the people there, who smiled then turned and waved at Lance.

"See? you've reached the voters with your message of truth, Lance. The rest of the state will do the same. We're not defeated yet . . . in fact, we've just begun to fight." Karamine's voice was reassuring and warm.

"Damn right," Richard cut in. "Your talk slashed straight to the core of those allegations, and any clear thinking person with one ounce of common sense or perception couldn't miss your sincerity and truth. You're not the same person you were then, Lance, and we certainly intend to back you all the way. Going on LIVE and dealing with it one on one was the best strategy. The voters heard you, and now no matter what spin the commentators put on it, they know the truth."

John waved his hand impatiently. "Meanwhile, let's get to the political impact of all this. First thing tomorrow, I'm going to call all the groups throughout the state to feel the pulse of the voters. They'll take surveys and canvas areas where our opposition is entrenched; that way we'll get some idea of their reaction to the broadcast. We've got to keep the momentum going." He paused to give the waiter his order.

Looking about the room, Lance sensed an atmosphere of approval and support as people looked in his direction, smiled, and raised their glasses. For the first time since his ordeal began he felt a lightness and a rise of optimism. Under the table, he grasped Karamine's hand and pressed it hard. Karamine understood.

"I'm glad its over at last. I hope they'll leave us and especially our families alone now," she said reflectively. "It will be good to lead some sort of normal life again."

"I know how horrendous these past few weeks have been for you, Karamine, with cameras and reporters trampling all over your property . . . your parent's property as well. I've been there myself, so I know what you've been through. They did the same thing to us a few years back when Richard was accused of bribery charges. I was bombarded with questions. They even asked me if I knew my husband was a crook." Alice Blair's voice trembled slightly.

Karamine placed her hand gently over Alice's. "Dear God Alice, how was it ever resolved?"

Alice smiled wryly. "Turned out the accuser was having mental problems, and was also on drugs. They didn't have a shred of evidence at the time except this so-called "reliable" source. Oh they apologized alright, but that didn't change what they had put us through. It takes time to get over something like that, as you'll see for yourself, Karamine."

"Yes, I know," Karamine agreed, sighing deeply. It's been difficult, especially for our families. Maybe we can put it behind us now, and just get on with our lives."

"There's something wrong with a system that allows innocent people to be dragged into court, simply because someone points a finger. First of all you've got to hire a lawyer, take hundreds of hours from your work time, then spend thousands of dollars defending yourself. We should have a law stating that if someone is charged with a crime, and it can't be proven in court, the accuser is liable for all court costs, including lawyer fees for the accused. You'd see a quick decline in these frivolous cases then, I bet. Not to mention the blow it would give to the ambulance chasers and contingency lawyers," said John, a mocking edge to his voice.

"Quite a speech, John," Richard declared, "except you know that lawyers run the country and you'd never get legislation like that passed, even if one hundred percent of the people wanted it. Thanks to lawyers, our Constitution's been prostituted. They've taken us from a country of absolutes to no absolutes whatsoever . . . no right, no wrong. If we're not careful we'll end up a totalitarian state. How many times have you fallen into the trap of thinking you want safety from crime, and don't care what kind of government gives it to you, huh? Think about it. I've toyed with the idea myself, and that my friends can really lead to tyranny."

"You're dead on, Dick," Lance replied, "I must admit I've thought about it every time I hear of another crime in the streets. It's out of control."

"That's why we've got to turn things around, and you're the right man for the job, Lance, the only man," John declared fervently.

"Look," Richard said with fresh enthusiasm, "first thing in the morning I'm calling all our field workers to canvas their areas to see what the polls look like throughout the state. I want a huge cross-section of their particular area, and I want answers to real pertinent questions like 'do you believe our candidate was telling the truth? Do you feel he'll work to change the way the state is going? Do you have confidence in him and mostly, will you vote for him?' These are things I want to know so we can see where we are, and where we're going. How does that sound to you, Lance?"

Lance gazed reflectively at both men before answering. "Sounds great to me. In fact, everything you've done so far has been great. And I just want to say at this point that I'd never be where I am today if you didn't have faith in me. John, your encouragement to be the best I can be, and the opportunity to have a program like ON TARGET was more than anyone could ask for. Together, we've tried to enlighten the people of this commonwealth, and now . . . thanks to both of you, I feel confident. No matter what happens from here on, I just wanted to let you guys know how much your support has meant to us.

"Don't forget the ladies," Karamine chimed, "Miriam and Alice have been there for us as well."

Richard smiled and raised his glass. "To the ladies!"

" . . . and a successful campaign," John added pleasantly.

Richard Blair stared thoughtfully from his office window to the city street below. On his desk, papers and charts were spread about in wild disorder as though confusion and disorder underlined the policy of the day. *I knew they wouldn't give up so easy,* he thought morosely, *the opposition is demanding Lance's withdrawal from the race, and they know damn well there's no time before elections to find another candidate.* He rubbed his chin then returned to his desk.

"Jim . . . bring in the latest reports from Springfield and the Worchester area. How's it look to you?"

Jim Roi entered, carrying an armful of papers and statistics. Jim was a young dedicated African American who worked hard at everything he did, and Richard appreciated having him on his team. A staunch Republican and avowed follower of conservative writers, like Thomas Sowell and Professor Walter Williams, Jim constantly surprised Richard with his penetrating insights and profound comprehension of current events. Although young, and still at university, Richard respected his views, and often called for his opinion and input on many issues.

"How's it lookin', Jim?"

"Dicy. According to these charts, we've lost a little momentum, but, it'll change I'm sure as election day gets closer.

"Humm . . . looks like a neck in neck situation that could go either way," said Richard scanning the charts intently. But hey . . . look at these Boston figures . . . we're slightly ahead there, and that's their stronghold."

"That's a good sign for us," Jim commented.

"You and your staff have done a good job there, Jim."

"Yeh . . . it's all those grassroot kids banging on doors and talking to people. It's really paying off," said Jim flashing a toothy smile.

Richard looked at Jim Roi in amazement, and shook his head. "Jim . . . how in the world did you ever become a Republican? A conservative one at that! Most African Americans I know are Democrats.

Jim Roi laughed with an easy rich tone. "Well, I guess it was my Mom . . . she was a great Southern Baptist lady who taught me to think for myself and gave me great values. She told me I could be the best no matter what obstacles I met. She made me study hard in school too.

Man, did she make me study!" Jim chuckled again. "But getting back to your question, Dick, believe it or not I actually considered becoming a libertarian, but, thinking it through, I found the republican party is the one party closest to the ideals and principles I believe in. I'm comfortable with candidates like Lance Bagdasarian. Personally, I think he's a libertarian at heart. That's why he's got to win."

"Damn right! So let's get back to work. Now, what are your projections for the western part of the state? Do you feel the figures will improve?"

"Well, as I said before, we need more numbers, and more interviews to bring the figures into a range where we can give a good projection. If we didn't have to deal with all this crap about Lance, we would've had more time to accumulate the proper amount of people to give a fairly accurate projection.

"Personally, at this point I feel the race is neck in neck," said Richard, scrutinizing the charts. "Meantime, let me call Lance and give him the information we have now. At least we can let him know he's not slipping in the polls. I'll call John too because his station is running a separate poll, and we can compare our notes and figures."

"Great. I'll get back to the calls and will monitor a constant update on the figures." He picked up an armful of papers then left Richard's office.

Still scanning the charts, Richard picked up the phone and dialed Lance. I wish I could give him better news then what we've got now, he thought dismally.

"Hi . . . Lance . . . yeah, Richard. Listen, I have the latest figures in the polls we've taken the last few days, but, I really can't give you an accurate projection."

"Why not? Don't you have the figures throughout the state? Just feed it to the computer and come up with a projection."

"Yeah, we could do that but it would not be a true projection because we don't have a significant number of voters polled as yet. As of now, you're holding your own and actually are slightly ahead of Senator Crawford, but that doesn't mean much. We have to figure an error of four to five percent, going either way. Look, at least you're not slipping, Lance, and that's important at this time. We'll let you know how things go as we do more polling."

"Thanks, Dick. Right, let me know whenever you get an update. Thanks."

Richard quickly dialed John's number. "Hey, John . . . how's it lookin' over there? Our figures here show Lance and the Senator running neck in neck. Anything coming in?"

"We're getting some calls, but can't get a good projection as yet. All we can do is get a feel of our audience, and hope they call in, then vote the way they said they would. Can't count on them though, we've been burned before, remember?"

"Hell! How could I forget. Look, John it's vital we get the blue collar vote or we might as well call it quits. We don't have enough registered republicans to bet the machine, and that's a fact. Hopefully, Lance has reached those hard-working people and they now see what the government is taking out of their paycheck for all those feel good programs. This whole episode has put a damper on things for now, but you never know what the voter will do once he's alone in the voting booth."

"Have to go, John. Jim just came in with more figures. Maybe we can get a trend here."

"Right. I'll let you know if anything changes. Meantime . . . let's hope for the best on election day."

10

Lance slept restlessly. The draining events of the past few weeks plagued his memory and disturbed his sleep. I never should have agreed to run for office, he thought dismally. Who was I kidding thinking I could beat the system and buck the powers that be. Had I ever had an inkling of the turmoil and anguish it cost Karamine, not to mention our families, I'd never have considered it for one moment. He sighed heavily and punched up his pillow in an effort to choke off his wrestling thoughts. But damn—you've never run from a good fight, Lance, and someone has to at least try and turn things around before we lapse completely into a totalitarian state. He watched as the first glimmer of light sifted under the window shade. God! It's here, it's actually here.

Tuesday, November 12 . . . election day! Well, in ten hours it'll all be over, one way or another, it'll be over, and that's all I want.

He got up and peered through the window. A sharp tint of crimson was bleeding fast into the murky darkness. Looks like it's going to be a clear day. Lots of republican voter turnout, hopefully. It's gonna be a long day though, but—whatever happens—surely our lives can get back on track again. He looked toward the bed where Karamine was still sleeping. I'm tired, but Karamine must be exhausted. She's taken so much time from her practice to help. I hated having to drag her all over this state to those luncheons and dinners—and those speeches! Somehow, I'll make it up to her.

Lance walked to the kitchen and plugged in the coffee. Karamine joined him shortly when the rich brewed aroma reached the bedroom.

"How are you this morning, Senator?" she teased lightly.

Lance smiled approvingly. "Senator? Humm. . . a little premature aren't we?"

"Oh I don't know, I'd say you have a pretty good shot at it. John and Richard seemed optimistic last night.

As she moved close to him, Lance reached out and put his arms around her. He nuzzled her neck gently. "Hey . . . will you still love me if I'm not a senator?" he murmured against her hair.

"All depends,"

"Yeah? On what?"

"On how fast you can whip up a pan of scrambled eggs."

"Just watch me, kid."

Karamine laughed, then walked to the living room and turned on the television. "Guess we'd better see what's going on."

Lance shook his head. "Well, it's hard to tell at this point. The last I heard was that its anyone's race. Polls didn't even show any trends as of yesterday when Richard called. I'm prepared for whatever happens.

Lance brought in a tray with breakfast and placed it on a coffee table before the sofa. He sat down by Karamine as she surfed through various channels hoping to catch some early hint of how things were going.

"At least you're holding your own, Lance. Remember the last election how one-sided it was? Any other candidate running against Senator Crawford would be overwhelmed in the polls by now. What time do you think we ought to head over to headquarters?"

"Oh I don't know, I'll check later with John and Richard at headquarters and ask them when we should go down. Personally, I'd just like to stay here with you like this for awhile without seeing anyone, till it's over. It seems so long since we've had some quiet time together, Karamine, I'm forgetting how it used to be with us."

Somewhere deep within her core of being, Karamine felt a stab. The note of longing in Lance's voice was something she had not counted on when she made her plans to travel to Armenia, once the election was over. Somehow the timing never seemed right to broach the subject, and her own plans and work had been suspended into a kind of holding pattern. She was happy, secure, absurdly in love with her husband, yet part of her responded to an ancient call, soul-stirring and strong. My people. My Armenian people.

During the year the group who usually accompanied her had managed to acquire pharmaceuticals and medical equipment, much of it hi-tech medical machinery donated by companies willing to help the cause of eleviating pain and suffering. Karamine was eager to get these supplies to Armenia, to set up programs and train technicians to operate the machinery. On every trip she was challenged to bring up the standards to western specifications, but the seventy years of soviet dominated mediocrity had taken its toll on the people, who were suspicious of progress and resisted change. Still, she was determined to enlighten them, to ease their suffering, and bring them into the modern age, where miracles of medicine and technology led to healthy and vigorous lives.

"What are you thinking, Karamine? You're miles away. Thinking about the elections?"

"Among other things, yes. I'll let you know when you're sworn in as the new senator from Massachusetts."

"Senator from Massachusetts." Lance laughed. "Do you really think it'll happen?"

"Yes, as a matter of fact, I do, and you'll make a great senator. That's what you really want isn't it, Lance?"

"Yep, sounds okay to me. The Don Quixote from the state of Massachusetts, tilting windmills for the glory of truth and justice. I wonder how many other young politicians have gone to Washington with those same noble thoughts only to be seduced by the beltway glitter and power. But, we'll show 'em something else in Washington won't we, Karamine mine. Personally, I think we make quite a pair," said Lance intimately, placing his arm around her and drawing her close.

"Now don't get yourself stirred up, Lance," she said gently pushing him back. You know I just can't up and leave my practice here. What would my patients do without me?"

"But, Karamine, if I'm elected . . . you will be coming to Washington with me, won't you?" Lance said urgently, his blue eyes suddenly filled with concern. "You can let your associate take over your practice . . . she's a capable physician, and has proven these past few months she's able to cover any situation."

"Look, Lance, let's just concentrate on this election right now and see what happens. If you win . . . we'll discuss it then. If you don't there'll be no need to discuss anything."

"If I don't win?" Lance queried. "Then you do have some doubts I'll lose this race."

"My God, Lance," Karamine said impatiently, trying to change the subject, "there's always a remote chance, you could lose you know. Things like that do happen especially to conservative republicans in a liberal state like Massachusetts."

"Yeah, for sure. Right now though, I'm not in the mood to discuss it," he said suggestively, pulling her close once more and allowing his hand to follow the curve of her body.

Karamine responded to the quickening fire he always ignited, and kissed him passionately.

"You're the most beautiful, desirable woman around, do you know that Karamine, mine?" he said, opening the tie of her robe, and slipping his hand inside her nightgown, to gently expose her breast.

"Lance . . . I do love you . . ."

The television continued to blast election news, but there was no audience in the living room to comment or care.

11

At Republican Headquarters, the whole area was charged with energy. People mounted numbers on blackboards and charts which were set across a stage; staff members wore headphones hooked to telephones throughout the state, where the latest information from all precincts was funneled to young runners. These in turn passed the figures on to workers at the blackboards. Most of the workers were young and full of raw zeal, their faces reflecting optimism and drive, especially when they noted their candidate was holding his own and had a chance.

Television crews saturated the scene, checking out their systems, talking into headsets. Others inspected cables and wires making certain no one tripped over them; Cameras were focused on the workers themselves, while one or two journalists carried on some interviews. Anticipating nothing short of absolute victory, one energetic group hung streamers from the ceiling, along with a huge netting of balloons to be released the moment Lances's victory was confirmed. Champagne and other liquors were brought and stored in a large refrigerator; the whole place buzzed with potent energy.

All across the state, numbers from each city were tabulated and the standing of each candidate from the various precincts indicated. As fast as the numbers came in, they were put on to stage blackboards that workers checked regularly to see how events were progressing. Desks were piled with papers and charts as analysis and evaluations were made; the results were then funneled to John Dixon and Richard Blair's office where a large television screen reported the latest developments.

"It's a big voter turnout, the largest the state has ever seen," Jim Roi announced excitedly bursting into Richard's office. Over sixty percent of the eligible voters have turned out as of now, and it looks like the trend will continue till the polls close. I think it's a good sign. Normally, we'd only get forty or fifty percent, as you well know, so this is great! Wow! It's what I was hoping for. I think we have a pretty good chance now with this voter turnout, don't you?"

John's expression was happier and more optimistic than anyone around him had seen in days. He beamed at Jim. "It's the best I've heard yet, which means we've reached a lot of voters who never come out to vote for whatever reason. Perhaps it's because they feel they have a choice for the first time. Lance certainly gave them plenty of reasons to come out and vote."

"Yeh . . . the good weather's also a factor. Some of these voters don't go out in bad weather, you know that, John."

"That may be true, Richard, but this trend seems to indicate a new group of voters who've been inspired for a change. There's a decided choice of candidate here, and I really think Lance's speeches throughout the state, and all that hype and hoopla over these allegations has stirred them into action. I have a feeling this thing's gonna surprise us all . . . even Senator Crawford and that liberal Democratic party. Give the people an opportunity and they'll come out in droves every time. In the past we haven't had good candidates, they were always compromising to the so-called moderate wing of our party. That's why we were so soundly defeated. Notice . . . they're not here helping Lance, and what's more they probably hope he loses so they can gloat and say 'I told you so' when it's over. I wish to hell they'd just join the Democrats and be done with it. As I said, we have a real challenger in Lance, and I've got a damn strong feeling about it all. Crawford should have been well ahead by now, and should be talking to the press. But, we'll know for sure in another few hours."

The frantic pace continued at Republican headquarters as the hours sped by. But suddenly, the figures changed abruptly toward Lance as new figures arrived from a substantially democratic area of Haverhill.

"Look at these figures, Jim!" a young worker cried excitedly waving a fist full of loose papers.

Jim Roi whistled a delighted response. "Wow! Lance is way ahead here. Crawford will never make this up. Hold on, I've got to get this information to John and Dick right away."

Jim bounded toward Richard Blair's office, full of enthusiasm and confidence. "Look at this," he shouted elatedly, "results from Haverhill. Lance is leading Senator Crawford in the town of Haverhill." He placed the figures in front of them and stood back to watch their reaction. John and Richard both stood up and gazed at the figures before them with disbelief.

"John, do you realize what this means? Can you see the ramification of these numbers from Haverhill?"

"Hell, yes!" Richard looked directly at John, then to Jim. "Two thirds of the vote is in, and Lance is leading by a large margin." He gave a slight whistle. "No way Senator Crawford can make that up, no way! But how can this be? That district is a democratic stronghold. Jim, you know we never counted on Haverhill to vote on our side, in fact, we'd written it off, for god's sake. This is quite a turn of fortune."

"I told you, Richard, but you weren't listening. Lance made a big impact on this state, and you're going to see it in the closing hours. The tide's turning. Get out there, Jim and find out what's happening in Lowell and Lawrence and some of the other smaller towns like Hopkinton . . . check Springfield and Worchester results as of now," he ordered.

As Jim rushed out to get the latest results, John turned to Richard. "We better get Lance and Karamine down here, because things are going to pop any minute. I'll call Miriam to get a cab here, and I'll ask her to pick up Alice."

"Aha! I have the smell of victory!" Richard said with a gleam in his eye as he picked up the telephone and dialed Lance's number. "Hello? Lance? Better get your butt down here pronto! Yep, things are starting to happen and it looks promising, very very promising. We'll fill you in when you get here. Richard hung up and looked at John. "I didn't want to tell him too much over the telephone. By the time he gets here, we'll have more figures to report."

Lance and Karamine arrived at Republican headquarters about an hour later. Walking to the entrance they were surrounded by reporters and workers who hurled questions and shouted remarks to them all at once. They crowded around and pressed in from every side. Holding Karamine's hand tightly, Lance managed to get through the throngs of people outside.

"What the hell's going on, it's bedlam out there," Lance gasped, when they finally reached Richard's office.

"Haven't you seen the results? Have you no ears, man? The tide's turned, and there's no way this momentum is going to stop now."

"You've done it, Lance . . . you've done it!" Miriam said, kissing him lightly on the cheek, then turning to embrace Karamine.

"Yes," Alice echoed, "against outstanding odds. It's going to be a real victory!"

For the first time in his life, Lance was lost for words. He placed an arm around Karamine and drew her close. Karamine's face was radiant, as the realization of what was taking place hit her. She felt giddy suddenly, and wanted to laugh and cry all at once. The euphoria of the moment was stunning, and its impact on both of them mesmerizing.

"We've done it, Lance . . . by god . . . we've done it!" John Dixon's mood was jubilant. "The latest results just came in from Worchester, Springfield and even Boston . . . and look at the figures from the small towns throughout the state. It's all the same. The polls will be closing in another hour, so there's no way the numbers can change now."

"When did it start, Richard?" said Lance finally recovering his voice to speak.

"About the time I phoned you to come down. You sounded half asleep."

"To tell the truth, Karamine and I were watching the election results coming in, and I guess we did drift off. We've been dead tired for weeks."

"Can't blame you for that," Miriam said, patting Karamine's hand. "But, all that difficult campaigning has paid off, it's over for now."

"We might as well stay here away from that turmoil out there," Richard suggested, making a motion for everyone to sit down. He called Jim aside and gave him some more instructions about the monitoring.

"Anyone want a beverage? Coffee, something to eat?" Jim inquired before leaving the office.

"Nope, we're all set for now, thanks, Jim."

Jim rushed back about an hour later in high spirits. "Line 5 . . . it's Senator Crawford," he announced jubilantly.

Richard picked up the telephone and keyed in line 5. "Republican headquarters, Richard Blair speaking . . ."

"You've put up a great fight, Richard. May I speak to Lance Bagdasarian?"

"Of course, Senator, here he is." Richard handed the phone to Lance.

"Hello Senator, how are you and your family?" Lance began awkwardly.

"Forget the amenities. We threw everything we had to stop your candidacy, but to no avail. I'm sorry about some of the tactics we've used, but it was beyond my control, you understand that, Lance, don't you? Your father and I are good friends. I hope this will not change anything."

"Well, that's up to him. What you have done to me and my family, I'd never have done, but, you didn't call here to have a friendly chat."

"No, we've been looking at the polls coming in from all over the state, and realize we've lost the battle. You've reached the voters, and it's obvious you are their choice, so I've called to concede the election and congratulate you on a well-fought campaign. Congratulations! May you do your utmost for our fair state when you are in Washington as I've done."

"Thank you for your call, Senator. I promise to do the best for my country and state, when I'm in the senate chambers. Thank you." Lance replaced the telephone slowly; this was it, the moment of victory, the culmination and apex of all his efforts. He glanced about the room and saw that all eyes were fixed on him. The crowd was quiet, expectant.

"Senator Crawford has conceded the race," he announced calmly, "He's conceded!" A sudden smile flashed across his face. He picked Karamine off her feet and swung her around wildly. "We did it, Karamine, we did it!"

"Bravo! We beat the machine." Suddenly, the whole room was a frenzy of excited comments, hugs and confusion. Richard shouted for silence. "We have to let the hard-working people outside know right now that Senator Crawford has conceded . . . Jim . . . get out there and tell them we have an announcement, then introduce me. Everyone else stay here until I bring Lance and Karamine to the podium. Go, Jim go!"

In the outside room, Jim stepped up to the podium and gave the microphone several sharp raps. His voice was resonant as he made the announcement. "Ladies and gentlemen . . . May I have your attention . . . please? I want to introduce the chairman of the Republican party, Richard Blair . . . Richard."

Richard quickly mounted the stairs, shook hands with Jim, then faced the audience who were whistling, clapping and drumming Lance's name. He smiled and raised his arms to silence the group. When the noise settled down, he cleared his throat then addressed them. "First of all, I want to thank each and every one of you who worked so hard on behalf of our great candidate, Lance Bagdasarian." Once again huge shouts and clamorings rose up from the audience; chants of Lance, Lance, Lance, filled the air. Again motioning for silence, Richard continued. "Lance is here now and wishes to say a few words to you." He stretched his arm toward Lance and Karamine who were making their way to the podium. T.V. cameras panned the crowd, and the roar of Lance's name reverberated through the hall. John, Miriam, Richard and his wife Alice stood in a line behind Lance and Karamine, smiling and waving, acknowledging the chants, the screaming and general high-spirits of the crowd.

When he finally managed to quell the crowd, Lance made the important announcement. "I have just received a phone call from Senator Crawford stating that he is conceding the election to me and . . ." the rest of Lance's words were totally drowned out by loud screams and shouts of victory. Balloons were released from the netting and they cascaded downward, charging the air with festivity and victory.

It was some time before Lance was able to quiet them, but, eventually, he gained control of the microphone. "As I said before, I want to thank all of you who had faith in me, even when we went through the darkest time of the campaign. My wife and I will never be able to tell you just what that has meant to us both, nor will we be able to express our gratitude for your persistent endeavors for victory. This is a turning point in our state, and let me tell you I shall never relent in my efforts to clean up, in the state or national level, all of those who abuse power through taxation and unlimited spending. When I go to Washington, I'm not just going to see what's good for our state, but what's good for our country." Another huge roar interrupted his message. "What is good for the country, automatically becomes good for our state," Lance continued, after the outburst had subsided. "We do not want huge, half-empty government office buildings set up here in Boston, merely to enhance the names of our politicians at tax payers expense. Let me quote something I read once . . ." Lance smiled broadly before continuing, "instead of giving a politician the keys of the city, it might be better to change the locks!" An explosion of unrestrained laughter and cheers rent the air. Lance raised his hand and continued. "I will strive to put an end to all this rampant, pork barrel spending, and help you keep some of your hard earned money.

It's your money, and that's something these politicians in Washington don't believe. They think it is theirs, an unending source to be tapped at will. I will strive to get rid of all regulations strapping our industrial strength. Our companies cannot compete with foreign markets, because foreign markets are not restrained with the rules and regulations imposed here. I could continue on and on, but, I want to do less talking and more legislating of these reforms. Once more, thank you for all your help and confidence in me. Without it there would be no victory tonight. My wife, Karamine and I are deeply moved and grateful. God Bless You all," he said, stepping away from the microphone and podium.

The place rocked with wild cheering, confetti and ribbons. Lance and Karamine tried to inch their way toward Richard's office, but were blocked by reporters storming questions at them from all sides. Lance looked contemptuously at one reporter from the EXAMINER, when he pressed in "Is this victory a surprise after your brother-in-law exposed your background?" he taunted.

"Your paper did its best to destroy me by not sticking to the facts and manufacturing some of your own, calling it a reliable source," Lance answered through his teeth. "I knew if I could speak directly to the people they would hear the truth and then make a valued decision."

"Are you saying the EXAMINER manufactured those allegations?"

Karamine felt Lance's body stiffen, and gently tugged his arm. They inched their way toward Richard's office, stopping to shake hands, and answer questions. When they finally made it, Richard and John were there with their wives.

"Boy, have you ever seen such wha hoo," Richard remarked, with a smile. "How about a celebration drink?"

"I think we could all use one," Lance replied.

"Let's go back into the conference room where we'll be more comfortable ," Richard suggested, pointing to an inner office door. "There's a long table in there and we can sit around and relax a bit, while the kids tear the place apart. They're entitled to it, they've worked hard and have done a fantastic job."

"How the hell did you recruit all those young kids to do the job they did, Richard?" John quizzed.

"Yes, Richard, how did you manage that. They look like college kids to me," Karamine added.

"They are," Alice Blair answered. "Richard and Jim have been recruiting them for the last few years. They've tried to get conservative students to unite and push some conservative ideas which we badly need in the universities. They also help in the leg work which these campaigns require."

Jim Roi returned to the room with a box full of assorted liquors and wines and placed them on the table along with a bucket of ice and plastic cups.

John Dixon raised his glass when everyone held a drink. "Here's to the first conservative ever to go to the senate from the state of Massachusetts . . . Lance Bagdasarian."

"To Lance" everyone responded.

Lance looked at Karamine first. She smiled warmly, then nodded her head for him to speak.

"Friends . . . again, no words can express the thoughts and affection I have for all of you at this moment. John, Miriam, your constant trust in me all these years, from a program like ON TARGET to your recent faith in me through the rough times of this campaign have touched me deeply. I'll never forget it. Richard and Alice who felt I would be a good choice to run on the Republican banner, and who did not falter when the going got tough . . . thank you." Lance turned toward Jim Roi with a broad smile and raised his glass. "Jim . . . who coordinated so many groups and molded them into a formidable force that defeated the opposition . . . Jim, my gratitude and thanks! Thanks so much to all of you. Finally, my wonderful wife, Karamine. Without her, I don't believe any of this would be possible." Lance hugged Karamine, and everyone cheered. Outside, the celebration continued. Victory is sweet . . .

It was after midnight before Karamine and Lance were finally able to leave the hall. Both expressed relief their parents had wisely declined the invitation to be with them, since the hectic, noisy scene would have been an exhaustive and draining experience. At every turn, cameras and microphones were thrust into Lance and Karamine's faces; over and over Lance was asked the same questions; over and over he gave the same responses.

"What turned the tide for you senator?"

"Truth, nothing but the truth. I gave people the full story without deleting a thing. Also, this time the voters had a clear choice between candidates and what they really stand for. The people registered their preference."

"Are you still a member of that secret underground group?" one brash reporter gibed.

Karamine felt Lance's body stiffen, and once again, she tugged his arm, sending him body language to ignore the remark.

"What will your main agenda be when you get to Washington, Senator?" someone else called.

"I'm hoping to work on legislation that will bind congress to the same laws and regulations they make for the rest of our American citizens," Lance responded, trying to get out the door.

"Do you think congress will give up their power so easily?" the follow-up question probed.

Reporters were still flinging questions as he and Karamine struggled to get into the car Jim had provided. Finally reaching it, they got in, slammed the car door shut and sank down into the back seat. Jim started the engine immediately and they took off.

"God, I'm glad that's over," Lance commented, with a sigh of relief . . . and did you hear that question from the EXAMINER reporter? Where the hell do they get their gall, trying to keep that scenario going!"

"Might as well get used to it, Senator," Jim commented with a laugh. "You know damn well they're never going to forgive you for defeating their candidate."

"That's true," Karamine added. They'll be on the prowl now for one missed word or action that will give them the chance to jump all over you and try to discredit you. You're fair game now, Lance, and you should know by this time that conservatives and republicans are held to a much higher scrutiny and standard than your counterpart, the liberal democrat. Just keep that in mind when dealing with the media, and don't allow yourself to be put off by their barbs and taunts."

"That's for sure. Maybe I should go with you and take care of you, Mr. Bagdasarian," Jim remarked pleasantly.

Lance laughed. "Well . . . how about it? What exactly are your plans now that the campaign is over, Jim? You know, I'd love to have you help me in Washington. I need people I can trust."

"Thanks, Senator. I'd like to very much, but, I still have one semester to go, and I want to have all my studies behind me. No . . . I'll work to get another good candidate like yourself for the next senate seat, also for the house seat. I'll stick with Richard Blair for now. I'll think about your offer when I'm out of school though."

As they raced through the streets of Boston, Lance leaned back in the seat and looked through the car window. It's hard to realize it's all over, he thought. Washington's the city now. He reached for Karamine's hand and pressed it, anticipating the new challenges that lay ahead. Karamine smiled warmly and rested her head lightly on his shoulder.

"Looking forward to Washington?" he whispered.

"Of course," she replied lightly.

The full implication of being a senator's wife was now a reality. The past weeks and months with its frantic pace had sped by rapidly; days and nights of intense activity left no time to think or sort out the complications of arranging her life. She thought about it now. Somehow she never actually believed she'd have to face the decisions and choices emerging so swiftly. Although she had put her life on hold, and had worked tirelessly to help her husband achieve his goal, she wondered now if somewhere deep inside she hadn't held out a secret hope that it just wouldn't happen, Lance would not be elected and their lives would soon be back to normal. God, she thought, frantically, how can I possibly go to Washington to live. How can Lance expect me to? I love him so deeply, and I'm so enormously proud of him, but, it's self-contradictory to think of myself in the lifestyle of a senator's wife. I'm a doctor with an established practice I've worked hard to build up. What about the commitment to Armenia and all the organizing and planning I've gone through to make that a reality? Surely Lance can't expect me to give up the work so close to my heart, or desert the people who've come to depend on me. Oh God, she thought miserably, why do these whirlwind events enter our lives and turn everything upside down. Everything was so perfect before, but now, I'm torn, fragmented, filled with doubts and guilt. I should be there with him, attending Washington functions and I will be for many of them. But, I can't live there and work here. One day at a time, Karamine, do it one day at a time. I haven't had an opportunity to discuss my upcoming trip to Armenia. Everything's in place to take off the first of the year. Well, I'll wait till then to tell him —after he's sworn in and installed in the senate. He'll be caught up and embroiled with politics, and maybe it won't seem so devisive then. Meanwhile, let's get through this next phase of living in Washington.

Lance was still carrying on a conversation with Jim when the car pulled up in front of their apartment house.

"Thanks again, Jim for all your help and support. Listen, keep in touch."

"Yes, Jim. Thanks, you've been a real friend to us." Karamine said warmly.

They didn't have conversation in the elevator. Both felt the strain of the past weeks and especially the last ten hours. Inside the apartment Karamine walked into the bedroom and wearily threw her pocketbook on a chair, and kicked off her shoes. Lance followed close behind.

"Shall I turn on the T.V. and watch your victory and Senator Crawford's conceding speech?"

Lance shook his head. "Oh . . . I don't think I could take any more just now, Karamine. All I want to do is to get out of these clothes, put on my pj's and relax for awhile."

"How about a cup of tea?"

"Yeah, sounds great. Maybe a slice of toast?"

"Maybe we should call our parents first. They've probably been trying to get us all night."

"Right. You dial them, while I make the tea."

Lance dialed his parent's home, and his father Antranig answered. "Lance, we're so proud of you. I guess I don't have to tell you how we both feel about your victory. I never would have thought it possible that you could beat Senator Crawford, but, you did it, son, by god, you did it!" Antranig's voice was jubilant. "Your mom's on the other line."

"Lance, we love you, and we're proud of you, whether you ever won an election," Lance's mother Kate added affectionately.

After a few moments of conversation concerning the day's events, Lance called Karamine's parents, Aram and Anahid Casparian. Anahid's voice trembled slightly as she spoke to Lance, but her greeting was uncontrived and sincere. They had been glued to the television all day and were genuinely happy and relieved to know Lance had survived the vicious damage and trouble their son, Vasken had caused.

"We're gonna have to get down there to Washington as soon as possible to find a place to live, Karamine," Lance remarked, when Karamine entered the living room with the toast and tea.

Karamine set the tray on the coffee table in front of them before answering. She sighed heavily.

"Lance, I know we haven't talked much about this, but, you must know I can't just pick myself up and follow you down there to Washington. Surely you don't expect me to do that, do you?" She looked at him quizzically.

Lance was silent for some moments before answering. "I guess I didn't think too much about it, Karamine. I just assumed you'd be there with me, by my side like any loyal and loving wife . . ."

Karamine gasped. "Loyal and loving wife? What else have I been all these months, all these years? The trouble with you, Lance is that you've been spoiled, spoiled rotten, and you take everything for granted. If you weren't so self-centered, perhaps you'd have thought a little about my role in your life, about me as an individual, and not merely as an adjunct to your career; I'm someone who's worked hard to build up a practice, someone who cares deeply about the suffering of children, especially in Armenia. Just understand one thing. My work is as important to me as your political career is to you."

"Oh, so now I'm selfish and self-centered, because I happen to love my wife and want her with me? Maybe you're the selfish one Karamine . . . you can work in any hospital. Washington is full of them."

"You just don't understand, Lance. You never do. All you can think of is what's good for you. All my arrangements are made here for my time in Armenia. It's taken me months of planning and organizing, but, you've been too involved thinking about yourself and your career to ever even ask me how it was going. In good conscience how could you even think of asking me to give it all up?"

"Good conscience?" Lance shouted. "Good conscience? Damn it, Karamine was it such a bad thing to think you'd be by my side, to counsel and support me. You know how much I depend on you. Had I known you felt this strongly about it, I may not have taken on this whole thing. I'd have chucked it."

Karamine sniffed with exasperation. "Knowing you, Lance, I doubt that very much; as far as counseling you do all right without me by your side."

"What's that supposed to mean?"

"It means, you're quite capable of making decisions when it's something you really want, and don't tell me now you haven't wanted this from the beginning. I don't remember your consulting my opinion on the subject when you were first approached to run."

"Oh great, great! So now I'm insensitive, thoughtless, ambitious, oh yes . . . selfish and self-centered. Anything else? I must say Karamine, your timing for telling me off is perfect." Lance got up and stormed into the bedroom.

Karamine put her head in her hands and tried unsuccessfully to stop the flood of tears. God, what are we doing? she thought. This is supposed to be our night to celebrate and here we are, fighting each other. She got up and followed Lance into the bedroom. He was already under the covers, his whole body facing the opposite direction from her side. Karamine walked to the edge of the bed and gently touched his head. "Lance . . . please . . . I'm sorry. We're both tired and overwrought. It's insane to fight like this. Surely you know how much I love you; how proud of you I am, have always been. I never meant to hurt you. I also understand how difficult these weeks have been for you, and your preoccupation with clearing your reputation. We should have discussed it more, and perhaps it's my fault, but then, you were always so busy and embroiled in the campaign. I'm not saying I'm not coming to Washington. Certainly I intend to help you find a place to live, help set it up, and I'll fly down to be with you most weekends. Weekends will be ours without interruptions, I promise. We have no children to consider, so there should be no problems. But you have to understand about these medical trips to Armenia. There are more people to consider than just myself. There are other doctors and medical people committed to the project, and I can't just bow out now."

Lance sat up and took Karamine's hand. "I do understand, Karamine, and I'd be the last person in the world to ask you to back off from a commitment. I guess I was pretty self-centered these past few weeks, and you're right, I am overtired. It's just that I'll miss you. It's that simple."

"Lance, you know I'll miss you as well. We've always done everything together. This isn't easy for me either you know."

"Well, maybe later on you can look around Washington and see what's available down there. They'll always have need of a good pediatrician there, and who knows . . . ."

"Right. In the meantime, Senator, I think we should both get some rest."

Karamine took off her robe and slid under the covers next to Lance. She felt drained and exhausted. Lance put his arms around her and five minutes later he was fast asleep.

12

The first few weeks in Washington were a kaleidoscope of activity. The unmistakable aura of pressure and power in the city was immediately discernible, as the tempo of government and decision making forces tapped out a steady vibration of supercharged energy. It electrified Lance and quickened all his senses. I was born to this, he thought, all of the strivings of my life have been to this end—to challenge and be challenged, to compete, to serve, to make the world a better place. Yep, this is really where the action is.

Karamine joined him every weekend in searching for a place to live. It wasn't easy to find a place in the city that suited their needs, but, finally, they discovered a brownstone townhouse on a shaded street that Karamine loved immediately. The caretaker explained that the owner was in Europe on an indefinite stay, but wanted to keep the property since it had been in his family for a long time. The place was completely furnished which was also a happy surprise, but a marble fireplace, fully workable, was the deciding factor.

"It's perfect, Lance," Karamine said, back in their hotel room, "spacious, roomy and a good address. I'm grateful we don't have to chase around looking for furniture just now, even the dishes are provided. It's exactly right for the kind of entertaining we'll have to do here. "You'll need to hire someone, Lance, a good housekeeper, to keep the place clean and neat. Have you thought about that?"

"Oh yes, as a matter of fact, I've already got someone lined up. She used to work for one of the senators who lost his seat in the last election. She's already indicated she'd be delighted to work for me. So things are pretty much under control."

Karamine flew down for the installation of new senators. The ceremony was impressive, and sitting in the senate balcony along with other senator's wives Karamine was deeply moved. Lance is certainly the best looking senator there, she mused, noting how well he carried his six foot frame. Her eyes traced the outline of his profile, and overwhelming pride surged through her. The senate chambers filled her with awe and respect. What history has been made here, what challenges met and overcome against great odds. How proud his grandfather would be to see Lance today. A secret smile played around the corners of her mouth.

After the installation ceremony, Lance took Karamine to the senate working area where the senators had their offices. He introduced her to his newly organized staff.

"Everett Mason, head of staff", Lance said, introducing her to a tall young man in a dark grey business suit.

"Happy to meet you, Mrs. Bagdasarian," Everett acknowledged pleasantly.

"So this is where all the dynamics of government are carried on," Karamine remarked, after the introductions. She looked around Lance's office and noted the piles of papers and documents crowding his desk. "You've scarcely been here a month and I see the work is already piling up."

Lance smiled and looked toward Everett. "Yep, but, Everett will go through all those papers, read them, then highlight all the crucial stuff, so I won't have to read every line. How do you like my office Karamine?"

"Impressive," she replied, picking up the gold nameplate with a Senator Bagdasarian imprint. You have arrived, Sir!"

The day after Karamine had returned to Boston, Lance and five other newly elected republicans met with the senate minority leader, who welcomed them with a few brief remarks before introducing them to the rest of their colleagues.

"We won five more seats here in the senate," he stated briskly. "Hopefully, this will help stem the tide of liberal democratic legislation. However, we're still a minority. We're still seven seats behind to make a majority; it's up to you, senators, to help us in our endeavors to control bureaucracy and all the red tape that binds our private sector to such a point they are unable to compete in world markets. If this continues, we'll end up a third world country or banana republic at worst. We've got to work together, to become a solid force that will enable us to overturn some of their astronomical budgets. These same liberal democrats want to fund all kinds of social programs that go beyond our government's concern and needs, and they don't understand or care, the money just isn't there. The taxpayers are already taxed to the hilt, but, somehow, these democrats don't see it that way. They seem to think all earned money belongs to them, and it's the duty of the taxpayer to turn it over to them.

He continued to show them around; the newcomers circulated, shook hands and discussed areas of interest, various committees they wished to be on, and their reasons for it.

While Lance circulated about the room, a slender built man with steel-grey hair and ruddy complexion approached him and extended his hand in a firm, western-style handclasp.

"Mr. Bagdasarian . . . a pleasure to meet you, sir! I'm Jeb Stuart, senator from Arizona. Welcome to Washington."

"Senator," Lance acknowledged with a smile. "Thank you."

"I followed those Massachusetts elections, closely, and was pulling for you all the way. Senator Crawford chaired the same committee I'm on, and I'm glad you unseated him. He was one spending fixture."

"Jeb Stuart! You're not by any chance related to the same man who fought the Civil War?" Lance flashed his engaging smile.

"The very same. James Ewell Brown Stuart! One of my relatives. He fought with General Lee behind the Union lines. A great southern officer and gentleman. My parents gave me the honor of bearing his name," he said proudly. "But that's not what I want to talk about today. I wanted to congratulate you for the great battle you fought up there in Massachusetts. I followed events closely, and saw what the media was doing to you. Being on Senator Crawford's committee I was anxious to see how you handled things. I always believed in you, and knew you were telling the truth."

"Thank you, Senator."

"Look, Lance, now that Senator Crawford is gone, I want to fill that vacancy on the committee with your name. Would you be interested?

For a moment Lance was speechless. He recognized the committee Senator Stuart spoke about as a very powerful committee, and for a few seconds he was uncertain. "I'm new, senator, and inexperienced. The question is, would I qualify?"

"I believe you could do anything you put your mind to Senator Bagdasarian. You creamed Crawford, up there in Massachusetts. If you're interested, I'll recommend you for the opening."

"Yes, I'm interested, Senator. I'd be honored to serve." Thank you for your vote of confidence."

After the day's formalities, Lance decided he needed a workout to loosen up some of his taut muscles and bones; he headed for the senate gymnasium which he'd found earlier, changed into his sweats then moved quickly toward a large, heavy punching bag in the gym. He would have liked a karati partner, but since there was no one available, he substituted the bag for an opponent. In one maneuver, he'd turn quickly, give the bag a hard back kick, and send it flying.

"You exposed yourself at the turn for an offensive jab" someone commented, after one of his moves. Lance turned to see a young attendent who'd been observing him. "If you want a good workout in the martial arts, you should go to the Martial Arts Academy located at the corner of Connecticut Ave. downtown Bethesda. It's nearby. Want the address?"

"Yes, as a matter of fact I would," Lance replied. I'm a little out of shape, and need someone to work out with. You stop for a while, and you go soft, fast."

The young attendent jotted a name and phone number on a piece of paper and handed it to Lance. Lance continued to work out until he was tired; he went to his locker then, took a swim and a shower before heading home to his empty town house.

He made arrangements to go down to the Martial Arts Academy the next evening. He was interested in finding a karati partner to get himself back in shape. Checking in at the desk, he walked to his assigned locker, stored his equipment and changed into the workout clothes. Arriving at the workout area, Lance focused on a man going through various moves. He admired his perfect timing and skill as the man leaped in the air, twisted, then gave his opponent a heavy blow to the chest, knocking him off his feet and onto the canvas.

"Is that what you had in mind?" he called to the instructor.

"Perfect. You did it perfect. As I said, relax, let your mind do the work, and the result is always flawless. Oh . . . here's a fresh candidate for you to work with," he added, noting Lance's black sash.

"That was a great maneuver. I've been trying that one for a long time, but can't seem to execute it properly." Lance said.

"It took me awhile," the man answered pleasantly. "Would you like to work out?" The man's medium height was deceiving to the ordinary eye but, Lance was immediately conscious of the sinewy format of his body muscles, the panther-like movement of a well-proportioned frame, and the penetrating focus of commanding black eyes.

"Why don't you two pair off," the instructor suggested. "I've a couple of others I want to get started."

"Sure, Ben",

"Oh, by the way . . . I'm Lance Bagdasarian from Massachusetts. I'm the elected senator from the state. I've just arrived in Washington a short while ago." Lance extended his hand.

"Welcome senator. Yes, I saw your name on the roster. You're Armenian, I see. So am I. *Parev!* Ted Sohigian from Racine, Wisconsin. I'm in the House of Representatives . . . second term." Ted extended his hand warmly to greet Lance.

Lance liked Ted immediately. They squared off in the traditional mode required, nodding, gesturing and manning the position. As they went through their routines of thrust and defense they seemed pretty well evenly matched. Toward the end, Ted went into an aggressive mode with turns and tumbles, perfectly executing the maneuver the instructor had taught him. Lance was knocked off his feet and onto the canvas.

"I couldn't resist it, Lance," said Ted, running over to Lance and extending his hand.

"Don't worry about it, I left myself wide open for that one. It was an excellent move. Will you show me how to do it sometime"?

"Be glad to. Let's work out a schedule right now when we can be here to work out together. You're married aren't you, Lance?" Ted queried.

"Yes, but my wife is in Boston. We're only able to get together on weekends. She's a pediatrician with a practice she can't leave."

"That's rough. My wife has been here with me the past seven years. Doesn't like Washington, though. Hates all the dinners, parties and luncheons I have to attend that raise havoc with my diet. She watches everything I eat, and hates it when I eat out so much. Worries about fat, salt, cholesterol, all that stuff." Ted laughed and shook his head.

"Do you have children, Ted?"

"Oh yes . . . two. A boy and a girl. Vartan's nine now, Alexis is seven. How about you?"

Lance shook his head sadly. "No, I'm afraid not. We've tried, but it just hasn't happened. It really bothers Karamine. I've suggested we adopt, but she's dead set against that idea. I wouldn't mind, but Karamine says its got to be ours or none at all. She's stubborn on that point. So . . . she throws herself into her work. She does love children though and she's an excellent doctor. Her trips to Armenia have given her a lot of satisfaction and fulfillment I believe. But, it does get rough at times. Like now. I miss her, damn it." Lance forced a little laugh.

"Hey . . . tell you what. Why not come to my house tonight for a good Armenian meal? I think that's what you need right now. You're not busy tonight are you?"

"Well I was going to go over a few committee proposals, but I'd be an absolute fool not to accept an invitation like that. Sure your wife won't mind?"

"Mind? She'll be delighted. Let's shower up, and I'll call her. Do you have a car?"

"No, I came by cab," Lance replied. "I've a rental on order, and should pick it up in a few days."

"Good, then we'll go in my car."

On the way home, Ted pointed out various points of interest. He also gave Lance directions to his home. "You just get on Rt. #1 south, and get off at the Alexandria exit. You make two right turns and you're at our home. Easy. Somehow I expect you'll be making a few trips out our way while your wife is out of town."

They pulled into the driveway of a stately white Georgian home, and entered the house through a small rotunda-type foyer. The house was tastefully decorated, with paintings and furnishings representing the colonial era.

"Tatiana . . . hello . . . we're home." Ted called.

"Hi . . . welcome," Tatiana Sohigian exclaimed, coming forward to kiss her husband lightly on the cheek and extend her hand to Lance. An attractive woman in her mid forties, Tatiana's body was trim and agile, her smile engaging and warm. Her steel-grey hair was worn simply, pulled back in a pony-tail, tied with a black ribbon. "It's so nice you were able to come," she said, her dark eyes reflecting friendship and sincerity.

The patter of footsteps attracted their attention. Two young children entered abruptly stopping short when they saw Lance.

"Woa . . . where did you guys come from?" Ted laughed as he hugged both his children, then introduced them to Lance. "Vartan, Alexis, I'd like you to meet Senator Bagdasarian from Massachusetts. He's Armenian too." They stepped forward and courteously shook Lance's hand. "Nice to meet you Senator Bagdasarian."

"Our houseman is off today, but I've already fed the children. This way we can have an uninterrupted and pleasant visit." Tatiana whispered softly.

"I hope you'll call me Lance when you get to know me better," Lance said, smiling at both children.

"Okay . . . you've had your dinner now, so go upstairs and do your homework. I'll look in on you later," Tatiana ordered gently.

"How about a drink?" Ted asked. "Tatiana?"

"I'll have a glass of chablis. I believe there's some chilled in the refrigerator, Ted."

"Bourbon if you have it, Ted. Just ice and some water."

Tatiana sat in one of the crewel-covered wing chairs and studied Lance intently. "I knew there was an Armenian senator coming from Massachusetts but, I'd certainly never take you for Armenian, Senator." She laughed lightly. "You look more Germanic or Swede. Forgive me, please, but I've never known an Armenian with such blue eyes."

"Please, call me Lance. I know. I've lived with it all my life. I even had to convince my wife, Karamine, when I first met her. Actually, I'm half-Armenian on my father's side. My mother is Canadian, of Scottish extraction, and she's quite fair-skinned. The blue eyes are from her part of the family. I've always felt Armenian though. I suppose it's because I was very close to my grandparents, especially my *meidz-hyrig*. He taught me so much Armenian history, and believe me, he experienced it first hand. He and my granduncle Avedis escaped here to America in the early part of the century. What stories he used to tell." Lance shook his head. "He had a tragic life over there. Saw the rape and slaughter of his village, experienced the murder of his young bride, Sonia Takhouie. I loved him dearly, till the day he died."

"Yes, I can understand that. Armenians relate many stories like that one. It's what bonds us together as one family I suppose. What hurts one hurts all. My grandparents and parents had similar stories; I wonder sometimes why our people have had so much suffering, and it still continues to this day."

"What continues," said Ted, entering with drinks on a tray.

"Armenian oppression." Tatiana replied.

"Well, I guess we'll never understand it, in the scheme of things," Ted answered, "but, let's not be downcast. I'd like to welcome Lance to our home and to the fun and games of Washington."

"Ted tells me your wife is a doctor, Lance. Is she Armenian?"

"Oh yes, thoroughbred Armenian. She goes over there once or twice a year and works with the children. She's done a lot to bring medical supplies and new technology into some of the more oppressed areas."

"How marvelous! She sounds like a wonderful person. I've always admired women who are able to become doctors, engineers or scientists. What a way to help others."

"Oh that's Karamine . . . helping others is what she does best. She's done so much it's incredible. She's even started a school there to train nurses and technicians. But, you have no idea how backward and dogmatic these people are about change. She has a lot to work through."

"That's impressive, you must be quite proud of her, Lance," Ted commented.

"Lance took a sip of his bourbon. "Yes, he said slowly, I am. She was a big support to me during my campaign. It really became a brawl and she stood by me all the way. I miss not having her here with me, I understand, her work is important to her but, it gets difficult. I miss her. She'll be here this weekend."

"Great! Then you both must come one evening for shish-ke-bob. It's Ted's specialty."

"I'm sure she'd love it. I would too. "Thanks to you both."

They had dinner in a softly-lighted diningroom. A crystal chandelier hung over the long highly polished table. Tatiana was proud of her efforts in producing a substantial Armenian meal, chicken and pilaf, with hot vegetables and salad, pita bread and from her freezer, she produced paklava dripping with honey and pistashios. The conversation was pleasant and easy; Lance felt as though he had known the Sohigians forever.

"Can I give you a ride home, Lance?"

"No, absolutely not. Your hospitality has been outstanding, but I'd prefer to take a cab back. I should have my own car in another day or so. I can't thank you both enough for this evening."

"Don't forget. Bring Karamine this weekend," Tatiana insisted, fifteen minutes later when the cab arrived.

"I'll see you down at the Academy, Lance. I'll show you the move that floored you," Ted added with a laugh.

Lance entered the cab waiting in the driveway. He turned to smile and wave once more before the taxi sped off into the night.

13

The days, weeks and months flew by. Karamine and Lance did their utmost to adjust their schedule of activities to spend time together, but there were many disappointments. At times, Lance felt isolated and lonely in Washington, and his mood vacillated from feelings of anger and frustration to sentiments of self-pity and mild depression.

But today, he felt slightly resigned to the situation. The Senate Education Bill lay spread out on his desk, and he studied it carefully. Basically, he was against it, and had been very outspoken in his opinions concerning it on the senate floor. His assertion was, that government was mandating unreasonable regulations, which would further cripple state and local authority, and take away options parents might have in the education of their children. Lance fought strongly against any Washington influence that would lessen the power of the state and local school boards in each town or city, even though some of his colleagues were for compromise—watering down the bill instead of out and out rejection. Lance was stubborn on this point however, and determined to stop it in its tracks. He was making notes and memorandums concerning the bill when his telephone rang. His secretary informed him it was Karamine calling from Boston.

"Karamine! Nice surprise."

"How are you today, Senator?" she said playfully.

"Lonely. Thinking of joining a bachelor's club. How are things back in old bean town?"

"Everything's fine in Boston, but we have a problem with the shipment of supplies we sent to Armenia."

"Oh? What kind of problem."

"Well, it seems the supplies were sent by ship to Armenia, and had to go through Turkey. The Turkish government seized it as contraband,

and now, they are refusing to release it. I warned them to send the shipment by air, even though it cost more. Had they listened, it would have arrived safely and faster as well. So, here we are, stuck in Turkey."

"Contraband! What the hell are they talking about?" Lance replied angrily. "That's medical equipment and supplies. How long have they held it up, Karamine?"

Karamine sighed heavily. "Over a month. We have no idea of how secure it will be or if indeed, they even intend to release it, Lance."

"Look, Karamine, I'll get in touch with the State Department and see if something can be done before they confiscate it. I'll call Ted immediately. Ted is the Armenian representative from Wisconsin I told you about. He knows his way around the State Department and perhaps he can get them to put a little pressure on the Turks to release the shipment. I'll get on it right away and see what we can do."

"Lance, it would be a godsend to have the shipment released. The people were looking forward to it and depending on the medical supplies."

"Oh . . . by the way, Karamine, changing the subject . . . when you come down this weekend, we're invited to the Sohigians for a shish-kebab dinner. You'll like Ted and his wife Tatiana, and they're really looking forward to meeting you, especially Tatiana. She's interested in your work in Armenia, wants to do something about it down here in Washington . . . you know . . . raise money to buy equipment, food, medical supplies or anything else they can do for the cause."

There was an awkward pause on the other end of the line. "Look Lance," Karamine began softly, "I'm not going to be able to make it this weekend. I was . . . "

"Can't make it?" Lance exploded, his voice filled with anger and disappointment. "This is the third time this month, Karamine. What the hell's so important you can't come down for the weekend? It's been quite a while since we've been together. Doesn't that bother you?"

"Of course it bothers me. I was going to suggest you fly up to Boston and I'll be down there next weekend for sure. But, with these supplies tied up in Turkey we're having an emergency meeting to see if we can't expedite the problem. I know you'll be working on it there, but we're also putting pressure on the U.N. to help us. It's critical those medical supplies get to Armenia, Lance. You have no idea how bad things are there."

"Why doesn't the soviet union help them out?" Lance cried angrily. "And why do they need you at the meeting, anyway?"

"I have to account for all the medical supplies, others for the food. There's a lot of red tape. You should understand that, Lance."

"All I understand is that I've flown back to Boston to be with you, but you don't seem to make a real effort to get down here to be with me.

It's been almost a month since we've been together, and it seems like a year. I'm getting to the point were I think your work and activities mean more to you than I do."

"You know better than that, Lance. How can you say such a thing?

"Very easy. It's always a meeting, seminar, emergency or some other damn thing that stops you from coming down. If you cared about me you'd give me a little priority once in awhile. Maybe I'd better make an appointment."

"Stop it, Lance. You're being immature. You know how much you mean to me. All I ask is a little understanding and patience. Why do you always have to be so cruel."

Lance gestured with his hand as the other held the phone tightly. "Cruel, she says! You know what cruel is, Karamine? It's being stuck down here with no real friends or family, but looking forward to seeing my wife for a few days. And what happens? She gives me excuse after excuse why she is unable to get here. I look forward to seeing you, and I'm let down week after week. It's damn disappointing, Karamine."

"Look, Lance, I feel the same way. Why don't you hop a plane up here on Friday night, and we can be together."

"Well," he said, cooling down a bit and flipping the calendar on his desk, "I can't, because the opposition is trying to ramrod this education bill through with all these changes and regulations we don't need. They always do it on the weekends when a lot of senators take off. This way they can shove it through. No, I've got to stay with my group and fight it through to its conclusion one way or another."

"Lance, look . . . "Karamine's voice pleaded, "I promise I'll be down next weekend for sure. I've cleared all appointments and have even arranged for emergencies. Do you think you could forgive me and try to understand a little? I really do want to meet the Sohigians, but most of all, I want us to get together. You know, I love you, Senator."

The persuasiveness of her words softened Lance's mood. "I love you, too. That's the problem. I miss not having you around. Okay, I'll see you at Washington International next Friday."

Lance had barely hung up when Everett Mason, his chief of staff entered and placed some papers on his desk. "Senator Howard, is in the outside office, and he'd like to see you, Senator," he announced.

"The senior senator from Massachusetts?" Lance said in surprise, "I wonder what he wants. Send him in by all means, Everett. We can't be discourteous now can we?"

A few moments later, a tall, slightly built man in early fifties entered. He was unsmiling, and seemed to project a mixed aura of ivy-league polish and subtle vexation. Behind his horn-rimmed glasses his eyes were cold, as he extended his hand to Lance. "I'm Senator David

Howard, your senior senator from Massachusetts. "May I ask you Senator Bagdasarian why it is you've never sought out my counsel on pertinent information going through the senate now, information concerning our state? That is the usual protocol accepted around here," he said in a haughty tone.

The color drained from Lance's face as he tried to control the fury he felt within. He thought of the many speeches made throughout the state by this man during the campaign, words echoing the unsubstantiated charges levelled against him. He remembered how much grief and hardship those speeches caused his family.

"Why should I seek your counsel after what you and your party did to me and my family with all those false allegations and lies. Why indeed should I have to answer any of your questions now, senator? I have no need of your help or input at this time," Lance answered cooly.

Senator Howard withdrew his hand. "Look Senator Bagdasarian that was the election, this is now. You won. Let's work together to formulate legislation to benefit our state. You know, I had nothing to do with the operation or conduct of the election committee. They do things on their own. I'm confident Senator Crawford himself didn't approve such extremes in their pursuit of victory, but, that is all behind us now, past history."

Lance deeply understood this was a most severe testing of his capacity to forgive an enemy; everything in him resisted. But, knowing the folly of holding grievances and bearing grudges, he grasped Senator Howard's hand as he offered it once more." You are right, Senator Howard, that was then, this is now. I hope we can work together for the good of our great state. This doesn't mean I necessarily agree with your political philosophy however."

Senator Howard smiled. "please . . . call me Dave. It makes for a more friendly atmosphere.

Lance shrugged his shoulders in acceptance of the premise, but remained non-committal.

"What I'd like to talk about, if I may Lance, are the new jet engines the Senate Appropriations Committee are considering ordering. I understand you're on that committee, and as you know, those engines are built in Massachusetts. I'm sure you realize how much this will mean to our state in the area of jobs and money. But unfortunately, we lack the votes to consummate it into a final decision. Do you think you can convince the senator from Texas to come aboard with his vote? He's trying to get an appropriation for the building of the Air Force planes for his state, and I believe that together, we could easily get the appropriations through the senate and benefit both our states."

Lance remained silent but it was obvious he was distressed.

"What's the matter?" Senator Howard queried.

"Senator, I've listened for some time to the people at the Pentagon, and they are dead set against ordering those jet engines. According to them, they have loads of them in crates, a real supply which they haven't even used. They have need of the money right now for other research and development; the new light heavily armed tank for instance. They have no wish to overload on jet engines they don't need. As for that Air Force plane, we've had the officers at our hearings and every one of them is against the building of that particular type of aircraft. They claim it is not suited to the type of warfare expected in the future. No, I have to tell you I'm not voting for either one of those boondogles, and that's all it is."

Senator Howard maintained his calm. "This is money and jobs needed for the economy of the state, a bill that would ensure jobs to the Boston area for a number of years. In good conscience how can you just deprive our people of this work?"

"Simple." Lance responded curtly. "First of all, the Pentagon does not want or need them, secondly, this is the American taxpayer's money, not yours or mine, or some other legislator's to throw around in reckless spending, just to placate some need back home. This is exactly the kind of thing I ran on as a candidate, and was then elected to stop. Abusive spending which has run amuck here in Washington. Sorry, but, I'm not voting for it, and furthermore, I'll do my best to stop its passage."

Senator Howard's face flushed as he regarded Lance with an expression of mixed anger and loathing. "I think you overstate your importance in this senate, sir. To think that a great senator like Jason Crawford was defeated by the likes of you. What a disgrace for our state and its working people. How the hell did they ever elect you!"

"They elected me, senator, to stop the likes of you," he said bitingly.

"This is not the end of this. Believe me, it's not wise to make enemies so early in your career, Senator," he said irately, turning abruptly to leave.

"Whew! What happened?" Everett Mason remarked as he entered Lance's office. "Senator Howard stormed out of here like a bat outta hell."

Lance shrugged again. "Well, I guess I made another enemy. He was upset because I said I was voting against one of his pet projects . . . those jet orders he wants for Massachusetts. He wants to push it through even though the Pentagon doesn't want any part of it."

"Senator Jeb Stuart is outside and wants to speak to you. Shall I send him in?"

"O.K. Send him in."

Lance rose to shake Jeb Stuart's hand. "Jeb . . . Come in, sit down."

Jeb Stuart seemed slightly exasperated. "Lance . . . just what are your doing by opposing the education bill? That speech on the floor was really something. I have to tell you . . . you are setting yourself up to alienate everyone in the senate with speeches like that. You've got to learn to compromise. Get it? Compromise. That's what the legislative body is all about. You get a consensus and write up a bill that almost everyone can agree on. This is the way things are done down here, Lance, so why are you fighting it?"

"Compromise. Yeah, I guess that's the way things have been done down here for the past thirty years. Thirty years of compromise. So . . . what's left? From what I can see we've compromised everything, morals, values, principles, character, and we're seeing the result and debris of it right in our culture. We've compromised our nation, a nation built on absolutes to a nation where nothing matters."

"Are you through making a speech? Let me give you a little advice, Lance. That type of rhetoric won't go too far here in the senate, so you better make up your mind that this is the way things are done here, and this is the way it's going to be, whether you like it or not. If we didn't compromise in congress we'd never get anything done or legislation passed."

"Huh," Lance sniffed, "perhaps it might be a good idea not to have legislation passed. It would save the tax payers billions of dollars for starters. All these new laws and regulations are binding our country's industry and stifling creativity to the point where we are unable to compete in world markets. The volume of mandates and regulations pouring out of Washington are subjegating the people to a despotic oligarchy . . . especially when they're not subject to the same rules and regulations they mandate for others."

"Despotic oligarchy for Christ's sake! What the hell are you talking about?" Jeb Stuart shouted. You forget we were elected by the people to formulate those very laws and regulations you seem to regard in such contempt. We're not bound by those laws in order to give us more freedom to work for the good of the country."

Lance laughed disdainfully, and his blue eyes flashed. "Some excuse. Some damn lame excuse, especially for a man of your stature, Senator. And how, may I ask, will you know or understand how these laws and regulations affect the private sector if you yourself are not subject to those same rules? It's no wonder legislators are so out of touch with the people. And that's something I intend to fight. I'll vote against every bill that stifles the freedom of the people to choose."

"Get real, Lance. Don't go off in a tangent. I'll agree. Government is too large and has many drawbacks that hinder our productive capacity, but, we're trying to get rid of some of the regulations that are cumbersome and costly to the manufacturing segment of our country. We can work it out, and you can help lead the way. But, you've got to work with the whole senate, get people together to back your reforms and legislation. There's no other way you can make headway. Keep up your obstructionist policies and you'll never get re-elected . . . a one-term senator, that's all."

Lance's strong jaw tightened and he gazed at Jeb Stuart with a granite stare. "I judge that remark to be a slightly veiled threat. Are you threatening me, Senator?"

Senator Jeb Stuart drew an exasperated breath. "Look, Lance I think I've caught you at the wrong time. From your mood I sense you're having a bad day. I didn't come here to antagonize you further. As a matter of fact I admire you, and think you have a great future here. I merely thought you'd like a little advice from someone who's been here a while and knows his way around the Washington scene, inside the beltway as we say. I only want to help you."

Lance smiled and shook his head. "You're right, Jeb, I am having a bad day as a matter of fact. Sorry."

Jeb Stuart stood up and laughed lightly "Don't worry about it, Lance. We all go through it. We come here as firebrands, idealogs hoping to change the world, then reality sets in and we discover, little by little, our oldest and most basic instinct . . . survival . . . you do what it takes to survive. That translates into compromise and flexibility."

Lance shrugged his shoulders and tried to manage a smile. "I appreciate your words, Jeb, and I know what you're saying is true. Nevertheless, something within me defies that premise, and urges me to fight for what I stubbornly believe is a higher instinct."

"Well, have it your way. Personally, what I think you need now is to get out and do some socializing. How about that affair the Department of Human Service is giving tonight in the Washington Hotel? That's really why I came over here. Are you planning to attend? I think you should get out and meet some people, find out how things work around here. There will be a lot of senators there you haven't met and hell . . . it'll be good for you. Get out and have a little fun."

Lance hesitated before answering. "I hadn't really thought about it. My wife isn't here in Washington, and I don't ordinarily attend social functions like that without her."

"I think you should go, Lance. Everyone goes out of necessity. That's where you find out what's going on. There'll be a few lobbyists there, usually pushing some bill or other, and it's a good way of sounding a bill out by seeing who's involved with it, and how much influence they have created. Come to the party, have a few drinks and loosen up. Make believe you're getting an education in Washington politics."

"Okay, Jeb, you win. Work the room for the good of the party, right?" Lance laughed.

Jeb Stuart patted Lance's shoulder. "You're learning . . . you're learning!" he said with a pleasant smile. "See you tonight at the function."

As Jeb left, Lance shook his head and wondered if he had made the right decision.

Lance entered the elegant lobby of the Washington Hotel, and walked briskly toward the SWAN ROOM. When he entered, the music from a four-piece combo band rippled and mingled with the strident hum of conversation, laughter and general excitement. Surveying the scene, Lance felt suddenly alienated, friendless and detached. He recognized no one. Damn, this is a stupid waste of time, he mused quietly. If only Ted and Tatiana could have made it tonight, but—they were tied up with other plans.

Somewhere in the Swan Room he remembered seeing a bar; Might as well get a drink—at least I can sit and relax, he thought moodily. He arrived at the party later than expected because of extra time spent with Ted at the Martial Arts Academy. Earlier, Ted had tried to coach him in the intricate maneuver Lance wished to learn. My stride was definitely off today, he thought glumly. I was unable to master that move, even though Ted went over it repeatedly. Perhaps I went about it with too much intensity; I let my emotions get in the way. Let me order a drink, I definitely need to relax. It's been a rough day all around, full of disappointment and hassles. He walked toward the bar and ordered a scotch and water. I shouldn't have talked to Jeb that way, he reflected. He really meant well. Bad timing I suppose, right after that confrontation with the senior senator from Massachusetts.

But, however much Lance tried to understand his mood, he recognized the bottom line of his short-temper and unsocial behaviour was loneliness—loneliness and disappointment. He had really looked forward to Karamine's coming this weekend, and it seemed an eternity to him since they'd been together. He took a gulp of his drink and glanced around the room. The chandeliers sparkled, scattering kaleidoscopic patterns throughout the room and over the lavish table straining with exotic foods. How many important functions and balls had been held here—how many world figures passed through—deals decided, bargains sealed, compromises made. There's enough food on that table to feed a nation—all paid for by tax payer's money. My, how we love to spend what is not ours, he mused abstractly.

"Glad you decided to come, Lance." A familiar voice sounded behind him. He turned to see Jeb Stuart who sat on the empty seat next to him and ordered a drink.

"Yep, I decided to take your advice after all, Jeb . . . and by the way, I want to apologize for my outburst this afternoon. It shouldn't have happened, even if I was having a bad day." Lance laughed lightly.

"Don't worry about it. It happens to all of us. We arrive here in Washington with our own ideas, only to find they conflict with set patterns and agendas of others. It gets chaotic at times, but, out of it all, this great republic somehow survives the clashes of time and politicians, and carries on our American tradition. You're right on one thing, Lance. There is too much compromise, and at times the hands of social agendas seem to get the better of us." Jeb Stuart took a gulp of his drink. "In any case, there are some people I want you to meet."

When they had finished their drinks, Jeb led Lance toward a group of senators, representatives and their wives and introduced him. Lance smiled pleasantly and made the appropriate cordial remarks. In the next hour, Jeb steered him from one group to another; It was some time before Lance was able to break away. He was bored and frankly tired of explaining Karamine's absence. Picking up another scotch at the bar he walked out to a small balcony, but quickly backed up when he saw he had intruded on a young woman who seemed wrapped in thought and unaware of him.

"Sorry," he said awkwardly.

The young woman turned and smiled pleasantly. "Why sorry?"

"Well . . . I seem to have intruded on your privacy."

"Oh, come on out here, join me in my privacy," she said invitingly. "I'm Rhoda Burke, and I'm with the Department of Education. I'm one of their directors and you . . . you look very familiar to me. I wonder why."

Lance looked at the attractive woman and noted her shining straight blonde hair and fair skin. Her black dress was cut low, held only by two slim straps, and her green eyes sparkled with amusement and curiosity. Lance felt a tinge of fascination.

"Lance Bagdasarian at your service," he said flashing his most engaging smile.

"Of course." There was a gleam of recognition in her eyes. You're the one who made that speech against the education bill, right?

Lance laughed a little awkwardly. "Yeah . . . that was me. How did you know about the speech?"

"I listen to all the speeches on the senate floor, especially the ones pertaining to education. Anyway, what's your beef about education? Don't you feel we need reform and more money to operate the new programs being administered by the legislature?"

"Reform, yes, but not by Washington bureaucrats who can't even run a post office efficiently, much less an educational program. Sometimes, I wonder if some of them can actually read, when you look at all the waste they initiate when trying to solve a problem. No, I believe in leaving the schools to the states and local towns and cities. They know the needs better than the people here in Washington who mandate rules and regulations without caring what results or damage it might create. I feel we should leave it to the locals to run their schools the way they see fit."

Rhoda Burke appraised him coolly through gem-colored eyes. "Wow! you're really gung-ho on the subject, aren't you?" A real fighter I can see. Wish we had you on our side. Here, come sit down, we have a lot to talk about," she invited warmly, sliding down on the bench to make room. "Are you alone at this party? Girlfriend, wife? what? Tell me about yourself. I can't imagine a good-looking man like you unattached." She laughed musically, with a sound that Lance somehow found fascinating. For a brief second, he longed to pour out his heart; He felt comfortable with her, and she eased his sense of displacement in a rather cold and friendless setting. But no, he thought cautiously, I'll just give her a few facts, nothing personal.

"I am married, but my wife is not here with me this evening. I'm only here myself because I was "advised" to come. Personally, I find it a bit hypocritical and useless. Those who believe in you will support you anyway, and those who don't . . . well . . . nothing can change their minds much less socializing at an affair like this."

"Oh, I don't entirely agree with you, Senator, some people change their minds more often than you think. Many are forced to change their minds, sometimes through cajoling or flattery, and of course, the last resort, threats. But never mind that, tell me, why isn't your wife here with you? Does she trust you with all these aggressive women here in Washington?" Rhoda Burke slid closer to Lance allowing her thigh to touch him lightly.

Lance felt a sudden awkwardness, that was not unpleasant. He was intrigued by her forwardness and he found himself slightly challenged by her manner. "My wife's in Boston . . . she's a doctor there, and finds it difficult to get away. We do get together on weekends, though." Why the hell am I confiding all this to her, he wondered with some vexation, suddenly annoyed by his own lack of restraint and confidentiality. "Hey . . . what about you, are you here alone, with a boyfriend or husband . . . significant other?" he asked abruptly switching the conversation to her.

Rhoda Burke regarded Lance intently, then shrugged. "Well, that's a long story. I was supposed to get married some time ago, but somehow the wedding was always postponed for some reason or another. The final upshot was, he was transferred to the West coast and wanted me to go with him . . . no marriage mentioned, just pull up stakes and go. To make a long story short, we got into a terrible argument, and said things which really pulled us apart forever. I won't go into that now, but it was quite obvious he didn't care that much about me. I'm glad the whole episode is behind me, and . . . I'm out here on this balcony now, with a handsome young senator . . . a married senator!" She laughed lightly, her gaze never leaving Lance's face.

"I'm sorry . . . about your relationship, I mean," Lance responded, somewhat awkwardly.

"Oh don't be," Rhoda answered in a half-whisper, "it was the best thing that's ever happened to me. Now I can live my life the way I want to, follow my career, and in short enjoy my independence."

"I notice your glass is empty. Can I get you a refill?" Lance queried, feeling the need to extricate himself from the spell of this captivating female. Maybe it's the scotch, he thought, or maybe I'm just lonely, but she's damn attractive. "What are you drinking?"

"Planters punch."

Lance walked to the bar and ordered her drink then a scotch for himself. Better take it easy on the stuff, he advised himself—you could head into dangerous waters here.

"That's a potent drink," Lance commented while passing Rhoda the tall glass." I watched them make it and the bartender put three kinds of rum in there, along with some triple sec. Will you be okay to drive?

Rhoda laughed, deliberately brushing Lance's hand as she took the glass from him. "I took a cab here, and will take one back . . . unless of course, you could drive me home?"

Lance could not understand his feelings of inner excitement and curiosity. The touch of her hand sent an unexpected tremor through him. "Where do you live?" he inquired politely. "I live in Alexandria."

Rhoda took a sip from her glass then threw him an appealing glance. "Well . . . it's on your way . . . I'll direct you."

They finished their drinks and Lance guided Rhoda to the lot where his car was parked. In the front seat she moved close to him, and Lance was aware of the pressure of her thigh as he drove along the highway. Her conversation was playful, flattering and full of subtle flirtation. "I can't understand why your wife would allow a handsome specimen like you to be here all alone in this town," she commented.

Lance laughed softly, but remained non committal. The last drink was getting to him slightly. He knew she was coming on to him, strongly, and he was struggling against a powerful urge to submit to the touch of her hand set lightly on his leg.

"Come up for a cup of coffee, Rhoda invited when they reached her apartment house. "It's still early and we could talk about your aspirations and hopes as a senator. Besides, it will give you a chance to sober up a bit before that long drive to Alexandria."

"That seems like an offer I can't refuse. Okay, I'll come for a cup of coffee, but I can't stay long."

Rhoda's apartment was tastefully decorated in light colors and sleek modern furniture. He noticed the modern deco-art hangings, the odd-shaped lamps and bold colored pillows; he had mixed feelings whether he liked the effect or not.

Suddenly Rhoda stood very close to him. "Are you sure you want coffee, Lance?" she murmured suggestively.

Lance was startled; a powerful urge swept over him. He felt Rhoda's lips tremble against his own, and the feel of her soft flesh as his hand wandered along her arm and to her breast. Everything in him yielded to the touch of her fingers, now knowingly, exploring his body, exciting him beyond all reason. The clamorings of guilt seemed only to enhance his passion. He slipped the thin straps of her dress over her shoulders, and the dress fell carelessly to the floor; her bare breasts glowed pink and white in the soft, indirect light. She was whispering against his cheek, and her breath was hot, perfumed, intoxicating.

Lance could not remember the precise moment he became chilly sober. It struck him suddenly, and filled him with remorse and self-loathing. He thrust Rhoda from him.

She gasped at him in disbelief. "What's the matter?"

"Nothing, Rhoda, nothing. It's me, not you," Lance said staggering back, struggling to gain some composure. "Look . . . I'm sorry Rhoda, I have no business being here, that's all. I'm sorry." Rhoda's eyes were a mixture of exasperation and disbelief. She watched silently as Lance left the apartment.

Outside Lance breathed in the cool night air. Although nothing happened, he felt dismay and a deep sense of shame. How could I even feel tempted to betray Karamine, he asked himself. I almost lost it up there. He started the car and hit the acelerator, then drove in the direction of his townhouse silently, he vowed he would never be caught in such a vulnerable and compromising situation again.

14

On Friday afternoon, Lance left his senate office early. The spring air was filled with the scent of cherry blossoms, now blooming everywhere in Washington; overhead the sky was clear and bright, a perfect day for Karamine's flight from Boston, he thought eagerly. To Lance's surprise and delight, she had phoned him earlier to announce her arrival on Friday afternoon instead of Saturday; this seemed to fill him with renewed buoyancy. He still felt a little guilty about his encounter with Rhoda Burke, even though nothing had really happened there. Still—it was the first time he had ever felt tempted to cheat in all his years of marriage, and it disgusted him to think he had almost enjoyed the experience. He had thought about telling Karamine, but, since nothing had really happened, he decided to charge it up to a learning experience and simply forget the whole incident.

He slid behind the wheel of his car and decided to put the top down. Karamine will love this little car, he reasoned. It will remind her of the MG we used to run around in. He smiled to himself, thinking of the weekend ahead. It seemed so long since they had been together. The realization of how much he missed her struck him acutely—life was meaningless and empty without her.

The big semi-trucks roaring past him on the Washington Beltway seemed louder than usual today, and interrupted his train of thought. He decided the Washington Beltway was no place to enjoy the open breeze of a convertible, and decided to put the top up once he reached the airport. On arrival at the airport, he turned into the private parking area especially reserved for senators and found an empty spot, then headed for the terminal. The flight from Boston was just disembarking.

Through the crush of people and confusion, Karamine finally walked through the gate, cool and poised in a light grey suit and overnight case. Her eyes darted quickly over the waiting crowd, then relaxed in a smile when she recognized Lance. They embraced briefly and tried to get out of the way of the crowds thick-pressing around them. "It's a madhouse on Fridays," Lance said, guiding her toward the exit and parking lot beyond. Outside, Lance put his arms around her and held her tightly. "God, I'm, glad to see you, Karamine . . . I've missed you . . .

"Lance . . . I just couldn't wait until tomorrow. I've missed you too."

"So . . . what do you think of this?" Lance waved his arm toward the sign indicating a parking area reserved for senators and congressmen only. "I guess I'm part of the privileged class now. Doesn't say much for the concept of the people's legislature though does it? Kind of unfair I'd say, but, right now it's kind of convenient, I must confess. Oh . . . here's the little rental I was telling you about. What do you think?"

Karamine threw back her head and laughed. "I don't believe it! Reminds me of the MG."

"Yeh . . . that's why I took it. It's a bit roomier and a little more comfortable though.

"Is your dad still using the MG, Lance?"

"Yep. According to him it's a real classic and the engine still runs well. They use it to visit the graves at the farm, or to run over to the yacht club."

"Why don't you buy this one, Lance. We could use it back home later on," Karamine suggested.

"No, it's cheaper this way. I don't have to bother with maintenance, insurance and all the other headaches that go with owning a car, especially here in this city. It's a good deal. Shall I put the top up? It's pretty noisy on the Beltway."

"No leave it down. I want to see the sights, and it is a beautiful day."

When they got settled in the car, Lance placed his hand lightly on her thigh. "This is the way it should be, Karamine," Karamine squeezed his hand. "I know, Lance. Don't you think I miss it too?"

"By the way, it's been working out very well with Emma. She comes early in the morning and leaves me supper I can warm in the microwave. She's a gem. I hardly ever see her so I call her my 'friendly phantom'. She's prepared some delicious food for this weekend, too. I told her you were coming down. I picked up some champagne by the way, the kind you like," he added with a grin.

Karamine smiled warmly. "You've thought of everything, I see."

They wound their way through the busy intersection of Alexandria and finally pulled up outside the townhouse. "It's beautiful here, Lance. I'm glad you have this place. I want to get down more often," she said, looking around and noting the new green leaves bursting forth on the ornamental shrubbery. Inside she was equally pleased and surprised. The place was immaculate, the table in the dining room already set for two.

Lance put her overnight bag on the chair and slipped his arms around her. "Yes, Karamine, it's all very nice, but there's just one thing missing. I'm glad you came today."

"So am I."

"Look, why don't you relax while I get things ready here."

"I want to help, Lance."

"I know where everything is, and it won't take a minute. It's all prepared. As I said, Emma's a gem. I'll just put everything on to reheat slowly, then we'll have a glass of champagne."

"You talked me into it, Senator."

Karamine took her bag into the bedroom and came out later in a loose sweater and comfortable slacks. She sat while Lance spun a bottle of champagne in an ice bucket, then placed two glasses on the coffee table.

"Hmmm . . . seems to me you do all right without me around," she commented lightly, "crystal glasses, silver ice bucket and all other creature comforts. I feel as though I'm on a date, and need to be wary of being seduced. I don't know if I like the idea of you down here with such a set-up . . . especially with all your charm, good looks and wit. Need I be worried?" she teased.

"Well now, I could probably say the same thing about you up north in our beautiful apartment, with all those young doctors at the hospital. I'm sure they're not exactly unaware of your charms." He filled her glass and raised his. "To my Karamine . . . the only woman I love, or will ever need. To us."

"To us." she echoed, taking a sip from her glass. "By the way, I read your speech on the senate floor regarding the education bill. I read it in The Examiner, of course, so naturally they weren't too thrilled about it, especially the part about bringing it back into the hands of the state and local authority, along with the PTA. They claim you're against education. That you're trying to destroy the public school system, giving parents vouchers so they can choose the school they want for their children."

"So . . . you're following my career in the Examiner!" Couldn't you pick a better paper?"

"Like what? What other choice do we have except that tabloid, The Journal. They're about the same aren't they?"

"You're right I suppose. At least you're keeping up with the debates here in Washington, even if it is in the enemy media."

"Sometimes it's good to know what the opposition is doing, and saying, Lance. Then you can counterattack their strategies."

"That's what Jeb Stuart said the other day when we had it out."

"What do you mean, had it out. I thought he was a friend."

"He is . . . but he didn't like my opposition to that education bill. He wanted me to support some watered down version which I dislike also. He informed me I'd have to compromise, which vexed me no end. Compared the whole political arena to a chess game where you have to give a little, then move into a position to checkmate your opponent. Those were his exact words. I blew up and let him have it. I felt badly about it, and apologized later for my outburst. Jeb's a good friend and has been a tremendous help to me. He showed me how to get a bill written so it can be introduced in the senate without obstruction, and gave me quite a few pointers and key elements that help me legislate. Every bill or resolution I write trying to cut the bureaucracy gets stuck in committee and that's the end of it. They don't want to relinquish one inch of power they've accumulated over the past thirty years.

Can't you get it out of committee and on the floor by a vote of all members, Lance? I thought there was a parliamentary procedure that could be used."

"Well, that's true, but you need two-thirds of the senate to do it. No way could we get that many votes with all the arm twisting that goes on down here. No . . . we need term limits, with some new fresh fighters on both sides. These career politicians become entrenched and become arrogant. They force everyone to abide by their rules and regulations. No, term limits is the only way this mess can ever be straightened out."

"How's that young lawyer John Dixon recommended getting along?"

"Everett? Oh, he's great! He's taken over the filing of the legal aspects of the bills we formulate. I'd be lost without his input. He's hired most of our personnel, so we have a great group of young people with the same political attitude as I have. There's a couple of libertarians with us, who claim I'm one of them . . . just don't know it."

"Libertarian" You? That'll be the day, Lance." Karamine threw her head back and laughed.

"I agree with them on some things, but they're a bit extreme. They're a nice hard-working group though. They go through those senate bills with a fine tooth comb, and pick up on every little loop hole. It's incredible."

"Karamine put her glass down for a refill. "I'm glad they're making your job a little easier."

"By the way, how did that shipment to Armenia go?" Lance queried. They told me at the State Department that the Turks would release it, but I really don't trust the State Department and their pro-Turkish sentiments. They do what they please no matter what the President or the congress says or thinks. We're calling constantly to light a fire under them and get them to move on it."

"It worked, and believe it or not the Turks apologized for holding it up and promised it wouldn't happen again . . . which of course we take with a grain of salt. Even at that, there were a number of crates and supplies missing when it arrived. Not much we could do," Karamine said, with a sigh of exasperation.

"Are you getting hungry?" Lance asked, changing the subject. Everything's ready . . . Emma's roast beef, potatoes, peas and a huge Greek s salad that you like. Oh and by the way, we're invited over to Ted and Tatiana's tomorrow for shish-ke-bob. Tatiana's been dying to meet you; she's really interested in the work you do in Armenia."

"I didn't bring any clothes with me, Lance."

"Don't worry, it's informal. What you have on is perfect. They're a warm couple, you'll like them. Anyway, Madame, dinner is served," he announced, walking to the table and holding a chair out for her.

The meal was leisurely. Karamine relaxed in the soft glow of candle light, good food and Lance's love. Their conversation was animated, heightened by their happiness in being together, after weeks of separation. Although Lance had made preparations to serve his own specially blended coffee, they forgot to turn it on; the currents of their love and mutual desire for each other exploded, when Lance bent over and lightly kissed Karamine's cheek. She was in his arms immediately, feverishly returning his kisses, moving her body closer to his. Lance picked her up then carried her to the bedroom; they undressed each other in a surge of mutual pleasure, speaking little, content to bask in the bliss and fire of their passion. Then, still clinging together, they fell onto the bed, their bodies merging as one flame, conscious of nothing but the hot, driving heat of their love.

It was late morning when Karamine awoke. The sunshine cast broad beams of light across her face, forcing her to turn her head and move closer to Lance. She pulled the covers lightly up over Lance's bare back and shoulders, then placed her arm gently around him. She sighed contentedly, her thoughts drifting back to the previous evening, a totally romantic night from beginning to end. I dearly love this man, she thought quietly, and when I'm here with him like this I wonder how I can ever bear to be separated from him. Why couldn't things have simply stayed the way they were—uncomplicated, simple. But, that's not the way life is, she reasoned, Life is change, challenges, surprise. Two careers. But why couldn't they run side by side, instead of in opposite directions? Why does it have to be this way? Well, I could apply to a hospital down here; but, would I have the same considerations about my trips to Armenia? I have a perfect set-up now, and it takes years to arrange a career to ones personal specifications. Lance won't be in Washington forever. But, can I bear these separations? It's tearing us apart. I have to make a decision one way or another. Lance stirred and turned over lazily, without opening his eyes. Karamine kissed him lightly on the top of his head then slid out of bed to take a shower.

After her shower, she put on her robe and went into the kitchen. She smiled as she saw the dishes were still on the table from the night before, the coffee beans unground in the coffee mill. Well—we'll just have that coffee for breakfast, she thought, picking up the dishes from the dining room table and placing them in the dishwasher. She opened the refrigerator and looked around the kitchen. She marveled at the order and neatness of everything—better than my kitchen she admitted with some amusement. Now let me see—what have we here. It's so nice to be able to make breakfast for my husband. She heard him stirring in the bed room.

"Lance? you up?" How about some ham and eggs this morning?"

"Sounds great. Just going to take a shower first," he called.

When he emerged, showered and shaved, Karamine had everything ready. Lance walked over to her and put his arms around her. "Have I told you how great it is to have you here, Mrs. Bagdasarian?" he said, kissing her on the side of the cheek.

"Not lately."

"Well, it is."

"What time are we due at Ted and Tatiania's"

"Oh, about four thirty. We have time to do some sightseeing if you like. We could take a ride around our fair capitol, or take in the Smithsonian . . . or . . . we could stay here and try the same exercise we had last night." He laughed mischievously.

"Are sure you're up to it? I wouldn't want to deprive your people of your superior strength and energy."

"I'm up to it," he said suggestively, slipping his arms around her and nuzzling her neck.

Karamine laughed gently. "Okay. I believe you. But, to answer your question, why don't we try to take in the Smithsonian this afternoon? There's so much to see there, and I've always wanted to go."

"Rejecting my overtures, I see." he teased. "Well, actually, on second thought, we'd only have a couple of hours there, and I think there's so much to see we'd really need a whole day. Why don't we plan it for some other time, and just stay home this afternoon, relax, listen to some music and talk. We rarely have an opportunity lately to do that. What do you think?"

Karamine smiled. "You're right, Lance. We'll do it some other time when we can really spend time and enjoy ourselves."

Karamine and Lance spent most of the day relaxing and talking about their favorite subjects—family, work and their prospects for the future. Lance was relieved to hear Karamine had no plans to visit Armenia in the immediate future, that there were several other doctors making the next trip.

"By the way, I heard reports from the C.I.A. and the state department that the Azerbaijani Moslems are pushing Armenians out of their homes and taking over their houses. Have you heard anything like that?" Lance queried.

"Well, they discussed it at our last Armenian Relief meeting, but, it was supposed to be just a rumor."

Lance frowned slightly. "I don't think it's a rumor, Karamine, the reports we've been getting are pretty reliable. Ted's checked it out too and he claims it's more than a rumor. God, I hope there's no trouble over there now at this time with the soviet union tottering. If it disintegrates completely, Armenia could be a free independent nation. No, we don't need trouble in Karabagh right now."

"Do you think the people there will have trouble with the Azeris?"

"Well, from the information we've gleaned, and its sketchy, we've found out the Armenians have formed a Karabagh Defence Force and intend to fight, if the Azeris continue to drive Armenians from their ancestral homes. I didn't realize it was ninety-eight percent Armenian there. It was actually part of Armenia until 1920, when Stalin wanted to break Armenian resistance to sovietize Armenia. So . . . he gave the whole enclave to Azerbaijan, and the poor people have been suffering there ever since."

Karamine shook her head sadly. "Will the trouble and pain never end. These people have suffered so much."

"Hey . . . look at the time." Lance blurted, looking at his watch and getting up quickly, "It's almost four and we're not even dressed."

"What will I wear?" Karamine mused half aloud.

"I told you, it's informal! Wear the slacks and sweater you had on yesterday. That looked pretty good to me."

"Okay, I have no choice I guess."

The trip to Ted and Tatiana's was fast and easy, and Karamine enjoyed all the sights along the way. Arriving at Ted's driveway on a tree-lined street, they parked, got out of the car and headed straight for the backyard. There they saw Ted was already at the grill. He waved and called to his wife as Karamine and Lance approached.

"You're everything Lance has said and more," Ted said appreciatively, when he was introduced to Karamine. "Welcome to our home, Karamine."

"Yes, welcome." said Tatiana, coming out to greet Karamine warmly. "I've been looking forward to meeting you, Karamine. I'm so interested in the work you're doing over there in Armenia. I'd love to be part of it in any way I can. You know, I'll do anything within my power to help."

Karamine responded with a broad smile. She liked Ted and Tatiana and immediately felt at ease with them. "Thank you, Tatiana, I'd be glad to talk about it to you anytime."

Two young children came bounding out from the sliding patio doors. "Easy there . . . just hold it down you two. We have guests," Tatiana ordered gently. "Karamine . . . my two children, Vartan and Alexis . . . Lance has met them before." She presented them proudly. After the greetings, they turned to their mother and discreetly whispered something in her ear. Tatiana smiled, settled a dispute over the computer, then sent them off.

"What will you have to drink, Karamine?" Ted inquired politely, after turning the meat on the grill.

"White wine, if you have it."

"Lance? bourbon and water or scotch?"

"Bourbon and water sounds great, Ted."

When he returned with their drinks, Tatiana motioned them toward a shaded patio, with colorful outdoor furniture.

"Just sit anywhere, Karamine . . . as Lance must have told you, we're very informal here." She laughed pleasantly.

"It's all very lovely. Somehow, I never pictured Washington this way, you know, back yards, patios, grills etc. I've always thought it was more black-tie affairs, cocktail parties, high powered entertaining."

"Oh it can be that, too," said Tatiana, laughingly. "But I think it can be almost anything you want to make it. Actually, Ted told me some of the new freshmen haven't even brought their families to Washington. They commute every weekend. That must be difficult though. How do you find it, Karamine? Do you mind living and working in Boston, while your husband is here in Washington? I don't know if I could do it . . . be separated from Ted."

"Well, its not easy. I do miss Lance, especially at night, when my work day is over. This is all new to us, but I keep myself busy in the evenings going to lectures and symposiums to upgrade myself in the medical community. The Armenian Relief keeps me pretty busy, also . . . I'm a board member there. We meet often to organize shipments and materials for the republic."

"I'm very interested in this aspect of your work, Karamine. As I said, is there anything I could do here in Washington to help your organization? What are their crucial needs? Food, clothing medical supplies?"

Karamine placed her wine glass on the table, and reached for a piece of cheese; she took a deep breath before answering.

"Much as I hate to say this, Tatiana, food, clothing and even blankets are cheaper when you buy them in Europe or the Middle East. We've found that by the time we gather all the food and clothes here in the States, the cost of the operation skyrockets. Mercenary as it sounds, it's really best to raise money and donate it to our organization, or some other, checking out their credentials of course, so you'll know the money is used properly. As for medical supplies, I, along with other doctors, do that myself in the Boston area. We get the best and latest equipment, and sometimes we even have to go to Armenia and train people there on how to use this new technology. But, that's what makes it all so worthwhile, Just the look on their faces when this medical equipment is unloaded. It means so much to them. They say they've never had such good equipment to work with because the soviet union had sacrificed everything for the build-up of their military. So, getting back to your question . . . raise the money and let the proper people handle it. This way we may get the most for our dollar."

"You know, that makes perfect sense to me," Tatiana agreed. "How would we be able to store the food and clothing anyway. It would be very difficult. It's settled then. We in Washington will begin a campaign to raise money, and we'll be in touch with your organization, Karamine."

"That would be much appreciated, Tatiana."

"By the way, changing the subject, have you heard the latest, Lance?" said Tatiana, directing her attention to him." Ted wants out of congress."

Lance was shocked. "What?" he shouted, almost dropping his glass. "What do you mean, he wants out, Tatiana. You mean as in go home?"

"Exactly! He wants out." she repeated.

"Wait," Ted exclaimed, pulling the grill cover down and quickly walking over to join the group, "please, Tatiana, let me tell him in my own way. Lance this is not something I've decided overnight. I've gone over the pros and cons of it for a long time."

"You'd leave before your term is up" Who the hell will take your place, you just can't do it, Ted," Lance protested strongly.

Ted raised his hand. "Listen, hear me out Lance. I want you to understand. Six years ago I came here with the high hopes and ideals of turning this country back to the standards of excellence drawn up by our founding fathers. Their concept of government was far ahead of its time, because they saw man governed by the smallest bureaucracy. They had planned for every aspect of our freedom from government; that's why they drew up the Bill of Rights, and the Constitution . . . to protect us. But through man's lust for power, we've prostituted every word they wrote. The Supreme Court is packed, and the rights of the people have been usurped through laws, mandates and regulations. And damn it, Congress is the worst offender of all. I just can't take any more of what's going on there in the Congress of the United States. It stinks to the core. As Mark Twain once put it so aptly, 'there's no distinctly American criminal class except Congress.' " Ted's dark eyes clouded.

"That's a hell of thing to say, Ted. What are you going to do, just quit and get out?" Lance's words were charged with emotion.

"I haven't quite decided. It's been burning in me for years as Tatiana can tell you. Lance, you're new and an idealist, like me, when I first came. But wait . . . wait till they grind you down, little by little, and you start compromising your belief principles. You either end up submitting and joining them or leaving," Ted said with a weary smile.

"Quit? No Ted, your Armenian roots won't allow you to do that," Lance argued stubbornly.

Ted smiled grimly. "Look Lance, in the House of Representatives, we should be, by design, a decision making body who rise beyond partisan, regional or factionalism to do what is best for the country. The Founding Fathers would turn in their graves if they could see what we've done to that noble concept. It's all a huge stage where we perform to the power brokers of the majority party, and this has been going on for the past thirty years. They set the rules of the House, they staff these committees, who by the way usually meet behind closed doors. They even make the rules of debate, so how the hell can you beat them? Issues are decided ahead of time, behind closed doors, and you're lucky to find twenty members out of four hundred and thirty five, debating. Hell . . . we don't even publicly debate issues as they did years ago."

Lance put his drink down and walked over to Ted, placing his hand gently under Ted's elbow. "Look Ted, you just can't do that to your constituents. They're the people who believed, voted and elected you. They sent you here to fight for them. You just can't let them down. Fight the bastards. I know they've killed the philibustering in the House, but be an obstructionist if you have to, to stop their rip-offs of the American people. Damn it, Ted, fight, and if you go down drag the bastards down with you. Don't compromise.

Ted sighed. "The battle's been lost, Lance, it's over and has been over for some time. Inch by inch they've encroached on our right to choose by stretching the Bill of Rights and the Constitution beyond what it was intended for. We even had a Supreme Court Justice say the Bill of Rights and the Constitution are what they decide it to be. Even our God given rights are not absolute any more. How can you deal with arrogance like that? No . . . the hell with it! Senator Jenner had it right when he resigned from the Senate. You should read his farewell speech in the senate. You'd understand my feelings about this, and I didn't come to it lightly."

"Senator Jenner? I've never heard of him Oh wait . . . wasn't he on that committee back in the 50's, the senate committee on subversive activities? Yes, I remember now . . . he was with Senator Joseph McCarthy and those inquisitors who destroyed peoples careers. McCarthyism, that's what that committee created I believe," Lance spoke assertively.

Ted put his drink down on the table and glared steadfastly at Lance. Tatiana got up quickly and put her hand on Lance's arm.

"You've hit a raw nerve, Lance. Can't we change the subject, Ted, please?" she said appealing to her husband.

"No, wait a minute, Tatiana," Lance said quietly, Have I said something to offend you, Ted?"

"What do you know about McCarthyism?" Ted asked Lance, calmly. "Do you know anything at all about him, what the man stood for?"

"Well, actually not much I'll admit, only that he was a bit of a radical . . . " Lance hesitated, sensing Ted did not share his sentiments.

"Let me give you a few facts about him, Lance. First of all, Senator McCarthy was from my home state of Wisconsin, and I'll admit there was a time when I held those same feelings about him as you. However, after doing a bit of research in the archives and senate hearing records I have a new perspective on the man, and realize now he was maligned by the extreme left and of course the press."

"Look, Ted," Lance said awkwardly, "I didn't know he was from Wisconsin, and the only information I have on him is sketchy . . . from school, old newspapers and the school library. I can see he means a lot to you and I'm sorry if I offended you."

"It's not you, Lance, and believe me I understand. It's just that label, McCarthyism, that sets me off. People toss it around without knowing one damn thing about the situation or the time these events took place."

"I guess we all need to be enlightened, Ted," Karamine commented. "I have to admit I've always understood McCarthyism to be a negative label also, describing anyone intolerant of someone else's views or opinion, an extremist actually."

"Yeah, that's the perception. With all the garbage and selective reporting out there, its hard to get the truth out. Senator McCarthy had his defenders as well as his detractors, but its the latter who've prevailed in the marketplace of public opinion. The relentless accusations and charges have silenced a lot of his defenders, and of course, a lot of them are gone now. Only the garbage remains."

Lance looked at Ted thoughtfully. "I guess I've never really taken the time to investigate or to even think much about it, Ted. But, I can see how you'd be involved, since he was from your home state."

"Well, you have to understand the time frame . . . the 1950's. We were at the height of the cold war with the Soviet Union; the Berlin Airlift, the wall separating Germany. Moscow had slaughtered the democrats of Eastern Europe, blockaded Berlin, raped Czechoslovakia, and exploded the atom bomb which they got through traitors in the U.S.A. My God! We were on the actual brink of war! The senate had a committee to investigate unamerican activities, especially communists in the government. Joseph McCarthy was one of the first members of that committee, the 'point man' to bring that information to the American public. He alerted us to subversives in the government . . . Owen Lattimore, Harry Dexter White and others. His job was to check out allegations made against people in government and other areas, such as Hollywood, to see if they were valid. Pertinent questions were asked, for example . . . 'within the last twenty-four hours, have you been in the pursuit of the violent overthrow of the United States government? Their usual response was to plead the fifth amendment . . . ' I will not answer on the grounds it might incriminate me.' At that time, being a communist was not illegal, but lying under oath to a senate committee was. That's how they got Alger Hiss, and the liberals have been furious ever since. They go after anyone, who may have been part of such investigation. Nixon for instance. They're an unforgiving lot and if you cross them, they'll wait years to get even, believe me. Even though the cold war was on with the Soviet Union, they felt no one had the RIGHT to ask such questions. As for McCarthy, they had a vendetta to get him . . . which they did finally, with the help of the liberal media."

"They censured him, I remember that part," said Lance in a quiet voice.

"Oh, yes, indeed they did. He was accused of an abuse of power and of ruining people's lives. But, contrary to what was being stated or implied in public forums, Senator McCarthy was never censured by his colleagues in the U.S. Senate, for the 'tactics he used in fighting communism'. All the charges were eliminated. He was condemned because of his caustic criticism of members of the Select Committee to Study Censure Charges, and the Senate session itself, Yes, that's what it was all about. His bitter attacks against his senatorial detractors, not for his tactics in fighting communism. True, he hit his detractors where it hurt them most, and that's why they wanted him destroyed. If you're really interested in the true account of what happened, Lance, go to the archives and read the senate reports for yourself, So briefly, that's why I no longer want any part of the House of Representatives. It's hopeless, I just want to go home, enjoy my wife and family, and to HELL with them all," he said bitterly.

Lance did not respond, but continued to gaze thoughtfully at Ted. Karamine and Tatiana also remained silent. After a few moments, Lance got up from his chair, walked toward Ted and touched his arm affectionately.

"Ted, I believe its more important than ever to stay here now," he said in a low, calm voice, Fight them. Senator McCarthy didn't give up, he fought them until the day he died from what I now understand. Stand and fight, and let that be his legacy for those of us who believe in honor, truth, God and country. If you think of him so highly, how can you ever consider giving up. No Ted, stay and fight . . . be an obstructionist to any more social legislation, and help get this country back to the people, the achievers and free enterprise system that made our country great. We can work together . . . you in the house, me in the senate; we'll give the bastards a good old-fashioned fight like our parents and grandparents did with the butchering Turks."

Ted's expression remained grave, but, soon his black eyes sparkled with their old vivacity. Looking squarely into Lance's face, he burst into laughter. "Now I know why I liked you right off, Lance, and why I consider you one of my closest friends. You're right. I've only been thinking of myself and not what might happen if the leftists take over completely. There are others in Congress who think as I do, and, we should unite, whether republican or democrat, for the good of the country." He patted Lance lightly on the shoulder. "Thanks for reassuring me of my purpose, and reminding me that I would be abandoning my children and their future to God knows what kind of system or country."

"I'm glad you'll reconsider your decision, Ted," said Lance. "I've had those same feelings during the election campaign, and more than once I'd thought of chucking the whole thing. Both of our families were harassed by the media, and the lies, the constant lies, were more than I could endure. It was Karamine who gave me a pep talk, and brought me to my senses. Why should we allow our opponents to take over? Not without a fight, for sure."

"How about changing the subject," said Tatiana, rising from her chair. "We're hungry. Will you see if the meat and vegetables are done, Ted?"

"Everything's under control . . . it's all ready," Ted called, walking to the grill and lifting the cover. The delicious aroma of shish-ke-bob floating in the open air reminded Lance of the old days at his grandfather's farm in New Hampshire. He smiled happily, remembering.

Later that evening, when they were leaving, Ted handed Lance a book with a hard, black cover. Lance looked at the title. JOSEPH RAY-

MOND MCCARTHY, LATE SENATOR FROM WISCONSIN. Memorial Addresses Delivered in Congress.

"Promise me you'll read it," said Ted earnestly.

"I'll read it, Ted, I promise." said Lance, getting into their car. They waved good bye, then headed for the freeway and home.

15

Everett Mason's expression was a mix of interest and amused curiosity when he walked into Lance's office to announce a visitor. Lance was going over some senate bills that had piled up, even though Everett had reviewed them legally, and made his recommendation. Still, Lance wanted to familiarize himself with the contents and understand the implications of the bill for future reference; he was determined nothing would get by him.

"There's a real good-looker out there who wants to speak to you, Senator, she's gorgeous," Everett whispered confidentially. "If you're not interested, get her number for me."

"Just give me her name, Everett, not the details of her physical assets," Lance replied abruptly, not raising his eyes from a folder he was studying.

"Rhoda Burke."

"Rhoda? What does she want I wonder. Send her in, but, leave the door open and make sure you're within earshot, will you?"

"Umm," said Everett, scrutinizing Lance's face. "Of course, Senator, if that's your wish."

"Good," said Lance with a serious expression.

Rhoda was smiling pleasantly when Everett ushered her in. Lance was perplexed, but stood up and offered her a chair. He hadn't seen her since their one encounter, and he couldn't imagine what was on her mind. He noted her well shaped legs when she crossed them, allowing her short skirt to ride up her thighs, the cool appraisal in her glance as she fixed her green eyes intently on him. He noted also, that Everett had left the door open, and Lance was discreetly visible within his range of sight.

"Well, Rhoda," Lance began, smiling pleasantly, "to what do I owe this pleasure?"

Rhoda assumed a pouting expression, before replying in a soft intimate tone. "You know, Senator, a woman could get a complex, a scar to last a lifetime, from the way you ran off and deserted me last week. I can't stop wondering what made you stop at such a point? Why? I need to know. Am I so unappealing?"

Lance smiled and shook his head. "Rhoda, I thought I explained it. It certainly had nothing to do with you, or your appeal, believe me."

"Then why, for God's sake?" she interrupted with impatience.

"It has everything to do with commitment, fidelity, being true to one's vows. I have no excuse for what happened, other than I had too much to drink, and perhaps got a little carried away by your charms?" He smiled awkwardly. "I should never have gone to your apartment."

"Oh God, protect us from doting husbands, please!" Rhoda commented with sudden cynicism. "Let's forget it shall we? That's not why I came over here anyway. Can you tell me Senator Bagdasarian, just what you and some of your cohorts think you are doing with all these social legislations, especially as they effect the education bill. That concerns my department you know, and its already been approved in the House, but, you guys in the senate have stymied it. What's going on?"

Lance clasped his hands together and fixed his blue eyes on Rhoda in a steady gaze. "Don't you think the states and the local communities with their own school boards know how to run their schools better and more competently than we do in Washington? We can't mandate regulations and order school districts to conform to each little whim the Department of Education puts out. No, schools should be left to the local school boards and state administrators, without any interference from Washington."

Rhoda's face flushed with displeasure. "What exactly do you think the Department of Education is for, Senator Bagdasarian?" We have some of the best qualified people to administer to each and every need a school might have. We have materials, money and regulations to force some of them to meet standards and social responsibilities that we deem needed. How can you brush off substantial benefits like that so easily, may I ask?"

Lance studied Rhoda reflectively, and wondered silently what her real motive was in seeing him. Was she truly concerned that he and his fellow senators were tying up legislation, or was she merely frustrated because he had not been wholly responsive to her charms.

"You know damn well, Rhoda, that you in that Department have a certain agenda. If you tried to get those mandates through congress you wouldn't get anywhere, so, by creating a Department of Education in the executive, you can force schools throughout the country to adhere to your agenda for them. Everyone knows Carter created that Department as a pay-off to the National Education Association, for their support of his election. Furthermore, since then, your people over there have been forcing schools throughout the country to go along with every hairbrain scheme they come up with. No, it's time to fight, to give the schools back to the people, states and local level. They know best what's needed, and also, it saves money for some real education, instead of supporting some bureaucrat in Washington whose job it is to oversee department mandates.

Rhoda was outraged. She pressed her lips together in an effort to control her emotions. "The die is cast, Senator," she said stiffly. "That department exists, and will continue to exist. There's no way you or your people could get a majority in the congress to do away with it. Are you aware, Senator, of what the media will do to you if you continue this obstructionist path?

I can just see the headlines now . . . obstructionist, anti-education, etc. Things could become extremely difficult for you in Washington. Believe me, the media will either drive you out or break you. You must know that they are our allies."

Lance's blue eyes flashed, and his expression became resolute. He spoke slowly and deliberately. "Surely you're not trying to threaten me, Miss Burke!"

Rhoda gasped. "Why on earth should I threaten you?"

"May I enlighten you on my view of the media," Lance began, smiling slightly, a thin edge of irony in his voice. They don't scare me. I've had my trial by fire with them during my campaign, and it taught me a lot. I know for certain, if you tell people the truth they'll always make the proper decision. I trust them more than I trust the media or anyone else."

Rhoda Burke tossed her head, and she lifted an eyebrow. "Really? Well tell me, Senator, just how do you intend to get your message out without the media and their outlets?" They'll silence you like they've done to others who've crossed them. You must know that."

"I don't give a damn about them, Rhoda. And let me tell you something else. Every spending bill that comes through with pork in it, unnecessary expansion of entitlements, educational spending to enhance the power of Washington, we'll attach amendments to it. We'll water it down to such a point, it won't pass. No one will want to vote for it and it will die. If that doesn't work, we'll filibuster it to death. The voters are sick and tired of the spending antics of congress, and we have supporters from both sides of the aisles committed to stopping this frenzied spending one way or another."

Rhoda gave an exasperated sigh. She studied him thoughtfully, for a few moments, then flashed her most dazzling smile, the smile that never failed. He's tough, she thought, a real challenge in every way,— and damn—so attractive! Maybe that's the secret of his charm—his power and unflinching fortitude for the values and ideals he believes. She rose from her chair slowly, smoothing her skirt over her hips, in a sensuous gesture.

"Lance, I like you," she said, speaking softly. "I just don't want to see you get hurt. You think you can turn the tide of one party's rules for the past thirty years? No way, Senator. You're a dreamer. They control and make the rules for the house and senate. Do you actually believe they'll relinquish that power to a few freshman and idealists like you? They'll chew you and your friends up and spit you out." She paused for a moment and shook her head. "What a waste! What a waste."

She moved toward the open door, where Everett Mason pretended to busy himself at a nearby file, but she was unaware of his obvious, deliberate appraisal of her anatomy. Lance however, noticed she stopped to make a few remarks to Everett on her way out. After she left, Everett walked into Lance's office, and whistled softly. As he was not usually effusive, Lance stared at him with curious interest.

"Wow! She's gorgeous, Senator! I'd really like to take her out. Do you have her phone number?"

Lance smiled. "Sorry, Everett, I don't. Didn't you get it when she stopped to talk to you out there just now? What did she say anyway."

"Oh I don't know, just something about getting an earful. I'm going to call her where she works."

"Everett, can I give you a little advice? That's no woman to fool with, take my word for it. She's trouble. Stay clear of her if you value your career or being."

"So, what's a little danger, now and then. Keeps life exciting," Everett protested.

"I thought you had a girl up in Boston."

"I have, but we don't really have a commitment of any sort. We just go out now and then for fun. Nothing serious.

"Well, what you do in your personal life is really none of my business, Everett. You'll do what you want anyway. But don't say I didn't warn you."

Their conversation was interrupted by a sharp knock on the open door to Lance's office. It was Senator David Howard, the senior senator from Massachusetts.

"May I have a few moments of your time, Senator Bagdasarian?" he inquired coldly, stepping into Lance's office.

"Certainly, sit down."

"Would you mind closing the door, I'd like to talk to you in private," he said, motioning toward the door.

"I was just finishing up some details. I'll get it on the way out," said Everett, backing up toward the outer office. "Thanks, for your input on that matter, Senator."

He had hardly finished speaking when Senator Howard confronted Lance angrily. "Just exactly what do you think you are doing, by holding up the appropriation for the new office complex in Boston. You and your allies have tied so many amendments to it, it will never pass the senate. Are you aware that bill will bring fifteen to twenty million dollars to our state, and will stimulate the economy of the whole area. It will provide badly needed jobs for the construction segment of the state. Doesn't that mean anything to you at all, Senator?"

Lance scrutinized him quietly a few moments before replying.

"All of my research and reports indicate that building complex is not needed," he answered calmly. Furthermore, there are thousands of feet of office space vacant in Boston at the present time, just begging to be rented. They're offering special deals up there for Gods's sake . . . three to six months free rent, just to get the space rented. No, we don't need another huge office complex, in one of your political crony's name. That's exactly the kind of spending we intend to stop. Why should other states have to pay for some boondoggle in Massachusetts anyway?"

Senator Howard's face flushed with hostility. "Because we voted for some boondoggle dam or other projects they don't need in other states. That's how the game is played down here, Senator, and that's the way it's been for the past thirty years. You better get used to it, because it's not going to change; there's not a damn thing you can do about it!"

Lance tried to control the agitation and contempt he felt for Senator Howard. The man was completely out of touch, he thought. He doesn't give a damn about the tax-payer, or the hard-working people who are burdened with extra taxes to pay for these unnecessary projects. What hypocrisy! He claims to think of the people in his state, when in reality he panders to the construction lobbyists and the millions of dollars they provide to his campaign and party coffers. His biggest concern is to perpetuate himself, his power and premise. Lance shook his head in disgust, and glared at the senator.

"I agree, the power game has been playing here for the past thirty or forty years, but understand this, Senator, we have people in both parties who see how this country is being destroyed, and we intend to fight you right down to the smallest piece of legislation, and you can bet on that," said Lance, forcefully.

"You're pursuing a dangerous course, Senator Bagdasarian. I'll address these when I return to the proper people. We'll see if we can have you returned, and your seat taken away from you. Believe me, I'll personally notify the newspapers and media of your obstructionist tactics. You'll not get away with hampering the will of the people.

"You mean the will of the lobbyist and contributors who want a fast buck at the expense of the taxpayers," Lance replied angrily.

"I see there's no use trying to reason with you. But understand this. There's more of us in Washington, and we'll see just how far you'll get with your persistence. As for your so-called party loyalty, I wouldn't depend too much on that if I were you. When the chips are down, they all move toward the buck, believe me. I've seen it happen. Often."

Lance shrugged, and smiled wearily. "Yes, I've known about that for quite some time, but, right now, I really don't care. I'm here to do a job for the voters, and I'll do everything in my power to save their money."

Senator Howard was infuriated. "I came here with the thought that you and I could come to some compromise and avoid a fight, but I see I was wrong. You're just too stubborn and insolent to give an inch. Good day to you, sir!" He walked toward the door, yanked it open and stormed out.

"What was that all about? Everett asked, after Senator Howard had gone. It sounded pretty heated from where I sat."

Lance sighed deeply and sat down behind his desk. I'm tired he thought, and a little weary. That's the second time I've been threatened today. And for what? For making the choice of upholding the trust of the people? God! What's happened to integrity and honor? Totally sacrificed on the altar of man's ambition and greed, that's what. No, I can't let myself believe that. I dare not. "He doesn't like what we're doing to his bill and other bills coming up from the Appropriations and Finance Committee. Just because it's been approved in the House, he thinks we should rubber stamp it," Lance replied.

"Hmmn! no wonder he stalked out of here. It's obvious he's not used to being opposed that way." By the way, Ted Sohigian called while you were tied up with Senator Howard. He'd like you to call him when you can."

"Good. I was going to call him anyway."

Lance picked up the telephone and swung his desk chair around to face the large picture window of his office with its view of the capitol. He needed to get together with Ted at the martial arts center to work off his frustration, and also, to practice the strategic maneuver Ted was teaching him.

"Ted . . . good to hear from you. I was planning to call you anyway to see if we could get together at the center tonight. Any chance?

"Sure, it's okay with me. I need the practice anyway. But, that's not what I called about, Lance. I've just heard a rumor that the Soviet Union is shaking and about to collapse. With all this Detente and Perestroika Gorbachev pushed for, the whole thing is getting out of hand, they're losing control. The Republics are clamoring for independence like Lithuania, and even Armenia is making overtures for independence. It's difficult to believe that Armenia will be a free and independent country after all these years. Have you heard anything?"

"Yes, I've heard a few rumors, too, Ted, when the Senate Committee on Foreign Affairs met with Intelligence and the C.I.A.. At that time, there was a lot of speculation but I didn't put too much stock in it. They've been telling us for the last twenty years that Castro is through in Cuba . . . and he's still there. I'd like to know how valid this information is. That's why I haven't mentioned it to you."

"Well, there's even some talk about the possible unification of Germany. There must be something to it. What a great thing it would be to see a free and independent Republic of Armenia."

"Yes, it sounds great, Ted, but independence means exactly that. Will Armenia be able to function and protect herself surrounded by Moslem countries like Iran, Turkey and Azerbaijan? They despise Armenia, and would want to destroy her. Armenia is land-locked, you know. The only supply route is through an unstable Georgia. Then, don't forget . . . there's that trouble in Nagorno Karabakh, where the Armenians are being pushed out of their ancestral homes, and their lands confiscated by Azerbaijani soldiers. Thanks to the Russian army all that was temporarily stopped. What's going to happen now if the empire is gone and the Russian army is returned to Russia? I fear our people would have to face some dire consequences."

"Yes, I thought about that myself, Lance. The only idea I can some up with is that we'd have to use all our diplomatic skills at that time to prevent chaos and suffering. I know, it's easy for us to talk here, but those Armenians will have to survive under that threat. There's no easy solution, but FREEDOM should be worth the risks after all these years. That's always been the goal of the people there, and now it's coming to a head. We'll just have to guide them through the perilous times ahead."

"Well, if it does materialize, we in the diaspora must make tremendous sacrifices to help them; even going so far as volunteering to go there . . . like Karamine has been doing with her medical team and supplies for years. If Armenia is independent and threatened, we must be ready to do whatever is necessary, even to fight, if necessary," Lance commented ardently.

"I agree. We should also do our best to make certain all the congressmen here are informed of the situation. In fact, some of the congressmen who've been alerted to what's going on there have already asked me about my thoughts and feelings. They want to stay abreast of what's happening there, and that's a good sign.

At least they show concern for the situation."

"Well, let's hope for the best, Ted, and let God in His wisdom release all the peoples held in bondage under any kind of tyranny, without bloodshed and killing. But anyway, coming back to the present, what time should I meet you this evening?"

"What about six-thirty?"

"I'll be there."

"How about dropping over to the house afterward. We can kick around the prospects of Armenia's future a little more, and we can have a little something to eat."

"Lance laughed. As long as Tatiana doesn't get tired of feeding me."

"Are you kidding. You're part of the family!" Okay then, I'll see you at six-thirty."

Lance hung up and swung around in his chair. What will all this independent Armenia mean I wonder. If it's true, Karamine might want to go there more often, and stay longer. She'll have good reason to do so then. The thought depressed him. I miss her now, even when we see each other on weekends. Its always so rough when she's out of the country on those needed missions. But now, there's added danger, especially if independence comes. Well, we'll just have to wait and see. Take it one step at a time. In the meantime, I'll give her a call. He glanced briefly at his watch, then dialed his wife's office. Her receptionist gave him the good news that Karamine was at her desk, and not tied up with a patient.

"Karamine . . . glad I caught you. Just wanted you to know I'll be leaving Washington on Friday afternoon. Not quite sure of the time, but, I'll call later to give you the details."

"Good, you'll be here on Friday instead of Saturday morning. Great, Lance. Karamine's voice was enthusiastic and seemed to fill a void that lifted his spirits. Yeah, I really need to get home. This place is getting to me."

"Why, what happened?" she asked softly.

"Oh, just a combination of things. First, the Department of Education is giving me a hard time for stopping one of their pet projects, then, our senior senator from Massachusetts, Howard, read me the riot act if I don't compromise on his new construction project. They're nothing but pork. Both of them! I'll be damned if I'll give an inch," he said vehemently.

"Why should you if you believe that's all it is. Why compromise, Lance. That's not you, and that's not what the voters sent you to Washington for."

"Well, that's not what I called you for, Karamine. Have you heard anything from any of your sources regarding the breakup of the Soviet Union?"

"Not really, just the usual information from the newspapers. Gorbachev, perestroika, detente, a little freedom for the republics, that's it. Why, what have you heard?"

"Well, Ted called and told me there are rumors that the Soviet Union is on the verge of collapse. He also said there's a definite push by the German government for unification with East Germany. There have been rumblings, too, that all the republics, including Armenia will be demanding their freedom. Wouldn't that be something, Karamine? A free Republic of Armenia!"

"Do you really think there's a chance of that, after so many years of fighting and struggling? Is it really possible, or just rumors?"

"No, I don't feel it's rumors this time, Karamine," said Lance, soberly. "Between our military build up under Reagan and his label of the EVIL EMPIRE, they've been seriously damaged economically. They've blown their wealth and efforts on the build up of arms to such a point, they've actually bankrupted themselves. Now, they're looking to the west for monetary wealth. They've been asking Europe and the U.S.A. for heavy loans, even though they've still not paid back what they owe us from World War 2."

"So . . . you do believe there may be a chance for Armenia's freedom. How do you think they'll survive when Russia pulls her troops out of the country?"

"That remains to be seen," Lance answered cautiously. "Don't forget the country is surrounded by moslem countries, Iran, Turkey, Azerbaijan, who are just waiting for the opportunity to destroy her. First of all, Armenia would have to have a formidable army to protect her borders. As I was telling Ted, she'd also have to form a new government fast, and write a constitution, with all the social and economic machinery to operate the government. The Armenians of the world will all have to donate their time and energies for this monumental task."

"Their freedom after all these years would be worth any of the sacrifices necessary, Lance," said Karamine firmly. Yes, we in the diaspora would certainly have to do everything we could for them, including you and I."

Karamine's words sent a slight tremor through him. "I guess if that happens you'll be heading there again . . . perhaps more often. I can't say that makes me happy, Karamine, especially if there's trouble over there."

"Look, Lance, we'll just play it by ear, and see what happens."

"Well, rumors say the Armenians are now being driven out of their homes by the thousands in Nagorna-Karabakh. Some of them are moving to Stepanakert. The situation there may get worse."

"I wonder if that's the reason Vasken said he'll stop in Boston, before going to Europe, Russia and Armenia?"

"Vasken? You've heard from Vasken?" Lance asked sharply.

"Just a postcard from San Francisco. He said his work there was through, and that he was on his way to Russia and Armenia and may stop over in Boston on the way. You know Vasken. No details, just a short note to let us know he's alive."

"He's alive alright, huh! It would take a major earthquake to kill him," Lance commented cynically.

"Lance, please! That kind of remark hurts me. Vasken is still my brother. Can't you find it in your heart to forgive him and forget what happened?"

"God knows I try, Karamine, but it's difficult. I know he's your brother, but, he has done things to me that go far beyond reconciliation. He sighed deeply. The election . . . all those lies and distortions, the hurt to our families. As I said, it's difficult."

"But you won, Lance, in spite of all his obstructions, you won, and that's what should be foremost in your mind. Anyway, for my sake, can't you put it behind you and look to the future."

"OK, OK," he said responding to her plea. "You always win. I guess you're right, Karamine, but, damn it, he sure makes it tough trying to forget and forgive."

"Is that why you're working so hard at the martial arts center with Ted? You want to tear him apart? To get even with him? Just try, putting it behind you, Karamine said, and leave it to the Lord."

"Alright, Karamine," Lance said wearily, "I'll release it to the Lord. What else can I do?"

"Good," Karamine answered softly, "then you'll call me back and let me know what flight you'll be on?"

"Yes, the staff is working on it now."

"Until Friday then, Lance. I love you."

"Love you, too kid," he said, placing the telephone on the receiver.

Vasken, he thought to himself, I bet he knows more of what's going on in Armenia and Russia than our own State Department and C.I.A. put together. I wonder what he's up to. He picked up his martial arts handbag and headed for the door.

"So long everyone, see you tomorrow. Everett, get in touch with your girlfriend this weekend. Lance walked out of the office and concentrated on the evening ahead. He smiled to himself. This is the evening to get the best of Ted, during their martial arts workout. He could feel it in his body. Tonight is the night.

16

Lance eased his way through the crush of people at Logan Airport to the exit terminal. The flight from Washington was smooth and fast, landing within minutes of its schedule, and, for the first time since leaving his office, Lance felt his spirits lift. He searched the waiting crowds for Karamine, then relaxed happily when he saw her familiar smile and wave.

"Did you rent a car?" he quizzed after they had met and greeted each other.

"No, I just got a cab to bring me down here. It's easier than looking for a parking place. He's waiting outside."

Inside the cab, Lance leaned back against the warm upholstery and stretched out both his arms, allowing one to rest lightly over Karamine's shoulders. "It's good to be home, and back with my girl. I miss you, honey." He pulled her close to him.

"I always miss you, Lance. It's empty without you."

"So, what are we gonna do about it?" Lance whispered.

Karamine sighed deeply. "What can we do about it? It's the way things are."

"There's lots of hospitals and children in Washington . . . "

Please, Lance, don't. I just don't want to talk about it now. Please?"

Lance withdrew his arm and settled back. "Okay. Just wanted you to think about it, that's all. We won't discuss it any further, Karamine." There was an edge of resignation in his voice. "Have you any plans for the weekend?"

"Well, I sort of made a commitment for you, Lance."

"A commitment? What kind of commitment, Karamine?"

"To give a little speech."

"A little speech? Ah c'mon, Karamine." Lances voice was slightly edgy. "Where and what is the occasion?"

"Have you forgotten? Sunday is Martyr's Day. The day our church remembers the million and a half Armenians slaughtered by the Turks."

"Oh, of course. So it's this Sunday. Where? The church in Watertown?

"Yes, Watertown."

"And you have me down for a speech? What will I talk about?"

"Well, why don't you just make some off-hand comments about what we were talking about on the phone this week. Sort of informal. I'm sure they would find that interesting."

"Well, that's not confirmed as yet, it's only what the department feels is happening. I suppose I could say it was unsubstantiated rumor, then get some of their reactions."

"Yes, but make it short. Short and effective. No one likes long speeches . . . oh, here's our stop."

When they got out of the cab, Lance took out his wallet to pay the driver, but the cab driver put up his hand. "That's Okay! The doctor pays me by the month. I give her a bill then." He smiled and drove off.

"What's all that about?" Lance asked in astonishment.

Karamine laughed. "Wherever I go now, I go by cab. It's safer than driving around by myself. I just call Pete and his wife radios him to pick me up. It's his own business and I like to help out. Anyway, I know him and feel safe in his cab."

"Great idea. I like it."

They took the elevator to their floor, and Lance took out the key to his apartment. Inside, he felt the rush of warmth and well-being he always experienced there. Nothing had changed. He noted the table set for two, the ice bucket, candles, flowers.

"Expecting somebody?" he teased.

"Well, I had to live up to your Washington standards, Senator," Karamine answered with a smile.

"You mean we're going to have an intimate, quiet, night at home?" Lance put his arms around Karamine and nuzzled her hair.

"Something like that. But call your parents first. They asked if you'd call them when you got in."

"Right. I'll call them now."

Lance dialed his parents number and faced the picture window overlooking the Charles River. The view was always restful to him, no matter what time of day; now in late April, he absorbed the soft glimmer of light from the setting sun, reflecting colored tints on the water; the early blooming trees; the unending line of cars speeding along the Drive. The air was cool and slightly damp in Boston, more so than

Washington, but Lance loved New England, and felt his perspective sharpened with a clearer focus whenever he returned.

Lance's mother, Kate answered the phone; almost immediately his father was on the extension.

"Great to hear from you, son," said Antranig, Lance's father in an enthusiastic voice. "I read you're giving them hell down there in Washington. Good. Let them know it's not business as usual." He laughed.

"Your father saw your old adversary, Senator Crawford at the Yacht Club last week," his mother, Kate, remarked.

"Oh, really? And what did he have to say," Lance responded cynically.

"Smooth as silk, charming to your mother, too. Said he had nothing to do with all that fiasco during the election campaign. Blamed it on over zealous underlings who got carried away with their positions. He even suggested we all go sailing sometime and let bygones be bygones."

"Look, Dad, you do whatever you want, but as for myself, I'm wary of him, especially after what he and his cohorts put us through. Right now, I'm getting flack from his other half, Senator Howard."

"You're right, Lance. You're better to keep a distance from him," his mother commented. "But, that's not why we wanted you to call. Will we be seeing you this trip?"

"Well, Karamine's committed me to speak at the church on Sunday. It's martyr's day. Any chance you could both come?

"Sounds pretty good to me. What do you think Andy?

"Fine with me. Will we meet you there?

"Yeah . . . perfect . . . About two then . . . see you there."

Karamine entered the living room as Lance hung up. She placed a bottle of champagne in the ice bucket then spun it around.

"Your parents coming? Great. I should call to find out if Mom and Dad are planning to attend. They usually do." she said.

"Call them now and get it settled," Lance suggested.

"Right. It'll be fun being together. Maybe we can all go to Anthony's later for dinner, if we don't eat at the church." She walked to the telephone and dialed.

Later, when Lance had showered and changed into a comfortable sport shirt and slacks, he popped the cork from the champagne bottle and filled two glasses.

"It's all settled," said Karamine elatedly. "Everyone's coming, and we'll take off after the ceremonies tomorrow. To your speech!" She raised her glass and touched his lightly.

"Yeah, my speech! What am I going to talk about, as an American senator? You put me in a tough spot, Karamine."

"I've never known you to be stuck for words, Lance. I'm sure you'll give them a few words of encouragement, tell them of the possibilities that are taking place, and, if we all stick together, how we can utilize these changes to build a stronger and more vibrant nation."

"Hey, that's pretty good. Maybe you should make the speech instead of me." He laughed.

"How are Ted and Tatiana, by the way?"

"Just saw them last night. Thank God for Ted and our encounters at the martial arts center. I can work off my frustrations there."

"Is Ted still getting the best of you in the karate?"

"Listen, believe it or not, Karamine, last night when I met him at the center, it was the first time I've been able to perfect that maneuver I'd been working on. I leaped into the air in a pirouette, and with perfect timing, slammed both my feet into Ted's chest, sending him across the mat and hard against the wall. Thank God, I only knocked the wind out of him. It was a bit too energetic. I'll have to learn a little more control and discipline from now on."

"Why do you continue to do it, Lance? You have your black belt don't you?"

"It's relaxing for me, especially after sitting at a desk or stuck all day in the senate, arguing and fighting. The arts rejuvenate and energize me. Anyway don't worry. The cardinal rule of martial arts is that it's for defense only, not for aggression."

"Well, it sounds dangerous. I don't want you two hurting each other. Does Tatiana know what you do when you go to the center?"

Lance smiled and shrugged his shoulders. "I guess she does. Ted never mentions it. Anyway, it's not as bad as you imagine. Our bodies are fine-tuned to take that abuse. Plus, it's a good way to get out our inner frustrations."

"What about what happened to Ted?"

"I told you, he just had the wind knocked out of him. He's done it to me many times. Our bodies are used to it."

Karamine shook her head, and put her empty glass on the table. "Let me check on dinner, I think it's ready," she said.

When she stood up, Lance put his arms around her and pulled her down on the sofa next to him. "Who cares about dinner," he whispered, intimately, kissing her hard on the mouth.

Karamine responded for a moment, then pushed him away gently. "Look, I've made a delicious dinner, and I'm not going to let it spoil, like last time."

"There you go, Karamine, putting dinner before a unique moment of passion," Lance argued, teasingly.

"Unique? Hummm. I think you're running wild down there living a bachelor's life," she said, getting up and straightening her hair. "We've got the whole night ahead of us, lover."

"Is that a promise?" Lance questioned, with a teasing smile.

Karamine touched Lance's cheek in a tender gesture. For a moment she fought a sudden urge to weep. It was so natural, so good to have him back home. How is it possible to separate from him, even for a day, she wondered. Everything fades when we're together; even my activities seem incomplete, diminished somehow and unsatisfying, compared to the priceless unction of our love.

"Promise." she whispered gently, before walking to the kitchen.

Martyr's Day, dawned fair and bright in Boston. This was the day Armenians everywhere honored the memory of one and a half million Armenians killed by Turks in the 1915 genocide. Pete, the cab driver, picked up Karamine and Lance as planned, and delivered them to the front door of the church at Watertown.

"What time will I come back for you, doctor?" he inquired politely.

"No need to, Pete," Karamine replied, "We're meeting our families, and there will be lots of transportation back. Thanks."

Inside, the church hall was already crowded. Karamine and Lance were greeted warmly by the chairman for the occasion.

"It's an honor to have you speak today, Senator. Thank you so much, Karamine for getting him on such short notice. Come with me." He guided them to the front seats where the *Der Hayr* (priest) and other guests were seated. Lance and Karamine looked around for their parents, and waved greetings when they spotted them.

The hall filled fast, and the function began with a benediction by the priest, and a few short speeches by some influential Armenians from the Boston community. Then, Lance heard the chairman introduce him. He squeezed Karamine's hand. "I hope they like what I have to say," he whispered softly, getting up from his seat. On the platform, he shook the chairman's hand, then placed his few cards down, and gripped the sides of the podium. He gazed out over the sea of faces before him in the hall; the people stared back with concentrated attention. He began slowly and deliberately.

"Der Hayr, noted speakers and fellow Armenians . . . once again we come together to commemorate the genocide of 1915. While we shall never forget our martyrs, it's not my intent today to focus on those terrible years, when our nation was torn apart, first by the moslem Turk, then by the ruthless bolshevik. Tomes have already been written about that and thousands of speeches describe it. No, my fellow Armenians, today, I'd like to honor our martyr's from a different perspective, and I'd like to begin with a quote from William Saroyan, if I may:

"I should like to see a power in this world destroy this race, this small tribe of unimportant people whose history is ended, whose wars have been fought and lost, whose structures have crumbled, whose literature is unread, whose music is unheard, and whose prayers are no more answered. Go ahead, destroy this race! Destroy Armenia! See if you can do it. Send them from their homes into the desert. Let them have neither bread nor water, burn their homes and churches. Then see if they will not laugh again, see if they will not sing and pray again. For when two of them meet anywhere in the world, see if they will not create a New Armenia!"

No one could have said it better. For here we are in this hall together today, where we have already created the New Armenia. Through the Grace of God, our people have survived the onslaught of the barbarian Turk, and we are flourishing throughout the world. In the field of music, art, politics, we are represented far beyond any other nation. And let me tell you, my fellow Armenians, there are rumblings in the Soviet Union which are now being heard throughout the world. The republics of the empire are fighting for independence, and with it the possibility of a free and independent Armenia. Think of it! The drumbeat of freedom is resounding throughout the republics, and it cannot and will not be stilled any longer.

So now, we must look ahead and not backwards. We must look to the future of our country, and not muddy the waters by old hatreds and revenge. Although many of these reports are unsubstantiated, believe me, the days of the Soviet Empire may be numbered. So, my fellow Armenians, with this in mind, let us think objectively of the possibilities for the future of our little country. First of all, if we achieve an independent republic, we have to recognize it is still surrounded on three sides by moslem countries. Armenia is also land-locked. Can she survive economically under these adverse conditions? What kind of relationship will we have with our neighbors, such as Georgia? These are just some of the questions to be answered for our people who live there. For their sake and their survival, we have to seek a different path . . . perhaps the path of reconciliation and forgiveness of all nations there, so everyone can live together in peace and harmony.

Considering the sufferings of the past, this is difficult and cannot be done physically. It's only through the help and guidance of God can independence, peace and unity be restored. We can pray my fellow Armenians, that the Turks will return the lands back to the Kurds, return the lands of Cyprus, Nicosia and other territories that historically belong to the Greeks; return biblical Mt. Ararat and the land of Karabagh, which was given to the Azerbaijani by Stalin, back to the Armenians; finally we could pray that Anatola, gateway to the Black Sea is returned so Armenia is not land-locked and dependent.

If, indeed, the Turks could make such gestures, they could be a guiding light, a homogenizing force for good, uniting the republics of the Caucasus into a stable, viable and prosperous economic force, which would not need the support of the west, nor the Russians. For centuries the Turks have used this area constantly for their own influence of power, costing millions of lives, hardships and turmoil for all the nations involved. It's time for the Turks to come out of the dark ages, to lead the way if only she could be convinced of these realities. War, killing, darkness and despair has been our legacy for generations. We're on the cusp of a new century. Can't there be light, wisdom, economic prosperity and peace? Is this beyond our understanding?

Today, my fellow Armenians, we've come to the threshold of change and transition. The world around us has become a global village, where, computers and satellite communications are able to change policy and procedures at a moment's notice. The only remaining absolute is God, and our faith in Him. This was the strength that helped us endure oppression and massacre. This is the faith that will help us heal, this is the hope for a liberated people, a new nation, as Saroyan says so eloquently, a NEW ARMENIA! Thank you.

There was silence in the hall, as people absorbed the impact of Lance's message. Then a slight murmuring as the crowd talked to each other and discussed this new approach to their usual Martyr's Day grievances. Always the speeches for that day were charged with frustration, hatred and talk of retaliations. Reconciliation was much too far beyond the pale just yet for most of them. On the way back to his seat, Lance encountered an old man who had survived the massacres. Slowly he got up from his seat and applauded, then shouted in a thick Armenian accent, "Bravo my boy!" "Bravo! Enough of killing! I agree." Others joined hesitantly, then loud applause and cheering vibrated through the hall.

The chairman raised his hand, and the crowd quieted.

"Thank you, Senator Bagdasarian, that was indeed quite a speech. We are a small nation and we have to be bold in our ideas to survive. I daresay your ideas will be discussed in many quarters, and I'm sure will meet with much opposition. However, I'm an optimist, and feel they could be implemented with the proper leadership."

The priest came up to the podium, then lifted his hand. "Let us all join in prayer now, and believe, this is the best way for our people. Let us pray for the leadership to carry out such bold endeavors." He bowed his head and began the Lord's Prayer in Armenian and then in English. The people prayed with him.

After the prayer, the priest and the chairman joined Karamine and Lance.

"How did you arrive at such a premise . . . Forgiveness? Reconciliation? Love must be somewhere, too. You must have been inspired by the Spirit, my son." He smiled and shook Lance's hand.

"You've given our people quite a challenge," said the chairman. "I'll depend on you to help me convince them, but it won't be easy. The hatred of the Turk and genocide is an old and painful grievance. It won't die easy. But as you say, with prayer perhaps, and God . . . who knows."

"Ah my pretty Karamine who's always there to help our people in their dire need," said the priest, turning to Karamine. I'm so happy to see you again, and to meet your husband, the senator. Karamine has mentioned you many times in reference to the Armenian Relief."

Lance studied the Armenian priest, with his well-clipped beard and penetrating eyes. The priest reminded him of pictures his grandfather, Sahag, had shown him many times—pictures of *"fedayees,"* (fighting mountain men) men filled with passion and fire, who fought and died for what they believed. I'll bet that same fury blazes beneath his venerable manner, he surmised, sublimated of course, but, in a crises, I believe this man would fight and die for his principles too. "Thank you, Der Hayr." Karamine answered. "I've been a bit tardy in attending church these past few months, but I've been occupied with meetings to see how we can help our country further. Setting up exchange programs with some of the universities in the Boston area is one of my main goals. We're trying to bring new medical technology to Armenia, but it takes time, with endless meetings."

"We're all very indebted to you for the work you do," said the chairman, especially for bringing your husband here today.

"Our parents are here today also, Der Hayr. I'm sure they'd like to say hello to you," said Lance, glancing toward the direction where he had last seen his parents. He saw they were speaking to a group of people, but caught his father's eye, and motioned to him to join them. When he looked around for Karamine's parents however, his attention was diverted to a small group deeply engrossed in dialogue. A tall man in a dark blue suit seemed to dominate, with opinions more vociferous than the rest. His face was turned, however, and obscured from Lance's view.

Lance's heart plunged suddenly. Vasken! God, no! he thought. A sense of sick frustration swept over him. Even before Vasken turned around, Lance recognized him, felt his presence and the undercurrent of his hostility. Karamine turned quickly when she saw the color drain from Lance's face and followed his gaze. She put her hand gently on his arm, greeted Antranig and Kate, then excused herself and hurried toward her brother. When she reached the group she took Vasken's arm and tugged firmly, pulling him away.

"Sorry," she said calmly, nodding briefly and trying to keep the anger from her voice, "but I'd like to speak to my brother a moment in private."

"What do you think you're trying to do, Vasken?" she said, hotly, when they were out of earshot. "Are you planning to make trouble today? Our parents are here. Are you going to embarrass and hurt all of us again? Haven't you done enough already?"

"Karamine, I have nothing against you or *Myrig*, or even *Hyrig*. He's the way he is. But that husband of yours is another matter. The program ON TARGET propelling him to the senate is too much for me to take. He's a coward and a traitor to the Armenian cause, and has sold out for his own aspirations of power. I know him damn well, and sooner or later, my dear sister, we will settle this thing between us, one way or another." Vasken's expression was dark and filled with enmity.

"How can you say such a thing to me, Vasken? How can you do this when you know how much my husband means to me? I love you and only want the best for you. I just don't understand you. At least come over and speak to Mom and Dad. Mom worries about you constantly and she misses you all the time. Is it asking too much to expect you to behave like a son and brother for once, if only for today?" Karamine's voice was pleading.

Vasken's expression softened slightly. He walked over to the people he was originally talking to, and excused himself, then accompanied Karamine to the area where his parents stood waiting. Anahid Casparian was the first to greet Vasken as he approached.

"Vasken . . . where on earth have you been? It's so good to see you, son. You know, I always worry something's happened to you when we don't get news from you. Those few cards you send are so short on news." She put her arms around him and held him.

Aram Casparian remained stoic and unsmiling. "Where has he been? Probably plotting the overthrow of some friendly country. As far as worrying about him . . . don't! The devil takes care of his own," he said bitterly.

Vasken laughed insolently. "You said it right, *Hyrig*, better a strong devil than a weak compromising alternative like the speech we heard today. Anyway, I'm glad to see your love for me has not changed and you still have those endearing feelings for me," he said sardonically.

Lance, still engaged in conversation with the priest and his parents, way trying to work through his agitation; he carried on the pretense as long as possible, but eventually he excused himself, and took both parents by the arm and led them outside the hall.

"I see Vasken Casparian is here today," said Antranig with disgust. "What does he want anyway, more trouble?"

Lance's blue eyes flashed with fury. "I don't know what the hell he wants, I don't know what he ever wants, except to hurt Karamine, and his parents. Look, folks, I have to go see Karamine's parents. I can't let Vasken think I'm intimidated and afraid to face him. We planned to go to Anthony's to eat, so why don't you wait in the car until I see what's going on."

"All right, Lance. We'll see you later, then. By the way, we loved your speech." His mother kissed him lightly on the cheek.

"I was proud of you today, Lance," his father said, patting him on the shoulder before taking Kate's arm and heading for the church parking lot.

Inside the hall people were still greeting each other and standing around in small groups. Lance took a deep breath and walked resolutely toward Karamine, where she stood with her parents and her brother. Lance greeted his in-laws warmly, but they were obviously uncomfortable. Vasken glared malevolently.

"Still making your hypocritical plebeian speeches I see, "bullshit rhetoric with no substance! You know, you're the biggest BS artist around, and you've gotten much better at it since you went to Washington. They must have taught you new ways of deceiving the unsuspecting voters," Vasken said unpleasantly.

"Vasken, please . . . you promised," Karamine said under her breath.

Lance's eyes flashed dangerously, as he tried to control his anger. "Vasken, I don't intend to fight you today, this is not the time," he said evenly, "I merely came over to collect my wife and her parents. However, I've got to say, I can still learn a lot from you in the art of deception and intrigue. I understand the KGB does a wonderful job in their training schools . . . especially in the art of slitting one's throat when they are least expecting it."

Vasken moved ominously toward Lance, but Karamine quickly stepped in between them, placing her hand gently on Vasken's chest to restrain him and avoid a physical confrontation.

"Can't you two be civil and remember where you are. We're in the church! Vasken . . . for heaven's sake! Put your views aside and think of Mom and Dad," Karamine pleaded urgently. "Let's not have any more hostility on this of all days. On such an occasion, let's at least make an effort to act like a family. Millions have died and we are here to commemorate their sacrifice. The last thing we should do today is to be divided in thought or purpose."

Anahid Casparian, glanced quickly at her husband; her eyes were filled with anguish. Karamine's father was clearly angered, embittered by his son's ethics and principles, crushed by his cold contempt and shattering scorn of all his values. He had disowned him long ago.

Vasken stepped back from Lance, but his face was contorted with wrath. "Where the hell do you get off, 'Sen-a-tor,' preaching to true Armenians, and telling them to forget their martyrs?" he snarled. "And as for the Turks giving back those territories, you're even more of a fool than I thought. Furthermore, all that crap about the soviet empire's demise, is nothing more than American propaganda funneled through the CIA. There isn't a shred of evidence to support it." People standing in groups nearby were suddenly quiet; they stared curiously when Vasken's voice grew louder and he continued his tirade. "Armenia should side with a strong powerful country like Russia. That way they'd have adequate support, and they could take back the lands that belong to the Armenian people. Then they'd have the force to do it with such violence and destruction our enemies would never dare touch us again. If need be we could nuke them into submission. And that sen-a-tor is my answer to your gutless idea of forgiveness."

Lance's eyes flashed blue fire as he faced his antagonist. "So that's your solution is it, to Nuke them? Nuke them? Turn the country into a nuclear battle ground where no one can win or live from the radio active waste for years?" You're as bad as the Turks and it's you who needs to come out of the dark ages. We're moving into a new century, and its about time to dispense with old paradigms and patterns of death and destruction."

Karamine tugged Lance's sleeve. "Lance . . . please . . . people are staring. Let's go. Coming Mom, Dad?"

"Same old hypocrite. Same old half-breed hypocrite," Vasken continued, "talks the talk, but has no stomach for the fight. If I ever had any doubts you're Armenian, I have none today, after the deliverance of such an appeasing speech. It's just about what I'd expect from you. And if you think the soviet union is about to crumble, dream on. Right now there are Russian subs patroling the east and west coast of this country . . . with nuclear warheads pointing to strategic targets throughout the United States."

All of Lance's senses converged on his anger. Hostility and rage welled up within him clouding his reason and he longed to smash Vasken, to wipe the arrogant sneer from his face, to silence his overbearing talk once and for all. But every discipline with the martial arts, with practiced introspection, with handling opposition in the media and senate, gave him control now. His anger submerged and gave way to deliberate calm. He turned from Vasken to Karamine's parents.

"Are you ready to join us, *Hyrig?*"

"Yes, we've had enough, let's go," Aram Casparian replied with disgust.

"Will you be coming home later, Vasken?" Anahid asked, timidly, her dark eyes filled with pain.

"This is no son of ours, Anahid, I don't want him in my home," said Aram with bitterness.

Vasken laughed in a mocking way. "My dear family, I wouldn't dream of intruding into your bourgeois lives. Continue on with your plans, please do. I have plans of my own. I'm leaving immediately for Armenia. It will be good to get over there and see for myself just how flawed and uninformed are the perceptions of our notable 'sen-a-tor,' here. Believe me, I'll report the true facts, not platitudes and wishful thinking, based on propaganda and capitalist guilt."

Lance stared at Vasken and his eyes sparked with rage. He longed to humble this arrogant bastard, to bring him to his knees and make him beg for mercy, to break him once and for all. Vasken invited it and was baiting him; this Lance understood. Nothing would give Vasken more pleasure than the opportunity to humiliate him before his wife, his family and his friends. Only this time it would be different, Lance thought confidently. Very different. This time I'd probably kill him. The group stood in deadly silence, then Lance felt the pressure of Karamine's hand on his arm. He saw her black eyes, appealing to him to ignore Vasken's words, to simply turn and leave. Lance saw her mother's stricken face, her father's fierce expression. He turned back to Vasken.

"I wish you well on your trip, Vasken. I hope, for your sake you do find truth," he said coolly. Somehow it was easier to say than he expected.

"You're leaving, again, Vasken? his mother said despondently. "We seldom hear from you, and now that you're here you're leaving again. Son, why can't you give us some time?" she questioned.

"I'm sorry, *Myrig*," he said, "I'm unable to stay longer. I have to leave tomorrow."

"Yes," Aram Casparian said, "he has to get to Armenia to show them how the bolsheviks should run the country. I'm quite sure you plan to have dissidents shipped to the Gulogs of Siberia."

"How right you are, *Hyrig*," Vasken said with slight sarcasm. "Your understanding of me is really brilliant. What have you done for your people? Your martyrs? Outside of fighting for the four freedoms in WW II. What have you done for your people lately; money, words?"

"Please," said Vasken's mother, "please, there's no need to speak to your father that way, my son."

Vasken looked at his mother and felt a slight twinge of remorse.

"You're right, *Myrig*. I'm sorry, *Hyrig*, but we never saw eye to eye on anything as far as I can remember. You're my father and I'll always respect you, but don't condemn what I'm doing until you fully understand my purpose."

He bowed slowly as he said his farewell and turned to face Lance. "I'll look forward to our next encounter, where we may continue our discussion of the ARMENIAN CAUSE in full detail, alone and without interruption."

"Yes," Lance replied, "till we meet again, brother-in-law."

Vasken's mother embraced her son. "Let us know where you are, my son."

Karamine kissed her brother gently on the cheek. I'll always love you, Vasken, no matter what. I pray each night for you, especially that He grants you light and wisdom."

Vasken threw back his head and laughed heartily as he walked away and headed toward the group he had been with earlier. They spoke for a few moments, then left the hall together.

Lance, Karamine and her parents watched as their son headed for the door without looking back.

"What is going to happen to our son?" his mother questioned sadly. "I feel I may never see him again."

"Aram placed a comforting arm about his wife. "Don't worry, as I said before, he's with the devil and the devil always protects his own," he said.

"Yes, perhaps that's why I'm worried. God be with you my son," she whispered under her breath.

PART TWO

ARMENIA and KARABAKH

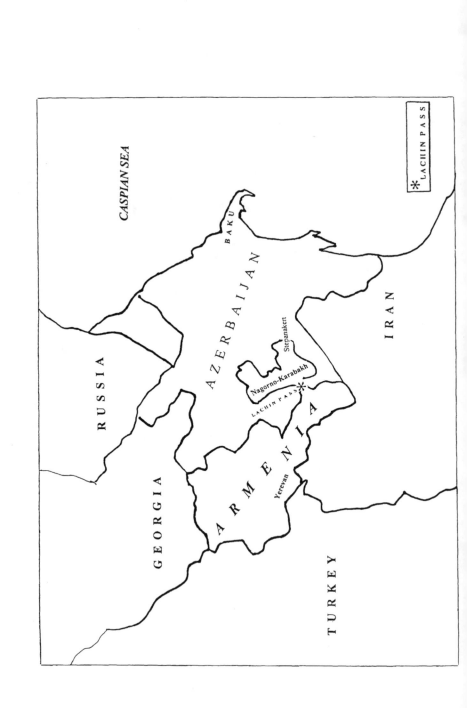

17

The seat belt sign flashed on in the cabin of Aeroflot Flight 35 from Moscow, as the plane began its approach for landing at Yerevan Airport in Soviet Armenia. Vasken Casparian leaned back and tightened the seat belt a little, when the flight experienced some turbulence and down drafts in its descent to the proper altitude and final turn for landing. His mind was active and teeming with thoughts and images from the past few days—the stops in Belgrade and Moscow; the meetings with fellow comrades there, who brought him up to date on what was happening to Armenians in the mountainous area of Nagorno Karabakh. He was agitated by reports of displaced Armenians, driven from their ancestral homes by Azerbaijani moslems; frustrated by news of the deportation and relentless confiscation of their lands and personal properties. Armenian refugees were forced to flee to the capital, Stepanakert, where the city's resources were already strained to the maximum from the influx of people. Schools, hospitals, barracks of the Russian army, every available space was utilized in ministering to the needs of the refugees. Vasken recalled his reaction when he heard the stories—"Where's the Russian Army?" he'd shouted. "Why aren't they protecting our people from those butchering moslems?" He flinched nervously now, recalling their answers. "Soviets don't want to offend the moslems, comrade— Armenians are in the minority; the Soviet Union is made up of many moslem countries, and the soviets don't dare provoke them, or take sides. They fear uprisings in the moslem republics as a result, so they merely close their eyes to the problem." Vasken cursed under his breath. "To hell with them," he'd blurted out savagely. "At least give us guns to protect ourselves, and let us fight. I don't want to see a repeat of 1915 where we were disarmed and the Turks slaughtered us. No! that will not happen, ever again," he'd stated emphatically, pounding his fist on the table where they were sitting, and rattling the cups on top. "Give us the guns, and I'll go there myself to fight if need be."

One of the men from Moscow lifted his hand. "Don't worry, comrade," he'd said, "we've organized a resistance force in Karabakh and they've raided Russian armories all over the mountain country. They've taken enough guns and ammunition to put up a good fight. They have some heroic leaders, whose names I shall withhold at present. They are organizing a formidable resistance force to protect the people against the Azeris. Young boys are being organized for courier duty throughout the mountain ranges. This way, they'll be informed ahead of any action being taken by those butchers. Later on, of course, we'll need radios and other modern equipment, but, for now, young couriers will do the job. But, even with all that, they're still going to need many more supplies to hold the line, especially if a war breaks out. New equipment . . . missiles, tanks and weapons of modern warfare are necessary, ground to air missiles in particular. The Azeris have planes and helicopters to bomb and straf us. If the Armenians are to survive, they'll need these things badly, and very soon. Just now, we'll have to wait and see. We have our people there to discern what the current needs are. Armenia has shipped food and clothing to help the refugees, but that problem of the refugees must be alleviated by putting an end to the deportations."

Vasken looked out of the window and tried to distract his thoughts from the situation. Below, for the first time, he saw the splendid peak of Ararat with its glacial-rimmed pinnacle projecting through the mist. He felt a deep stirring and an awesome sense of wonder. There it is, he thought, the symbol of Armenia; imperial, proud, strong. And so it has been for all these centuries. The landing place of Noah's Ark, if one chooses to believe the bible. But, then again, the bible is historic, I'll give it that much.

The plane descended to the altitude necessary for a final approach. Toward the right, Vasken was able to observe the borders of Armenia and Turkey, with its barbed wire barriers and stockades. The land they stole from us, he thought, fiercely. Those borders will be removed one of these days, and Ararat will be ours again. We'll wrench it away from them one way or another. This I vow.

The aircraft flared out for its touchdown, and Vasken heard the screech of the tires as they made contact with the hard concrete. The aircraft rolled down the runway with tremendous speed and Vasken felt the strain on his seat belt as the pilot reversed the engines, and applied the brakes slowing the aircraft down rapidly.

"Yerevan Airport." The pilot announced. "Please stay seated until we taxi to the proper gate for disembarkment and customs."

Vasken looked out the window and viewed the panorama of terminal, tower and other buildings; It was difficult for him to realize he was actually in Armenia, mother Armenia, he thought. I've always dreamed of being here and now, here I am. He was filled with enthusiasm and expectant hope. I'll work hard here, improve the workers standard of living, help the country develop her full potential. Yes. This is what I've always dreamed of doing, and now I'm here to do it, he thought resolutely.

The passengers got up from their seats and reached for their bags and articles they had purchased in Moscow—toasters, mixers and other items in short supply in Armenia. Slowly Vasken secured his handbag and worked his way out of the plane and over to the customs terminal. The passengers were herded into a stuffy room, where they were asked to produce their passports and papers before being permitted to enter the country. The customs officer spoke in English, Armenian and some French. Vasken moved his free hand into his breast pocket and pulled out his passport along with identification as a high party member. When he reached the desk, the customs agent looked at his passport, his party I.D., then looked up at Vasken and smiled. "We have been expecting you, comrade. There is someone here to take care of your needs," he said in broken English.

"I speak Armenian, I also read and write it, comrade, no need to speak to me in English," Vasken replied in clear Armenian, but with an American accent. The customs officer raised his eyebrow and nodded slowly.

"Good, comrade, Good! It will be a great help to you here, as not all are able to converse in English. Have a good stay, comrade," he said, handing Vasken his papers. The customs officer motioned to a young man who came over to the desk, then he pointed to Vasken's bag. "He will drive you to your hotel, comrade. Just let him take your bag. We have been informed that arrangements have already been made for your stay in Yerevan."

"Thank you," Vasken replied.

Vasken shuddered slightly as he followed the young man through the airport terminal. The air was heavy with a foul smell of stagnant filth. It surprised him to note the large plate glass windows were dingy and streaked with grime, giving the place an aura of neglect. Vasken was perturbed slightly by his first impression; this was not quite the way he had always envisioned it. They walked through the grimy glass doorway toward a waiting vintage car parked at the curb. An official insignia was prominently displayed on the windshield. The young man opened the door for Vasken, then slid in on the driver's seat. But, everywhere Vasken looked, he saw that no great thought had been given to cleanliness or mechanical maintenance. The driver was friendly, however, and smiled at Vasken when he introduced himself.

"My name is Rouben. I'm to be your guide and friend while you are a guest here in Yerevan. Please let me know what I may do for you at any time, to make your stay more comfortable and pleasant," he said.

"Thank you, Rouben," said Vasken, scrutinizing the young man carefully. "I'll take you up on that very soon." He took a pack of chewing gum from his pocket and handed it to him. "I hear the people here love American chewing gum."

"Chewing gum! We love it, comrade," Rouben replied with a broad grin. "It's like currency, more than currency. I could trade this pack for many things, a stick at a time. We barter a lot here. Chewing gum and American cigarettes are at a premium in the black market. Chewing gum is the best though," he said turning to look at Vasken.

"Black market?" Vasken queried, raising an eyebrow. "I thought this was a worker's paradise where everyone was equal. How is it possible to speak of a black market? How does it exist in a socialist state?"

Rouben laughed heartily. "Worker's paradise? You must be living in a dream world, and listening to all the socialist propaganda for western consumption. Don't tell me that you've fallen for all that garbage they put out daily . . . you of all people." He laughed loudly again. "Listen, comrade, there are black markets everywhere in the Soviet Union Republics, including Moscow and Leningrad. Our great leaders know all about it, but don't lift a finger to stop it. If it weren't for the black markets, people would be starving to death, and they know it. At least you can barter something to get food from the farmers when they bring in their produce. Even clothing shipped to relatives from the west can be bartered."

Vasken listened quietly, with a growing sense of disillusionment. Still, he reasoned, these things would stop once the economy of the state improved, and better distribution procedures were initiated for the various products produced. "How come the airport terminal is so dirty and neglected?" he asked bluntly. "Don't they have workers for the job?"

Rouben shrugged his shoulders. "Sure they have, twice the number they need, and all paid the same. Some show up and others do not. Why should they? They get paid one way or another, so why bother working when you don't have to. There's no reward for working hard. Those who do are scorned and ostracized. No, comrade, we're all the same, and you better stay that way if you want to survive."

Vasken was incredulous. "Don't you have supervisors who take charge and see that the work is done properly? What about rules and regulations governing worker's actions on the job?"

"Where have you been all these years of our great socialist progress, comrade?" Rouben answered, shaking his head and turning to look at Vasken. "You are naive or totally blind to the ways of socialism. As you said, it IS a worker's paradise and the unions control everything. If a supervisor complains of a worker's deficiencies, the worker merely goes to his union and registers a complaint. The supervisor is then reprimanded for harassing the worker. And, many times, people have been stripped of their positions and shipped off to unattractive places, if you understand what I'm saying. So . . . the work is done when it is done. Usually, at the convenience of the workers."

"Is it this way in all the republics? or just Armenia?"

Again Rouben shook his head. "It's the same throughout all of the republics. We're all socialist states, and have powerful unions who dominate the party. The party wants to stay in power so it gives them anything they want."

"But what about the space programs? The Astronauts? The military complex of the Soviet Union? It's the most powerful in the world. If what you say is true, why is the power of the country so great?" Vasken questioned sharply.

"Oh that," Rouben answered indifferently, "those air and space projects have their own towns and cities where engineers and workers live and work under a more capitalistic system. They're highly paid for their efforts, and they're able to afford and buy the best the republics can produce, whether it be food, clothing, cars, anything! Incompetence is not tolerated there as it is in the rest of the soviet union, comrade. I've been to some of these cities, and I've seen their supermarkets and stores where they even sell foreign products, like dishwashers and other appliances unheard of in the rest of the republics. Some of those people attend foreign schools for advanced education in whatever field they are in. Because they're the elite, they have all the privileges. The military get the best, too. Don't forget, comrade, they're the ones with the guns, so they have the power." Rouben shook his head sadly.

Vasken sat back in his seat and stared blankly at Rouben in disbelief. It was some minutes before he spoke. "I don't understand. Are you telling me there are some workers considered "elite"? I though we are all the same, working equally for the glory of the Soviet Union. How can this be under the rule of the proletariat?"

Rouben shook his head and laughed. "You have a great deal to learn of our socialist experience, comrade. In the West, you've been exposed to the greatest propaganda machine ever devised. It's been so successful that a person of your knowledge and understanding has been totally taken in by their propaganda." He brought the car to a stop before the hotel. "Here we are," he said, getting out of the car, opening the door for Vasken, and handing him his bag. "Do you want me to come later and show you around our city, comrade?"

Vasken thought for a moment before answering. "Yes, I think I'd like to drive about and see the city, get the feel of the place. Pick me up in about two hours. That will give me time to clean up, relax and get the flying out of my system. Seems all I've done in the last few days is fly."

"Must seem that way. You've come halfway around the world so you're probably dead tired. Why don't you rest, and I can pick you up early in the morning, and take you about," Rouben suggested.

"No, no!" Vasken asserted, "I want every minute of my stay to count for something. I'll be tied up in meetings and briefings later, which will probably take up most of my time. So, pick me up in a couple of hours." He turned and entered the front door of the hotel and headed for the desk clerk.

"My name is Vasken Casparian. I believe the party has made arrangements for me to stay here," he announced to the desk clerk in a crisp commanding manner.

"Vasken Casparian?" the clerk repeated, squinting through horned rimmed glasses. "Just a minute." He looked through an ancient ledger following a few names down with an index finger.

"Ah yes, comrade ... they've made arrangements, and have detailed us to take care of all your needs, including a good woman for company if that is your desire. You must be an important visitor to rate all this attention," he said unsmilingly, peering over the top of his glasses.

"Humm," said Vasken looking around with disdain, "if I were that important they would have gotten me better accommodations than this antiquated place. "No, I'm just an American here on a mission of understanding, and to see for myself how the five year plans of the past twenty years have been working. I've come to enjoy the ... ah ... worker's paradise," he said sarcastically.

The clerk glowered at him through his glasses. "You have to understand, comrade, that no matter what, our nation has survived, through the blessings of the Soviet Union. It has keep the Turk at bay, and for that we're real grateful."

"Yes, I noticed the border barbed wire and stockades separating us from our lands and Mount Ararat," said Vasken in a disdainful tone. "Look, I'm tired after this long trip. I want to clean up and rest for an hour. Please ... my room."

The clerk motioned to a young boy and gave him the key to Vasken's room, along with his bag. Vasken followed the boy down the hall where they took an old elevator to the third floor. Entering his room, the boy placed the bag on the bed, then walked to the window and opened it. Vasken put his hand in his pocket and took out some money to give him for his effort, but the boy shook his head in protest.

"No, you are a guest of our people, no thank you," he said, leaving the room.

Vasken looked around the room, then went into the bathroom to check for a shower. He was disappointed. The tub was longer than those in the West, but, equipped with only a pan and scoop to rinse off the soap suds. I guess we're back to the twenties and thirties when people didn't think much about showers, he thought, smiling to himself. Oh well, I'll just make do. He was surprised however to find the hot water was in plentiful supply, and it gushed forcefully from the tap.

He stretched out in the long tub and relaxed in the water, which he found pleasantly soft. He thought about Karabakh. One way or another I've got to get to Karabakh to see how things are going with those deportations, he thought. I wonder if Rouben can give me any information on how I may do this, and exactly whom I'll have to see to give me clearance for the trip. I'll find out what he has to say this evening when he comes to take me sight seeing. He soaked for awhile, then rinsed himself from the bucket of warm water; he wrapped a thick towel around his lean body and walked into the bedroom and lay down on the bed. He drifted into deep sleep almost immediately.

He woke up suddenly, however, with the sensation of violent shaking. For a moment he couldn't remember where he was. He sat up and wiped his forehead with his handkerchief, then slid his legs over the side of the bed and held his head between his hands. The nightmare! That same damn nightmare! It's plagued me now for months, he thought impatiently. What the hell's goin' on anyway. At one time, he had mentioned the dream to a friend. His friend had advised him to see a therapist, but Vasken had shrugged off the suggestion, believing it to be, the mere spilling over of a too active, too aggressive, subconscious mind. Besides, Vasken didn't trust therapists, calling it a lot of "psycho babble." He truly believed it would pass in time, but the nightmare persisted, and always, it left him shaken and unnerved. There was a fight in the dream, a battle for his life. The face of his assailant however, remained obscured. No matter how hard he tried, he could never quite see his adversary, nor understand the message. There was confusion, shouts, a shining piece of metal like a sword or bayonet, wielded by a shadow who tried to pierce his heart; a desperate struggle followed, then darkness, cold sweat, trembling, agitation on awakening.

He wiped his forehead again then walked to the bathroom and washed his face, allowing the cold water to bring him back to reality. He pulled out clean underwear, then dressed comfortably in slacks and a pullover sweater, appropriate for the chilly evenings in Yerevan. Before leaving he checked his wallet and papers, put out the light, and heard the lock click shut to his room. When he left the hotel, he was happy to see Rouben waiting by his car. He was casually reading a newspaper when Vasken approached.

"Rouben, can you arrange a passage for me to Karabakh?" he asked authoritatively when he got into the car.

Rouben laughed in a good-natured way." No problem. I've done it many times before. It's just a matter of getting the proper clearances and papers, and you being an important member of the party, that should be easy."

"I don't know about being an important member, but whatever you say, just as long as I'm able to get there."

"No problem", Rouben repeated again with a grin.

The car sped off for a tour of the city of Yerevan.

18

The Aeroflot helicopter leaped from its pad at Zvartnots Airfield in Yerevan and lifted at rapid speed to its assigned altitude. Vasken felt the steep climb in the pit of his stomach, as the aircraft vibrated from the powerful surge of the engine. When things had eased, Vasken relaxed in his seat and stared out the window. He thought about the last two days, touring the city of Yerevan with Rouben as guide. He's been a good guide, Vasken reflected, and he's certainly a storehouse of information and know-how. Rouben's stock answer "no problem" to any of Vasken's wishes or demands, amused him; his amusement soon turned to admiration, however, when Rouben followed through on everything he promised. He introduced Vasken to the proper people, provided the correct papers for the trip, as well as the necessary mode of transportation.

"Is this fantastic acceleration and climb to altitude the way it is all the time?" Vasken inquired of the passenger next to him.

"Yes," the passenger replied, "the pilot has to climb rapidly to get safely over the mountains of Nagorno Karabakh and to the East safely. It's always the same, I've made the trip many times." He pointed to the mountains on the horizon before them. "There it is, our ancestral lands, which were usurped by the Azeri's, thanks to that bastard, Stalin."

"Yes, I know the story of the treachery full well. But, have no fear, it will be ours again."

The passenger lifted an eyebrow and stared curiously at this foreign dressed man who spoke Armenian with a peculiar accent. "How will it be returned? Do you know something that I may not?" he inquired.

"We will get the Soviet Parliament to rescind what Stalin has done; through Mikhail Gorbachev's Glasnost and Perestroika, we will petition our cause in Moscow in the Soviet Parliament. Even the Azerbaijani's know it does not belong to them."

The passenger studied Vasken closely before answering. "What is your name, and where are you from, my friend? You speak with an accent. Is it English, or American? My name is Armen Tackvorian, from the village of Spitak Karabakh," he said, extending his hand.

Vasken took his hand and shook it. "I'm Vasken Casparian, and yes, I'm from America."

Armen laughed. "Oh that's why you are so naive my friend. All of you who come here from America are dreamers, and you have simple western solutions to our problems."

Vasken observed Armen cautiously. His thick curly hair and ruddy skin reminded him of old pictures he had seen of Armenian mountain fighters, who had fought furiously and had saved Armenia many times from the Turks. There was a rugged quality about him, a maturity beyond his years, which Vasken calculated to be somewhere in his late thirties. "Why do you say that?" he asked.

Armen laughed again. "Petition the parliament? First of all my friend, you do not petition the Soviet Parliament. It's not allowed. Then there's the question of millions of moslems living in other republics of the Soviet empire, Turkastan, for instance. What makes you think the Russians or other republics care what happens to us. No, my friend, never will they do that. The only way is with force. The Armenians need weapons of all kinds to arm themselves, or there will be another massacre like 1915 in these mountains. That is why I'm here, to ascertain their needs and to see how this can be accomplished."

"But, what about all the equipment taken from the Russian armories? Won't that help?" Vasken queried.

"For the moment," Armen replied, shrugging his shoulders. "But, I'm afraid a war between the Azerbaijani and the Armenians of Karabakh is inevitable, my friend, if things continue going the way they are. The displacements are still going on, and people are pouring into Leninakan and Stepanakert. Sooner or later the Azeri will move in units of their army, and try to push all the Armenians from their homes. We have to move fast and stop this before it gets out of hand. That's why I'm here. I'm meeting with Varoujan Torossian who's in the process of organizing the KARABAKH DEFENCE FORCE. We'll know it later as the KDF. We will need everyone's help if we are to succeed in our mission.

"Are you a TASHNOG, a member of the Armenian Revolutionary Federation?' Vasken asked through narrowed eyes.

Armen's eyes shifted and his face took on a wary expression. He countered Vasken's question with a question. "Are you a bolshevik, my friend or should I say, comrade? Are you a follower of that Armenian butcher Migoyan, who had thousands of his own people executed when he took over Armenia? Why ask about the ARF? You must know that organization is outlawed in our republic, and anyone espousing those ideas would be arrested immediately and executed. You don't really expect me to answer such a question do you?" He laughed scornfully.

"Yes, I am a communist," Vasken admitted, "and you must understand that Migoyan felt justified in his actions at the time. He did not want any opposition or resistance from the intellectuals until the new regime of the communist state could be put in place. We could debate that one way or another."

"Debate?" Armen shouted angrily. "Half a million Armenians, doctors, teachers, scholars, all the intelligentia were brutally murdered, but you understand his motives? How many more do you feel it will take to satisfy the security of your proletariat appetite? Worker's paradise! What a joke, when the likes of Gorbachev and his family enjoy their summer homes on the Black Sea, along with their staff of servants, living the life of a capitalist baron. So much for the redistribution of wealth and the equality of workers. Just another group of thieves taking power and subjecting the masses again in the name of the revolution and communism. What a bunch of crap!"

Vasken was clearly taken aback. He had to admit he had heard those rumours before, but had dismissed them as capitalist propaganda. He had refused to believe the stories circulated in the past, even those stories told to him in Yerevan by his guide, Rouben. But now, he was confronted again by the same information, and it seemed to validate everything he had heard. He shook his head and looked at Armen. "Impossible!" he protested weakly. "I can't understand how that could exist under Marxism. How could it happen?"

Armen looked at Vasken and saw the disillusionment in his eyes. "How could it happen? Very easy, my friend," he said gently. First they control the parliament without opposition, the bureaucracy, and most importantly, the guns and the army. They even control all facets of information, like newspapers, TV and radio, all communication, so the people never know what's happening nor the source of frustration in their daily lives. The corruption and deceit is worse than in the days of the Czar. You have to understand that whenever you create a government bureaucracy, you have to insure that what you have created does not become tyranical through laws, rules, regulations or mandates of any kind. Look at your country . . . the Founding Fathers of your nation originally created a government of checks and balances for the purpose of insuring freedom for the people. They saw how people had been subjugated, and wanted to make sure it did not happen in America. They even established a Bill of Rights to guarantee individual freedom. They gave the people the right to bear arms, and made it the second ammendment, not the eighth or ninth, but the second right after the first, the freedom of speech. Why do you think they did that? There was a purpose to it. To bear arms against a tyrannical bureaucracy in the future, if need be. But look what's happening there." Armen shrugged his shoulders in a deprecatory gesture. "Under Roosevelt your Supreme Court was packed with justices stating the 'Constitution and the Bill of Rights is what we say it is.' Unelected bureaucrats making rules and regulations and mandates to impose their rules on the people. I see your country and I see your whole nation has drifted from its original concept of one's individual freedom . . . and it's slowly becoming a tyranny . . . no better than here. You have to fight to protect freedom. Never forget that, comrade."

"What makes you such an authority on our history?" Vasken asked accusingly. "Where do you get your facts?"

Armen loosened his seat belt and turned to look directly at Vasken. "First, I read everything I can get my hands on about American history, then I read all the newspapers and magazines that people like yourself bring into the country. Lastly, I have visited your country, many times in the past, have gone into the libraries to learn all aspects of what made your country great. I was most impressed with Thomas Jefferson. I have read a lot of his writings. He warns the people constantly against giving one inch of freedom to the government; he calls it the first step toward tyranny. And from what I observe, my friend, you now have excessive taxes, rules and regulations imposed by unelected bureaucrats, and the people are being enslaved little by little, hardly noticed by the masses. It will soon be no different there than here in the Soviet Union."

"You still haven't answered my question," Vasken queried abruptly. "Are you a TASHNOG?"

Armen slapped his knee and laughed out loud. "You're damn right I am, and I really don't care who knows it or what may happen to me, comrade," he said in a challenging tone, staring straight at Vasken. "Turn me in if you want to, but when we land at Karabagh, there's not a damn thing you can do to me. We are there, and we're the ones helping the people arm themselves; we're also teaching them how to fight, if the Azeri become a threat. Yerevan? Humph! They don't even want to hear of the plight of these people. No, they want to negotiate, while Azeri disposses the people. Thanks to the ARF and other parties joining us, we WILL prevail!"

Vasken's face was pensive as he considered the weight of the man's words. "No, I'll not turn you in, or any other member of your organization, even though we may differ politically. I only wish to help in your efforts for Karabagh and its people. Please believe me in this. I will not do or say anything that may jeopardize your organization's efforts in achieving its goals. Frankly, that is my true reason for coming here . . . to help Karabagh in any way that seems fit. It's good we met this way," he said, extending his hand in friendship.

Armen took his hand and responded to Vasken's firm hard hand-shake, even though he silently wondered whether he was wise to trust this product of American Marxism. "I'm in a position to let you know what's going on, but I'm sure you realize you may be jeopardizing your safety and position by association with the likes of our group. I hope you take that into consideration before doing something you may regret in the future."

"No, no, I wish to help our people in any possible way," Vasken in-sisted emphatically. "From all I've heard since my arrival here, I'm more interested in the survival of our people."

"Good. We're just organizing for the purpose of arming our men to stop the Azeri's from driving our people from their ancestral homes. Guns from the armories, hunting rifles and other materials will be dis-tributed. There are ex-Armenian soldiers of the soviet army who have joined with us, and who will train the men. We will need people like you to funnel guns and ammunition to hold the Azeris back. We're calling ourselves the Karabagh Defence Force. Look, I'm to meet the comman-der of the Force after we land this evening. Do you want to join us? I'm sure you'd be a help in many ways."

"There will be someone there to meet me when we land," Vasken said quickly, "also, I don't think it's a good idea for us to be seen together. Does the KGB know of your activities, or what you are planning?"

Armen thought for a moment. "You're right. We can't be seen to-gether, at least not yet, Not until we're organized, and then, we don't care who knows. There's a communist element in Stepanakert who get their orders from the KGB in Yerevan. They claim all they want is peace, but, so far we haven't had any trouble from them." Armen took a piece of paper from his pocket, wrote an address on it, then handed it to Vasken. "Give this to the apple merchant at the Bazaar. He'll guide you to our meeting place. Take care that note doesn't fall into the wrong hands or there will be Armenian blood spilled for no reason. Take care of it."

Vasken took the note and put it into his pocket, then glanced out of the window to the terrain below. He had never seen anything quite like it before, not even in the High Sierras or rockies of America.

"There it is, Nagorno Karabagh, my family's homeland for cen-turies," said Armen, noting Vasken's interest.

Vasken shook his head. "It's quite a sight. I've seen the rockies at home, but never anything to compare to these mountains. They are so formidable and solemn. How can people live in these mountains? What do they do there? What kind of people would want to live there?" he asked in amazement.

"People like myself," Armen replied, smiling broadly. Tough, hardy people who don't expect too much from the land, only that which helps them survive. It may not be your cities with all the libraries, museums and universities, but there's a pristine purity here, an exhilaration and energy that not too many people would want or be able to endure, but, it's home for most of us who love it. Did you know the true Armenian name of our country is ARTSAKH before Stalin gave it to the Azeris? It will be called that again in the near future."

Vasken glanced again into the valleys below, where streams ran from the mountains and cascaded into rivers. He noted the small towns and villages surrounded by towering mountains, and wondered about their isolation and remoteness.

"What about the young people? Don't they crave the cities and perhaps want to be educated, become acquainted with the arts and sciences and other things civilization has to offer?"

"They do, and they go to Yerevan and get their education in medicine, engineering and other vital areas. But most return to Karabagh, and try to help their people tame these wild mountains with what they've learned. It's in their blood. Hell . . . look at me, I've been educated in Yerevan, schooled in Germany, studied in America. I'm a civil engineer, but, here I am, on my way back to pick up another challenge." He stretched across Vasken's seat to look down at the land below. "No, this is our home, and we know every little hill, bush, mountain and cave here. Let those bastards come with their tanks, and see what good it does them. We'll fight the next hundred years if need be before we give up our ancestral homes to those moslem hordes. They've taken enough of our lands and what we have, we'll keep, no matter what the cost. Every man, woman and child down there is ready to fight to the finish," he said with grim determination.

Vasken looked out of the window of the helicopter to the rough landscape below, and was fascinated by its wild beauty. No wonder armies had been defeated fighting in such terrain, he thought. The Serbs had held three German Panzer Divisions at bay in such mountains during World War II. He agreed heartily with Armen. Let the bastards come and die in these mountains before we lose it.

"By the way, shall I call you friend, or would you prefer I call you comrade?" Armen questioned.

Vasken turned from the window and saw Armen's friendly smile. "Please . . . call me friend from now on, for that is what I am to you, and to the CAUSE. At the moment I'm slightly confused regarding the soviet way of life. There are contradictions in what I believe and what I see in practice. I'd hate to discard everything I've believed all these years, I've sacrificed too much to do that, but I have to admit, I'm disturbed by what they've done in the name of Marxism."

The helicopter began its slow descent, zigging and zagging around the tortuous mountain peaks to the helicopter pad in Stepanakert. It circled a few times to discern which way the wind was blowing, then it slowly hovered and descended, tip toeing to the pad and lurching to an abrupt stop. The blades were still turning slowly, and the engine was idling when Vasken stepped out of the machine behind Armen. They walked from the pad to the makeshift terminal where a group of men and women were waiting.

"Try to make it tonight," Armen whispered, before breaking away from the group of passengers, then heading for an attractive woman with three children.

Vasken changed his bag from his left to his right hand and looked around for his contact. He had been informed that a party member would be there to meet him, and take care of his needs. Shortly he noticed a young man in late twenties who motioned to him to come his way. Vasken nodded and picking up his pace headed in that direction.

"I'm Vasken Casparian. Are you the one sent to meet me?" he inquired briskly.

"Yes," said the young man taking Vasken's bag, "my name is Toros Balian, and I'm to take you directly to headquarters where you'll meet Zaven Torrissian, the communitarian of this area. He put Vasken's bag in the back seat of the car, and motioned Vasken to the front. Walking to the driver's side, he slid behind the wheel then turned the starter key a few times until the engine spit to a start. The car, which was an old model, and well past its prime, lurched forward as Toros hit the gas pedal and drove through the streets of Stepanakert.

"How did you know who you were to meet?" Vasken asked in a preoccupied manner, while studying the houses and stores they passed along the street.

"Oh easy. Your clothing and the way you dress." He laughed. "Clothes here are at a premium. They're made strictly for warmth, and to last forever. We don't have anything like your western clothing here." He laughed again.

Toros stopped eventually before a two-story building, with a sign on the door showing the party seal. Vasken mentally noted the bleakness of the building, as well as those across the street. They seemed uninviting and cold. Not like Yerevan, he thought, where the buildings at least displayed some artistry and attractiveness of design.

"Here we are, comrade, this way," Toros said, motioning with his arm.

Inside, they walked through a dimly-lit lobby and up a flight of stairs. The steps creaked with age and dust, and there was a stagnant smell in the air. Vasken took out his handkerchief to clear his nostrils. "Don't you people ever clean up the place?" he asked in an irritated tone. "The dust is heavy."

"We have people who are supposed to clean and polish, but they do not show up most of the time. You have to understand, they belong to the people's union, so we do not want to offend them," Toros explained.

They reached the landing and turned left toward an office. A matronly lady with brown hair and dark eyes greeted them and guided them into an inner office. "Mr. Torrissian is expecting you," she said quietly.

Zaven Torrissian was a portly man about five ft. six. From his general stance and drooping shoulders, Vasken determined he was part of the general bureaucracy, and had probably never done a day's work in his life. There was no soft benevolence about him, only an aura of power and self interest. Vasken disliked him immediately.

"Welcome, to Stepanakert," he said, taking Vasken's hand firmly. "It's good to meet our comrades from America." He motioned his secretary and Toros from the room, then closed the door. "Why is it you come to such a god-forsaken place as Karabagh? You probably would have been much happier in Yerevan with their superior hotels and accommodations, and also their museums and libraries.

"I'm not here in Karabagh as a tourist, nor do I care for the sights of Yerevan or here," said Vasken in a clipped voice. I've come to see for myself what's being done to alleviate the suffering of our people who are being displaced and driven from their homes. Have you gotten in touch with the Central Committee in Moscow and informed them of the conditions here? Where are the Russian troops to protect our people and prevent all this?"

Zaven's smile was gracious, but his eyes remained unfathomable. "You have to understand, comrade Vasken, the party doesn't want us to create a problem about this situation, and they inform us they're doing all they can to stop the displacements. They have contacted Azerbaijan, but the Azeri's deny that anything is happening. They claim it is nothing but propaganda the Armenians are putting out. You have to understand, comrade, there are many Islamic republics with hundreds of thousands of people that Moscow does not want to offend. To come to our aid would seem as though they were taking sides. Can you imagine what those republics would do if they were united? No, my American comrade, we must move slowly and cautiously. In fact, Moscow wants us to give up Nagorno-Karabagh completely, and evacuate all Armenians to Armenia . . . or live under Azeri rule."

"Give up Nagorno-Karabagh? What do you mean the party wants Armenians to give up Nagorno-Karabagh or live under Azerbaijan Islamic rule?" Vasken shouted angrily. "How would that be possible? History has shown that when our people live under Islamic tyranny, they're usually slaughtered without mercy. No! Never! Karabagh is Armenian, culturally and historically. It's been part of Armenia for centuries, and it should continue as it always was. You of all people should know and understand how we feel."

Zaven shrugged his shoulders indifferently. "But, I'm told what to do and think, comrade."

"But you're the leader here. The people look to you for leadership and guidance in order to survive. Are you going to allow these continued deportations and ethnic cleansings to continue? And what about these so-called "neutral soviet troops who are supposed to be protecting the Armenians? I've heard in Yerevan that Soviet Interior Ministry troops are surrounding Armenian villages, and are now disarming, arresting and brutalizing the people. I hear of no such action taken against Azerbaijani villages." Vasken's anger mounted as he faced Zaven.

"Patience, my American comrade, patience," Zaven said patronizingly, lifting his hand.

Vasken exploded with rage. "Patience be damned. Haven't you heard of the streams of refugees arriving at Leninakan and Spitak? Soon there will be thousands. How the hell do you propose taking care of their needs? How are they to be sheltered and fed? Why aren't you fighting the Central Committee to have them settle these people? What kind of a leader are you anyway, and what the hell are you good for!"

Zaven Torrissian stared incredulously at Vasken. "Who do you think you are, you American upstart, storming into my office and speaking to me this way. You're not talking to an obscure underling, but the Communitarian of Karabagh. Do you understand what power I have in this area? By what right to you speak to me in such a manner. I could have you arrested and shipped off in a matter of minutes where no trace of you would ever be found. And your America be damned! You come to our country where we Armenians have suffered under the yoke of bolshevism for years, and you make comments and demands not knowing or understanding the precarious line we walk trying to survive as a nation. You . . . a Marxist, who has condoned all that has been going on in the Soviet Union. I've had all your background here before you arrived. Now you come and complain about conditions. Where have you been all these years while we were suffering all sorts of indignities? Espousing bolshevik doctrine . . . revolution of the proletariat, trying to overthrow a free society for the good of all. Bah! People like you make me sick. People like you who have never lived under a communist system, and have no idea of its awesome power of subjugation." Zaven took a step toward Vasken and looked fiercely into his eyes. "Listen to me, you son-of-a-bitch bourgeois, and get it straight, I'm the power here, and don't you forget it. I want you to hold your tongue and weigh your words carefully while you are here in our country. Be careful how you speak, especially to me. Your American citizenship means nothing to us. As I said before, you can disappear quite easily . . . just by my word, and believe me, your country will not raise a finger to help you if that happens, it has happened many times before."

Vasken placed his hands on Zaven's chest and gave him a quick, short shove, sending him against his desk. Then, stepping forward, he seized both lapels of Zaven's jacket, and pulled him closer, breathing heavily into his face. "Listen, you son of a dung heap," he said through his teeth, you don't frighten me one bit. "You call me bourgeois," he shoved him hard again. Zaven tried desperately to break Vasken's hold, but was unable to do so. "I and my organization have taken this battle directly to the Turks for years. Do you know how many Turkish officers and diplomats we have killed in this battle for freedom? Do you know how their representatives shake in their boots when they move from country to country, never knowing where or when we will strike? And what have you been doing my little bureaucrat? How many of our people have you sent to the slave camps of Siberia? How many families have you deprived of food and shelter, my fat comrade?" Vasken tightened his grip and continued to shake Zaven. "You seem well-fed to me. I notice coming from Moscow that you bureaucrats get special privileges for your rations of food and clothing. The workers have their ration lines, while you people have the food centers. Equality, what a bunch of rot! You damn people should all be shot for abusing your position. I could be an anarchist very easily, just to get rid of the likes of you! Shit! It's the same in the States!" Vasken pushed Zaven to the side and stalked out of the office. He ran down the stairs, with Toros close on his heels behind him. On the street, he took a breath of fresh air, inhaling deeply. "I need fresh air after talking to that bloated bureaucrat!" he said scathingly. "Take me to the bazaar, Toros, then you can leave."

"There are many bazaars here, comrade, which one do you wish?"

Vasken took out the paper Armen had given him, scanned it, then turned again to Toros. "The one on Haig street."

They drove through the streets, making a number of turns, then finally stopped at an open air bazaar.

"Here you are, comrade, hope it is the one you are looking for."

Vasken got out of the car and looked around cautiously. "How will I be able to have you pick me up this evening?" he inquired.

"Just call headquarters, and we will get someone to pick you up fast. Here's a card with the proper number. Are you sure you will be all right here? You don't want me to stay with you and guide you around?"

"No, I'll be all right," Vasken reassured him. "I speak the language, so if I get lost I'll always be able to get a taxi or transport. No Toros, I'll be fine. If I'm in a bind, I'll call headquarters as you said. Thank you."

Vasken watched until Toros was out of sight, and then made sure no one followed him before asking the nearest person for directions to the apple merchant. The person took him through a maze of merchants, then stopped and pointed. "There is the apple merchant," he said quietly, before turning and leaving without a backward glance.

Vasken walked quickly to the vendor. The man was about six foot one with black curly hair, trimmed close to his head. His ruddy skin was stretched over high cheekbones, and his hands were large and roughened from heavy field work. Vasken approached him and extended his hand. "I'm Vasken Casparian. I was told to come and meet you for directions to the home of Armen Tackvorian. He said it would be enlightening for me."

The vendor smiled amiably, but his eyes scanned Vasken, carefully evaluating him. He took his hand and held it so firmly, Vasken felt suddenly vulnerable, as though he could be struck down without a defense. This was against everything he had ever been taught in the martial arts. "Look, I have a note," Vasken said awkwardly, fumbling in his jacket pocket for the note Armen had given him. When he found it he handed it to the vendor, who read it and recognized Armen's handwriting. Slowly he released his vise-like grip on Vasken's hand. "We have to be careful, the KGB is everywhere," he said quietly.

"Yes, I understand that," said Vasken rubbing his hand to start the circulation again. "Armen told me to be careful."

"How did you get here?"

"I was driven by a guide from communist headquarters."

"Communist headquarters?" The vendor raised an eyebrow. "Are you a communist?"

"Yes, yes I am," Vasken admitted, "but believe me, you have nothing to fear from me. Armen interrogated me quite well. I'm only here to help the cause in any way possible. This is my only mission."

"Well, if Armen gave you that note, it's all right with me," he said, looking about him. "I'm Arshog Hovsanessian." He motioned to a young man to take over. "Take care of the business for awhile, I have to leave with this man on urgent business," he explained. He guided Vasken to a private coffee house nearby, where they sat down at a corner table with their backs to the wall. "It's safe here. Are you hungry?"

"Yes, I haven't had anything to eat since breakfast," Vasken replied.

"How about shish-ke-bab in some pita bread, a little salad, and some good Armenian tea?" Arshog suggested.

"Sounds great to me."

Arshog ordered the food, then sat back and continued to observe Vasken. "You're a foreigner, what country?" he asked pleasantly.

"America."

Arshog nodded his head approvingly. "Good country. You have that Bill of Rights and, . . . what do you call it? The Constitution?"

"Oh yes, we've got that all right, but its been prostituted over the decades by unscrupulous lawyers and power-hungry men," Vasken replied, somewhat cynically. "For the most part, I was a collectivist, a fighter for the proletariat, seeking equal justice for all. To say the least, I was a dedicated bolshevik."

Arshog studied Vasken for awhile, and wondered why Armen had trusted this foreign bolsehevik. It puzzled him and he could not fathom why this stranger, from a great land like America, would choose to become "A bolshevik? How can that be with all the freedoms you have in your country? Both here and in the Soviet Union, we have secret police, KGB and other organizations of terror and intimidation everywhere. How could you? Were you born there?"

"Yes. I am first generation, but as I went through school I saw the injustices of the law and how it was manipulated by clever lawyers and judges, using semantics to mean something other than what was intended. Little by little, I was taught in the school systems there, how the collective ideas as outlined in the Communist Manifesto, and the writings of Fredrick Engles, could free the world of deceit and corruption, ultimately liberating the real workers from their shackles of economic slavery. I dreamed of a worker's paradise, and dedicated my life to it."

"And now . . . here you are in the worker's paradise," Arshog said in a curious, double-edged tone. "Can you imagine it? It's taken seventy years to get to where we are, and look at the freedom we have. Observe the primitive life we have after butchering millions of people in the name of comradeship. Lenin and his dialectic materialism! Bah! We live here in an atmosphere where we trust no one. We are constantly looking over our shoulder wondering who may be informing on us. We are careful to whom we confide our feelings and beliefs, for fear they may be communicated to the authorities. Any mis-statement or indiscretion and you may be charged and sent away. This is all we know and see. We've never seen anything better or different, so how are we to know, my friend, how are we to judge? You in America have had it all. How did they hoodwink you?"

Vasken sighed wearily. "As I said before, I was an idealist who merely wanted justice for our people, and believed the collective system was the way to wipe out hunger and need. Since being in the Soviet Union and Armenia, however, I have seen such an abuse of power, and such mediocre attitudes toward everything, my mind is confused. It seems my whole premise of what I believe and have dedicated my life to, has been a sham, and yet, if I accept that, I must also accept myself as a worthless fool, a rebellious buffoon and master of lies, a betrayer of principles and philosophies dear to my family. I have to believe the Soviet way has something still to offer . . . the Aero space development, the military, something."

"Does that balance the butchering of millions, my friend?"

Vasken did not respond. The waiter arrived with their meal, and Vasken began to eat in silence. Arshog ate heartily, and maintained a lively account of his family life, his wife and two children, the struggle to sell the produce from his collective farm on the black market. "It's the only way we can survive," he explained.

Later, they finished their meal, left the cafè and walked out to the street. "It's a walk to Armen's house, let's get started."

They walked for some distance until they reached a two-story building. Arshog gave three solid knocks and one soft on the second-floor door. It opened slightly, then Arshog and Vasken were welcomed inside. There were others in the room including Armen, who came immediately to Vasken and shook his hand. "I'm so glad you decided to come. This is an important meeting, and we're going to need your help. I'll explain later. In the meantime, let me introduce you to my wife, Tonya, and my son and daughter, Serop and Anahid." Vasken shook their hands, and remembered them as the people who had met Armen at the field that morning. He was introduced to Varoujan Torossian, a tall man of six feet, two, with the body of an athlete. Varoujan Torossian was a handsome man in a strong Spartan way, sinewy and well-knit, he moved with decisiveness and the grace of an eagle. His complexion, tanned beyond its normal dark hue, marked him as a man who had lived outdoors, or fought outdoors under countless suns; His iron-grey hair was straight as an arrow, accenting the powerful flash of jet-black eyes. His mouth was full, but sharply carved, the expression mobile, sensitive or severe. No one could doubt that Varoujan was a leader, a man of compelling authority. Vasken studied him carefully.

"Armen tells me you are from America and want to help us in our struggle. Why?" Varoujan's eyes held Vasken's in a grip of powerful concentration.

Vasken was taken slightly off guard by the question. "Simple," he answered, "I want our people free from the deportations and killings going on here. I may be from America, but I still feel for the people here. I am after all, Armenian."

"You are also a bolshevik and have worked in the underground in America, from what I understand from Armen. Why should we trust you?"

"I've questioned him this afternoon, Varoujan, and feel he can be trusted," Arshog said, stepping forward. Since he's been in the Soviet Union, he's seen the hyprocrisy of the worker's paradise, and has come to his senses."

"I've also questioned him," Armen interjected, "and I'm willing to vouch for him. Anyway, he would be an ideal candidate for what we intend to do."

A young woman in her late thirties stepped forward. Her bright auburn hair was tightly braided into a pony tail, and her steel-grey eyes flickered with determination and purpose. "My name is Shakie Tamarian, and I'm also a member of this group willing to fight and die if necessary." She extended her hand to Vasken. "I'm glad you're with us, and yes, Armen, you are right. This is the perfect man to do the job for us."

"Ah yes, Shakie, our most ardent patriot," said Armen, smiling. "Vasken, let me introduce you, and don't let this woman fool you. She's a hard fighter, who's been right in the forefront of it all. She's Varoujan's second in command. Shakie's husband and son were killed by Azeri hoards when they tried to evacuate them from their ancestral home in Martuni," he explained.

Vasken took her outstretched hand and felt its firm grip. He also noted her trim figure, under the heavy tunic and skirt she wore.

"Look," he began, glancing around the group, can't you forget my past and what I may have done. Being here in Armenia and seeing for myself has shaken my beliefs to the core. At present, all I want to do is to help."

"Good," said Armen, motioning for everyone to sit down. He turned to Vasken. "Conditions are quite bad here in Karabagh, Vasken, and we don't see any change in the future. We believe the Azeri plan to drive us all out of the area and back to Armenia, just as the Turks did in 1915 in Anatola. But this time, we will not leave like sheep or be tricked by their overtures of peace. They talk of peace while undercover they are moving military units and equipment to our borders. We can't depend on the Russian army to protect us. They haven't in the past, so why should they now? We have to do it ourselves, which means we have to arm our people to fight. We need guns and ammunition, along with medical supplies, if we are to fight the Azeri army."

"I understood you had broken into the Russian armories and had already secured guns," Vasken remarked.

"Yes, we managed to get some," Armen replied. "However, they are on the alert now, and what we have is not enough for a sustained war."

"War? You feel there will be a war?" Vasken asked in surprise.

Armen smiled grimly. "Yes, I'm afraid that is what it will come to. There is no other alternative. So, we intend to arm every single person in these mountains for the inevitable battle of survival and retention of our homeland. Armenia does not want to help us. They are trying to get on friendly terms with the Azeri Turks for economic reasons. Karabagh is nothing but an embarrassment to them."

Vasken looked at him in disbelief. "But we are all part of the Soviet Union. We are comrades, all of us. Turkey is part of NATO, the enemy of the Soviet Union. How can this be happening?"

"The Azeri are cousins of the Turks, and there's no difference between them," Varoujan declared bitterly. "Their main concern is to finish the job they started in 1915, the genocide of our people. This is the first step toward that goal. These mountains and plains belong to us, the Armenian people. Our centuries old churches are buried underground to protect them from desecration by the Azeri. No moslem butcher is going to drive us from what belongs to us. We could hold out for years here in the mountains, but we need more guns and equipment for a long siege."

"And that's where you come in, Vasken," Shakie interjected. "You're the perfect person for the job. You're an American bolshevik with a good background in the underground of your country. You're respected for the work you've done in America and you can travel about freely in Armenia without suspicion of any kind."

"Job? What job?" Vasken queried impatiently.

"We want you to make a contact in Leninakan, Armenia, with an officer in the Russian army there. He has the perfect cover and is able to get all the necessary papers to transport the supplies across the border and into Karabagh without problems. He has supplied us with weapons before, for a price of course, and, I'm sure he'll do it again. This time we require large supplies, which will mean a lot of money for him. We need you to contact him and to get as many weapons as you can from him, then have them delivered to us in Shushi. He has been there before."

"A Russian officer taking a bribe?" Vasken commented in a disillusioned tone, once more seeing his ideals of the Soviet people's paradise take another hit.

"Yes, and he has to deliver it to us as soon as possible, before things get worse here," said Shakie. "We'll need the equipment fast. Tell him the money will be deposited in his Swiss account as soon as the equipment arrives there. No money until the goods are delivered safely. We've done business with him before, so it shouldn't be a problem."

"Where's the money coming from?" Vasken asked curiously.

"The money? Oh we have contacts abroad who are helping us, contacts who have helped us before. Don't ask too many questions," Armen said sternly. "You can be of great value to us in supplying what we need now and in future. That is the best way you can help. We have many volunteers to fight, but, we need men of your calibre to do the real work of supplying us with arms."

Vasken did not reply.

"Well will you be our arms negotiator?" Varoujan asked, concentrating his gaze on Vasken.

Vasken smiled slowly, then nodded his head. "Yes, you're absolutely right, I'll do it. Then every shot fired, and every Azeri killed will be through my efforts. Yes, I'll do it," he said confidently.

Armen and the group gave Vaskenthe information on the Russian officer and how to contact him in Leninakan; they assured him this had been done before, and that the money would be dispensed in the same manner. "I have a fair idea where the money for supplies is coming from," Vasken said, shaking hands with Varoujan. "They did a great job fighting the Turks in 1920. Thanks to them there is an Armenia."

Varoujan smiled but remained noncommittal as he took Vasken's hand and held it firmly. "Be careful. We're depending on you. When you meet the officer, ask this question, 'do you believe in revolutions?' It's the password to identify your mission."

"I'll drive you back to your hotel," Armen offered, when the group began to break up, and he walked to the door with Vasken. "Tomorrow, Shakie and I will take you to the frontier. We want to take a look at the build up of Azeri forces."

The car moved swiftly through the streets of Stepanakert, with Armen at the wheel. Vasken was exhilarated by the idea that here at last he would be doing something to really help his people; he would also see the results immediately. He laughed to himself. I've become a munitions procurer. He shook his head, and leaned back against the seat and quietly thought about his new role.

19

During the next few days, Varoujan and Shakie took Vasken to the border of Azerbaijan. Hidden in the dense undergrowth of the area overlooking the frontier, they scanned the build up of military hardware in the neighboring towns of Fzuli, Aghdam and Shahumian. Vasken's heart sank when he saw the vast strength and number of tanks, cannons and personnel carriers the Azeri's had acquired; for the first time he realized the monumental task that lay ahead of him. Compared to the strength of the KDF force in the neighboring towns, he was distressed to see how ill-equipped they were, with nothing but a few ancient shot guns and hunting rifles. There were some rifles taken from the Russian armories, but not enough to go around. They would have to depend on weapons from their slain enemies.

"How are we supposed to succeed? The KDF doesn't stand a chance!" Vasken cried out with frustration.

"Look Vasken, I was a commander in the Russian Army," Varoujan explained, "I've gone to their academy in Moscow and graduated top of my class. I understand strategy, and especially fighting in these mountains. The Azeri will have to come on narrow roads and pass over mountainous terrain we all know well. With those odds we'll be able to stop them temporarily, even with our archaic weapons. They'll suffer losses, and when they do we plan to take their good equipment and use it against them. We'll be buying time until your contact delivers."

"What about those tanks? How in hell are you going to stop them from slaughtering your forces?" Vasken demanded sharply.

"Gasoline bombs, wedging rocks, timber, steel into the sprockets of their tracks, disabling them," Shakie said coolly, her grey eyes unwavering. "On the narrow roads, we will build tank traps, and create

181

boulder slides in the mountains. We'll do everything we need to do to give us time to arm. No," she continued bitterly, "this is not 1915 or 1920 where they slaughtered our unarmed people. This time they are going to find an avenging force to reckon with. We'll also advise our men they have no right to be taken alive or be killed until they have taken at least five Azeris with them. That's the approximate figure they outnumber us. Each one of our men who falls must account for five of them, no quarter given, none taken. They come to plunder peaceful villages and towns? Let them pay the price for their transgressions against us."

"Now you understand why she is second in command of our forces," Varoujan said with a smile. "She's our Joan of Arc to push the bastards out of our homeland, and lead us to victory."

"Are there other women like you ready to fight?" Vasken questioned, awed by her uncompromising spirit of courage and grit.

Shakie shook her head affirmatively. "Yes, many throughout our forces. Women who've lost their homes, husbands, children, parents, families. Oh yes, they're ready to fight alongside the men and do their part, right to the bitter end. This is a battle for survival."

"Now you understand how critical your mission is to the success of our homeland." Varoujan said, "you've seen how desperate our position is, and time is important at this juncture. We'll get you back to Stepanakert as soon as possible. Go to Leninaken then and secure the arms we need. Tell our contact we need a lot of arms this time. Make sure he understands that, Vasken."

"Yes, I understand, but I don't understand why he would do it without receiving at least half of the money up front. What guarantee does he have he'll receive any money at all?" Vasken asked.

"Don't worry, he will deliver," Varoujan reassured, "he knows us and understands how we operate. The money will be in American dollars."

Vasken shook his head and his voice was skeptical. "I've never done business like this, but you seem to know what you're doing, so I'll do my part."

"Good," said Varoujan, as they started back to the car and drove back to Stepanakert.

On the way back, they stopped at Martuni, a town near the Azeri border. It was one of the first towns the Azeri had hit, driving the Armenians out and torching their homes so they could not return. The ragtail army of the KDF had forced them back across the border, but the people who had returned reported to Varoujan and Shakie that they had been driven out, and their homes had been ransacked for valuables. The Armenians were told never to return or they would be slaughtered, even though this was the land of their ancestors; many stubbornly refused to leave.

"Don't lose heart, and don't leave," Varoujan advised, "An army is being formed to protect you, and it should be ready and in the field within weeks. Your army will be known as the Karabagh Defense Force, or the KDF, and everyone will be armed and ready to fight for their homes and properties. No, they will no longer get away with these atrocities against our people," Varoujan vowed. The Azeri will pay dearly for every inch he moves into our country."

"How long will it take before the KDF will move in?" someone asked.

"Well, time is an element and we don't have much of that. The Azeris are bringing up reinforcements along the border, so we have to move fast. At present, the whole KDF force is moving to the frontier with whatever weapons they have. They'll fight for time, and may lose a little ground, but don't be dismayed. Stand your ground, no matter what you may see. We'll be armed rapidly and will return to drive the enemy out. You have my word for that."

Leaving Martuni, Shakie, Varoujan and Vasken drove over the narrow and treacherous mountain roads to Stepanakert. When they arrived at his hotel, Varoujan reminded Vasken again about the gravity of the situation, and reviewed the code phrase once more. "Do you believe in revolutions? The answer should be . . . not all." "Remember, we are depending on you, Vasken." He clasped Vasken's hand firmly.

"Good to have you with us," said Shakie, shaking Vasken's hand before he got out of the car.

After they drove off, Vasken entered his hotel and was greeted by an anxious voice. "Where have you been these days? Everybody's been wondering what happened to you," said Toros, his guide. "I left you at the bazaar and wondered if someone had done you in. Some of us felt we should have an emergency call for you."

"No, I just met a few friends and they gave me a tour of the city, as well as a few of the neighboring towns," Vasken replied in a matter of fact way.

"I hope they didn't take you too far. You know the Azeris may strike anytime and anywhere. I wouldn't want you to be trapped by them."

"No," Vasken said non-committedly, "it was just a little tour. By the way, what is the party doing to help fight these Azeri invasions? What are they doing to protect the people?"

"Well, we have the Russian army to protect us."

"From what I hear in Belgrade, they were helping the Azeris, not protecting our people," Vasken said cynically.

"It's a delicate matter for the party, comrade. Moscow runs the army, and, as you know, they don't want a moslem uprising on their hands," Toros explained.

"So in the meantime, our people suffer atrocities while the party looks the other way. Great!" he said with exasperation, reinforcing his decision to get to Leninaken. "I want you to get me on the first helicopter or plane leaving for Yerevan, Toros. I want to go there and see what I can do to shake the party into helping us here in Karabakh. Can you arrange this?" he asked crisply.

Toros glanced at his watch. "Yes, comrade. I believe there is one leaving in about an hour for Yerevan . . . a mail helicopter. I can make arrangements to have you on that if you wish."

"Good. Make the arrangements while I go to my room and get my things together. Get in touch with Yerevan and make arrangements for the same guide to pick me up at the airport. His name is Rouben. They know who he is."

In his room, Vasken placed the pistol Varoujan had given him in his overnight bag, and remembered his words spoken in confidence when he gave it to him, "take this Vasken, in case you need it. There are some Armenians who do not believe in our fight for freedom and autonomy. They feel we should not be sanctioning such a desperate venture, and would rather negotiate and achieve what we want through diplomacy, which of course is impossible. While they are negotiating, the Azeris will drive our people out of every town, village and hamlet. There simply won't be anything to negotiate." Vasken smiled to himself as he picked up his shaving kit and headed for the bathroom. He was more resolved than ever to succeed in his mission.

He had just finished cleaning up when he heard a tap on the door. "Come in, it's open."

"Everything has been arranged for the flight back to Yerevan," Toros informed him.

"And my guide, Rouben?"

"Yes, he'll be there, comrade."

"Good. Thank you Toros for your help while I've been here. Can I give you anything? Cigarettes, chewing gum?"

"No, comrade, I don't need anything. I was just doing my duty." Vasken walked over to his handbag and searched for cigarettes and chewing gum. Finding a couple of packs, he passed them to Toros. "Here, Toros, if you don't want them, there must be others who do, take them," he insisted.

"Thank you," said Toros, putting the packs in his pocket.

"Let's go," said Vasken closing his bag and picking up his gear.

The waiting car drove them quickly to the airport and to the helicopter pad where the aircraft's rotor blades idled, while crews filled the ship with sacks of mail. There were a few passengers boarding also. The car came to a screeching halt, and Vasken got out and extended his hand to Toros.

"Thanks for everything, Toros. Hope we have the opportunity to meet again."

Settling into the helicopter, he sat in his assigned seat and strapped the belt securely. From the window he waved at Toros one last time as the aircraft turbines blasted, and rotors turned rapidly, lifting the craft, cargo and passengers in a fast vertical climb. Vasken was amazed at the rate of climb, when he saw the tarmac and its people diminish rapidly in size. The pilot wants to get as much altitude as possible before flying over those high elevations, he thought. He remembered reading somewhere that mountains created tremendous downdrafts that could overtake a craft's vertical climb and smash it into the mountain side.

The helicopter leveled and stared flying west toward Armenia and Yerevan. It swept around high mountains and crossed valleys of breathtaking scope. Vasken settled in his seat and let his mind drift over the past few days spent with Varoujan and Shakie. He smiled to himself. They're right, let the bastards come and die by the thousands in these unforgiving mountains. These mountains and plateaus have been a haven for our people since the days of the Persian Empire. It's also ideal for fighting, which the old *"fedayees"* (mountain fighters) did successfully against invaders, years before. Now it's the Azeris' time.

Some time later, Vasken noted the terrain below them was changing radically to a smoother less rocky surface. They were informed they had just crossed the Azerbaijan border, and were in Armenia. Yerevan was just ahead. Since Karabakh was surrounded by Azeri territory, they had to get permission to fly over their territory even though that territory belonged to the Armenians for centuries. However, it was now under the domination of the Azeris.

The aircraft began its slow descent toward Yerevan. Flying over the city now, Vasken observed the buildings and layout of the view below, and tightened his seatbelt for the touchdown. He wondered if the resourceful Rouben would be there to meet him. It was urgent that he get to Leninaken as soon as possible, and he didn't want to be side tracked for any reason whatsoever. Varoujan had convinced him that time was of the essence. The helicopter hovered, and the pilot adjusted the rotors for touchdown. The craft tiptoed down until it touched the tarmac, then the pilot cut the engines and the craft settled on the ground. The rotors were still turning, idling as the passengers and crew came off.

Vasken stepped out of the craft and immediately saw Rouben wave to him. He headed towards Rouben and greeted him. "You got my message, Great."

Rouben greeted Vasken with his usual smile. "Yes, here I am to serve you again," he said, gesturing to the car. He opened the door for Vasken and put his bags in the rear. He got behind the wheel then and headed toward the hotel.

"I saved your room when you left. I knew you'd be needing it again. We heard of your encounter with the Party leader in Stepanakert. He called and gave us a rundown on what happened. I'm to take you to headquarters as soon as possible. The Commusarit wants to talk to you."

Vasken felt an upsurge of irritation. "Look Rouben, I can't waste time with them just yet. Make excuses for me, but one way or another get me to Leninakan. I have to get there in a hurry. Can you arrange it? I need time before I get involved here, but keep this between you and me, understand?"

Rouben studied Vasken for a moment before giving his usual answer, "no problem. I can arrange it with no questions asked. Coming from Karabakh it must have something to do with the problem there," he added soberly. "Something about helping the people. Well you can count on me. I want to do all I can to help those people."

"Yes," Vasken agreed, "It is to help the people, and I appreciate your help and cover for me until I get back."

"Look," Rouben said, "if fighting breaks out there I'm going to help. I'm joining up and will go there. That's how I feel about it, even though the party has other thoughts on the subject. I'll do anything I can to help now, or in the future."

"Good, Rouben. They need you now. I knew I could count on you. Behind that smile and carefree attitude of yours is a man of deep conviction and honor. I can't give you any information, so don't ask questions. Just do as I ask. As I said, it is to help the people of Karabakh, so just cover my tail until I do what has to be done and return from Leninakan. Then I don't give a damn what the commusarit or anyone else has to say or do to me. Understand?"

"Yes. I'll make some excuse for you, and make the arrangements for you to leave as soon as possible. That might be sooner than you think."

"That's O.K. with me, Rouben. I'd leave right now if you could make the arrangements so fast. Just get me on anything that's moving."

They pulled up in front of the hotel. "You have the same room as before." said Rouben, turning to wink at Vasken. "As I said, I knew you'd need it again. I'll get back to you as soon as I get the arrangements made for your trip."

"Good. I'll go to my room, clean up and get some rest until you return."

The clerk recognized Vasken when he entered the hotel, and he passed him the key to his room. Vasken placed his handbag on the bed as he entered, then went into the bathroom and turned the hot water faucet in the tub. When it reached the level he wanted, he stripped off his clothing and stepped into the soft, relaxing water. He felt the stress and strain of the last few days receding somewhat, but his mind was busy with details and plans. He went over them again in his head, the Russian officer's name, the address in Leninakan, the code word, the urgent need for reinforcements. When he got out of the tub, he dressed and lay down on the bed, closing his eyes. He drifted off. Once again the familiar dream hit him. It was always the same—the battle scene, the mist, the unknown assailant, the bright shining metal; He was jolted awake by a light tap on the door; but as always, he was shaken by the sharp realism of the dream, and the curious shrouding of its recurrence.

"Come in, it's open," he called.

Rouben opened the door and walked in. "It's all arranged for tomorrow morning at eight o'clock. I was able to get you passage on a twin-engine military plane. It was impossible to get you out today, everything was booked. I even got you an old motorcycle if you really had to get out today. It's an old vintage BMW, but it still operates. But, on second thought, that was not a good idea. You'd probably get lost, especially on that dark mountain road to Leninakan. Do you ride motorcycles?"

Vasken smiled slightly. "Oh yes, I used to do quite a bit of riding many years ago, and was very good at it. But, you're right. I can't trust not getting through, and it would be too dangerous on the roads at night. I'll take that morning flight, and will be there approximately at the same time, without the danger."

"Good. One more thing. You'll need a guide there, so I've taken the liberty of notifying a cousin of mine to meet you at the field and guide you to your destination."

Vasken hesitated. He did not want too many people involved in his mission. He had confidence in Rouben, but was wary, and determined his venture would not fail.

"Look, my cousin will not betray you, believe me," said Rouben, noting Vasken's expression of distrust. "We grew up together as kids, fighting Turks and driving them out of our lands. I would never compromise your position. Hell, my cousin wouldn't even join the party even though it meant he couldn't go to school and be an engineer. You must be a party member for that privilege. No, you can trust him. He feels the same way I do about Karabakh, and its suffering people."

If you believe in him so much, Rouben, then it will have to be the same with me. I'll need a guide there, and your cousin will do fine. I know I can trust him. Good."

Rouben handed Vasken the documents he would need to clear him.

Vasken placed them on the bureau, then shook Rouben's hand firmly. "Thank you for all your help, Rouben. Our people will be proud of what you're doing for the cause."

Rouben took Vasken's hand. "My cousin's name is Dikran, and I described you to him. He will meet you at the field and will guide you to your destination. I've informed him to protect you, no matter what until you have completed your mission. He understands and will do everything you ask with discretion. I've also told the commusarit that you were delayed and would not be available for a few days."

"Good. Then you'll be here tomorrow morning to pick me up for the field?"

"No problem. I'll be here early, as they don't wait one minute from their departure time. What are your plans for the evening?"

"I'll just take a walk around the place and retire early. The last few days have been pretty rough, and I do need some rest. I haven't practiced my martial arts for some time. Is there any place in this city I could go?"

"Martial arts?" Rouben asked with curiosity.

"Yes, the ancient art of self defense, Karati.

Rouben smiled. "Oh, I see. No, we have nothing. Only the military has training like that. Have you been doing it for a long time? What is it like?"

Vasken was amused. "Here, punch me with all your strength and I'll demonstrate what one can do with the martial arts."

"No, I don't want to hurt you," said Rouben, backing up and rubbing his hands on his thighs. "It's not right."

"You can't hurt me, here, let's try it in slow motion."

Rouben thrust forward toward Vasken's jaw, and as he did, Vasken grabbed his wrist and twisted it around, using the momentum and weight of Rouben's body, then he seized Rouben's elbow and held him in a strong arm lock, much to Rouben's surprise.

"That's an easy move, but one that comes in handy many times," Vasken explained. "There are many others, that can be done with deadly force, but, the body has to be in tune, like a musical instrument; your mind has to be clear and alert as well."

"That's very good. I'd like to learn that," said Rouben in admiration.

"Sometime, I'll teach you a few simple moves to get you out of a jam. They're basic, but deadly against an unsuspecting opponent. Well, Rouben, I'm going to take a walk and get something to eat later. Want to join me?"

"No," said Rouben, looking at Vasken's warm, sheepskin coat. "I never saw a coat like that before. It sure must keep you warm on cold nights like we have here."

"Yes, it does, Rouben. Look, when I leave for the United States I'll leave the coat for you. How about that?"

"No, no, I couldn't accept such a gift," Rouben protested.

Vasken laughed. "Don't be silly. When I get back I'll get another one, and will be glad you have this one to keep your backside warm. No, it will be yours."

Rouben was speechless, and didn't argue.

"So, it's settled. Now, either join me or I'll be off." Vasken said with a smile.

"Yes, I'll have to leave," said Rouben sheepishly. Until tomorrow for your trip to Leninakan then, I'll be here at seven AM, so be ready."

"I'll be up and ready," said Vasken.

True to his word, Rouben was at the hotel by seven A.M. knocking on the door of Vasken's room.

"Come in, Rouben, I'm ready."

Stepping into the room Rouben was dismayed to see Vasken packing a pistol that Varoujan had given him.

"Do you know there's a heavy sentence for the possession of a firearm in the Soviet Union?" he questioned with concern. "Even in Armenia."

Vasken eyed him stoically. "No, I didn't know, but, it doesn't make any difference if I need to use it fast. I was told there might be people who may try to stop me . . . people who don't believe in the Karabakh struggle. And that, my friend, will not happen as long as I'm alive," he said unflinchingly, stuffing the pistol deep into the handbag.

"Why didn't you ask me to get you a permit? I could have arranged for it very easily, as you know." Rouben argued, nodding his head in a meaningful way. "I simply would have said your life was threatened and you needed a gun for protection. It would have been as simple as that. After all, you are a good party member in high standing."

"Don't worry about it now, there's no time anyway," said Vasken, leading Rouben out of the room. "Let's get to that plane, I don't want to miss the flight."

In the car, Rouben slid in behind the wheel and hit the starter, putting the car in gear. He pushed the excelerator and the car leaped forward. Arriving at the air field, they parked the car quickly, then headed toward a camouflaged twin-engine military plane parked on the tarmac with one of its engines running. As Vasken and Rouben approached the plane, they were stopped by an armed guard who checked their papers, then nodded for Vasken to get aboard the plane.

"I'll let you know when I'll be back, Rouben. Will you meet me?"

"Of course. I'll want to know if your mission was successful. Make sure you ask for me again or leave a message of your arrival at headquarters."

"Good." Vasken turned and saluted Rouben sharply before board-ing the plane. Inside he took the first empty seat and buckled his seat belt. There were only three other people on the flight—two officers of some high rank, and one civilian which Vasken had sized up as KGB.

The plane got its taxi clearance and headed for the active runway. Just before taking off, the pilot checked both engine mags, propellers and controls, making sure that all was in proper order. The co-pilot followed the check list with his manual. The tower cleared them to the active runway, where they took off without delay heading for Leninaken.

The plane climbed to its cleared altitude, then leveled out allowing the passengers to relax in their seats. Vasken loosened his seat belt and took in the landscape below, which he noted was not as rugged as Karabakh. The flight was smooth, without incident, and in very little time Vasken saw the safety belt light come on as the airplane began its descent to the Leninakan airport. Vasken observed the city from the air as the plane banked sharply for the base approach. With its low build-ings and few factories, it reminded him of the many small midwestern cities in the U.S.A. He noted there was one tall building, and a central square with a big clock tower. This is actually Armenia, he mused qui-etly, and there's about one quarter million people living there—all Ar-menians. The plane descended to pattern altitude turning final for the landing. The aircraft glided smoothly in its flairout, and as the pilot pulled the throttles back and held the control steady the wheels gently touched the runway allowing the plane to decelerate. They taxied to the tarmac the tower had assigned and the aircraft swung around, stopped and slowly cut engines. The co-pilot opened the cockpit door and the passengers began to descend.

Vasken unbuckled and pulled down his bag from the upper com-partment, then quickly headed out. The huge Leninakan letters on the side of the Administration building was the first thing he noticed. As he approached the gate, he wondered if Rouben's cousin would be there to meet him. After presenting his papers to the guard at the gate he noticed a slim young man with black hair who eyed him closely. His nervous smile reminded Vasken of Rouben.

"Dikran?" Vasken queried.

"Yes, I am Rouben's cousin. He told me to take good care of you. Come, this way. I have a car to take you where you want to go."

"Did Rouben say anything else?" Vasken inquired pointedly.

"No. He told me not to ask questions, just do as I'm told. He said it had something to do with our people in Karabakh, that's all."

As they got into the car, Vasken showed Dikran the paper with the officer's address which Varoujan had given him.

"I know that part of town," Dikran said with youthful confidence. "It's not far."

Racing through the city, Dikran pointed out some of the sights along the way. They passed the central square which Vasken had seen from the air, and Vasken also noticed several small museums and churches.

They stopped finally outside a two-story building, and Dikran glanced at the paper Vasken had given him. "This is the place."

Vasken opened his bag and pulled out the pistol; he checked it closely, making sure it was ready with a live bullet in the firing chamber, before stuffing it into his waist. Then, he got out of the car and glanced about cautiously, to make certain no one had followed them.

"If anything happens here, Dikran, don't worry about me. Take off fast. Just give me time to get back, and if I don't come back, just go . . . disappear, understand?"

Dikran attempted a response, but Vasken put his hand up. "Just do as I say. Please."

"Yes." Dikran said reluctantly.

Vasken walked to the entrance and checked the list of tenants. Then he climbed the stairs and stopped outside a solid door with a small nameplate. Checking the name, he knocked assertively.

"Yes . . . who is it?" There was an unmistakable ring of authority in the response.

"A friend who would like to talk to you in confidence."

"A friend? Who has friends nowadays?"

"I have a question for you."

"A question?"

"Yes . . . do you believe in revolutions?"

There was silence for a moment, then the door opened slightly. "Not all." The door opened wider and a heavy-set man in his late forties scrutinized Vasken intently as he motioned him to enter. About five foot ten, he had a strong stocky build; his sand-colored hair was combed straight back and the expression in his blue-grey eyes was a mixture of wariness and distrust.

Vasken gazed about the room and noticed the officer's tunic lying carelessly across a chair. He seemed to be the process of having tea. Vasken also observed his service pistol on the table. It was still in its holster, but the flap was open and Vasken saw it was cocked and ready for action. The unwelcome thought flashed through Vasken's mind that this might be a trap planned by the KBG or the military; He touched the pistol under his sheepskin.

"Well . . . what have we here? I know you to be a foreigner, but how did you know the password?" said the officer looking sharply at Vasken. He moved closer to the pistol on the table and placed his hand near it.

"I'm sent from Karabakh with a message of importance for you."

"By whom?"

"Varoujan Torossian."

The officer raised one eyebrow. "Varoujan? Good. We have done business before." He stepped back from the table, and Vasken felt an easing of the tension.

"I am Colonel Sergei Ivanavich, commander of the forces in Leninakan, at your service." He clicked his heels and saluted smartly. "And who are you, may I inquire?"

"Vasken Casparian. I am here because I was informed you could help us. I'm sure you are aware of what is happening to the people of Karabakh. The moslem Azeri are massing equipment along the border for what Varoujan and I believe to be a massive invasion of that area, and the disposition of the Armenians. We need arms to fight back. The Armenians there will need arms to defend themselves. Will you help us?" he questioned coldly.

The colonel nodded his head. "Yes, I know what's happening there. I have been briefed about it, and find out that the Turk, as usual, is at it again. I am dead set against this ethnic cleansing they are initiating." He threw his hand into the air. "Stalin did that stupid thing in 1923. He gave all that land that is really part of Armenia to the Azerbaijani; and now they've subjugated all of the Christian people there. You know, he did this out of frustration and spite to you Armenians because you stubbornly refused to forsake your heritage for that of the soviet union. He shook his hand again to stop Vasken's protest. I know . . . it was wrong, and now we have this situation. I agree, these Turks have been killing for centuries, and I wish they'd come out of the dark ages. But, that's another subject. What does Varoujan want? Arms I'm sure. I'll help in any manner I can . . . for a price."

"They're willing to pay, don't worry. They need guns, ammunition, grenades, anything you are able to secure for them."

The colonel understood Vasken's mood and observed him closely.

"Where are you from?" he asked crisply.

"The United States."

"America," the colonel nodded. "Humm! You don't know what's happening under our great leader Gorbachev with his Glastnost and Perestroika. The republics are rebelling and demanding freedom. Not too far in the future the soviet union will collapse. I can see it coming if he continues his present course. Do you understand what that means? The whole soviet union will come apart at the seams, and this leader is not doing a thing to hold it together. For what? All for western money and technology to buy time. Believe me, I am not going to be around when these republics release all the pent-up passions that have been smoldering for centuries. I'm getting out of the army and this country before it collapses. I've moved my family to Switzerland and when I have enough money, I'll follow them there and never return to this god-forsaken country."

"Yes, Switzerland. That's what Varoujan told me to tell you. Just as before, the money, American dollars for the equipment will be deposited into your bank account there."

"Sit down for a minute," the colonel answered. "The Azeris have tanks which you will have to destroy if they are to be stopped. We have a new anti tank gun that will rip those tanks into small pieces as though they were tin cans. I'll send a number of them. They also have aircraft that the Turks have given them, and they have trained pilots. That means the Azeris will be able to straf and bomb the towns and villages. You will need portable ground-to-air missiles to shoot them down as well. But," the colonel rubbed his chin, "this will cost big dollars. You know, I hope this will be my last business deal. I'll have enough then to leave this dreary country once and for all."

"Look," said Vasken, "get as much as you can and deliver it one way or another to the village of Shushi in Karabakh. Once delivery is made, word will go out immediately to deposit the money, American dollars into your numbered account. As I said before . . . delivery to Shushi in Karabakh, no other place, understood?"

"Understood. I know where Shushi is. I'll make out papers for transfer of the equipment to Karabakh and take it there. There will be no question once I get the necessary papers of transfer, and will easily get through Azerbaijani lines into Karabakh. We are the Russian army just moving equipment up to a potentially dangerous area, so don't worry. I know how to do it. Inform Varoujan he will get the latest the Russian army has to offer, and tell him, good luck in the fight."

The colonel walked over to a closet and took out a bottle of vodka and two glasses. "Now, we'll have a drink," he said with a laugh. He set the glasses on the table and slipped into his military tunic and buttoned it. He took the pistol and belt off the table. "Oh incidentally comrade, I saw that bulge under your jacket. Did you plan to shoot it out like in your country's western movies? His laugh had a slight mocking edge. And do you have a permit to carry that weapon?" He laughed again, knowing the answer beforehand.

He filled the glasses with vodka and passed on to Vasken. "Let's drink to my getting out of here and the soviet union. Good hunting for your comrades in Karabakh."

They drank the vodka quickly and Vasken felt the burning liquid in his throat and stomach. He felt alert and quickened.

"Another," the colonel shouted. But before he could pour the second drink, a sharp cracking sound shattered the air; the whole room and building shifted to the left, then right, throwing both men from one wall to the other like rag dolls.

"What the hell's going on," Vasken shouted, getting up off the floor, as a section of ceiling fell on top of them knocking them both off their feet again.

Earthquake! It's a damn earthquake!" the colonel shouted loudly. "Let's get out of here and to the street before the whole building comes down on us."

Rushing toward the stairs, Vasken heard a hissing sound and then, once more, a loud thundering crack, like the sonic boom of a plane breaking the sound barrier. The stairs gave a lurch to the right, then to the left, throwing and tumbling both men halfway down the steps. Vasken had an eerie feeling of doom as the whole building shook again; he reached down to pull the colonel up to his feet, then rushed down the rest of the stairs and out to the street. Outside, the ground seemed to shift violently, sending them to their knees. They braced themselves for balance. Raising his head, Vasken saw the buildings across the street sway in horrible rhythm, while the outer side of the structures gave way, exposing people and furniture inside. Again the ground shifted, knocking Vasken and the colonel off balance and on to their knees. A young woman on the second floor of an apartment screamed in piercing terror as the rest of the building collapsed around her in a rubble of dust and debris.

Panic hit the streets. People ran out of their houses as once again the ground shook leveling many of the structures and buildings that crumbled like a house of cards. Above the confusion, fear gripped everyone and settled on the town like a mantle of doom.

Vasken looked about him in disbelief. "Damn . . . damn . . . shit" . . . he gasped, as the panorama of destruction registered within him. He wiped the dust from his face and turned toward the colonel. "Are you alright?"

"Look comrade, I have to get to headquarters and see what can be done here," he answered soberly. "This is devastating. I'll get all my men to help in whatever manner they can.

"What about the arms?" Vasken queried.

"Don't worry my zealot friend, the arms will be at Shushi in less than a week. This earthquake will be a good cover to move the equipment without suspicion. Tell them to hurry with the payment, as I want to get out of the soviet union fast and on to Switzerland after the transfer." The colonel took off without delay.

What's happened to Dikran, Vasken wondered, and squinted his eyes to scan through the dust-filled, hazy atmosphere. He made his way to the spot where he had left him parked; he saw the car was covered with wood, glass and mortar. With desperate movements he dug through the rubble with his bare hands, until he found Dikran's body slumped over the wheel. Vasken pulled him out gently and lay him on the street, then felt his pulse. Vasken was relieved to see he was still alive. Dikran coughed suddenly, then raised his arm slowly to wipe dust from his eyes. Vasken felt for broken bones. "Don't worry, I'm OK. Just shook up a bit," Dikran said somewhat unsteadily.

Under the collapse of tons of material about them, they could hear the cries and groans of people caught beneath.

"Let's see if we can help some of these people," Vasken ordered, looking around and surveying the catastrophe. With their bare hands they lifted mortar, pieces of wood and timber trying desperately to reach the voices of victims pinned beneath. Their hands were cut and bleeding, but they struggled on relentlessly, as though driven by some force, potent and overwhelming as the quake itself. The nightmare continued. Vasken tripped, fell on his knees and ripped his clothes.

Finally, after hours of frustration, pain and grief, he collapsed, exhausted and drained, realizing his desperate efforts were all in vain. He lay there pounding on the ungiving mortar, "Damn damn damn," he repeated over and over. He twisted and turned on his back, staring absently through the heavy mortar dust to the sky, wiping his face with a grimy handkerchief. Confusion was everywhere, and somehow he and Dikran became separated. Hysteria replaced shock and terror, as buildings continued to collapse and women screamed and tore at piles of concrete, trying to save their children and pull them out from what had once been a school. Vasken moved in a trance-like state. Nothing seemed real to him. He stared with fascinated horror as broken electrical cables sparkled and cracked in a dance of death, striving to attach themselves to anything that moved. He watched as an exposed cable touched a man trying to get out of its way. The man shook violently before he collapsed in a heap, sparks playing their deadly game and burning him till he ceased to move. An after-shock jolted them. Vasken quickly pulled a woman and her baby to the ground as a huge explosion erupted nearby and flames shot up to the sky. A gas main, Vasken thought, "what else, what else" he screamed aloud, shaking his fist in the air. As though responding, an underwater main pipe burst, cascading tons of water high into the air.

Vasken rubbed his eyes, now irritated and burned from concrete dust, and put his handkerchief around his face to keep the dust from his nose and lungs. He helped a woman and child to a safer place, then continued to help other people digging with boards and timber pieces, trying to reach helpless victims, relatives and friends.

"Hurry" a man shouted from a group working to extricate a young girl covered with dust, frantically crying *"Myrig, myrig"* (mother). Slowly they pulled her free, and stretched her flat on the ground. Vasken felt gently for broken bones, while the child looked at him with undisguised fear. He was relieved to see she had no broken bones, only outside cuts and bruises, and was badly shaken.

He continued to help the group working with their bare hands, working feverishly against time to free victims trapped beneath.

"Where the hell's the heavy equipment?" Vasken lashed out impatiently. "We can't go on digging like this with our bare hands. Where do they keep the bulldozers, cranes and other heavy equipment? Damn it! Where the hell's the army? What happened to that damn colonel and the bloody army?"

There was a sudden rumble and a whole section of wall collapsed on top of them, burying them under heavy debris and dust. Though Vasken lay half buried under the crumbled wall, and was only barely conscious, he wondered why the buildings came down so easily. Who the hell designed these buildings he thought vaguely—this whole area is quake prone. The architects and engineers should be shot for incompetence.

There was a rush of activity around him, and Vasken felt himself being dragged free to a clearing. "I'm O.K.," he gasped, slowly opening his eyes. "Don't waste your time on me, go to the others who need your help." He raised himself on one elbow and grabbed a man's leg. "Where's the heavy equipment? Where's the army?" he asked weakly.

"There isn't any, we've never had any of that sort of equipment. The builders who came here, build, then leave and take the equipment with them. But, we've managed to get the message to Moscow before the lines went dead, and they've promised to send help immediately. Help should be flown in very soon my friend. You're alright, just the wind knocked out of you. Take it easy for awhile."

Vasken was given a hand, as he got up on one knee, then shakily stood up on both feet. "I'm OK, no broken bones," he said weakly. Glancing about, he was horrified to see the city of Leninakan totally leveled. Nothing was left standing. As he surveyed the scene, he wondered how many people were trapped and dead beneath the grisly piles of rubble and confusion. How many were still alive, and how could they be reached without heavy equipment. Rage and bitter fury welled up within him, subsiding gradually into a sense of desolate helplessness. The lightless day deepened, then, night descended, bringing darkness and unbearable quiet. For the first time in his life, Vasken Casparian sensed emptiness and despair. He was not in control, and the unfamiliar realization overwhelmed and dazed him. He remained still for a long time, before clenching his jaw with a renewed sense of purpose. Leninakan and its people will rise again, he vowed silently. They will, and I'll defy the elements or anyone else who tries to prevent it.

20

$\mathbf{B}$ack in Washington, Everett Mason, Senator Bagdasarian's assistant, keyed the hold button on the telephone, and walked toward the closed door of Lance's private office. He knocked twice before entering.

"Sorry to disturb you, Senator, but Congressman Sohigian is on line one, and he indicated the call was urgent.

Lance looked up from the speech he was dictating, then picked up the telephone. "Ted . . . what's up?"

"Obviously you haven't heard the news, Lance. The word just came in from the State Department, and I've confirmed it with the C.I.A. There's been a devastating earthquake in Armenia, and as of last report, thousands have been killed."

The news hit Lance directly in the solar plexus, and for a moment he was speechless. "Thousands dead in an earthquake? My God, Ted, No!" he gasped. "How much more can our people take. What's being done?"

"The only information I have here, is that Gorbachev has cancelled the rest of his trip and is returning to Moscow immediately. They were supposed to see New York, but according to Soviet Foreign Minister, Shevardnadze they'll fly directly to Moscow, and then on to Yerevan to survey the quake; from there they can determine what needs to be done and what Russia can do to help. As far as what's being done from this end, I just heard the Pentagon is getting aircraft ready to fly out equipment and supplies to dig out the people trapped under debris. From what I understand, they don't have any heavy-duty equipment there at all, and people are using their bare hands. They're sending dogs over, too. Remember how they used them in that big quake in Mexico? Dogs are excellent for locating trapped victims. That's about all I know right now, Lance."

"How many do they estimate are lost, Ted?"

There was silence. "The reports coming in figure about seventy thousand people . . . men, women, children. It's a mess, Lance, a goddamn mess," Ted replied, heavily.

"Well it's certainly a disaster of huge magnitude. It will be difficult for our people to bear," Lance said soberly. "I don't know how they will ever bear it, or recover. What about Yerevan, is that city still standing or is it levelled?"

"No, Yerevan is not too bad compared to Leninakan, Spitak, and Aghourian. From what I hear those towns were levelled. The houses and buildings were never built to sustain quakes like that, for God's sake, and those damn engineers who built them knew it. There's a fault running under the area, but they went ahead anyway, using cheap materials with no concern whatsoever for the quality of the work, or the safety of the people. The result is, these areas have taken the brunt; the heaviest loss of life is there. I heard the schools collapsed with the first shock, and many of the children were trapped and killed under the debris. The worst of it is they don't have any heavy equipment, bulldozers, or cranes, for Christ sake! Time is crucial, and from what I understand about the Russians, they're damn slow when it comes to rescue efforts. So, it's up to us to get the needed materials over to them as soon as possible, before the victims die of dehydration or suffocation."

"Look, Ted, let's see if you and I can get over there as observers on a fact finding mission aboard the relief planes. That way we could let Washington know what needs are critical. I'll speak to the Senate Democratic Majority leader here to get his approval, you check with yours. Let's see if we can't get on the first cargo planes leaving here."

"Great idea. We speak the language, and we'll be in a better position to quickly communicate the needs to Washington. We'll have to get on it right away. Bring something warm to wear. It will be cold there. Why don't we get together this evening and see what needs to be done . . . come for dinner. Tatiana will want to know what's happening too."

"Yes, okay, Ted. Karamine will want to make a trip over there again, I'm sure of that," said Lance, thinking aloud.

"She'll be needed, Lance, believe me, so don't make it hard on her."

"She just got back a few months ago, God, I hardly ever see her anymore, Ted, and I miss her," said Lance. His tone was slightly edgy.

"Look, Lance, this is a major catastrophe, and every one of us will be required to do whatever is necessary. We here in Washington to expedite equipment and supplies over there, Karamine in the hospital medical end. That's the way it's going to be, Lance. Miss her but don't try to stop her by giving her a guilt trip. She's a great lady, and she's really needed there now. She could save thousands of lives."

Lance sighed. "I know, Ted, I know, but, it's just that we've been apart so much since I've been in Washington. I wonder sometimes if it's really worth all the sacrifice."

"Hey! You feeling sorry for yourself? Think of how much you've done for the taxpayers of this country by fighting for what you believe in. But, I don't have to remind you of these things. Right now, let's just think of our people, and how we can help get them through this crises."

"You're right, Ted. I was feeling sorry for myself. I will throw myself into this foray and do my best for them."

"O.K. then . . . tonight at six thirty at my house, right?"

"Right. See you then."

Lance had just placed the receiver down when his telephone rang again. He picked it up and heard a familiar voice.

"Lance? Karamine . . . "

Lance laughed softly. "No kidding. Don't you think I know your voice by now?"

"Hmm . . . perhaps not. We are apart so much. But anyway, I just wanted to know what kind of information you have about the earthquake in Armenia. The Committee just got a call from Moscow, and I wanted to verify it."

"Unfortunately it's true, Karamine. I just got off the phone with Ted, and he filled me in." He hesitated before continuing. "It's bad, Karamine . . . devastating. The reports say there's about seventy thousand victims, men, women, children."

Karamine gasped. "NO! Oh God, no! Moscow didn't give us the details. We only heard there was an earthquake!"

"Well, we just got the information from the State Department and the C.I.A. It doesn't look too well for our people, Karamine. School buildings with the children in them collapsed like houses of cards. I understand they never built the structures to sustain earthquakes, even though they knew there were quake faults all over Armenia. The worst of it is they don't have the basic heavy-duty equipment to rescue victims from under the debris. The people are using their bare hands and a few shovels to do the work of cranes and bulldozers."

Karamine sank to her chair, as blood drained from her head making her a little weak. She put her hand to her head as though to block out the gruesome reality of the news. "Vasken is in Armenia. I hope he's all right," she said softly.

"Don't worry about your brother, Karamine, the devil takes care of his own."

"What's being done in Washington, Lance?"

"The Pentagon is getting military planes ready now, to send over equipment, medical supplies and dogs. Ted and I are making arrangements to go with them on a fact-finding mission to assess the damage and see what other needs they may have. We speak the language, so we shouldn't have any problems to get the assignment from the house and senate majority leaders. We should be on the first cargo plane that leaves from here."

"And that's the one I'll be on," Karamine stated firmly.

"No, Karamine, you can't. These are military planes, made for troops and heavy cargo. They don't have the basic comforts of an airliner. They're not made for passengers. Ted and I may be sitting on crates, for all we know. I know you're upset and want to help, but it would be foolish for you to leave with us. Anyway . . . you just got back a few months ago, and now you want to go again?"

"This is entirely different, Lance. I'll be needed there and you know it, so don't try to stop me. I'll be on that plane with you when it's ready to leave and I won't listen to another word about comfort, cargo or what have you. I'm going on the FIRST PLANE, so make the arrangements. Make sure they have lots of antibiotics, splints and the medical supplies needed for broken bones and head injuries," she said adamantly.

Lance shook his head. "It doesn't matter to you what I say or think, does it Karamine? My words just bounce off you. Don't you realize my concern is for your safety and comfort? We seem to be on two separate paths lately. I don't know what else to think."

"Lance, please! Our people need us now, and there's no sacrifice too big or small that we shouldn't make to help get them through this devastation. For once, let's not think of ourselves; let's just put all our efforts into help and assistance. As soon as I hang up, I'll get someone to take over my practice again, my old friend, like last time. Then, I'm going home, throw some things together and come to Washington immediately. Make sure you take some warm clothing, Lance. It gets mighty cold there this time of year, especially at night. I'll call again, soon as I know the flight number."

Lance hung up and leaned back in his chair. He was upset by Karamine's unflinching determination to overrule his wishes. Just like that, he thought, it's decided. Ever since I've been in Washington our time together gets shorter and shorter, then, when we do get together lately, we seem to argue about her work, her trips out of the country and the hundreds of reasons why she has to go. I know she'll be needed, I know lives will be saved because of her efforts, but, damn, it still creates an emptiness in me when I don't get to see her for months on end. This time it will be more difficult than ever to get in touch with her; all the lines are down in Armenia. He sighed disconsolately. I better start making those arrangements for the trip. He reached for the telephone and dialed the office of the Republican minority leader to make plans for leaving. He also checked to make certain no important legislation would be voted on in his absence, and that his committee would be notified of his trip.

21

Vasken Casparian scanned the sky impatiently. Behind the plate glass windows surrounding the tower at Zvartnots Airport, he watched and waited for the first flight of supplies from America. It was lucky that Moscow had cleared the plane directly to Yerevan, instead of having it make the usual first stop over in Moscow, he thought. He was listening attentively now, hearing the communication from the C-141 Lockheed Starlifter cargo plane. The Pentagon had originally planned to use the larger C-5 Galaxy with its jumbo size payload, but decided to use the C-141 due to the short length of the runways in Armenia.

Vasken decided to sit down until he heard the communications tower clear the aircraft for its approach. The last few days in Leninakan had been traumatic; he was lucky to be alive, he mused, especially after being trapped under a collapsed wall. Others had not been so fortunate. His mission there had been successful, however, despite the earthquake. He had gotten Varoujan's message of much needed arms for Karabakh to the Russian Colonel, and had remained in the stricken city for two days helping where he could. When he heard of the supplies for earthquake victims arriving from America however, he had decided he would be of more use back in Yerevan. He had even called headquarters there to have Rouben meet him at the airport. The headquarters personnel were surprised to learn that Vasken had been in Leninakan, and questioned him at length on his reasons for going there. "It's a great city, I just want to sightsee; I didn't feel the need to check with you," he'd answered glibly. When Rouben met him at the airport, however, he was accompanied by Sylvana Markovian, the Commusariat of the Department of Stores and Distribution. She had been ordered to meet him on his return to Yerevan aboard the Aeroflot helicopter from Leninakan.

She had also heard rumors of his outburst with the Karabakh Central Committee leader, but was unaware of the facts; she wanted him to know the party was displeased. Vasken was then informed that since he had been in the center of the quake, where thousands were killed, he may have sustained some injuries as well, so, to make certain he was in good physical condition before doing anything else, Rouben had been ordered to take him to a hospital first for a check up.

In the hospital he was examined thoroughly for broken bones and ribs, but found to be in excellent form. The doctor remarked on Vasken's solid physical shape, especially after his harrowing experience of being caught under a collapsed building. Vasken shrugged it off indifferently, however, replying that "he'd always stayed active."

After the hospital visit, he was taken immediately to the Central Committee Headquarters, where he was reprimanded by the party head for his outburst with Zaven Torrissian. The Communitarian of Karabakh had called reporting Vasken's insolence. "Control your temper while you're here, comrade, we need your help but please don't antagonize the party members," the party head had warned. "You will work with Sylvana to coordinate the shipment of supplies, and also make certain none of the materials end up on the black market. We need to get all the supplies to the disaster areas as soon as possible. Understood?"

"Understood." Vasken replied.

"There's also a Fact Finding Committee aboard from the American Congress to assess the quake. Since you speak English, comrade, you are assigned to meet with the committee, and expedite whatever they want to know or do in getting all the information concerning the devastation here. Please be polite and courteous to them at all times. We need all the help we can get from America and the rest of the world . . . and take care of their needs," the party head had ordered, turning to Sylvana.

One day later, Vasken had gone out to the airfield in Yerevan for the arrival of Mikhail Gorbachev. He recalled the scene with a tinge of cynicism—"Where's the army to help us" the supplies? the heavy equipment? Question after question had been hurled at the communist leader from the crowd of people, pressing in to welcome but also to challenge him.

"What about the deportations and bitter conflict in Karabakh?" Gorbachev's answers were not reassuring, and his reaction to the Armenian questions Vasken sensed, seemed hostile and impatient. He denied the Russian army was helping the Azeris but his remarks fell on deaf ears, which also angered him.

Vasken got up from his seat and walked once more to the window to scan the sky. The American C-141 cargo plane was turning on final for its landing. Sylvana Markovyan joined him. Vasken had dined with her the previous evening, and had enjoyed it. He liked her stride of confidence, her short-clipped auburn hair and dove-grey eyes, her lack of intimidation in the company of powerful men, with whom she made no secret of enjoying. Outspoken and direct, she wasted no time in conveying the message to Vasken that he appealed to her, both intellectually and physically. Vasken smiled to himself remembering the way she had rubbed her knees sensuously against his during dinner. I'll have to pursue that further he'd thought at the time.

He watched the cargo plane flare out for its touchdown, then the screech of tires and billows of smoke rising from the friction of the runway as it touched down. Vasken watched it mechanically but was jolted by a sudden thought. What if my brother-in-law is on that plane—no, not a chance, he argued with himself—still, they did mention a few American politicians were coming along on a fact-finding mission. Damn, it would be just my luck to run into that bastard now! The controller in the tower motioned to Sylvana. "The names of the people aboard the American cargo plane," he said, handing her a list, when she approached him. "A crew of five, several dogs and their trainers, Representative Ted Sohigian, Senator Lance Bagdasarian, Dr. Karamine Bagdasarian."

Sylvana raised an eyebrow, "Dogs and trainers?"

She walked back to Vasken and passed him the list of passengers and crew. "There are some important people on this list who will need accommodations immediately," she said curtly.

Vasken took the list and quickly scanned it. "I knew it, KNEW it, I just felt it in my bones that he'd be on that first plane, and I was damn right," he remarked heatedly, "Just wait till he sees who'll be here to welcome him." He laughed spitefully.

"Who? Why are you laughing? What's going on?" Sylvana asked impatiently.

"The list. The list of passengers. Dr. Bagdasarian is my sister, Senator Bagdasarian is her husband and my illustrious brother-in-law! We're not exactly the best of buddies. I detest the bastard if you really want to know."

"Dr. Bagdasarian is your sister?" Sylvana questioned in surprise. "Your sister is a doctor?"

"That guy has the damndest luck. Talk about a Nemesis!" Vasken said, ignoring her question.

"Look, Vasken, I'd better call the Central Committee and make some arrangements to have them put up in a good hotel. The Yerevan Hotel would be ideal. We didn't expect persons of this calibre to be on a cargo plane, plus the others with dogs. I'd better do it right away. The Committee wants to take good care of them while they stay here in the city." She headed toward the nearest telephone and dialed.

The plane continued its roll out, reversing its turbine engines, and blasting hard until the plane shook and slowed down. The tower cleared them to taxi then guided them toward the assigned tarmac where men and trucks were waiting to unload the cargo.

"Are all the trucks and personal carriers ready to go? I want them on their way to the disaster areas immediately. Lives are depending on our speed," Vasken barked sternly.

"Yes. I've already instructed the committee to go straight to the hotel to greet them there, rather than coming here as originally planned. I realized we would have a lot of work unloading cargo, and they would only be in the way."

"Good. It's better that way. Let them handle the protocol there, and leave the men to do their work here, without interruption. In the meantime, Sylvana, see that the trucks and fork lifts are ready for unloading. I want to surprise my sister and her husband. I doubt very much they expect to see me here to greet them. Meet me by the plane when you get things moving, and I'll introduce you."

Moving toward the cargo plane, Vasken and Sylvana realized for the first time how huge the aircraft was. Slowly the cargo doors were raised to an open position, and a ramp was lowered to the ground. They heard barking dogs, happily released from the confinement of kennels; they watched as dogs and trainers made their way down the ramps first, followed by a small group of people. Vasken recognized Karamine among them, and called her name.

Karamine stared incredulously when she saw Vasken. Then her expression changed to relief and excitement.

"Vasken! I don't believe it! What are you doing here? We knew you were in Armenia, but I am surprised to see you here. What about the earthquake? Are things as bad as we heard?" Karamine embraced her brother enthusiastically. "Why haven't we heard from you, Vasken? Mom and Dad have been so worried . . . so have I."

"Well, the towns of Leninakan and Spitak and a few others have been hit pretty hard, Karamine, but I'll talk about that later. In the meantime, let me introduce you to Sylvana Markovyan. She'll attend to the unloading and distribution of the cargo, and also to your needs of transportation and lodgings. That's her job here . . . to see that nothing ends up on the black market. I'm helping with that also." Vasken stopped abruptly when he saw Lance and Ted Sohigian approaching them. He glared at Lance coldly.

Karamine shook Sylvana's hand warmly and smiled, then turned to present Lance and Ted.

"I'd like you to meet my husband, Senator Lance Bagdasarian, and Representative Ted Sohigian, Sylvana. As you may be aware, they're here on a fact-finding mission to assess the immediate needs required to get the people through this crisis. Right now, we have water tanks, blankets, sixty-four thousand pounds of food, heavy equipment, and medical supplies aboard the aircraft. Let them know your immediate needs so they may expedite your requests. There will be other members of the fact-finding mission coming later, but, since we speak the language, we all wanted to be on the first plane here. Ted, this is my brother, Vasken."

Ted shook Vasken's hand. He felt the strength of his grip, and immediately recognized Vasken as a practitioner of the martial arts. Ted greeted him cordially.

"Glad to meet you. I hope our country will be of assistance here. There will be more planes arriving shortly from the States."

Vasken turned from Ted to face Lance, who observed him silently.

"We're on a job here, a mission of mercy for the Armenian people. Let's forget our personal vendetta for the moment, Vasken, and just get on with it, without hostility or trouble, if that's possible," said Lance, frigidly.

"O.K. with me," Vasken replied, bowing his head in a mock gesture. "I can live with it."

Karamine placed her hand gently on Lance's arm. "Please, let's keep it in the family, you two," she said, lowering her voice, before turning to Sylvana.

"Sylvana, I want to work with you to get the medical supplies where they will be most needed; where would that be?"

"Leninakan should be the main storage place, I think," Sylvana replied. "Leninakan was hit badly, but they have the airfield there so we can use that as a center of distribution. From there, trucks can take over with deliveries to the other towns."

"Good. Then you'll make sure that all the supplies get there fast as possible?"

"Yes. I have my people at the field with trucks and helicopters, ready to move," Sylvana answered in a businesslike tone.

"There's heavy equipment which will have to be transferred along with the dogs and trainers," said Ted. "As you know, the dogs will be invaluable in locating people buried under debris."

"Yes, we will take care of everything. The dogs and their trainers will be helicoptered in. I have the men, trucks and equipment ready for the transportation. Medical supplies will also be air lifted by helicopter . . . it's important to get those in first, as medical supplies are in short supply."

"Sylvana, if it can be arranged, I'd like to be on that first helicopter," said Karamine. "I know the hospital and staff there from my previous visits, and I'd like to be there when the medical supplies arrive. They'll need all the assistance they can get I'm sure."

Sylvana glanced toward Vasken for his approval. "For whatever is left of the hospital," he said cynically. "However, my dear sister, if that is your wish, so be it. Sylvana has made some comfortable accommodations for you at the Hotel Yerevan, which I believe is one of the more pleasant hotels overlooking the Hraztan River. You'll probably want to clean up after your long trip. We can pick you up later for dinner and take you to one of the better restaurants here in Yerevan. In the meantime, the crew out here has been given their instructions and, as you can see, they're moving as of now." He pointed to the trucks and forklifts in action.

"That sounds fine, Vasken," said Karamine looking toward Ted and Lance for their approval. "But, to repeat myself again, my main concern is to be on that first helicopter out of here."

"Good, then it's settled," said Sylvana. "Let's see the city of Yerevan on our way to the hotel. Have you ever been here before?"

"Yes, I've been here a number of times," Karamine replied, "but my husband and Ted have not, so it will be nice to take a short tour."

Before guiding the party to the waiting limousine, Sylvana gave instructions to the crew to load the medical supplies on one of the Aeroflot's large helicopters, and to wait for further instructions. "You'll have a Doctor Bagdasarian on that first trip to Leninakan," she informed them. She also instructed the lead truck driver to load up and leave immediately for Spitak and other small towns without delay. "Make sure the dogs and trainers are on that first helicopter when Dr. Bagdasarian arrives. Time is of the utmost now, so move fast. The longer the people are buried beneath debris, the chances of finding them alive is lessened."

The limousine was a large one, made to accommodate a party of eight; Lance, Ted and Karamine sat in the back seat, Sylvana and Vasken sat on two jumpseats set to turn and face the visitors.

"Take the long route to the hotel, driver, we want to give our visitors a tour of the city," Sylvana ordered.

"Yes, comrade," the driver answered, not turning his head.

During the drive through the city of Yerevan, Lance and Ted caught their first sight of Mt. Ararat, bare and glacier-coated standing like a sentinel on the horizon. They'd felt cheated not being able to see it from the air on their approach to the airport, since, as had been explained to them, "the aircraft was built to handle cargo, not passengers." Now however, staring at it through the limousine window, Lance felt he had waited for this moment all his life. The mountain gripped him fiercely, imaging every story his grandfather had told him . . . of Noah's Ark still rumored lost there, of mountain people, proud and free. He felt an upsurge of emotion and bit his lip hard to keep his reactions in check. He felt a link with the past sharply now, and the tangent presence of his grandparents; the old bitterness recharged once more by the sight of the barbed-wire fence on the border of Turkey, enclosing the lands stolen from his people.

"Ah, there's the statue of David of Sasoon, one of our greatest heroes," Karamine exclaimed, pointing to the left. The car headed northeast and on to Republic Square, where Sylvana pointed out the National Art Gallery of Armenia and the History Museum of Armenia.

"Would you care to stop and take a look?" Sylvana questioned.

"No thank you, Sylvana, our trip here is not for sightseeing, we're here to find out how we may help," Ted replied graciously.

They sped north past Opera Square, a meeting place for artists to get together and discuss their work and the politics of the day" Yerevan is a city of the history and culture of the Armenian people, "Sylvana explained. "The city was redesigned in 1920 by Alexander Tamanian," and it is one of the oldest, continuously occupied cities in the world.

They continued on toward Sayat Nova Boulevard, then left into Paronian Drive where the Hotel Yerevan was located. The classic hotel was well designed for the area. Stopping the car, the driver jumped out and assisted the passengers through the door, where the party was met by the Communitarian, and a delegation of grateful people. Sylvana motioned the driver to take the guest's luggage, then, one by one she introduced them to the delegation, specifying their title.

The Communitarian, a stocky built man in his early sixties, recognized Karamine and approached her with a generous smile. "Welcome, Doctor Bagdasarian. We are so happy to have you back to help us again, especially at this time of crisis. Thank you."

"We came with the first cargo plane to expedite the country's needs. May I introduce my husband, Senator Lance Bagdasarian, and Congressman Ted Sohigian.

Lance extended his hand toward the Communitarian and noted the quizzical expression in the man's eyes. Lance smiled. "Yes, I'm definitely Armenian . . . don't let these blue eyes and light skin fool you, sir."

"Oh I'm so sorry. I know, I shouldn't have stared. We have a few light-skinned blue-eyed Armenians here, but I must say that they are rare. It is so wonderful of your people in America to come to our assistance in this troubled time. America is generous, and helps every one in the world. We do appreciate all you do for our little nation."

"We Armenians of the diaspora will always do our utmost to help the people of Armenia," Ted commented, when the Communitarian turned to shake hands with him. "We are here now and don't want to waste any time . . . lives are depending on our quick action."

The Communitarian agreed quickly. "Yes, you are absolutely right. Our delegation here simply wished to show our gratitude and thanks to the people of America. You must have a great deal of work to do, and you must be tired after the long trip. Again . . . thank you from the people of Armenia." He turned and made a motion to the delegation, then led them away. He stopped short however when he caught sight of Vasken. "Ah! Comrade Casparian," he said smiling and wagging a finger at him, "I hear you were a very bad boy at the Communitarian's office in Karabakh. You'll have to learn to keep your temper in check and curb your tongue. I wish the best for you, and know you only want to help, but please . . . no more temper."

Karamine stepped forward quickly when she saw Vasken's expression. "You know my brother, Vasken, Communitarian?" she said with a smile.

The Communitarian was taken by surprise. "Your brother?" he said, raising an eyebrow. "Even more reason for you to do as I ask Comrade Vasken. You have a wonderful, beautiful sister you should be proud of. She is an asset to our nation, and we owe her a lot."

Vasken bowed stiffly, but did not reply.

Sylvana walked into the hotel and got the keys for their accommodations, then motioned to one of the housemen to direct the party to their respective rooms.

"Are you staying?" she asked Vasken.

"No." He turned to Karamine. "Look, we'll be back later when you've had time to clean up and get some rest. We'll have dinner then, and make plans about the next move."

"I know I'm repeating myself, but when that helicopter is loaded and ready to leave, I want to be on it," Karamine restated. "You have to understand my urgency."

"Yes, that's absolutely right," Lance added. "We want to get there as soon as possible so we may ascertain the imperative needs and send back a report to Washington. We only have a day or two to get this done, then we must get back. The quicker we return, the sooner the supplies will be sent here. This is winter, and those people will need shelter, heat and clothing."

"No, there's no time to lose. We have a job to do and the faster we get on with it, the better." Ted added.

"Well, you have to eat, right?" Vasken said. "We'll pick you up later and then we can decide what comes next." He took Sylvana's arm and headed out of the hotel to the waiting limousine.

Upstairs in their room, Karamine and Lance stepped out to the small balcony, facing the Hraztan River.

"I can't believe we're actually both here in Armenia together," Karamine said, touching his arm. "Look at that view, Lance."

"Yes, it's difficult to realize, or even understand how deeply we're touched by the genes of our ancestors. If I was never aware of it before, I am now."

"I know exactly what you mean," Karamine answered with a sigh. "And that's what draws me here. It's part of my blood and soul, Lance."

"This is not a bad hotel, Karamine," Lance said, when they went inside. Seems comfortable."

"Yes, it's one of the better ones in Yerevan. I've been here before. Some of the accommodations are not as nice, in fact, some are almost primitive, as you may soon find out, Senator." She laughed.

"I don't care, I'm here to do a job, and that's my first concern. You're right. We'll leave on that first helicopter, and get to work immediately. In the meantime, I wonder if we could get something to drink. I'll ring the desk."

Lance walked to the telephone and picked it up.

"Yes, do you by any chance have a selection of liquors? Vodka?" He looked toward Karamine, who shook her head.

"Ask if they have wines."

"Do you have wine? Wine of Armenia? Yes, that's great, a medium dry white wine. Would you send up a bottle . . . and a couple of glasses? Thanks."

The hotel houseman arrived a few moments later and set a bottle of wine, along with two glasses on the table. He lifted the cork and smelled it, then offered Lance a small portion for approval. Lance however, simply nodded then motioned him to fill the glasses. He offered him a tip, but the houseman refused.

"You're a guest of our country," he stated emphatically.

After he left the room, Lance picked up the filled glasses, passed one to Karamine, then led her out to the small balcony. He gestured ceremoniously then lifted his glass.

"To *Myir Haiastan* (the Motherland) and the spirit of our ancestors."

Karamine touched the edge of his glass gently with hers. "*Ayeu . . . To Haiastan.*"

They sipped their wine slowly, gazing silently outward toward the River. The landscape on the opposite side was peaceful, its fields of contrasting ochre and yellow green colors contradicting the conflict and unrest present everywhere in the land.

"Such a beautiful country," said Lance quietly. I still can't believe you and I are here together, Karamine. Too bad it had to take an earthquake to get us here. I noticed some bad cracks in one or two of the buildings along the way here."

"Yes, but thank God, the museums and other outstanding buildings were not damaged. Leninakan and Spitak took the brunt of the quake, from what we were told. I'm anxious to see for myself. Lance, I'm so glad you and Ted will be able to see the hospital I set up there, and I'm eager to have you meet some of the doctors and nurses I've trained on my last few visits."

Lance took a sip of his wine and continued to stare thoughtfully at the view. It was some minutes before he spoke.

"Karamine . . . have you ever had any regrets about marrying me?"

Karamine gasped slightly. "What on earth motivated a question like that?" she replied, turning to face him directly.

"Well, I don't know, Karamine, you seem almost like another person when you're here . . . you're so alive and absorbed. I can understand the passion you have for this country, I have it too, but, somehow I get the feeling you'd like to stay here forever. You said this afternoon you felt it was your real home."

"Well yes, Lance, I do admit I have deep feelings for this country. There's just something here. I find it difficult to explain. It's just a sense I get whenever I'm here."

"A feeling of belonging you said, a feeling of wanting to be part of it," Lance replied dismally.

"A sense of belonging, yes, I guess that's true. I thought you felt the same."

Lance paused slightly before answering. "Karamine, of course I feel a sense of belonging here. It's only natural I should. When I first saw Ararat it seemed that every story my grandfather told me came alive; for the first time I truly understood his passion and fire, his courage and tenacity in the frustrating fight for liberty and freedom through the centuries. I felt connected, rooted to all of this and I'm deeply moved now by this new calamity. I'll do anything to alleviate the pain and suffering here, but unlike you, I don't feel it's my homeland. America is my home. That's where my family lives; that's where all my childhood memories reside.

Karamine sighed slightly. "Well perhaps my sense of belonging here is reinforced by my strong sense of purpose. You have your work in Washington, Lance, and you love it. I love the work I'm doing here. Helping the people, especially the children, is quite fulfilling. The children here endure so much. Surely you can understand that, Lance. It has nothing at all to do with my love for you. How could you doubt that?"

Lance turned to face Karamine directly, then he placed an arm around her. "I don't know, Karamine. I suppose at times I'm afraid . . . afraid of our drifting in two different directions. I miss you so damn much. I miss our walks by the Charles River in Boston, our long talks about everything and nothing in particular. Somehow we never seem to have time for anything now, except our careers, and when I finally have some time with you, I see a new light in your eyes, for something I'm not quite part of. I get the feeling I'm losing you and it scares the hell out of me. I don't know what to do about it."

Karamine put her arms around Lance and kissed him gently. "Lance, Lance . . . how can I convince you?" she whispered. "How could you ever think you could lose me? You are the deepest part of my life. I'll never belong to anyone else. Just try to be patient for a little while, and don't ask me to make choices. That would tear me apart. I love my work here, as you love yours. We don't have children so we're free to follow our chosen professions. You wouldn't deny me that would you?"

Lance held Karamine close to him. Her words were reassuring and he did trust the truth of her love. Still, from somewhere deep within, a nagging doubt persisted. Will things ever really get back to the way we were?

22

Early next morning, Lance, Karamine and Ted were met by Sylvana, Vasken and Rouben. They had breakfast together, then Rouben drove them directly to the airport. In the car, Sylvana scrutinized Karamine intently; it was some moments before she spoke.

"Your brother tells me you are a doctor with a good practice in America. So tell me," Sylvana said with a slight smile, while watching Karamine's eyes for her reaction, "why have you come here, to Armenia?" She gestured, extending her hand out over the countryside, "this country, compared to the United States, must seem backward, and somewhat alien to you. True, you know the language, but, forgive me . . . I am curious."

Karamine laughed lightly. "Contrary to what it must seem to you, my dear Sylvana, I'm very comfortable here. It's like a second home. Yes, I must admit, I found it a bit difficult on my first visit, especially adjusting to the limitations, and, I must say there was some resentment because I'm a woman doctor. The old ways die hard. However, once the people understood the reasons for change, and the advantages, and realized I knew what I was talking about with the newer techniques and equipment, they began to trust. Actually, they're quite supportive now, and they learned fast; all the doctors, nurses, and students have become my good friends and, this encourages me to do even more. I'm impressed with their attitude and desire to learn. It's beyond what I expected, so its completely rewarding for me, Sylvana."

Sylvana nodded her head and smiled thoughtfully. "Yes, the old ways are hard to change, especially here in Armenia. But I'm sure it can be done with time and patience. Remember, Moscow has been thinking for the people for seventy years. Very few decisions are left to the people, so you may find it difficult for us to change at first. But, I know we can. Now Gorbachev's Glastnost and Perestroika will be real challenges to the people. They just don't understand these new concepts and standards that you take so much for granted in America. You have to understand the people here have always been led. They don't understand the responsibility of decision making for themselves.

"I understand that," Karamine replied, "and that's one of the reasons why many of us come here to Armenia, to show how this can be done peacefully, without revolution. To think and take responsibility for one's action is one of the most important aspects of a free society. Learning to change and accept new, valid ideas that don't encroach on another's rights. This is precisely why we send students and other professionals in sociology, economics, engineering and environmental issues to help Armenia and its future. They are the visionaries who want to bring the country to a new dawn of freedom . . . and, that's why I come. True, communism rules now, but not in the future. I want to be part of the transformation. I believe, like many others in the diaspora, that we have an obligation to see our motherland change . . . but change peacefully, without turmoil or revolution. It's vital for us to do this for a smooth transition when the time comes."

The car arrived at the airport gates and stopped. Rouben presented his identification and papers of clearance. When the guard was satisfied, he waved them through; they headed for a tarmac where a huge cargo helicopter with double rotors waited. Sylvana got out first and spoke to one of the ground crew who was busy logging all the supplies being loaded into the craft.

"Everything's ready for you to leave immediately," she announced, turning back to the group. "The dogs and trainers left moments ago, so you people will arrive in Leninakan right after them. You can get aboard immediately."

"Will you be travelling with us?" Lance asked Sylvana, as he stepped out of the car with Ted and Karamine.

"No. Vasken, Rouben and I will stay behind to meet the other planes coming in," Sylvana replied, shaking her head. "We have work to do here. It's our job to expedite the supplies and make sure they get to wherever they are needed most. We've just been talking to one of the controllers who had word that your fact finding mission has arrived with their civil engineers, architects and other personnel. I understand they are to join you in their assessments and recommendations for the damage to our cities. We'll take care of them and see they are flown to Leninakan as soon as possible. But right now, all is ready for your flight, so just get settled aboard. Rouben's cousin, Dikron will meet you in Leninakan with the necessary trucks for the supplies aboard the copter.

He'll guide you to whenever you choose to go with him. He's an excellent guide."

"Yes," Vasken added, "Dikron is young, but he knows his way around Leninakan. He was my guide while I was there, so I can recommend him. That was before all hell broke out of course. I was lucky to get out alive. We were both lucky."

Karamine glanced sharply at Vasken. "What were you doing in Leninakan, Vasken?"

"That's what we'd all like to know," Sylvana interjected, "especially how he got there."

Vasken smiled knowingly, but ignored the question. It'll take more than an earthquake to kill me," he said, casting a brief look toward Lance. "Meantime, let's get you all aboard."

"You didn't tell me you were there in the earthquake, Vasken," Karamine whispered softly.

"Look, you're holding things up, and time is of the essence. Get going." Vasken kissed Karamine's cheek and gave her a gentle push toward the helicopter.

Karamine boarded first. "That brother-in-law of yours doesn't have too much use for you, does he?" Ted commented under his breath while extending a hand to Lance to help him aboard.

"Long story, Ted," Lance replied briefly, "I'll tell you about it sometime when we get back, over a shot of bourbon."

The rotors of the helicopter roared, as the RPM increased and the craft lifted vertically off the ground till it was clear of surrounding buildings and obstructions. It hovered for a moment then, with its precious cargo aboard, headed northwest toward Leninakan.

"How far is it to Leninakan, and about how long do you think it will take to get there?" Lance asked, turning to Karamine, when they were settled.

"It's not far, really. We'll be there in no time. There was an old railroad that ran between Yerevan and Leninakan. I wonder if it's been damaged by the quake. I hope not. We'll need it for the heavy equipment transport and tons of supplies that will be arriving daily. Freight cars are a much better way to transport supplies. Better than helicopter. Anyway, I'm sure Sylvana knows what she's doing." Karamine paused a moment before continuing. "I wonder if there's anything going on between her and my brother. I see the way she looks at him."

Lance turned to look at her. "Really? I hadn't noticed," he said indifferently. He leaned forward and tapped Ted gently. "Did you happen to find out the extent of the damage from anyone you spoke to in Yerevan last night, Ted?"

"Everything was sketchy, and they were quite pessimistic. Just kept saying it was bad and kept repeating that tens of thousands are dead in a city of a quarter of a million. Those figures don't include the other towns, villages and cities in the whole quake area. They still don't have any idea of the death toll there, with thousands still buried under collapsed buildings and rubble. They're worried about dehydration if they remain buried much longer. They have to be pulled out. God! It's difficult to get things done around here, from what I've heard," he added with exasperation.

"Please . . . enough! Don't talk about it any more," Karamine pleaded, placing her hands to her head. "I can't stand it. Let's just get there and see what we have to do to save as many as possible. Right now, I don't want any statistics or numbers about victims. I don't want to hear anything. All I want is to get the healing process started."

Lance placed his arm around her gently, noting her deep expression of concern. Karamine turned to look out the window, and Lance settled back in his seat. They remained quiet for the rest of the trip, absorbed in their own thoughts.

Some time later, the seat light flashed on and the craft began its decent. The pilot announced he intended to fly over the city to give them a better view of the damage. Ted took the camera from its leather case and tried it for focus. The craft made a wide turn and dropped down to about eight hundred feet before banking sharply to the right. The first view of the city was devastating. Karamine gasped sharply.

"No . . . oh God, no!" she cried in disbelief, when she saw the stricken city for the first time. Ted and Lance remained in shocked silence. Never had they witnessed destruction of such mammoth proportions.

"The people in Yerevan were right when they said you had to see it for yourself to understand the scope of damage," Ted said at last. "There's not a building left standing down there."

Lance felt a sharp stab of pain as he strained to see the people below, scrambling over debris, searching for families and loved ones. He felt sick inside, when he realized the full impact of the disaster. "The death toll must be astronomical, Ted," he commented finally. He turned in his seat and talked to the pilot, who informed him that forty-five miles to the north, the town of Spitak with a population of 30,000, had been wiped off the face of the earth. He had flown there to bring some victims out, and had been informed that most of the population was gone. "Buried alive" he said. "The surrounding towns and villages as well, erased from the face of the earth those few seconds during the quake, and then, the aftershock."

The craft made a wide circle over Leninakan before heading for the airfield where it hovered until it was directed to the proper tarmac. It hovered over the tarmac for a few seconds while the pilot checked the wind direction, then slowly it descended until the wheels touched the ground.

When Karamine, Lance and Ted got out, a truck with a crew aboard pulled up to the tarmac. A young man jumped from the truck and walked toward them.

"Parev" (hello), my name is Dikron," he said extending his hand. "I was told to meet you, and help with anything you might need. The other helicopter arrived just before you, with the dogs and trainers. They're already on their way to the city to do their job. I was wondering of what use they'd be, and from what I've learned they must be great."

Lance shook Dikron's hand. "This is my wife, Doctor Karamine Bagdasarian, this is Ted Souhigian, and I'm Lance. We represent the United States government."

Dikron flashed a friendly smile then led them to a waiting car.

"Where do you want to go first? You know, most of the hotels have been destroyed. You'll have to do with whatever is available."

"Don't worry about that," Karamine replied, "just get me to your hospital immediately. I want to see what's being done, and I'm anxious to get started."

"You mean what's left of the hospital," Dikron answered glumly.

"Is it totally destroyed?" Karamine asked anxiously.

"Well, not entirely. Part of it is still there, but we don't know for how long. Another tremor and that could go. There's no electricity, water or needed supplies. We're lucky you brought some with you."

"Then get the supplies unloaded and brought out to the hospital without delay," Karamine ordered firmly. "There's a full army field hospital aboard. Bring it there for assembly as soon as possible. We've also brought large tents along with hospital equipment used during wartime. It's a temporary hospital that can be set up fast with little trouble, so don't waste time. I want it set up today, if possible. As I said, don't waste time."

Dikron and Karamine walked over to the crew unloading the supplies from the helicopter, and gave them orders to unload the crates marked FIELD HOSPITAL, first. Then, Dikron ordered them sent to the hospital immediately. Ted was taking pictures while Lance made notes. They were silent when they finally got back into the car, and drove by the gates and into the streets of Leninakan. The ghastliness of the landscape depressed them, and filled them with wrenching pain. Misery was evident everywhere; men with nothing more than timber and shovels, worked desperately with frenzied effort to reach the victims trapped beneath the heavy rubble and debris. Small groups huddled around bon fires seeking warmth and light from the chilling dark, now falling swiftly over the bleak landscape. Here and there Russian soldiers attempted to lend a hand, but the lack of heavy-duty equipment for such an emergency was painfully obvious.

Lance wrote feverishly on his clipboard; Ted kept snapping pictures. Karamine sat quietly in the front seat staring straight ahead. The pain and suffering from every side seemed to her too engulfing and oppressive. She knew she had to steel herself against it if she was to be of any effective help. She thought of doctors and nurses in wartime; she wondered how they coped. Her training had taught her to block out the outer appearances, the emotional responses, to remain cool and level-headed. But, it's difficult, she thought despondently. When we actually come face to face with the reality of a situation, it's difficult.

The grim facts of the situation hit her still more forcibly when she saw the twisted remains of the hospital. The whole building looked as though it had shifted, and the right half was totally collapsed in a heap of metal, mortar, broken cables and twisted steel. Her heart sank. She had worked so hard on her last trips to set up this hospital, and it had been one of her proudest achievements. It had serviced the children, mothers and families of Leninakan. Karamine fought hard to hold back the tears.

"I put so much hard work and effort into this hospital," she said, turning to Lance. "So much. Now look at it. Ruins. Total ruins."

Karamine turned when she heard her name called, and saw several doctors and nurses approaching her. They greeted her warmly, and in spite of her resolutions, she broke into tears. After the greetings and introductions, she turned to Lance.

"My job is here, Lance. I'll be supervising the setting up of the field hospital as soon as it arrives. You and Ted take off and do what you need to do. Make sure they know at home the full extent of the damage here."

Lance looked at her with concern. "Will you be all right, Karamine? You look tired already. Can we be of help in any way?"

"No, I'll be all right. You and Ted go ahead, and get all the information you need for your report. Let them know back home how bad things are. I'll be staying right here."

Lance embraced her briefly, kissed her cheek then left with Ted and Dikron.

The supply truck arrived within the hour. Karamine watched and supervised the unloading of the crates; some, containing delicate instruments, were marked HANDLE WITH CARE, and these were carefully unpacked and set aside. The directions for assembling and setting up the field hospital were more involved and complicated than she had imagined, however. Karamine and her colleagues struggled with the directions but were unsuccessful in deciphering them. Tents, and lab equipment lay strewn about the area, and the darkening evening sky added to their problems. Karamine was frustrated and struggled against her feelings of discouragement. The mechanics of things were not her strong point. She was impatient and anxious to begin helping people. Fortunately, a group of Russian soldiers passing by stopped to ask a few questions. "Could they help?" One of Karamine's doctor friends who had been educated in Moscow spoke fluent Russian. He explained the situation to them, and the soldiers responded enthusiastically. They informed Karamine's friend that they were quite familiar with the setting up of field hospitals, and would be more than happy to assist. Karamine whispered a silent prayer of gratitude when she saw the soldiers take over. The men worked for many hours, and eventually, the temporary hospital took shape—the equipment set in place in operating areas, separate tents set up for intensive care. Karamine's spirits lifted and she felt a renewed sense of hope and optimism.

The Russian soldiers were proud of their efforts. The hospital staff brought them hot tea and biscuits, for which the men thanked them warmly. Karamine's friend, Dr. Papken, who had been the interpreter with the Russians, appeared suddenly from the hospital waving a bottle of Vodka. He approached the Russian sergeant in charge of the group.

"This escaped the quake," Dr. Papken announced with a smile, "and I believe it's only fitting that it be given to you and your men in appreciation for what you have all done for us this day." There was a ripple of approval from the soldiers.

The Russian sergeant bowed slightly as he took the bottle. "My comrades and I thank you, and when we drink it, we'll toast your brave people, and vow to do all we can to help them alleviate their suffering in this time of need." He gestured with the bottle. "Thank you for my men. Thank you for me." He shook the doctor's hand vigorously, before leaving along with his men.

When they left, Karamine took one last tour of the area, checking out the units, and testing each piece of equipment. The noise of the generator pierced the late afternoon air with a light humming sound. Suddenly, Karamine felt weariness in every part of her body. It had been a long and exhausting day. She stretched out on one of the bunks in the Intensive Care unit to rest momentarily, but within seconds fell into a deep sleep. She was still sleeping soundly when Doctor Papken came into the area about a half hour later. The tenseness in his face relaxed somewhat when he saw Karamine, and a faint smile traced his features. He checked the flame in the kerosene heater to make sure it was burning cleanly and throwing heat, then, walking to a large carton, he picked up an army blanket and gently covered her.

"Karamine drives herself to the limits," he said to the nurse who had just entered the unit. "She'll drive herself as hard tomorrow. She gives beyond what is expected of her. We could do with a few more of her caliber."

The nurse nodded her head and agreed. "You are so right, doctor. With people like Karamine, we have new hope for the future, and know our Armenian people will heal and survive this disaster."

Dr. Papken tucked the blanket lightly around Karamine's feet. "Sleep, *"anush archigus"* (sweet girl) sleep. You deserve it. Tomorrow will bring its own troubles." Quietly then, they left the area.

23

Lance felt uncomfortable leaving Karamine at the site of the wrecked hospital, yet he knew he had to move on and get his report done as soon as possible in order to expedite supplies to the stricken area. He also knew he would be heading back to the States without Karamine when his report was finished; the thought depressed him. He had resigned himself to her staying, but, he was not quite prepared for the emptiness and sense of desertion the separation suggested. We've been apart before when she's come over here to Armenia, he reasoned with himself, so why does it seem more difficult than usual? She'll be coming back in a month or so—or would she? He knew Karamine and her resolute determination; he had witnessed first-hand her undisguised pleasure to be there in Armenia; a 'sense of belonging' she'd called it. He sighed deeply, remembering his helplessness and frustration at the hospital scene when he knew Karamine didn't need him. He was unable to assist in any way. After all, what did he know about the setting up of field hospitals, or the assembling of medical supplies? I'd probably have just gotten in the way, he thought bleakly.

Dikron hit the brakes and the car stopped suddenly. A collapsed building blocked the road and they were unable to pass. "I've got to find another way, I want to get to the center of the city where the damage is heaviest," Dikron said, backing up and turning the car. Lance looked around and continued making notes in a renewed effort to concentrate on the job he was there for. He noticed some Russian soldiers had joined the search for missing persons trapped beneath the collapsed buildings. "Stop the car, Dikron," Lance said urgently.

Dikron pulled the car to a sudden stop and Ted and Lance got out. The air was heavy with fine particles of powdered mortar, and smoke from nearby fires. Ted addressed the soldiers in English at first, but switched to Armenian when they shook their heads to indicate they didn't understand him. Fortunately, one of the soldiers understood Armenian, so Ted quickly turned to him and communicated his message.

"We're representatives from the United States," he began, "and we're here to help the people through this disaster. We're assessing the damage to see what further supplies will be needed; where's the heavy duty equipment . . . cranes, backhoes and bulldozers?" he demanded, waving his arm and noting the soldiers were working only with rough shovels and boards in their attempt to rescue people trapped beneath collapsed buildings. The Russian soldier shrugged his shoulders indifferently. "Equipment? Everything we have is being used right now. More was reportedly sent from Moscow, but you know . . . red tape . . . bureaucracy." The soldier shrugged again.

"Yeah, red tape and bureaucracy . . . I know all about it. It's the same everywhere. Wherever you have a bunch of know and do nothing freeloaders for a government," Ted barked with frustration.

"Take it easy, Ted," Lance cautioned. "We won't get anywhere this way. Let's try to get more information."

The soldier informed Ted and Lance that a Russian military plane carrying troops for the earthquake rescue, had crashed at the airport killing 79 soldiers. Some of the heavy duty equipment was being used to clean the wreckage from the runways. This was necessary since other transports carrying supplies were due. However, they were assured, as soon as the wreckage was cleared away, the equipment would be brought back to the city.

Lance was glad he had the conversation translated on tape, as the soldier spoke to Ted. It would be a powerful tool to convince congress and the people back home of the desperate needs in Armenia. From that scene they continued on, where Lance once more put his hand on Dikron's shoulder and asked him to stop. When they got out of the car, they approached some people who appeared to wander aimlessly through the desolate landscape. Ted and Lance approached them, raising their hands in a gesture of friendship. Ted attempted to ask questions, but the people's answers were incoherent and vague. They seemed to be in shock, staring vacantly and answering in disjointed phrases; they muttered names and asked repeated questions. Ted and Lance tried to give them some encouragement and hope, assuring that help was on the way but, the words fell blankly. Confusion and denial was apparent everywhere, and a suffocating melancholy permeated the area.

Lance and Ted got into the car again and continued their mission. Soon they arrived at the central square of Leninakan. "This is what I wanted you to see for yourself," Dikron said, pointing to a huge clock tower that had crumbled and plunged to the ground. The frame of the tower was twisted and distorted, but the hands on the face of the clock itself were locked at 11:41 A.M. recording for posterity a violent, terrifying moment when a city of 290,000 was destroyed. Lance stared at the clock and clenched his hands together. He continued to stare as though what he saw unnerved his soul. Ted broke the silence.

"I believe those people over there are the rest of the fact-finding committee," he said pointing to an official looking group. "Let's join them."

When they joined the group, Lance and Ted were informed that the official fact-finding committee had arrived on the Presidential Aircraft about one hour behind them. They had looked for Lance and Ted, and were relieved they had caught up with them. They were interested in every detail of the information Lance and Ted had gathered so far. Lance guided them to the spot where the tower clock grimly recorded the exact hour Armenia felt the brunt of a killer quake.

"We're witnessing a tragedy of major proportions," one of the men from the group commented sadly. "It's really something beyond our expectations. We have a mammoth task ahead . . . to alleviate this suffering and help with the rebuilding of this country."

The others nodded briefly, feeling the impact of the featureless city around them.

"Where's your wife, Senator?" one of the members asked, turning to Lance. "We understand she came along with you."

"Yes," Lance replied, brushing mortar dust from his clothing, "she's over at the site of the field hospital. They're setting it up now. Thank God she had the foresight to insist it go along with us on the cargo plane. We left her there with the medical staff."

"That was foresight indeed, on her part, Senator. From the looks of this city they could probably use several field hospitals."

That evening the entire group were billeted in an old Russian army tent and informed that this would be their official headquarters during their stay. Kerosene stoves were supplied to keep out the chill autumn air, and several wash buckets and latrines had been crudely set up for their use. Food supplies were limited. However, a few locals managed to bring in some coarse dark bread, and the Russian army supplied fresh water from tanker trucks, as well as a small quantity of tea and potatoes. After the meager meal, Lance and Ted along with the rest of the fact finding group, that included engineers, and seismologists, gathered around the kerosene heater to assess their information. The earthquake had measured 6.9 according to statistics by Armenian and Russian geologists and seismologists; the epicenter was located twenty-five miles northeast of Leninakan; the fault rumbled about twelve miles below the surface of the earth, spreading out to a radius of thirty miles. Every house over two stories in that whole area had crumbled like a house of cards. Neighboring towns and cities like Kirovakan, Spitak, Stepanakan and Leninaken with a population of close to 700,000 were largely destroyed. The death toll was rising rapidly.

"Why did the buildings crumble that way?" a civil engineer in the committee questioned sharply. "We'll have to examine the design and building materials closely."

The next morning, the entire fact-finding committee, along with Lance and Ted were out on the streets early. They examined many of the collapsed buildings including the elementary schoolhouse on Gorky Street, where all but fifty of the children attending classes perished. They were shocked to discover that nothing was reinforced, and the mortar used in the buildings was of poorest quality. Thick, eight inch concrete slabs, were held together with flimsy metal hooks. "Those buildings should have collapsed long ago," one of the engineers stated, shaking his head sadly. "There's such a poor and disproportionate mix of sand and cement." They also discovered that some of the people in poverty areas of the city lived in houses of unreinforced mud and rock. These collapsed with the first tremor. The committee were horrified by the negligence and complete disregard of good building standards obvious everywhere they went.

They continued making their investigations and were amazed by the speed and efficiency of the dog teams and their trainers as they searched and found people trapped under debris. When the dogs located someone, they were rewarded by their trainers, then, with precise accuracy and speed they moved on to the next location. The people were deeply impressed by the team's performance when they witnessed rescue after rescue, and the dogs were treated like heros.

But the populace in general were weary and confused. And, as Lance discovered, there was resentment as well. Because of the ethnic cleansing taking place in Karabagh, Armenian refugees driven from their ancestral homes by the Azerbaijans had been arriving steadily at Leninakan over the past weeks. This compounded the needs of the people, and strained the already short supply of resources. Ted and Lance included these observations and documented everything they saw and heard, as part of a complete record for the President and his cabinet.

The time passed quickly; Lance, Ted and the committee were gathered together the last evening before their departure for America to finalize notes and go over their findings and recommendations. Lance was silent as he gazed beyond their faces and the small circle of lamplight to the darkened contours of the tent. It's been days since I've seen or heard from Karamine, he thought despondently. I'm leaving for home tomorrow and I don't even know how she is. With all telephone communications down, it's impossible to get in touch with her. I just hope she's not overdoing things. She looked exhausted the last time I was with her. He ran his fingers impatiently through his hair, as if to wipe out the troubling and persistent thought that he and Karamine were slowly but surely travelling two separate courses. I've got to see her before I leave, he thought desperately, I've got to get to that hospital somehow.

Some of the men began to pack their gear, briefcases and bags. A few others stretched out on their cots for a few hours sleep. They were due to leave first thing in the morning.

"Ted, I've got to see Karamine for a few minutes before we leave for the States," Lance whispered urgently in Ted's ear.

Ted hesitated a moment before replying. "You know we have to be on that plane first thing tomorrow morning, Lance. There's not much time. You realize the importance of all of us being together as a unit when we make this report to Washington. We as a group can exert more pressure and convince Washington of the necessity to act fast in sending aid here. Anyway, how would you get to the hospital and back before we leave?"

Lance motioned to Dikron who was already stretching out on his cot. "Hey Dikron, I want to ask you something. Do you think you could get me over to the hospital and back here before we have to leave for the airport in the morning?" he asked.

Dikron looked a little dubious. "Well . . . we'd have to leave early, and time would be short. But we can go if that's what you want," he answered with a slight smile.

Lance looked at his watch. "O.K. let's grab a few hours sleep, then we can leave before the others wake up. I wouldn't ask you to do this, Dikron if it wasn't vitally important to me, but it is. I've got to see my wife before I leave. Lord knows when I'll see her next. Do you understand?" Lance placed his hand lightly on Dikron's shoulder.

Dikron nodded his head pleasantly. "I understand. We'll go."

Lance barely slept during the next few hours. He checked his luminous watch dial continuously. It was still dark when he decided to get up and wake Dikron, but he was determined not to oversleep and miss the opportunity of seeing Karamine before he left the country. He felt a slight edge of guilt as he nudged Dikron gently, rousing him from deep sleep.

"I'll see you in about an hour or so, Ted," he whispered tapping Ted lightly as he passed his cot.

Outside, they climbed into the car and navigated the dark streets of Leninakan with as much speed as they were able, avoiding the routes they knew were impassable. The sky was still black, but the car head-lights provided enough light to manoeuver. Dikron drove the car hard. It took about one hour to reach the large tent hospital; the outline of the bulky tents blocked against the first hint of morning light seemed firm and steady, suggesting permanence and stability in a world of devastation and ruin.

Lance got out of the car. "I won't be long, Dikron. If I don't show up in half an hour, just come in and get me, O.K.?"

Dikron nodded and looked at his watch. "O.K. If you're not back here in thirty minutes, I'll come in and get you."

Lance headed for the tent marked Field Operations. Entering the tent, he met a nurse leaving what seemed to be the operating area. Its an ungodly early time, he thought, I wonder if Karamine is here or resting.

"Is Doctor Karamine Bagdasarian here?" Lance inquired, in his best Armenian. "I'm her husband. It's important I see her right away."

The nurse nodded and smiled. "She is inside the operating room, but they are almost finished. Please . . . take a seat." She pulled over a collapsible chair from a large stack.

Lance sat down and waited impatiently, as precious minutes passed. He glanced nervously at his watch. "How much longer do you think she'll be? I've only got a few minutes left."

"She shouldn't be long. They're washing up now."

"How is she holding up with all this?" Lance looked around and pointed to rows of patients lying in bunks.

"She's holding up well under the pressure of tremendous long hours. She doesn't get much sleep, even when we urge her to take some rest." The nurse shook her head. "Perhaps you can convince her to rest a little."

Lance laughed wryly. "No, I doubt if Doctor Karamine will listen to me. I know how determined she is once she sets a course. But, I'll try. I really don't want her to get sick."

The curtain of the operating room was pulled aside and Karamine walked through still wearing her operating mask. She saw Lance at once, and quickly ran over to greet him.

"Lance . . . " she cried excitedly, throwing her arms about him, "Lance . . . where have you been? It seems like years since I've seen you."

Lance held her tightly. She felt thin in his arms, and she reeked of strong antiseptic.

"It's been a hectic few days, Karamine. We travelled all over Leni-nakan, the surrounding towns and villages to get as much information as we can. We've been documenting everything for our report. You have no idea how bad the situation is, Karamine." He took a deep breath and shook his head.

"I thought at least you'd be able to get back here at night. You have no idea how much I've missed you. I've longed to see you, Lance."

"I know, I know," Lance murmured, "it's been the same for me. What made it worse was not being able to call you. We had our meetings at night, which lasted for hours without a let up. Then there were trips to other towns and villages. We stayed at some of the damnest places. We even slept in the open one night, without shelter. Our main quarters were in a Russian tent. There was no way I could have gotten over here. If there was any possible way I would have done it. As it is, I could just about make it here now, and I've only got a short time. I have to join the others. The helicopter is leaving for Yerevan and at six thirty our plane is leaving for the States; I have to be on it."

"Oh no! No!" Karamine's voice broke and she buried her head deeply in her husband's arms. Lance felt her body tremble, as emotions, pent up and strained through days of fatigue and stress were released.

"Karamine . . . " Lance whispered tenderly. "God, Karamine you seem so tired. How long can you keep this up? It's driving me crazy. Come home with me, please Karamine. It's killing us both." Lance's pleading was urgent.

Karamine stepped back and shook her head. We've been all over this before, Lance. You know I can't leave now, and I know you wouldn't really expect me to. Please, dearest, try to understand. I'm needed here."

Lance's mouth closed firmly and grimly. He tried to control the red-hot resentment he felt rising within. "Damn it Karamine, I need you! I love you and I'm worried about you. Or doesn't that mean anything to you any more! I need you!" he repeated.

"Don't, Lance, please. Don't make it any more difficult than it already is. Karamine's voice broke before she continued on. "If you really love me, you'll understand how important this is to me. All I'm asking for is a little time."

Lance cursed himself under his breath for losing control. What am I doing, he thought miserably. We've only got a few short minutes, and here I am giving Karamine more grief, adding to her stress. He sighed deeply and put his arms around her. "Karamine, Karamine, the last thing I ever want to do is to make you unhappy. It's just that I love you and miss you so damn much. And I worry about you. Forgive me, sweetheart."

"Couldn't you stay over a day or two and take another flight?" Karamine asked softly.

Lance shook his head. "No, that's just it. I have to leave, and leave now! I have no choice." He glanced at his watch. The flight's taking off in a couple of hours. I just barely made it over here, as is, and Dikron's waiting outside. I gave him orders to come in and get me if I was longer than half an hour."

"So this is it," Karamine said, smiling drearily. "We didn't have any time together at all. Just these few minutes."

There was silence between them, and the air in the tent was laced with heaviness. "Do you have any idea when you'll be coming back, Karamine?" he asked dully.

"Just look around, Lance. You see the need. I can't make a guess at all. But, you know how much I love you, and long to come home. I promise, when the real crises is over, I'll be on the first plane out of here."

Lance sighed heavily, and glanced at his watch again. "Just promise me you'll take care of yourself, Karamine. Don't overdo it, please. For my sake."

Karamine took his face between her hands forcing him to look at her. There was tearing pain in his blue eyes. "Lance, my love, I promise I'll take care of myself. And believe me when I say, this is not forever. I'll be home, before you know it."

Lance pressed closer to her in a final embrace before he turned and walked quickly to Dikron and the waiting car. Karamine watched him leave, turn once more and wave. Her gaze followed the car through the shattered city until it was out of sight. She was seized by intolerable loneliness. Everything dimmed but the clear comprehension that she was alone, alone on a mission that she herself had chosen. She shivered slightly, then with steely determination, turned and walked back into the hospital.

24

It was three months since Lance returned from Armenia. The emptiness and pain he felt leaving Karamine persisted, coloring his thoughts with a deep and brooding heaviness. All during the debriefing by the State Department, President and congressional committees his thoughts were with Karamine, still there in Armenia, its cold winter now in full progress. He was concerned about the fuel, in short supply because of the tightening blockade by Turkey and Azerbaijan. There was also the continuing conflict in Karabagh. Due to pressure by Lance and Ted however, the State Department and Pentagon were taking action, sending shipments of kerosene heaters and fuel to the devastated country. But relief was unable to get through, despite State Department pleas to the blockading countries to open their borders. The best efforts of the State Department were met by hostile resistance from the Turks and Azeris, who were determined to crush the Armenian people.

Lance reviewed events of the past three months while driving through beltway traffic en route to Ted and Tatiana's home. He was pleased his efforts had paid off and that the State Department and Pentagon had fully cooperated with him. Still, he couldn't shake the emptiness and depression that overshadowed all his waking days. It seemed years since he had seen Karamine, even though phone lines had been restored and he was able to get an occasional call through to her. Still, he reflected, her voice sounded weary and had lost its buoyant enthusiasm. "You're burning yourself out, Karamine," he had pleaded, uselessly, put off by her now familiar response, 'soon . . . please be patient, Lance, it's coming to an end.' He worried constantly about her physical well being, and wondered if she was able to keep warm. How she hated the cold New England winters, he thought wretchedly, but at least they were comfortable and lived in a well-heated home.

The blockade was hurting Armenia badly; food, clothing and fuel were scarce. Karamine had mentioned seeing her brother, Vasken, a number of times. He had been in Karabagh, but she was unsure of his mission, she had said. "I feel it has something to do with the Karabagh Defence Force, but, you know him, he just smiles whenever I question him." Lance shrugged his shoulders and tried to put the thought of Vasken from him. He fumbled with the radio of his car and tried to find some music. He was grateful Ted and Tatiana had invited him to their home for the evening. They were good for him, and were usually successful in picking up his spirits.

He saw the exit to Ted's address, and put on his signal light. Soon he was in Ted's driveway, exchanging greetings with the family.

"Have you had your dinner, Lance?" Tatiana questioned, after the children had left the room and the excitement had died down.

"Yes, thanks, Tatiana. There's a little restaurant I like near my place so I've had a good meal."

"How about coffee then?"

"That would be great."

"So," said Ted, making himself comfortable in his favorite chair, "what information have you had from Armenia, lately? What's new with Karamine?"

Lance was silent for a moment. "You know, Ted . . . same old thing. 'It's almost over, I'll be home soon.' Karamine and I are thousands of miles apart, and I just don't mean miles," he said bitterly. "I've got the feeling I'm losing her, and . . . I don't want to lose her, Ted."

"Come on, Lance, you're not losing her. You're building this separation thing all out of proportion. I know it's hard having her thousands of miles away, with just minimum communication by telephone, but, she's doing what she feels she has to do, and doing a fine job, too. She loves you, for God's sake. Get behind her and give her some encouragement. Let her do her job and . . . stop feeling sorry for yourself."

Lance looked at his friend, and smiled. "Yeah, I guess that's what I'm doing, feeling sorry for myself. But, I do miss her. It seems light years since we've been together, and I'm worried about her Ted, her physical well being. Everything's scarce there, food, clothing, fuel, everything! The Azeri blockade of the rail shipments is hurting Armenia badly."

"What about the Karabagh Defence Force, Lance?" I heard that's a force to be contended with, and they've been successful in breaking through that blockade."

"Not entirely. They don't have much by way of arms and ammunition. But, they have some good dedicated men and women in the KDF, according to Karamine, and her sources."

"Fighting women?" said Tatiana, who had just entered the room carrying a tray of coffee and cake.

"Well, I guess if you saw your children starving, and your home burned, you'd do anything, Tatiana," Lance replied.

Tatiana's expression was thoughtful. "Yes, Yes, I would. What do you hear from Karamine, Lance?"

Lance gazed silently at Tatiana a few moments, as though considering his answer.

"Well, she sounds weary, Tatiana, and I'm worried about her. Frankly, I just wish she'd come home."

"It's not that easy, Lance. Karamine is a zealous and dedicated doctor, a woman whose sentiments run deep. Would you have her any other way? Isn't that why you fell in love with her in the first place?

Lance gave a short laugh, then shook his head. "Yes, I've been all over that myself, Tatiana, and I realize the truth of everything you say, but that doesn't make it any easier. I miss her and that's that."

"Certainly you miss her, Lance, that's only natural. And don't you think Karamine misses you as much? But, a woman's love when it's real, has many components . . . dedication, loyalty, compassion, fierce defensiveness and a willingness to sacrifice, as you are witnessing yourself in those fighting women of Karabagh. Without these elements, what is love? Selfish emotionalism, turned in on itself. Karamine's love for you is real, so try to think of that, and all you mean to her when doubt and resentments flare. Give her space to fulfill her role, and believe me, you'll never regret it."

"Sound advice, my friend," Ted added, with a smile. "But, Lance, getting back to our original topic, what other information have you had on Armenia? Has anything improved? And what about Karabagh?"

"Well, this is the first time the Kremlin has ever made a formal request for American help," Lance replied; "even before the quake, the Armenians of Karabagh were demanding to be returned to Armenia, but Gorbachev continually rebuffed their demands. He felt the Armenians had no territorial claims against Azerbaijan for these lands. He damn well knows the history of how Stalin gave away the territory to punish Armenia for not sovietizing and becoming Russian. The timing of the quake was bad in that sense . . . nationalism for the Armenian people and the demand of Nagorno Karabagh back . . . then the quake." Lance shook his head.

"Yes, I heard things have turned from bad to worse in Azerbaijan because of the resistance taking place in Karabagh. I heard they're burning the homes of all suspected Armenians, in the Azerbaijan city of Baku." Ted commented.

Lance shrugged his shoulders disgustedly. "Well, outraged Armenian intellectuals went to Moscow to present their case of ethnic violence against the Armenians by the Azeris. I heard they were only given a finger waving lecture by Gorbachev, told to return and tell the Armenians to submit. You can imagine how well that was received. The last I heard was they were protesting in the streets of Yerevan, demanding independence from the Soviet Union, just like the people in Eastonia, Latvia and Lithuania. But," Lance continued, "the good news is that medical supplies, rescue equipment and other trained teams have arrived from France, West Germany, Switzerland, Bulgaria and Poland. This has brought down the death toll considerably. The first estimates were around sixty or seventy thousand dead. Last I heard it's been brought down to about twenty-five thousand, dead. They've been sending prefabricated shelters for the people as well."

"Don't forget the people of the Diaspora, here in the United States," Tatiana interrupted. "We've collected over seven million dollars in pledges, from Glendale, California alone. About three hundred thousand Armenians live there, then from Cambridge, Mass., sister city to Yerevan, we've collected tons of winter clothing and shipped it out. We're proud of our Armenian community's outpouring of relief. Remember, this relief effort is all done privately, and not through any government agency."

"Hey, I'm not underestimating the American Armenian Relief efforts, in the slightest," Lance protested lightly, "but, the downside to all of this is, the Azerbaijans are holding up some of the shipments to rebuild Armenia because of the trouble in Karabagh. We here in America have got to put more pressure on them to release the shipments. So far, its been useless. Ted and I will try to get resolutions through on the floor of the senate and house condemning the blockade. But, even the Turks have joined the blockade to stop the shipments."

Tatiana gasped. "How will Armenia survive?"

"The way she has for centuries, through ingenuity, know-how and sacrifice," Ted replied determinedly. "The first thing we have to do is set up flights there to bring in all the necessary supplies. Remember the Berlin Airlift when the commies tried to cut the city off from the west? Well that's what we'll do. Get some airline set up with cargo planes that will fly directly into Yerevan. I know we can raise money from many sources, especially wealthy Armenians, who would help if it was presented to them in the right way. If they understand it's for the survival of Armenia, they'll help. We'll need aviation experts for the formulation of the presentation. We'll also need advice on the type of aircraft required to carry the largest payload, with enough fuel for just one stop-over in reaching Yerevan. They will have to stay out of Turkish air space. Our contributors must be convinced of the value of such an endeavor if they're to approve the plan. Everything must be considered, gas, navigation, feasibility of landing, pilots, everything. Each detail must be considered with utmost care. We've got to convince our contributors of the dire need, if Armenia is to survive. Once she is totally blockaded, it will be too late. This is the point we have to hammer to them."

"You've hit on a damn good idea, Ted," Lance said with enthusiasm. "An airline direct to Armenia with one stop for refueling. Let's get started on that project right away, and see who can make up a great presentation. Have you any leads on who we can approach once we have the presentation?"

"What about the man in California who had been active in starting an airline some years ago? I believe he owned a movie studio, too. Now that's a shrewd businessman and details would be important to him. We'll need a damn good presentation. I'll look up his name and address," Ted replied.

Lance lifted his hand. "I met a man some years ago who worked for IBM on a consultant basis; he was in charge of presentations for any type of endeavor. As I recall, he owns his own ad agency and public relations firm. We could probably get hold of him, and he could work up the presentation."

"Great," said Ted approvingly. "We'll get on it first thing in the morning."

"Don't forget, they're three hours behind us, Ted."

Ted laughed. "No, I'm not forgetting."

Lance looked at his watch. "Speaking of time, it's after nine. I'd better get on that beltway and head home. I hate driving the beltway at night."

"Yeh, it's rough," Ted agreed.

When they walked to the front door, Tatiana took Lance's hand and looked seriously into his face. "Remember what I said about Karamine, Lance. She'll be home before you know it. In the meantime, just be patient."

Lance bent down and kissed her gently on the cheek. "Good night, Tatiana. Thanks for the coffee and sympathy! I guess I just needed a little reassurance."

Alone on the beltway, Lance settled into the traffic. Light from the winter moon seemed pale and distant above the string of oncoming traffic lights; frosty mist drifted in from the Potomac. Tatiana's words of comfort and advice came back to him, and he pondered their meaning.

I know Karamine loves me, but can love survive these grim assaults of loneliness and pain? Lance hit the steering wheel with his gloved fist. Damn, It's just that I miss her, and Hell yes! If I mind competing with her dedicated work, then yes, I guess I'm guilty of 'selfish emotionalism', as Tatiana calls it. It's easy enough for them, he reasoned—she and Ted aren't apart for months unend, with minimum contact. He drove the rest of the way home torn by a flood of uneasy and contradictory thoughts.

25

Spring arrived early in Leninakan with blustery winds and torrents of warm rain. The elements did little to lift the spirits and general pessimism of the people, who grieved endlessly over their losses and shattered lives. Things were moving slowly in the city's rebuilding, and there were days when Karamine's endurance hit bottom. Work had begun on the new hospital, but, there were many delays and complications, due partly to the blockade of supplies in Azerbaijan. There was more volunteer help now at the field hospital, but, the overload of patients and their desperate needs continued; Karamine was on call morning, noon and night. Her only consolation was the comfort of the small prefabricated housing unit, one of the many shipped by Germany to house the quake victims over the winter. She had been pleasantly surprised to find the unit well equipped with many small conveniences—heat, furniture, cooking area, refrigerator and most importantly, hot water and shower. The units were powered by diesel generators, located some distance away from the pre-fabs and hospital, because of the noise they generated.

At times, Karamine felt guilty having the entire unit to herself, when there were so many destitute families coping with hardship. But, Doctor Papken, in charge of the field hospital, had convinced her—she worked hard and needed the rest and convenience of her own place. Besides, this was little enough payment and appreciation for the magnanimous contribution she was making in their time of crises, he'd said.

Today had been particularly long and strenuous. The stream of patients seemed endless. When will it ever ease up, she thought, wearily, as she entered the small unit and kicked off her shoes. She dropped onto a small sofa, closed her eyes, and tried to block out the images of crushed limbs and broken bones. Amputees were the worst. Here I am a pediatrician doing surgery; Thank God, I had operating room experience during internship, she thought. Her eyes wandered over the small room, with its utilitarian furniture and neatly built-in cupboards and seats. It reminds me of the waiting room on the ferry boat we took to Nantucket once; She smiled to herself, thinking back to her apartment in Boston, her luxurious carpeting, silk drapes, the damask-covered chairs . . . and . . . that view of the Charles River! It's like a dream, those days with Lance. Wonderful weekends with nothing to do but sleep late, go to church, have leisurely breakfasts, and read the newspapers. God! how we take it all for granted!

She got up and walked slowly into the bathroom, where she took off her clothes, and turned on the shower. The hot water was soothing when she stepped into it. She stood there for some time, allowing its warm flow to melt away the stress and tensions of the day. She lathered herself carefully with a bar of white soap. It was the last of the supply she had brought from home, and it was too precious to waste. Soap was a rare commodity now, even at the hospital, where it was used constantly for cleaning hands and instruments. Rinsing off, she replaced the bar in a plastic container away from the splashing water.

After the shower, Karamine put on a warm robe, stretched out on a cot, and covered herself with a heavy Russian blanket. One of the soldiers had given it to her as a gift, in gratitude for her medical services to him as well as to many others in the Russian army. Karamine admired their youthful vitality, and thanked them for their generosity and help. She had grown to love these people—her heart had opened a wide fissure of compassion for them, and she had discovered within herself a nobility and strength in ministering, unselfishly to their sufferings. How can I leave them, she asked herself again and again. Can I abandon them to new levels of despair and wretchedness, when a situation is within my skill and ability to treat and make whole? Never! To do so would contradict every noble passion and truth I've held dear. Yet the cost is supreme. I've put my own private world on hold, and challenged the depths of my husband's love. She sighed deeply, and her eyes filled. Lance, Lance, she thought, When will we ever be together again? I need your strength, love and support. I have never missed you as much.

She was aroused suddenly from her musings by a sharp rap on the door. The imperious tone startled her. Not another emergency, she thought, groping for her slippers and removing the towel from her damp hair.

"Who is it?" she called out cautiously.

"Vasken, your brother, who else. Can I come in for a few minutes?"

"Vasken! Well of course, come in," Karamine said opening the door and embracing her brother. "What on earth are you doing here, in Leninakan?"

"Well, I don't have much time, only a couple of hours, really, but I wanted to see you. Hey . . . not bad, not bad at all, Karamine, for a prefab," he said approvingly, looking around her small quarters.

Karamine smiled. "Well, considering what some people are suffering, I suppose I'm pretty lucky. I've all the comforts of home. What else could I want for, except perhaps a year off to do nothing and recuperate."

Vasken eyed her sharply. "You do nothing? That'll be the day! I must say though, you do look a bit down at the heels. Not overdoing things are you, my dear sister?"

"Thanks, just what I need to hear, Vasken," Karamine replied irritably. "Why are you here anyway?"

"Well, I didn't come here to upset you, Karamine, but, I do seem to have a knack of saying the wrong thing to you, as always. How can I make it up?"

Karamine turned to face her brother. "Well, for one thing, you can tell your comrades in Azerbaijan to release the supplies they are holding up in the railroad yards. We're out of important medical supplies here, like antibiotics and disinfectants. You're the one who believes in the brotherhood of the proletariat, under the banner of bolshevism. How come they have no compunction about holding up supplies to a fellow communist country? They know how badly we need those supplies and the dire straits we're in. If they're comrades, why don't they release the supplies if they believe, according to your dogma, that there is no country or national boundaries."

An uneasy expression flashed across Vasken's face. "Well, I wouldn't admit this to anyone, but you have a valid point, Karamine. I've seen and heard a lot of things lately that bother me and shake my core beliefs. I have this feeling there is something frightfully wrong. You know me . . . I've never been afflicted by so insignificant a thing as 'bourgeoise conscience'. For me there's only been one goal . . . the promise of Marx and Engles and their worker's paradise; some of the things I've witnessed here, however, inspire me with doubt. But . . . about those shipments held up in Baku, Karamine, I've given that a lot of thought myself. In fact, I'm way ahead of you. I've already approached some people at headquarters in Yerevan, and with Sylvana's help, I'm trying to get permission to go to Azerbaijan and talk to the head of the party there. I'd say to them exactly what you've just said. I'd ask them to inform me, as a comrade, just why they are doing this to a fellow communist republic. Since we're all members of the Republics of the Soviet Union, damn it, it's their duty to help us, especially now after this devastating quake. I'll put the question to them. I'll say, how does it look to the world when a fellow soviet republic blockades supplies to another in need. I'll do my best to get the supplies released to Armenia."

"Do you think the resistance in Karabakh has anything to do with it?"

Vasken shook his head. "That's an internal matter, and entirely different issue. Those people want self rule, which has nothing to do with Armenia and the quake. Hah!" he remarked with slight contempt, "those damn Azeris are sure getting their fannies kicked off, but good! They thought they'd just walk in and push the Armenians out, like the Turks did in 1920. Surprise, surprise . . . for them! They met a formidable defense force they hadn't reckoned with. Up to now, it's been easy for them with their ethnic cleansing, no one but old men, women and children. Now they're up against a force they can't deal with so easily."

Karamine remained silent. She took a deep breath then gazed at Vasken thoughtfully. "What have you to do with the fighting in Karabakh, Vasken? Are you connected with that?"

Vasken smiled warily. "Let's just say I've tried to do my small bit for the people of Karabakh. That's about all I can say at the moment. I want them to be a free country like Nakhichevan. Look Karamine, don't repeat one word of this conversation to anyone, it's strictly between you and me, OK? It's very important, lives depend on it."

"So, you're coming here to Leninakan to see me is merely a cover for something or other, is that it?" Karamine snapped.

Vasken laughed a little, and shook his head. "You always jump to conclusions, Karamine. True, there are things I have to do here, but, believe it or not, I was concerned for you and your safety. I wanted to see for myself how you were doing. As for my other involvements, they are no concern of yours. Furthermore, I want to emphasize the importance of your silence regarding my being here. If anyone asks questions, tell them I'm here to see you and that's all. Most of my stay has been with you, do you understand?" he questioned sharply. "Even if anyone from Yerevan inquires, don't say anything about our conversation. I'm visiting you and that's it. Got it?"

Karamine nodded her head. "Yes, I've got it," she responded dully.

"Dare I ask about this Sylvana Markovyan, Vasken? Now there's a woman with a mind or should I say will of her own."

Vasken laughed. "Yeah, she's that all right. That's why I have her with me, to push them along with what I want. Like the trip to Baku to release the shipments. Everyone's afraid of her in Yerevan. When she speaks, they jump, and damn, she usually gets what she wants."

"Oh? And does that include you, Vasken? I got the impression she did."

Vasken laughed again. "Well, like I said, she's all woman, warm-blooded and strong. Take my word for it."

"Oh so you've already explored those talents and find them satisfying. Somehow I never thought of you in that kind of role, Vasken. You're a mystery, and you never disappoint me."

"See . . . you don't know me as well as you think. Good. It amuses me when people think they know me. Only I know the intricacies and passions of my own mind, and that's the way I like it."

Karamine shook her head. "Soft grace was certainly never one of your virtues, Vasken," she said with exasperation. "Well, if you want some female advice, take it easy with this woman. Since as you say, she doesn't take no for an answer from anyone, that may include you as well."

"Look, I know how to handle Sylvana. She has everyone jumping to her tune. Not me. I give it to her squarely without pretense, and she appreciates that. Right now, she's working on my clearance for the trip to Baku. I hope to talk to the leader there about the release of these supplies. I'm damn sure she'll get the clearance for me. The only trouble is, she wants to go along with me, and that's a problem. I want to go alone so I can move fast and easy if things don't work out. I don't want anyone holding me back. From what I've heard, Armenians in Baku are being beaten and driven from their homes."

"Will you have some sort of immunity or protection if it is so dangerous there?" Karamine inquired with alarm.

"Hey look, I don't need a babysitter. I can take care of myself as long as I'm alone, so don't worry. I just want to see this Gamal Arshod, Commussariat of the Party, and see if I can get him to influence the Azeris to release those supplies for Armenia, sitting in their freight yard. I'll be short and to the point. I'll simply explain and remind him of his duty as a fellow communist; I'll convince him it's to their benefit to help and not hinder the recovery of Armenia. Comrade helping comrade. If anyone can move the shipments, he can. I've heard he's a power to reckon with in Azerbaijan."

"Do you really think he'll help?" Karamine inquired.

"I have no idea at all what I'll accomplish there, but it has to be done. By everything that's communistic, he has an obligation to help, and he's got to be approached before all hell breaks loose in Karabakh. The people there are getting impatient and are arming fast. If a full scale war breaks out . . . those supplies are gone. The Azeris will keep them for their own use." He glanced at his watch. "I have to go."

Karamine was filled suddenly with inexplicable apprehension. "You will take care, Vasken," she said, softly, placing her hands on his shoulders. "You are my brother, and I do love you."

Vasken laughed. "In spite of everything?"

"Yes, in spite of everything you did to hurt Lance. Forgiveness opens the channels of love and success. You should try it sometime."

"Now don't go preachy on me, Karamine. I'll be all right." He embraced her briefly. "And remember . . . my visits here to Leninakan are always to see you, Right? It's very important."

"Right. I'll remember, Vasken."

He kissed her on the forehead as he did years ago when they were children, then gently, he pushed her aside and walked out to the waiting car. He stepped in and waved once, as the car pulled out and headed for the airfield and a new challenge.

Vasken settled into a comfortable position after adjusting his seatbelt, when Aeroflot flight 35 took off from Yerevan for the city of Baku in Azerbaijan. He looked out the window and tried to catch a glimpse of the landscape below, but a grey, heavy overcast blocked his view. He breathed a sigh of relief. Finally, he was on his way to Baku. Through Sylvana and his own determined efforts, they were able to convince the Armenian Communist Party in Yerevan to allow him to make the trip. The permission was granted with some reluctance, however, and Vasken was strongly cautioned of the many perils he might encounter there. "Remember, they are Muslims," the Yerevan commussariat had advised, "and Gamal Arshod hates Armenians and has always given us trouble. Nothing may be lost in your attempt but your life, my fellow comrade. So, be warned." He was relieved, the Commussariat had refused to allow Sylvana to accompany him. He knew how to take care of himself, and he didn't want the responsibility of someone else to worry about. He smiled to himself recalling her outrage and angry words the night before, "I can take care of myself. I'm worth two of those whining mealy-mouthed Bolsheviks in headquarters. They're nothing but a bunch of blood sucking bureaucrats, and you, Vasken Casparian, know it." Vasken had laughed then, and pulled her solidly toward him in a strong embrace. He felt her body against his, the pressure of her full rounded breasts against his chest. He recalled kissing her into submission and silence, as he undressed her, and placed her on the bed. Sylvana had responded with burning pleasure and mutual desire. They delighted in each other's ardor, forgetful of everyone in the world around them, except the union of their bodies, and the exploding ecstasy of their passion. Vasken closed his eyes, and smiled, recalling once more the pleasure and delights of the previous evening, and Sylvana's urgent message to him the next day before boarding the plane "Be careful, my proud strong stallion; Sylvana wants you back!"

Vasken closed his eyes and continued to indulge himself in the pleasure of his private inner world for almost an hour. It was only when the plane hit turbulence, and they were advised to buckle up their seat belts, that Vasken looked around and took note of the piercing eyes and malevolent scrutiny of some of the passengers. A sixth sense told him he was the only Armenian on board heading for Azerbaijan, that most of the passengers were Islamic Azeris returning home from Moscow. He knew instinctively they were suspicious of his western clothing and ruddy complexion, which marked him as a foreigner, someone to watch. This amused him. He could read their minds and he delighted in adding to the mystery, challenging them by fierce looks and body language. He returned their hostile gazes defiantly. They are so blinded by their own hatreds and fanaticism, they react in the manner of all ineffectual men, he reasoned. Only the man who subordinates his reflexes to the power of his will can attain mastery and control. These fools subordinate their passions to the power of their fear, which makes them a treacherous and unstable enemy. They fear us, and what we Armenians may accomplish if left alone and free to accomplish our own goals. He sighed heavily. And so it has been for centuries. The Armenian people have been tormented perpetually by these same Islamic Turks to the West, Iran to the south, and Azerbaijan to the east. They are bordered on three sides by Islamic fundamentalists. Sometimes I wonder if the persecution of the Armenians is the result of their embracing Christianity, a fool's religion to the moslems, and no wonder—the meek shall inherit the earth, turn the other cheek, love your enemy. What bullshit! No wonder they think they can push us around. Yet, on the other hand, they fear us. They fear our ingenuity and spirit. They know damn well the Ottoman Empire was nothing without the creativity of the Armenian architects, artisans and builders. We gave life, culture and meaning to the empire.

Once I get to Baku I'll go to see Gamal Arshod immediately, he thought, bringing his mind back to the purpose of the trip. I'd better rehearse the approach I'll use and just exactly what I'm going to say to him. He's a shrewd weasel from what I hear so I don't want any slip-ups. I'd better have my facts straight. I'll approach him first in the name of comradeship and good will; I'll ask him to release the supplies stagnating in the rail yards of Baku, and to allow them to enter Armenia. I'll persuade him as a communist in good standing, that it's his duty to do so, since, after all, we are brothers under the Soviet Union. Then, I'll appeal to his egotistical self-importance, by explaining the need as a great humanitarian gesture, which would be reported throughout the world; I'll convince him that this would demonstrate the profound compassion and understanding of the Azeri people, which would naturally reflect on their great, great leader. Yeah! How can he possibly refuse? Vasken thought, pleased by his fondness for flattery, when used as a weapon of guile.

The Karabakh Defense force is not going to make things easy in my negotiations, however, he reasoned. Unfortunately, the timing is not good. Wish it all could have waited, but, I can understand why the Armenians in Karabakh had no choice with all the deportations and persecution of our people. Well, it's too late now, the die is cast. We have to take it from here. Christ, if Gamal Arshod had any inkling of my part in all this, he'd have me shot before I got off the plane. Vasken smirked to himself. Well, what the hell does he expect? Arshod must know the history of Karabakh, and how Stalin gave it to the Azeri back in 1920 against the will of the Armenian people. Ninety percent of the population there is still Armenian; their churches and buildings in that area are centuries old. But, I'll have to weigh my words carefully with Arshod. It's vital I don't offend him or his country. Won't be easy, but I'll play along. I just won't mention Karabakh or make any demands pertaining to that particular conflict. I'll get it across to him that Karabakh is an internal problem, that it has nothing to do with Armenia, and Armenia is not helping them in any way.

Vasken felt the airplane slow down and its turbines decelerate and begin the descent from its altitude. He tightened his seat belt when the landing light went on and the pilot announced they were arriving in Baku. Slowly the aircraft descended to pattern altitude, as the Baku controller indicated the runway to use for landing. Looking over the fast approaching landscape, Vasken noted the sprawling city of Baku, and the outlines of derricks in the numerous oil fields. The craft's wheels touched the ground with a slight jerk, rolling out its landing. He felt the pressure of his body's forward motion as the brakes were put on and the turbines reversed, slowing the aircraft down to taxi. The pilot taxied to the assigned tarmac, and was guided around for the disembarking of the passengers.

He reached for his handbag and brief case from the overhead compartment, then headed toward the exit door. The line moved slowly. Craning his neck, Vasken saw the passengers going through the customs area, where they were interrogated and their passports and papers checked. He had no difficulty getting through, however. In his most authoritative tone, Vasken informed the customs officer he had an appointment with Gamal Arshod at headquarters, and his papers and passport were immediately stamped, allowing him to pass.

Once outside the terminal, Vasken approached a parked, unmarked car. "Is the car for hire?" he inquired, in his best Turkish.

The driver nodded. Vasken pulled out the slip of paper with Gamal Arshod's address and passed it to the driver, then got in the car.

"It's the communist headquarters, in the old part of the city," the driver informed him, taking the cigarette out of his mouth. "Gamal Arshod is the commusariat of the whole party."

"Yes. He's been notified of my arrival and is expecting me," Vasken informed him.

The driver eyed him suspiciously in the rear view mirror. "That last plane . . . it came from Armenia, yes?"

Vasken returned his gaze stoically, wondering if he should answer the driver's question correctly. "Yes, that was the last stop before Baku."

"You don't look like anyone from the Soviet Republic. Are you a foreigner?"

I wonder if this guy is KGB, Vasken thought to himself. If he knows I'm Armenian he'll dump me in the street, or worse, try to have me arrested on some pretense.

"I'm an American visiting Armenia, and I have business here in Baku with Gamal Arshod."

Again the driver studied Vasken in the rear view mirror. "You're Armenian, aren't you?" he asked.

Vasken was taken aback by the directness of the question, and he tried to control his annoyance. "Yes, I'm an American citizen, of Armenian descent, if it's any concern of yours."

The driver broke into a wide smile. "Good, good I am Armenian also! My name is Setrog Nazeri. I cut my name from Nazerian so they do not suspect I am Armenian. If they knew, I'm afraid my family and myself would be thrown out of our home, beaten, and Lord knows what else." He shook his head sadly. "Things are bad here for Armenians ever since the resistance started in Karabakh. Coming from Armenia, you must have seen all the refugees there and heard their stories."

"Yes I have heard the stories, and I'm sorry to see our people in such dire circumstances. But, don't despair. I'm here to see if something can be done to release the supplies so badly needed by Armenia. I intend to plead the case with Gamal Arshod, and try to enlist his help. I am Vasken Casparian," he stated, extending his hand.

"Yes, I know of the supplies, but I doubt if you'll get any help from Arshod. He hates us. There's a group of us here who are trying to plan a way of getting into the freight yards and taking off with the train, along with our families. We have railroad workers who know their way around trains and know how to head the trains for Armenia. We thought we'd take the freight, and all Armenians who were willing to chance it and make a dash for the border and into Armenia. We want to escape this country."

An expression of alarm crossed Vasken's face. He admired Setrog's courage and fortitude to devise such a plan to get his family out, but, realized the desperation of the situation, and desperate men often make foolish errors. "You'd be a fool to take such a risk, my friend. The Azeri have airplanes the Turks have given them, and they have trained pilots. Believe me, they would strafe and bomb the train before you ever hit the border. Worse, they'd blow up the tracks leading to Armenia, and that would be the end of you and your families."

"At least we'd die trying to escape. That's preferable to living in constant fear of sooner or later being put to the torch," Setrog commented dismally.

Vasken remained quiet the rest of the trip. They were entering the old section of Baku now, passing outdoor vendors selling vegetables and other foods. Here and there, the driver pointed to the fascade of some Islamic structure, rock turrets which centuries ago were strongholds against advancing armies of Mongols, Tartars and Alexander the Great's armies. He pointed out some archways, commenting that these were typical Armenian structures, designed and built by them at that time for the great Khan. They passed heavy and ornate wooden doors that had borne the assault of centuries; mosques with glistening minarets, dating back to the eleventh century. They turned a corner and entered a huge plaza; the buildings here were ancient with time-worn columns and richly-wrought Arabic embellishments. There were steps leading up to one of the structures from the plaza. The driver stopped in front of them.

"Here you are . . . communist headquarters," he announced. "Just go up those steps and through the entrance. You can ask for Gamal Arshod's offices. Anyone there can show you."

Vasken was impressed with the plaza and the buildings with its Arabic design arched over the entrance. He looked at the steps leading to the upper section and wondered how many there were to the entrance. It reminded him of the steps leading to the Lincoln Memorial in Washington.

"It's quite impressive," Vasken admitted to Setrog. "I've seen pictures of that memorial in books."

"Yes, it is. During peace times, we Armenians would come down here often and sit and talk. Not anymore, my friend. It's too dangerous. So . . . be cautious and careful."

Vasken got out of the car, and noticed a large crowd milling about someone, and several shouts as people joined in. "What's going on over there?" he questioned.

"Probably an argument of what to do about Karabakh and the fighting. It's always something. That's why I warned you about your safety. Take care. Being American will not help you one bit in these times."

"Will you wait for me?" Vasken asked with a laugh. "I may have to leave in a hurry. Would it be asking too much of you to wait around this place?" He thrust a generous amount of rubles into his hand.

"You don't have to bribe me. You are Armenian. I'll wait."

"Take it, you may earn it yet," said Vasken, thrusting the rubles into Setrog's jacket pocket. He headed for the steps, skirting around the crowd who were becoming unruly. He walked through the heavy doors, and into a foyer, then stopped an attendant and asked directions to Gamal Arshod's office. The attendant did not understand Vasken's broken Turkish, but recognized Gamal Arshod's name, and indicated the direction with two fingers. On the second floor, he looked for the most prominent office, then entered boldly. A plain-looking woman glanced up from where she sat behind a large oak desk, and surveyed him coldly.

"What do you want?" she asked bluntly in Azerbaijan.

"My name is Vasken Casparian," he answered in his best Turkish. "I have an appointment with Gamal Arshod." The woman conveyed no warmth, but motioned Vasken to a seat, then picked up an antiquated inner office phone and spoke rapidly, referring to Vasken, while appraising him astutely.

Vasken picked up a magazine from a table nearby and scanned it with detachment. It was an industrial magazine depicting Azerbaijan's plants and chemical companies, machine factories, textile mills and oil rigs rising from the Caspian Sea. The pictures were excellent in themselves, but Vasken's interest was jolted suddenly by the equipment demonstrated in the photos. Through Industrial Processing courses taken in college, he had acquired a smattering of knowledge, pertaining to industry, logging and farming. He knew enough to recognize that the equipment displayed in the Azerbaijan photos was of ancient vintage, and had been out of use in most modern countries for years. That's odd, he thought, studying the pictures more closely. They have all the raw materials they need to compete in today's world; certainly the Soviet Union is a modern, industrialized country, or so he had been informed in the United States. So, what's the dichotomy here? Looks like they're not as modern as we've been led to believe, he concluded, tossing the magazine back on the table.

The door to the inner office opened. Gamal Arshod stood framed on the threshold, like some forbidding portrait of an ancient Tartar. A slanting ray of sunshine from an inner window fell obliquely across the upper half of his face, highlighting awesome brows, narrow and thinly drawn over obsidian-black eyes; His beard was thick, but finely cut, meshing neatly into a mustache, that lay like a cropped brush above the curved, and much too reddened lips. He stood there for a moment, his hawk-like glance darting, swiftly and coldly over Vasken's presence.

Vasken stood up and took a few steps toward him. The play of light accented Gamal's high cheek bones, his deep, olive-tinted skin and greying black hair, combed straight back. Vasken extended his hand, which Gamal took in a steel-like grip. His hand felt hard as flint. Vasken felt a deep foreboding.

He tried to speak a few words of greeting to him in Turkish, but Gamal put his hand up quickly to stop him.

"Please . . ." he said in English, "your Turkish is worse than my English, so if we are to understand each other, let's converse in English."

Vasken was surprised. Gamal smiled guardedly. "I see you are surprised. I learned your language at the university, where we were informed that it was most important for one to learn English, especially for foreign trade and politics. It also helped me to get ahead in the party, as very few of the students learn other languages. So . . . we speak English, please."

Entering Gamal's office, Vasken took in its appearance at a glance. The furniture was old, with the distinct smell of time, and the windows, set in deep mahogany frames were grimy and unwashed. An oriental rug, thrown haphazardly on the floor was stained and worn, showing abuse and neglect; the walls and ceiling were dull, as though they hadn't been painted or washed in decades, and the air in the room was stale, and oddly scented.

"Now . . . what is the purpose of your trip to Azerbaijan at this time, and why do you wish to see me in particular?" Gamal began.

"Sir . . ." Vasken began with measured artfulness, "I have come here as a fellow comrade from the Soviet Republic of Armenia, on a mission of humanitarian nature."

Gamal raised his hand. "Wait. Are you saying you are Armenian? This I cannot believe. Your whole manner of dress, and speech, would lead me to believe you were born and raised in the United States. You are American, yes?"

Before Vasken could respond, Gamal continued speaking, pacing back and forth, darting occasional sidelong glances toward Vasken. "I've had you investigated since we first set up this appointment, comrade. I know quite a bit about you, and your activities as a communist in America. You are aware of course, that we do keep records of our members throughout the world. I must say, your record is impressive, comrade, especially among the American Armenians . . . oh yes, and among the Americans also." Gamal paused to stop directly in front of Vasken and look piercingly into his eyes. "Do you still believe in the overthrow of your American government, comrade? Do you still like and respect Gorbachev? Do you still adhere to Lenin's teaching of world socialism, or have you become a renegade and joined the bourgeoisie?"

Vasken met Gamal's gaze coolly, while trying to control his mounting agitation. He took a deep breath before answering, choosing his words carefully. "If you have done a thorough investigation of me, as you say, comrade, you will have discovered that I am much with Lenin's teaching, in the class struggle, and the ultimate destruction of all capitalistic systems. Surely you've been informed of my activities with peace groups, demonstrating and recruiting young activists for the cause against the war in Viet Nam. That war wasn't lost in Viet Nam for Americans. It was lost in the streets of America through the turmoil we created by our demonstrations on college campuses. And . . . the American media willingly played right into our hands."

Gamal Arshod smiled, his red, bearded lips parting scornfully. "Yes, I've read that account of your activities, and found them to be quite impressive . . . for what it was. But the applauding and congratulations must go to your congress in the USA. They are the ones who refused to resupply the South Vietnamese, comrade. They, South Vietnamese were unable to use their equipment against the Viet Cong forces, for lack of gas, ammunition, and other necessities of fighting." Gamal laughed heartily. "The action of your congress there was better than an ally." He looked at Vasken quizzically. "Have you ever read Von Clauswitz's book ON WAR?"

"No, I don't believe I ever have. I haven't even heard of him," Vasken replied.

Gamal shrugged, then gestured dramatically with his hand. "Hah! That's a must in our soviet republic schools. Every comrade should study and absorb it. As Von Clauswitz says, the first step in defeating your adversary is to destroy the will to fight. Wars are not won on the battle field only, comrade. You and your cohorts in America with your demonstrations and turmoil, as well as your very cooperating congress helped us achieve our goals. Read for yourself. That book is a must to understand the politics of war. And remember, war is an extension of politics. From what I understand, the military schools in the USA no longer teach Von Clauswitz's ON WAR. Good! That's to our advantage." Gamal turned and looked out the window. "If I seem to get carried away on the point, comrade, I merely wish to indicate how stupidity and treason can destroy a country. It's important to understand the large picture, and you, comrade, are part of it, and therefore call it to mind." He turned from the window to face Vasken, and resumed speaking. "Now, comrade, just what is it you have come to see me about?"

Vasken, aware of the veiled contempt in Gamal's speech, lowered the tone of his voice, and decided to appeal immediately to his ego and sense of power. "As I've stated," he begun, "I've come on a humanitarian mission, for a fellow communist republic, Armenia. You are surely aware that with over 27,000 killed, and many of the smaller towns and villages destroyed, the people are in dire need of the supplies held here in the freight yards of Azerbaijan. Food, piping, clothing, machinery and medical supplies, donated by nations all over the world are stagnating, while your fellow comrades in Armenia are freezing and dying. In the name of what we both believe, our commitment to communism and our cause, in the name of humanity, I appeal to you to intercede and release the supplies; allow them to enter Armenia. I understand you have great influence with the party here in Azerbaijan, and people listen to what you say and do. This would be a tremendous gesture of the Azerbaijani people, which the entire world would note and applaud. It would open many doors for your country's development."

Gamal Arshod listened to Vasken with cynical amusement. He lifted an eyebrow and surveyed Vasken coldly.

"You wish me to intercede?" he said scornfully. "Intercede? For those Armenian *Gavoors* (Christian Dogs)? He threw back his head and laughed unpleasantly. "Never! We've got those supplies and we'll hold them hostage until those *Gavoors* in Karabakh lay down their arms, and submit to the will of the Azerbaijan people. We want every Armenian out of Karabakh, do you understand? We will drive you Armenians out one way or another. Karabakh will be completely Islamic. That is my answer to you and your people. Humanitarian," he mocked, "Bah! Never!"

Vasken stared at Gamal, his anger mounting, but, he realized there was too much at stake to lose his temper. I've got to play it smart, he thought, I'm in a precarious position here with this madman. He remained silent while Gamal resumed his ranting.

"Anyway, all of that territory belongs to us. Stalin gave it to us in 1923, and it's now part of Azerbaijan, and has been since that time. You may be sure, comrade, we are going to keep it. Armenians have been a curse to us ever since our acquisition. We intend to clean it out and populate the place with believers, our Islamic people. Had you *Gavoors* embraced the Islamic faith we could have lived together in peace and harmony, as brethren. It's your damn women who rebuff Allah and our people. They turn you against us and think they are better than we are. The Islamic faith and women's place in it is abhorrent to them. The problem is with you men. You treat your women as equals, and this makes them arrogant and independent. Our brother Turks have known how to bring them into a more, shall we say, manageable cooperation with our society? Many a female *gavoor* (Christian Dog) has decorated our harems, and many thousands lay dead by our Islamic swords, and will continue so in the future."

Vasken felt every muscle of his body strain. For all his training and success with maximum control under all circumstances, and subordinating his reflexes to the power of his will, the quick and independent blood of his ancestors rushed into his face, and he was filled with sudden rage and hatred for this contemptible *Vad Shoon* (perverted dog). He longed to seize his throat, to choke back the brazen, insulting words, and rip the loathsome, lying tongue from his mouth. Only a supreme act of will restrained him. Stay cool, he cautioned himself. He's looking to draw me into a heated confrontation, and I'm not going to fall for that, and entrap myself, especially here in his country. There's too much at stake, and the release of those supplies is critical for our people. Look for a point of weakness to address him on his own ground. For all the cool assurance in his voice, Vasken's eyes held a deadly expression of contempt, although he smiled and spoke with calm deliberation. "Let the past be forgotten, comrade, and all our old enmities. As for Karabakh, there's only a few hotheads stirring the pot. The demonstrations in Yerevan do not reflect the will of the Armenian people who only yearn for peace, and the rebuilding of their homeland devastated by the earthquake. Karabakh is an internal Azeri problem, which could be solved without bloodshed. As a demonstration of good will and faith, let the supplies through, and I will go back and tell the Armenian people of your generosity. This will help reconcile the Karabakh situation, I promise you, and you will be a great shining light of understanding between the people. Your premise and the views of the Azeri people will be presented, and I shall try to have it resolved to the benefit of both our nations. Don't let personal feelings overcome the need for peaceful resolution, comrade. The fighting there is not good for Azerbaijan, nor is it good for Armenia. The differences must be reconciled. Don't let hotheads on both sides make a bad situation worse. I appeal to you . . . make this gesture of good faith to a fellow communist republic in need. Release the supplies."

"Never!" Gamal Arshod shouted. "We have those supplies and we will never let them go until you Armenian *gavoors* lay down your arms and accept our domination, as I said before, or leave . . . one or the other." He walked to the window again and stared down, then wheeled around to face Vasken once more. "You and your people don't understand. The earthquake that killed so many of you and destroyed your towns, was the will of ALLAH. He punished your people for not embracing the Koran and for refusing to follow Him. Fools! That's what you people are, fools!" Gamal continued his violent denunciation of the Armenian people. "You Christian Armenians have to understand. You are alike wheat growing in the fields. We Islamics allow you to grow, ripen, multiply and prosper, we allow you to feel secure. Then, when you are ripe for our harvest, we harvest you with the sword. All for the glory of ALLAH! You must understand . . . to kill an infidel Christian, guarantees us a passage to heaven and eternal peace. In Karabakh, comrade, it is harvest time, and no one can stop us."

Vasken opened his mouth to protest, but Gamal raised his hand. "I know . . . the Soviet Army! Well, comrade, they have other things to worry about at this time. Besides, they have no wish to offend other Moslem nations, Islamic republics, like Turkastan, Chechnya, and similar republics. Do you think they want uprisings? I think not, comrade." Again Gamal laughed unpleasantly. "No, they won't help you! The time has come for the Azerbaijan nation to use its power and break the barriers that separate us from our brother Shites in Iran. Armenians want Karabakh as an independent state . . . we want to leave the Soviet Union and join our brothers in Iran and Turkey. Let us see who survives."

Gamal's outburst left Vasken speechless. He didn't expect him to reveal so much of the ultimate goal of the Azerbaijani people, but he was glad for the revelation. He would have to inform the people in Yerevan as soon as he returned.

"Do you think Moscow will allow you to secede from the soviet union?" Vasken asked calmly. "They would send thousands of troops down here to prevent that, and you know it. If they allowed you to do such a thing the Balkans and other republics would follow. No, there's no way Moscow would allow it."

"We shall see, comrade, we shall see. Take some advice," he warned, lowering his voice menacingly, "don't stay here in Baku too long; Armenians are not safe, much less welcome here. Return to your people and inform them the supplies will never be released to Armenia. You can also inform them if they join or assist the rebels of Karabakh in any way, they will have a war on their hands. As for you, you'd better get out of Azerbaijan as fast as you can. As a comrade, I'm giving you this warning if you value your life. We don't want Christian dogs here in Azerbaijan polluting our land. Leave on the first plane out of here, and advise your fellow Armenians to do the same."

Vasken gasped incredulously. "Is this actually a warning and threat to me, and our people, comrade?"

"Threat? Of course it is a threat. Take it for what it is worth," Gamal stated bluntly. "We're sick and tired of the sight of you, especially here in Baku. You take all the good jobs, leaving nothing but menial work for our own people. This is going to change and change fast, comrade."

"Don't give me that crap," Vasken shouted, raising his voice finally, in an outburst of anger, "The Armenian people have been an asset to Azerbaijan, and they've helped upgrade the country and living standards through medicine, engineering and the arts. Where would you be without their ingenuity and talents? As for your threats? Bullshit! The Armenian people and I have had all of that before from your brother Turks. Oh they're good when it comes to defenseless women and children, but when it's a fight man to man we've always defeated you and your kind, so don't waste your threats on us. The supplies? We've asked for them in a humanitarian manner, and have been rebuffed. So be it. But believe me, supplies will get through with the help of Armenians abroad who have already set up the mechanism to airlift into Armenia. The hell with you and all Turks. I hope your nation rots in hell! And another thing . . . let me warn you . . ." Vasken pointed a finger in Gamal's face, "don't try to invade Karabakh, or your men will die by the thousands. Believe me, the men there are well armed and will be ready for you, that I can promise." Vasken stomped furiously out of Gamal Arshod's office, and headed for the street.

This is the last straw in a fool's illusion, he thought bitterly, while racing down the steps and looking for Setrog and the car. This dismal city of Baku with its seventy years of Bolshevik rule looks like time passed it by. My whole experience since coming to Armenia has been nothing but disillusionment and frustration; first the earthquake, and lack of heavy equipment to help the people there, then, the inferior workmanship of the buildings in Leninakan; I thought I would find a happy people, working for a better future here in the Republic of Soviet Armenia, but instead, all I find is apathy, despair and hardship for the people. And from what I've heard, Moscow and Leningrad are no different. This is not the Marxism I've been taught back at university in America. They never mentioned the stagnation and appalling bureaucracy stifling progress everywhere. Well shit! What could I have been thinking of anyway? How the hell could I have been so taken in. Talking to that bastard Gamal was the last straw. Withholding survival supplies to a desperate soviet country in need is too much to bear. This is a depressingly black day, he thought bleakly.

His attention was drawn suddenly to the noisy mob he had passed earlier on his way into Gamal's office. They were screaming and gesturing loudly now, and circling someone. He saw Setrog waiting by the car, and noticed the crowd had retreated to the sidewalk.

"What the hell's going on over there, Setrog?" he said when he ran down the steps.

Setrog shrugged. "Can't tell . . . hope it's not an Armenian."

"Get in the car and start your engine," Vasken ordered. "We may have to leave here in a hurry. Be ready."

Vasken inched his way closer to the mob, who were frenzied and shouting loudly. He tried to get a look at what was happening, and was propelled closer by the pressing in of an angry crowd. Suddenly he caught a clear view of what was happening. To his shock and amazement, he saw that a woman was the object of their attack. She had fallen to her knees and was now being dragged, kicked and spit upon. Her face registered intense fear, while she raised an arm in a futile attempt to shield herself from the jeering mob. Vasken elbowed his way closer and was horrified to see a man douse the woman with clear fluid. He couldn't identify the liquid until the vapors reached his nostrils. Gasoline! Christ! It's gasoline! He thought with alarm. Those bastards intend to incinerate that woman, they're going to burn her alive! He heard the woman's cries for mercy, and although her voice was weak and broken, Vasken immediately recognized her words as Armenian. *"Myrig . . . Myrig, Dervormier"* (Mother . . . Mother, Dear Lord help me). He also saw she was several months pregnant.

Vasken was filled suddenly with inexplicable rage and fury. Shoving hard he beat his way through the crowd intent on reaching the woman. When he got through the circle, he seized her by the arm with a steel grip, and pulled her apart from the crowd and close to him. *"Me vahknar, yes kezzy goknam* (don't be afraid, I'm going to help you)."

With one arm around her, he began to move toward the car, pushing and shoving his way through. His action was so swift, the mob near her didn't quite realize what had happened. He continued to smash and kick anyone who tried to block his way. As he got nearer the car, the man with the can of gasoline loomed up suddenly in front of him. Vasken gave him a straight hard jab with the bone of his palm, smashing his nose and causing it to bleed. As the man fell to his knees, Vasken struck him again in the face with his knee, sending him back in a heap. He dropped the can of gasoline and it started pouring out rapidly. Seizing the can, Vasken flung the remaining contents in a wide arc onto the crowd and on the ground in front of him; then, rapidly, he reached into his pocket for a book of matches, lit and threw one, igniting the gas. The explosion of fire panicked the crowd, dispersing them in all directions. Vasken made a run for the car, pulling the Armenian woman with him. Reaching it, he opened the door, thrust her inside quickly, then jumped in beside her.

"Quick, get going, before they know what happened and come after us," he barked to Setrog.

The car sped away from the plaza at top speed. Only when they had safely escaped from the older part of the city, did Setrog stop the car and turn around to look at the woman they had saved from a fiery death.

She sobbed hysterically in Vasken's arms. "Why? Why are they doing this? They killed my husband some weeks ago, for no reason except he was Armenian. And now me. They said it was an accident, but I know they killed him. Friends have turned against us, and we have no where to turn." She continued to cry uncontrollably.

Vasken held her gently until she finally settled down. Her face was swollen, and bruised, and there was a slight cut near her right temple. Her long black hair was disheveled, and her dress was torn and soiled.

"I owe my life to you both," she said at last when she had become calmer. "They would have burned me alive if it weren't for you. How do I ever repay you?"

"Repay? There's no repayment necessary for what we have done," Setrog said. "You're Armenian, one of the family, our flesh and blood. No need to speak of repayment, dear lady. We did what had to be done and thank God, Vasken was a match for that craven mob."

"So, your name is Vasken," she said softly, staring at him.

"Yes, Vasken Casparian, and this is Setrog Nazarian, who has shortened his name to Nazeri." He laughed.

"My name is Andreas Sassoni," she smiled slightly, also cut short. "I'm head nurse at the Lenin hospital here in Baku."

"You said your husband was killed? How?" Vasken inquired.

"He was an engineer on an oil rig in the Caspian Sea. He told me that some of the Azeris working with him had warned him that since the uprisings in Karabakh he was in danger, and should leave the country. They said it was unsafe for him and his family to stay in Azerbaijan, as there would be reprisals. A few weeks ago, I was informed at the hospital that they had brought in an accident victim who needed immediate attention." Andreas covered her face with her hands. "When the victim was brought in, I saw it was my husband. He was barely breathing." Her voice broke slightly. "I turned immediately to the head surgeon there, who is also Armenian, and told him what had happened. He did his best to save him, but it was to no avail. My husband passed on leaving me pregnant, and nowhere to turn."

"How do you know it wasn't an accident?" Vasken inquired.

"One of his fellow workers who was close to him, told me so. He said they deliberately let a heavy overhead pipe break loose and fall on top of him."

"How do you know he wasn't lying?" Setrog asked.

"No . . . he liked my husband, he is telling the truth, I am certain."

"What were you doing at communist headquarters, and how did you get involved with that crazed mob anyway?" Vasken asked.

Andreas shook her head sadly. "Since my husband has been killed, and I knew we Armenians were unwanted here in Azerbaijan, I wanted a visa and permission to leave the country. I was also informed my apartment had been broken into and ransacked. Everything I had of value was stolen, but the police would not do anything about it because

I am Armenian. They made a mess of the whole place and now, I am afraid to go back there. I don't know where to turn, much less what to do." She covered her face with her hands and began to cry again.

"Were you able to secure the visa?" Vasken asked gently. "Where would you go?"

"No, they refused me a permit to leave and a visa. Where would I go? Anyplace to get away from Azerbaijan. Anyplace."

"But why would they refuse you, *"archig"* (girl), they hate us and want to be rid of us. So why hold you here?"

"Simple. I am a head nurse and a certified anesthetist, with much experience in operating rooms. People with my training and credentials are in short supply here. So, they hate us, but don't want to get rid of us," she said bitterly.

"What turned the mob on you?"

"Someone recognized me from the hospital and shouted, 'There's one of them, those butchers of our sons, she's Armenian!' They began to gather around me, and wouldn't let me pass. It didn't take much to stir them up. Someone shrieked 'the Armenians are killing our sons, and we will kill you.' The police came, but did nothing. You saw them."

"Are you hurt?" Vasken asked.

"No, I seem to be all right," she said, inspecting a cut on her knee, "a bit shaken, however, and some bruises."

"Look, your clothes smell of gas, and that's dangerous. The vapors may ignite, so you have to get out of them and get cleaned up," Setrog said.

"I can't go back to my apartment," Andreas answered.

"It's all right, I'm going to take you to my house where you will be able to clean up and take care of those cuts and bruises. I'm sure my wife will have some extra clothes you can wear. Later, we will go back to your apartment and pick up anything you want to save, then you'll stay with us until you decide what you want to do. You will not be safe in your apartment. Those people may come back and try to finish the job they started," Setrog said decisively.

They drove through the streets of Baku, until they arrived finally on the outskirts of the city. The car stopped before a modest house, with a small lawn and some well trimmed shrubbery. Setrog entered the front door first, then returned to the car with his wife.

Setrog's wife bent down and looked into the back seat where Vasken and Andreas sat.

"*Parev* . . . (hello), please come in. I have fresh clothing for you . . . we will take care of you." She took Andreas by the arm and escorted her into the house. Vasken followed behind with Setrog, who took him into a small kitchen.

"Would you like some tea? Something to eat?" he asked.

"No, but I could sure use a drink if you happen to have anything around," Vasken answered.

"Good thinking, my friend," Setrog answered. "Yes, I do have something on hand." He searched through a lower cupboard, and came back with a magnum of vodka. "My wife thinks I drink too much, so she hides the bottle way back there," he laughed. He brought two glasses from a shelf, and placed them on the table, then pulled out a chair.

"Sit . . . be comfortable," he ordered. He poured out two healthy servings, then raised his glass, "to Armenian brothers and sisters, heaven preserve them."

"If there is such a place," Vasken replied cynically, before smiling and raising his glass.

"What are we to do with Andreas?" Setrog asked, after taking a few gulps of this drink. "She says she wants to go to Armenia."

"Yes, I know, but, she says she has no papers, and they won't let her out of the country without them. You know that." Vasken answered.

"Ah, papers!" Setrog exclaimed. "Papers!" He raised his hand in the air and stared at Vasken. "That's it. That's it!"

"What the hell are you talking about," Vasken replied.

"Let me see your clearance papers for a minute, I want to see what they say."

Vasken took an envelope from his inside coat pocket, and passed it to Setrog. What the hell are you up to, Setrog?"

Setrog's eyes raced over the papers. Suddenly he pointed to a sentence on the form. "There . . . there it is. It will be perfect. No one will suspect or question." he exclaimed, excitedly. "See here, where it says your name on the document? All we have to do is add . . . *and wife!* Simple! She will leave with you today."

Vasken looked at the document and to the line where Setrog pointed. "You know, they'll see it's been added, we'll never fool them, Setrog. Do you think it'll work?"

"Look, you are a member of high standing in the party, and when you go down to the field, you will be impatient, demanding to move along quickly. Bully them around with comments that you will report them to Gamal Arshod, and that'll scare the hell out of them. Don't allow them to examine the papers too long, push your way through. You can do it if anyone can, and take her with you."

Vasken remained silent a few minutes, while he thought over the idea. "Why not," he said, slapping Setrog on the arm, "yes, why the hell not. I'll give them such a hard time they'll be glad to get rid of us." He smiled at the prospect of a new challenge. "We've got to move fast, though, the plane will be leaving soon." He glanced at his watch.

Setrog found a pen and carefully added the words 'and wife', then he and Vasken had another drink.

Andreas and Setrog's wife came back into the kitchen. Andreas looked much better in a tan skirt and sweater, with matching boots. "The clothes fit perfectly," she said, "and you have all been too kind to me."

"We have a plan, but we have to move now." Vasken said.

"You, Andreas have a plane to catch."

Andreas eyes opened wide with surprise. "Plane? What on earth do you mean?"

"You'll be leaving with me within the next hour for Armenia, as my wife," Vasken told her with a smile. "You have just acquired a husband by Setrog's stroke of the pen."

Setrog laughed. "Yes, by simply adding 'and wife' to Vasken's documents, you have a new husband. You're leaving today . . . right now is more like it."

"Yes, we'll make a quick stop by your apartment, in case there's anything there you want to take with you. But, we haven't much time. It's now or never."

Andreas smiled slightly. "Well, I guess I don't have much choice. I'm ready." She turned and hugged Setrog and his wife. "How can I ever repay what you and your husband have done for me," she said tearfully. "I have only just met you both, and now I have to leave, but I will never forget you . . . never!"

"There's no repayment required, we're happy to help a fellow Armenian. Go now, my dear, and good luck to you both," Setrog's wife said gently.

Vasken, Andreas and Setrog got into the car and waved, then carefully, Setrog followed Andreas' directions to her neighborhood. Things looked quiet and normal, when they arrived. After scanning up and down the street, Vasken and Andreas entered the building. Setrog waiting in the car lit up a cigarette, and kept the engine running. Warily, he watched the people passing by and counted the minutes until he saw his friends come back. Andreas held a small overnight case. "It's all I want from this life, here," she explained, getting into the car.

By the time they arrived at the airport, the plane had already loaded the passengers aboard, and the crew was making last minute checks. They rushed into the terminal and Vasken thrust his papers and visa toward the guard. "Don't waste my time," he said imperiously in a loud voice. "I have to be on that flight!"

The guard looked at Vasken and Andreas suspiciously, then studied Vasken's papers. "I see you are a member of high standing," he commented.

"Yes, and I'm on a mission to Yerevan for Gamal Arshod; he wants me on this flight, so let's move it!"

"Of course, the guard said nervously, returning the papers to Vasken, then motioning them to pass through. Vasken put the papers in his breast pocket, then turned to Setrog. He emptied his pockets of all the money he had with him, and thrust it into Setrog's hands.

"No, please, it's not necessary . . . it's for a fellow Armenian," Setrog protested.

Vasken held his arm in a steel grip. "Listen Setrog, . . . use the money for your wife and family. Bribe your way out if you have to but get out of this bloody country as soon as you can. Don't wait. Travel light and fast. Don't look back. There's nothing here for our people but death, my friend."

Setrog embraced Vasken and Andreas. "When you come to Armenia, I'll be there to greet you," Andreas promised, tears welling in her eyes.

Setrog watched them pass through the gate and on toward the plane. He waited until he saw the plane taxi down the runway and lift off. He watched until it was out of sight, then he turned and walked back to his car and headed for home, making plans for his own escape.

26

Karamine was awakened suddenly by loud, persistent knocking at her door. She snapped on the light by her bedside table; It was 11;30 p.m. Who on earth could that be at this hour, she wondered wearily, while slipping into her warm robe and slippers. The impatient knock had now become a raucous banging. Someone called her name. "Open up, Karamine! I know you're there!" The words were slightly slurred.

"Who is it, and what do you want at this hour?"

"It's me, Karamine . . . your one and only brother."

Karamine opened the door to see Vasken, swaying unsteadyily on his feet. His appearance was disheveled, and lacking his usual sartorial bearing. He was accompanied by Dikron, the driver who had picked him up earlier at the airport. Dikron held his arm to steady him, when Vasken put a bottle of liquor to his mouth, took a deep gulp, then waved it wildly.

"Vasken! What on earth are you doing?" Karamine said irritably. "How dare you come here like this, at this hour. What's the matter with you anyway. What will my associates think?"

Dikron shook his head and looked apologetic. "I tried to stop him, doctor," he explained, "but, he insisted you were the only one who would understand. He just keeps singing that old folk song . . . "*sood eh, sood eh*, (lies, lies, everything's a lie)" Then he takes a drink out of that bottle. Believe me, I tried to talk him out of coming here, but, I don't know what to do with him. He missed his plane back to Yerevan, and I've been driving him all around Leninakan trying to get him sober. But he got another bottle of vodka somewhere. I tried to take him home with me, but, he insisted he wanted to come here. I've never seen him like this."

Karamine shook her head. "Neither have I," she said taking Vasken's arm and leading him through the doorway. "Don't worry, I'll take care of him, Dikron, that is your name, right?"

Dikron nodded.

"Has he seen anyone since his arrival in Leninakan?" Karamine questioned, leading Vasken to a chair and making him sit down.

"Yes, he went to headquarters and had a meeting with the communitarian. He came out of there flustered and angry, and he said he wanted a bottle of liquor. After I got him the bottle of vodka he told me to drive around. He began drinking then, and hasn't stopped since. Something happened in there, but, he won't say a word. I can't get anything out of him."

"Thank you for taking care of him. It was right you should bring him here, Dikron. I'll take care of him now, and you can come round early tomorrow and get him on the plane for Yerevan."

"Yes, I'll be here in the morning. I'm glad you'll take care of him. I like him. I don't want him to get in trouble with the party here. They seem nervous nowadays."

Karamine smiled at Dikron. "Well thanks for all you've done, Dikron. You needn't concern yourself further. He'll be fine by morning."

Karamine closed the door and leaned against it. She looked at Vasken as he took another drink from the bottle, then offered it to her. "No, I don't think so, Vasken, and I think you've had enough for tonight as well. Give me the bottle," she said firmly, reaching out for it.

Vasken pulled the bottle closer to him guarding it. "No! Why don't you have a drink too, my bible thumping sister? It will do you good, loosen you up." He laughed mockingly. Besides, we have something to celebrate . . . death of the proletariat!" Once more he picked up the strains of the old Armenian ballad and began to sing the words in a disdainful voice. "*sood eh, soodeh, sood eh,* (lies, lies lies, in this crazy world, everything's a lie)."

Karamine walked over to her brother and pulled the bottle from him abruptly. He resisted for a second, but then slumped down in the chair. "You can have it, it doesn't matter anyway," he said gloomily.

Karamine walked to the cupboard and filled a pot with coffee. Then she added water, and placed the coffee pot on a small propane stove. "I'm making coffee to help sober you up.

Now, Vasken, tell me . . . what's this all about?" she asked, gently placing her hand on his arm.

"It's all been a lie, Karamine . . . my whole life, nothing but lies, lies lies," he kept repeating himself.

"Vasken, you're not making any sense. Lies? What lies?"

He struck the end table next to the chair with his clenched fist. "Just that. My whole life's been a damn lie. Everything I've worked for and believed in all these years . . . school, university, the party, nothing but a sham. Engels, Marx, the fathers of the great proletariat revolution who promised a people's utopia. What a crock! They lied!" He slumped further into the chair.

"What are you trying to say, Vasken, I don't understand you. I've always known you to be a dedicated bolshevic, someone who worked for what he believed in. And, I've understood that. True, I disagreed with your philosophy, but at least you were always true to your beliefs. You didn't try to hide them from anyone. I admired and respected you for that, because you weren't like a lot of hypocrites who hide behind slogans of reform and liberalism, but espouse the same ideology. On the other hand, what you did to Lance was totally wrong, in my opinion, and unforgivable. But, you are my brother, and through the Lord's help, both Lance and I have found it in our hearts to forgive you." She took his face between her hands, and forced him to look at her.

Vasken violently thrust her hands from him. "Okay. You have your God whom you trust and believe in with all your heart. Well, what if you found out one day that your religion, God, the bible, was all a fraud? How would you cope with a situation like that? Huh? How would you cope?"

Karamine listened quietly. "First of all, Vasken, that's an erroneous hypothesis, it would never happen, God is absolute."

Vasken shook his head impatiently. "You don't understand, let's just say hypothetically if that were the case, what would you do?"

"It would never happen, Vasken," she said stubbornly.

"Damn it, Karamine, can't you just put yourself in that position for a moment?" he shouted, his voice rising to an angry pitch.

"Yes, alright, Vasken. I'd be devastated. I don't think I'd know how to cope with such a situation. I'd feel that I lost my soul. I'd be dead."

"Damn right. Well, that's the way I feel right now."

"What's happened to make you feel this way, Vasken," Karamine said softly.

Vasken stared blankly, not responding for some minutes, then he turned to face her. Karamine saw nothing but the black fire and pain in her brother's eyes.

"How can I express it into words you can understand," he said haltingly. "I'm sick, Karamine, tormented by lies, deception, hypocrisy and deceit." He reached for her hand and held it in a strong grip. "I've failed, Karamine. I've failed. My trip to Azerbaijan was a complete failure. I was unable to persuade them to release the supplies they're holding. All the medicines, food, everything you need are right there in the freight yard in Baku, but your badly needed medical supplies will not be coming through." Vasken stood up and began pacing nervously. "That Gamal Arshod . . . that bastard, just laughed at me, Karamine. He laughed and mocked the Armenian people. He said we were like wheat in the field, which THEY, allowed to grow and prosper until harvest time. Well now harvest time is here, he said, and it's time to reap. That's what's happening in Karabakh . . . harvest time. Do you understand? they want us all deported, or dead."

Karamine listened and hardly breathed. She had often seen Vasken filled with fervor and fanatacism, but never before did she feel his passion held the elements of futility and defeat she sensed now. His suffering was obvious, his pain compounded by rage and indignation. She longed to comfort him, but she knew there was nothing she could say or do to ease her brother's anguish.

"Did you plead for help as a humanitarian gesture"? she said quietly.

Vasken laughed scornfully. "Of course. I also told him it was his duty as a bolshevic to help a fellow soviet country in need . . . brothers of the proletariat, united world wide. Never! That was his answer, Never! So much for the unity of bolshevism."

"So . . . what has that to do with you getting yourself in this state, Vasken? It's no surprise that's the way they feel, that's the way those moslems have always felt, and they'll continue to do so. You said yourself you expected as much when you went to Baku. You felt there was only a slim possibility they would release the supplies."

"Right, I expected that, but not the kind of hatred that goes with it. Right after I left Gamal's office I saw a crowd of people shouting and encircling someone. Do you know what they were doing? They intended to burn a woman alive."

Karamine stifled a cry. "What? For what reason?

"For being Armenian, that's why. The feeling is bad there. They blame us for Karabakh, and for their sons being killed, for having all the good jobs, hell, they blame us for all their ills. You can feel the hate the minute you cross their border."

"What happened to the woman?" Karamine asked.

"I managed to break through the crowd and rescue her. I also managed to grab the can of gasoline from the big hero about to douse her. I sprayed it all over the ground then lit a match. That dispersed the crowd in a hurry I can tell you. I had a car waiting, so we all got away before they knew what happened.

Karamine was shaken. "The poor woman. She must have been terrified. You know you saved her life, Vasken. What happened to her, after that?"

"She was hysterical, for quite a while, but when she realized she was safe, she calmed down. Her name is Andreas Sassoni. She told us her husband was killed on the job, because he was Armenian. Anyway, I managed to get her out of Azerbaijan and bring her to Yerevan. Setrog, my driver in Baku forged my papers by adding 'and wife' after my name. I left her there in the hotel in Yerevan. Oh . . . yeah . . . that's one of the reasons I wanted to talk to you. She was a head nurse at some hospital in Baku . . . an anesthestist I believe she said. I don't know. All I know is she said she's a nurse and mentioned something about an operating room. I thought you could use her talents here, or find her a job in Yerevan. You know about that stuff." Vasken took a mouthful of coffee.

"An anesthestist? That's miraculous, Vasken. We're in dire need of good help here. You've been quite heroic in all of this, I'm proud of you, Vasken."

Vasken shook his head. Don't try making some sort of hero out of me, Karamine. You know me, I'm no bloody hero."

"Drink your coffee, Vasken. And cheer up. You have every reason to be proud. What you did was risky and courageous. That has to count for something, and make you feel good."

Vasken looked exasperated. "You still don't understand, do you, dear sister. Don't you hear what I'm trying to tell you? It's not just what happened in Azerbaijan, Karamine. It's my whole life. I gave up everything, EVERYTHING, for the cause.

Family, friends, my very identity, all for world socialism. My whole life, I've never allowed people to get close to me, I've shut them out, and branded the slightest expression of love or compassion as a crutch of the powerless. I believed that only impotent and simple-minded weaklings fell under the tyranny of sentimentalism." Vasken sat down, put his head in his hands and began to sob. "It's not a bad thing to love home and country, to love one's family . . . it's not a foolish tyranny . . . " he continued, brokenly, "but I've sacrificed them all to the mythical ideals of the greater good. I've felt obligated to crush love, desire, yeah . . . sentiment, out of my life, and for what, Jesus . . . for what! He hit the table again with his fist.

"My whole life has been shattered and wasted. Since coming to Armenia, my eyes have been opened to the fallacy and chimera of my philosophy. I've been had, little sister, had!" He laughed bitterly. What I've found and witnessed is corrupt bureaucracy, mediocre workers, engineering shoddiness, poor building standards which took such a toll in lives in the earthquake, and who cares? No one. The lack of heavy duty equipment after the earthquake disaster is something beyond my conception and belief. How could a modern country like the Soviet Union lack these basic needs? Where's the progress in seventy years of bolshevic rule that would justify the liquidation of millions of people for the cause? Where's the worker's paradise we were promised in the universities and media of the United States? From what I've seen, some of them don't even have the barest necessities, while the party elites enjoy their villas on the Black Sea. All that killing and suffering for the revolution. Damn them, damn all those radical professors who brainwashed me into believing Marxism and socialism was the panacea for all our ills. It's all been a lie, a God damn lie!" Vasken beat the table so hard he made his hand bleed. "You've had your God, Karamine, I've had Marx. If I had those lying bastard professors and apologists of Marx here now, I'd blow their bloody heads off." Vasken reached to an inside pocket and took out the pistol Varoujan had given him.

Karamine had listened sympathetically, but was suddenly alarmed when she saw the gun in Vasken's hand; she made an effort to grab it. Vasken however, held it out of her reach, then staggered backwards against the kitchen sink with such force, he knocked down a couple of dishes.

"Lies, lies, lies, he shouted, it's all been a fucking lie. Dialectic materialism, Marx and all that other shit they've spoon-fed me for years . . . LIES! Do you hear me, I've been had by those bastards . . . how could I have been so taken in. I must have been some damn fool." Vasken's eyes glittered with rage, as he continued his ranting. "My life is worthless. I've been a fool all these years. Who needs it," he said slowly and deliberately pointing the cocked pistol to his temple.

Karamine was horror-struck. She had seen her brother's explosive temper many times, but never the violent, darkened rage that filled him now. The volcano within him suddenly erupted, flinging the debris of all his life's worth and meaning into nothingness; only a dark and gaping emptiness remained.

"Vasken!" Karamine screamed, trying to remain calm. "What do you think you're doing? How could you even think of committing such an act in front of me, your only sister, who loves you dearly. Can't you ever think of anyone but yourself? What about our parents, your friends, the woman you saved? Vasken . . . look at me," Karamine put her hands on Vasken's face and forced him to look at her. "Dear Vasken, she began, her voice pleading, don't you think I understand what you're suffering, and the extent of your disillusionment now. Believe me, I've been where you are now, and tried to kill myself too. Don't you remember? I told you about it. We were in university at the time and you called me weak for even considering such a thing. I felt life was not worth living any more and wanted to end it all. Then a friend showed me the way to make my life worthwhile and brought me to God's grace. Life is so precious, Vasken. Don't waste it."

Vasken's expression was both cold and fiery as he looked at his sister. "God's grace? precious? Is that your answer? Don't make me laugh. A lot of good He has done the people of Armenia. Where was He during the earthquake? Where was He for the woman who lost everything in Baku? Did you know she's pregnant, so your good God was ready to sacrifice both her and the baby too." He took a deep breath and pointed the pistol to his temple.

Karamine put her hand over Vasken's and tried to move his hand slowly from his head. "Vasken, please dear, I don't expect you to believe as I do, but I beg of you, don't waste your life this way. All is not lost. Make use of your life in another way, serve the people, your people, the Armenian people, here in Karabakh," she pleaded desperately. "You're needed in Armenia and in Karabakh in their fight for freedom. The hell with Marxism and bolshevism. Don't be a fool and play into their hands, moslem hands. That's what they'd want you to do, pull that trigger. That's what Satan wants, but you're better than that, Vasken. Don't let them do this to you." Karamine began to weep uncontrollably. "Don't do this to me, Vasken," she sobbed, Slowly she released her hand from his, and sank to the floor. She leaned against his knees. "Vasken, I can't fight for you any more. I'm drained. Dear God, forgive me, I tried my best. I just don't have any more strength, THY WILL BE DONE." She continued to weep.

Vasken broke out in a cold sweat, but felt a certain tenderness as he looked down on his sister at his feet. He was suddenly sober and alert, as he bent down and gently lifted her to her feet. He kissed her wet cheek, and stroked her hair.

"Karamine," he said softly, "you're right. What would my suicide accomplish. Nothing, and not a damn thing for our people. Look . . . " he showed her the pistol, and released the trigger from its cocked position "it's not cocked any more. The safety is on." He shook her gently to bring her around. "You're right, Karamine, everything you've said makes sense. That's exactly what I'm going to do. From now on I'll live my life for the freedom and preservation of our people. They'll need men badly in Karabakh if a full scale war breaks out there."

"Thank God, I reached you, Vasken."

"God had nothing to do with it. It was you and what you said that convinced me of the foolishness of the moment."

"That may be true, but He gave me the words to convince you, and I praise Him for that," said Karamine taking a handkerchief from her pocket and wiping her reddened eyes.

Vasken laughed a little. "Look if it makes you happy to think that, so be it. I won't fight you. What happened to Dikron, by the way?"

"I sent him home, but he said he'd be back in the morning to try and get you a flight to Yerevan."

"Good. The first chance I get I'll return to Karabakh and get in touch with Varoujan. I'll join his forces, the KDF and help them. Things look bad there. From what Gamal hinted, there may be a full scale war. They'll need every able bodied man to keep those Azeris at bay. Yes, that's where I'll focus all my efforts from now on, Karabakh!"

Karamine was dismayed hearing her brother's latest plans, but remained silent. She was relieved that he'd been motivated in another direction, even though she realized this would be a dangerous mission. But, it was a better alternative, and she would pray for God's protection for him.

Vasken glanced at his watch. "We still have some time before Dikron comes back, Karamine. Why don't you try and get some sleep? I'm sorry to have come here like this . . . drunk, and disturbing. I must have awakened you rather abruptly. Sorry, Kid."

"Don't worry about it, Vasken. I'm glad we talked, and that perhaps now you feel better about your life. You are my only brother, you know, and I do love you dearly," she said embracing him. "Do you remember when we were kids and you'd protect me from the bullies? Perhaps I've protected you now, from yourself. Anyway, I hope so."

They talked the rest of the night, and Karamine made him breakfast before Dikron arrived. She held his hand tightly before he left in the car with Dikron. She waved him off then took a deep breath, and tried not to think of the difficult days that lay ahead for both of them.

27

A full scale war now raged between the Karabakh Defence Force and the Azeris for the territorial mountains of Karabakh. The Azeris bombed and strafed the cities and villages throughout the region in an attempt to force the Armenians out. Determined to break the will, morals and courage of the defenders, the capital city of Stepanakert was struck by air attacks constantly, causing additional hardship and death to the civilian population. The Azeri planes bombed and strafed any moving object, including children's playgrounds and schools, where children were wounded and killed by the hundreds. With no adequate hospitals or medical centers left standing in Stepanakert, victims were temporarily bandaged and treated, then flown by helicopter to Yerevan, Armenia. The hospitals in Yerevan, already strained by the never ending flood of wounded persons brought in daily, were pushed beyond their medical staff's capacity to cope.

Karamine had left Leninakan when she felt the medical personnel at the hospital there had enough training and equipment to carry on without her. Her plans were made to return immediately to the United States, but arriving in Yerevan and observing the urgent state of emergency existing there because of wounded personnel brought in daily, she decided to delay her departure a few extra weeks and lend a hand.

Lance was distraught. Karamine's heart was heavy when she informed him she was extending her stay for the third time. She heard the anger and frustration in his voice, heard his pleading note of apprehension and dismay, but still she persisted in her deep response to a hurt and wounded people who needed her ministrations more than ever. She had argued with herself a hundred times—the drama of life and death is in my hands, she reasoned, Lance doesn't understand—

and how can he? He's unplagued and free from pain. He's not witnessing the abyss of suffering or the misery on faces of loved ones who depend on me for hope and consolation. There's so much to be done, and so few to do the work. Can't we sacrifice a little longer? Our world is safe, secure. If we can't go beyond the boundaries of ourselves and our own interests then what is our value in living? She shook her head as if to release herself from an uncompromising space. Dearest Lance, she thought passionately, I miss you so. You'll never know how much I need your understanding now and the comfort of your arms; but, over and over the resentment and anger in his voice was replaying and he argued "the war in Karabakh could go on for years with no forseeable end in sight. It's not a matter of making sacrifices, it's a matter of your safety, Karamine. Because of the war in Karabakh, the Turks have now blockaded Armenia, which makes it next to impossible to get supplies in, of any kind; there are so many dangers and problems facing the small countries now, especially with the soviet union breaking up and republics clamoring for independence. I just want you safe."

But suddenly, their telephone conversation had been cut. Telephone communications in and out of Armenia were unstable. When all her efforts to call her husband back had failed, Karamine finally decided to write him a letter. She wanted to reassure him of her love and longing to join him once more at home in America. Lance was also unable to reconnect his call, and now, it seemed to Karamine, that all her emotions, reasonings and explanations were left somewhere in space, hanging and unresolved.

Her spirits lifted somewhat when she entered her office and saw a large bowl of soup along with a thick slice of homemade bread sitting on her desk. This has to be Andreas' doing, she thought, smiling to herself, who else would do this for me. She sat at her desk and took a sip. The soup was hot. Karamine savored the gentle flavor of barley with onion and chicken and broke off a piece of bread. She was interrupted by a light tap at her door.

"Come in," she called, taking another mouthful of soup.

"Well . . . I'm happy to see you taking a few moments to eat," said Andreas, entering Karamine's office. "That soup should revitalize you for the rest of the day."

"So . . . it was you, Andreas. I knew it. When did you ever have time to make soup, and how on earth did you heat it?" Karamine questioned.

"Easy . . . I just used one of the lab bunsen burners. Andreas laughed.

"Well, that's a new one on me. By the way how's that son of yours?"

"Alex? He's fine . . . growing fast! Before we know it, he'll be a man."

Karamine shook her head. "Where does time go? It just seems like yesterday that Vasken brought you here, pregnant and so frightened." She shook her head again.

Andreas' expression was serious. "Yes, I think of it often. Had it not been for you and your brother Vasken, my son and I would not be alive today. Vasken will always be my savior, my champion. How he rescued me that day in Baku from those barbarians . . . then took a chance to bring me here to Armenia and safety. And you, Karamine . . . what you've done for me! God, I can never thank you enough or repay all your kindness. You saw me through my pregnancy, delivered my baby, set me up here at this hospital then helped us to find a place to stay." Andreas' eyes filled with tears. "Karamine, I truly love you and your brother. You two are my family . . . It's beyond anything I am able to express."

Karamine smiled tenderly, then reached out and touched Andreas arm. "Andreas . . . you have been my right arm here at the hospital. You're such a valued asset to me and everyone else. You've helped me so much in the operating room, and as a nurse. The hospital staff knows your worth even though they don't have time to express their feelings. They thank me constantly, and praise your work and cheerful attitude. They're grateful to have you here. And . . . speaking of your help in the operating room, I've observed how much you know in that area, how well you know the instruments used, the procedures. I feel you'd make an excellent novice surgeon. Did you ever think about that?"

"No, I couldn't. I'd be scared to perform such an operation."

Karamine laughed. "Look, I'm not talking about brain surgery here, I'm talking about simple operations . . . setting bones, removing schrapnel and bullet wounds, that sort of thing. You'd be supervised until you felt comfortable. This way, other surgeons and I would be free to do the critical and major operations, where there's more than one doctor required."

Andreas shook her head. "I'm not a doctor, Karamine, I'm not certified or qualified to do such things."

Karamine placed her hands on Andreas' shoulders and looked firmly into her eyes. "We're in a state of war here, Andreas, and this is an emergency. We need every qualified person available, and if I and the staff feel you are qualified to do this, you are capable, and that's all there is to it. If we're to survive this war, we're going to utilize everyone's talents to the fullest. This is no time to worry about protocol. I feel you can do the work and I've taken it up with the hospital staff. They agree, so that's that. But, changing the subject for a moment, have you heard from my brother lately?"

"No, not lately," Andreas answered sadly. He's been at the front with Varoujan, and from what he's told me, the fighting there is fierce. I worry about him constantly, and pray for his safety and well-being. I don't know what I'd do if anything happened to Vasken.

Karamine felt a warm rush of affection for this woman her brother had rescued and brought to Armenia, but inwardly she was troubled and plagued by doubts. She secretly hoped something would come out of this relationship between her brother and Andreas, but since his disillusionment with Marxism and socialism Vasken was filled with so much bitterness and pain there seemed little room for any other emotion, much less a woman like Andreas. Most of his frustration and hostility was vented against the Turks and Azeris in Karabakh, but Karamine, in spite of her doubts, hoped Andreas could somehow restore his spirit, and find some sort of relationship together with him.

Andreas walked to Karamine's desk and picked up the empty dish and spoon. "Now, don't you feel a bit more energized she said cheerfully.

"Yes, I do, Andreas, it was delicious," Karamine answered, smiling and interrupting her train of thought.

"Good. And remember, you're to be at my place tonight for dinner, Alex and I demand it," said Andreas with a smile as she left Karamine's office.

Alone in her office, Karamine picked up a pen and paper and tried to pour out her thoughts and feelings in a letter to Lance. Most of all, she needed his understanding, his absolute and unconditional trust in her love for him. She finished the letter and was sealing it in an envelope when Andreas suddenly burst into the room once more.

"Helicopters have just arrived from Stepanakert with badly wounded soldiers and civilians," she announced nervously. We haven't been told the exact number, but they feel there are at least twenty or more. My God, Karamine, how are we to take care of them? Our supplies are so low, where will we put them all? When will the fighting end?" Her voice trailed off.

"Get hold of yourself, Andreas, calm down and tell me again, slowly."

"We just got a call from the airfield to say that helicopters have landed with wounded patients, both military and civilians. They were brought in from Stepanakert, and the city is under aerial bombardment. These patients are the most critical that have been evacuated. What are we going to do about supplies, Karamine? And where will we put them?"

Karamine pushed herself away from her desk and walked over to Andreas. "Damn the Turks for their blockade, damn them and damn those Azeris!" she said in anger and frustration. But as quickly as her outburst of rage had erupted, she reproached herself. "I'm sorry, Andreas, what am I becoming? I'm exhibiting as much hatred and rage as our enemy. She lowered her head and prayed silently. Forgive me Lord, release this hatred and anger from me. Guide me as you have in the past with your wisdom and strength. Help us to minister to these suffering people in this emergency, to bind their wounds, and comfort their pain. She sighed heavily, then looked at Andreas who waited anxiously.

"Clear the first floor as soon as possible. Remove the patients there to other areas and billet them, even if you have to double them up in the rooms. Set up the cots we received last month from that American cargo plane, and utilize the hallways if need be; I want the first floor cleared and ready to accept the patients when they arrive," Karamine ordered. "make sure all the equipment in the operating room is checked out, operational, and properly sterilized, Andreas. Get out whatever stores we have of morphine and anaesthetics . . . we'll use them sparingly, ration and recycle everything. We'll take care of the most desperate cases first. Don't worry, Andreas, we'll do the best we can," she said, touching the nurse's arm gently to reassure her.

When Andreas left, Karamine returned to her desk feeling suddenly drained. She put her head in her hands for a moment as she recalled her angry outburst and tirade against the Turks; Oh God, she whispered silently, forgive me. It's so difficult to do as you ask, to forgive our enemies, especially when I see so much suffering. Give me strength to continue, physically and spiritually; Make my work here count for something, and let me be a true channel of your light.

A sharp knock on her door announced the arrival of the patients. Karamine joined Andreas and they both watched as the first ambulance arrived with the most critically wounded. The ambulance backed into the receiving area where drivers and helpers jumped out and hurried to the rear of the vehicle. A truck filled with patients able to fend for themselves pulled in behind the ambulance. When the back door of the ambulance opened, Karamine saw stretchers, three racks high, filled with patients. Some women and children were bleeding profusely through their unchanged bandages, and the moans and sounds of death pierced her heart.

"Move those women and children first! Do it as quickly and gently as you can," she ordered. "bring them to the receiving area, so I can discern what each one needs, before we billet them."

Everyone, including nurses, drivers and aids assisted in removing the patients from the ambulances and transport trucks. Karamine quickly read the tags attached to each patient; the information described briefly their wounds, and what medical procedures and medicines had been prescribed and dispensed to them. As she checked out the tags, her attention was forcibly drawn to a fair-skinned young woman who reached out and grasped Karamine's wrist. The grip was surprisingly strong. The woman's dark eyes were filled with pain and pleading.

"Please . . . " she gasped weakly, "my children, take care of my children, doctor . . . don't bother about me, just save my children . . . " The woman's voice trailed off in a high wailing sound, and tears welled up and spilled down her face.

Karamine's heart wrenched when she saw the tense emotion and unselfish concern of this woman for her own pain and needs; she was touched by her unselfish display of pure unconditional love for her children. Karamine took the woman's both hands in hers and held them firmly.

"I'll do as you ask. I'll take care of your children immediately, I promise you," she said softly. "Please try to rest now."

The woman barely managed to mouth the words "thank you" before slumping back into unconsciousness.

Karamine felt her pulse and put the stethoscope to the woman's heart. The beat was weak. Checking the medical tag she noted the description—deep chest wounds, pierced right lung, bad internal bleeding, prognosis negative. She read her name—Azniv Torossian. Karamine lifted the blanket covering to check the bandage, and found it soaked with blood.

"Andreas," she called urgently. "Take her immediately to the operating room and prepare her . . . we'll need to operate fast or she'll bleed to death." Andreas motioned to two of the stretcher bearers to follow her into the operating room.

Karamine walked out toward the back of the ambulance which was still in the loading area. She saw two makeshift stretchers carrying a young boy and girl. The boy gazed about apprehensively, his dark eyes filled with fear and confusion. He appeared to be about ten years old. Karamine read his medical tag—Sabu Torossian—shattered arm, shrapnel wounds on the right side of his body. She touched his forehead gently—his fever was high; she noted the instructions on the tag to administer antibiotics to prevent infection. His sister lay on the other stretcher, a small girl about seven. Karamine read the medical tag— Arax Torossian, then the information on the severity of her wounds. The girl's black eyes expressed the shock and terror she had experienced; she shuddered when Karamine softly placed a hand on her forehead to reassure her, then took her temperature.

"Hello Arax, how are you feeling? We're going to help you here, so don't be afraid . . . you're safe now! No one will hurt you," Karamine said gently.

These must be the Torossian woman's children, Karamine thought, they have the same name. She took the small girl's hand in hers and smiled. "I'm going to take care of you, your mother and brother. Your mother is hurt badly, but we're going to do everything we can to help her, do you understand, Dear? I promised your mother I'd take good care of you, so don't you worry about anything except getting well." Karamine gave the little girl another reassuring pat before turning to the orderlies.

"Keep her with her brother. That was the young boy they just took out. They can help and encourage each other."

Turning from the ambulance, Karamine walked toward the hospital, but was stopped by an older patient who called to her.

"I can see why you were affected by the two children and their mother," he said. The old man shook his head. One of those low flying planes shot a missile into a civilian apartment complex and hit their apartment. I still can't see how they survived. The place was completely wrecked and in shambles when we got there. They are luckier than the others."

Karamine shook her head. "Does that happen a lot now?"

"Yes, they've been coming over daily. The killing of women and children is horrible, but, we have to stand up to them. We'll fight to the bitter end," he said resolutely.

Karamine put her hand on his arm to calm him down. "You've done enough fighting," she said, looking at his wounds. Let the young ones take over now."

"No! Those are my boys in the field, and I will never desert them. I've been at the front lines with them, leading them on for my commander Varoujan Torossian. We put up a powerful fight and we held them back until reinforcements came . . . then we routed them." He laughed. "Patch me up quickly, doctor, so that I may join my comrades again."

Varoujan Torossian, Karamine thought quickly. Torossian! That was the name of the woman with those two children. "You mentioned the name of your commander, as Torossian. Could they possibly be related? Karamine queried.

"Indeed yes," the old man replied quickly, that's Azniv, our commander's wife, and those are his two children." He shook his head despondently. "Varoujan is the leader of the Karabakh Defence Force, and with his leadership we've been giving those Azeris a taste of Armenian justice and vengeance! We've been driving them out of the Armenian villages in Karabakh, and now out of Karabakh itself, back into their own territory of Azerbaijan"!

Karamine saw the old man was becoming over-wrought; She covered him with a blanket and motioned to the men who were standing by to take him inside to the hospital. She continued on, attending the wounded, and giving instructions for their care. When she had seen to the last one, she hurried to the operating room, to wash up and prepare for surgery. Andreas was already there, scrubbed up and waiting. Karamine washed, then Andreas pulled the sterilized gloves on her hands. Karamine glanced toward the lifeless form on the operating table. The patient was Aziv Torossian. Karamine took a deep breath, and silently spoke the quick prayer she always said before major work. A hundred thoughts flashed through her mind when she gazed down at Commander Torossian's wife, her face white and expressionless now, revealing nothing of the intense agony and turmoil she had so recently endured. Karamine glanced at the monitor for pulse and heart beat. The rate is very slow, she thought. She must have lost a lot of blood. "She needs a blood transfusion, fast, or we'll lose her . . . Quick . . . check her blood type and see if we have any to match," she directed, turning rapidly to Andreas.

"It's type O," Andreas replied. "I'm sure we have it."

"Get it fast!"

Andreas had barely returned from the hospital blood bank and begin to administer the transfusion when the monitor registered and hummed NO RESPONSE. Karamine worked vigorously with shock treatments to revive Azniv Torossian, but her efforts failed. She had tried her best, but it was not enough to pull her patient through. Azniv Torossian had simply passed on, leaving a husband and two children.

Karamine felt defeated and drained. She also felt an overwhelming burden of grief for this stranger who had reached out to plead for her children a short while ago. Her heart ached for Commander Varoujan, the woman's husband, who currently fought courageously to protect his home and family against such violence and destruction as had now descended on them. Karamine continued to stare silently into the young woman's face; Does her husband feel the loss at this moment, she wondered, did they love intensely as Lance and I? Karamine leaned toward Azniv Torossian's lifeless body. Sleep in peace, *anoush* (sweet one), and join our other exalted martyrs. I'll take care of your two children, as I promised," she whispered gently, before covering her face with the sheet and silently watch as she was wheeled from the room. Karamine took a deep breath before turning to the orderlies.

"Bring in the boy, then the girl," she ordered crisply. The promise made to Azniv Torossian to take care of her children was brought sharply into focus now. Andreas and the nurses responded swiftly to prepare the young boy for surgery when he was brought in. The bone in his arm was badly fragmented, and the operation taxed Karamine's skills to the maximum. Meticulously, she placed all the fragmented parts together like a complicated jig-saw puzzle, joining each piece with a surgical screw so the bones could adhere and heal properly. But, Karamine reasoned, the only alternative to this slow and methodical procedure, is amputation, and everything in her spirit fought against it.

When she finished the major part of the operation, Andreas took over the stitching up and bandaging. Karamine went on next to the boy's sister. She was relieved to find the the girl's wounds were simpler. Karamine supervised as she watched Andreas remove shrapnel from the girl's side, checking to make certain there were no remaining pieces to give trouble later on.

She returned after Andreas had dressed the wounds, and the young girl was taken away to the recovery room and placed next to her brother.

From so much concentrated emotion, Karamine's gown was damp with perspiration, and her hair was wet under the surgical cap. After the operations, she walked to the wash-up area and pulled off the gloves, careful not to tear them so they could be reused in future. She let the cold water run over her hands, enjoying momentarily the refreshing coolness. Then, she took off her surgical gown and mask and threw them into a hamper, where they would be disinfected and recycled. Once again she returned to the large sink to wash with sterilized soap and allow the cool flow of water to wash over her hands. She splashed it on her face, and looked thoughtfully at her reflection in the mirror. There were small lines of strain about her mouth, and her eyes reflected the brooding sorrow she felt for the shattered lives of the family she had just treated. Andreas entered and placed a large towel over her shoulders, rubbing them gently.

"How do you feel, doctor, tired?" she questioned.

Karamine nodded, still gazing at herself in the mirror. "How are the boy and girl doing?"

"They're asleep, last time I checked."

"We lost the mother, you know," Karamine said sadly. "How will I be able to tell the children?"

"I'll talk to them and explain it, if you wish."

"No, Andreas, thank you. I'll explain it to them myself, and tell them they will be staying with me until their father comes for them. The children are strong and have been through a great deal. I made a promise to their mother I'd look after them, and I must honor that, but, if I take them to my apartment what am I to do with them when I'm here, at the hospital? I'm sort of in a quandry. I just can't leave them alone."

"Don't worry about it Karamine. We'll have the woman who takes care of my son take care of all three while we're here at the hospital."

"Do you think she will?"

"Yes, I'm sure of it. I'll ask her when I go home tonight, and prepare her for when they're able to leave the hospital."

"That would be a wonderful solution, Andreas," Karamine said, sounding relieved.

Both women finished cleaning up in the scrub area, then left the room to begin their rounds. Karamine felt a faint trace of warmth rising when she thought of keeping both children with her; In spite of everything, the heaviness of her mood lightened.

28

Varoujan Torossian, Commander of the Karabakh Defence Force, was so heavily involved in a major battle for control of the Lachin Corridor in Azerbaijan, he had not received news of his wife's death, nor the wounding of his children. The Corridor, a small pass from Karabakh to Goris, was the only link between Karabakh and Armenia. Controlling the Corridor was vital because it was the only route where critically needed medical supplies and equipment could be transported and provided to the KDF. Varoujan Torossian realized the corridor must be held at all costs, despite a never-ending attempt by the Azeris to break through with planes, artillery tanks and a non-stop stream of troops. Although Varoujan and his men were vastly outnumbered both in manpower and equipment, they fought so ferociously the enemy finally retreated. Terrain and weather conditions were favorable to the KDF. Ultimately, the Azeris suffered tremendous losses in manpower and equipment, and the capture of the enemy's equipment and badly needed supplies, encouraged the KDF to hold on more tenaciously than ever. Damaged enemy Turkish tanks were trucked out to Stepanakert where they were repaired and refurbished for use against the Azeris in future battles. The captured supplies were then spread out to the men along the perimeter, the front lines of Karabakh.

Varoujan was devastated when news of what had happened to his family finally had reached him. The realization that women and children had now become targets of war infuriated him. Why—why didn't my wife listen to me, he thought bitterly. I tried to warn her—I begged her to take the children and leave Stepanakert. Beads of perspiration broke out on his forehead. He removed his cap and ran his fingers nervously through his dampened hair. He remembered his wife Azniv's spirited words when she had faced him, the flash of boldness in her eyes . . . 'No, my husband, we will all stay. This is our home. We will remain here and take care of our wounded men, and if worse comes to worse, we women will fight beside them.' Azniv had always been courageous, ferocious as a young lioness in her zeal and loyalty, particularly regarding the protection of her family. Her fortitude and determination reminded him of Armenia's invincible heroines, legends of ancient warrier-queens who fought tenaciously beside their men to preserve and protect a way of life. It was useless to argue with her. Women like Azniv and my first officer Shakie Tamarian have sustained our nation throughout history, he mused. As long as we have such women, how is it possible to lose?

But despite deep concerns for his family, Varoujan was unable to leave until the positions occupied by his men were secured. They had dug in now to counter any offensive the Azeri might make to retake the Corridor. The Azeris knew how important it was to sever the Corridor connecting Karabakh, and to destroy the supply route from Armenia. But they were also well aware they fought on unfriendly terrain, where narrow roads and treacherous mountains provided perfect conditions for guerrilla warfare.

Checking now with his first officer Shakie Tamarian and Vasken, Varoujan spread out charts.

"We are well entrenched here and here, on the high ground," he said, pointing to several areas on the chart, "the Azeris will have a hell of a time trying to get through here. I want these areas mined," he said authoritively, pointing to another spot on the chart. "Make sure we have each mine marked accurately on the chart for the future. We might want to pass through the area ourselves later and may want to remove them. We don't want to be killed by our own mines, now do we?" He laughed grimly. Turning to look at Shakie directly, Varoujan's compelling eyes were grave. "While I'm away, I want these positions held at all cost. If anything happens, get in touch with me immediately, send a courier if need be, but let me know. If the Azeris mount an offensive to retake the area they must be stopped, at all cost, do you understand?" He glanced sharply from Shakie to Vasken who were studying the positions on the chart. "Let me repeat, get in touch if anything happens, and I will return as quickly as possible. Don't give up one inch of that territory. We have paid dearly for it with the blood of our comrades."

"Yes, we understand, Commander," Vasken replied. "We know how crucial it is and we will hold it. Go now . . . go and see to your family and don't worry about things here. As you have put it so well, it is ours and it will remain ours from now on."

Varoujan gripped Vasken's forearm firmly, and looked intently into his face. "Vasken . . . I'm glad you're here. The help you've given us, right from the beginning in securing weapons, and now . . . fighting here beside us have made you indispensible to our cause. You're an asset to me with your knowledge of tactics and fighting," he paused, knowing Vasken was rarely, if ever moved by emotion. "There's only one thing I hope you'll keep in mind . . . adhere to the rules of the Geneva Convention regarding prisoners."

Vasken laughed irreverently, his white teeth expressing scorn. "You know, Commander, I've studied all this in American universities. As for the Geneva Convention I don't recall mistreating prisoners. I don't take prisoners . . . they refuse to give up!" He laughed again.

"That's the point, Vasken, you don't take any."

"Look Varoujan, I'm here to kill Turks and Azeris. That's one reason for joining this fight. They started all this with their killings and deportations when we were helpless and unable to fight back. So let them fight and not surrender. I'll never surrender to them. No way!"

"He's right," Shakie Tamarian added vehemently, her grey eyes cold as glittering steel. "They're the ones who began this ethnic cleansing, raping our women, killing our elders. I'll never forget how they murdered my husband and son and pushed us out of our ancestral homes in Martuni. At least we give them a chance to fight. That's not a choice they ever gave us." Shakie Tamarian pressed her lips together, and shook her head. "No, we will not take prisoners, Varoujan. Why should we? We'll have to feed them, and we have hardly enough food for ourselves."

Varoujan stared intently at both of them, his black brows arching decisively. "Now you listen to me, both of you, I don't want to hear this kind of talk from any of my officers or men. If the enemy wants to surrender . . . you allow them to do so. Do you understand? Take them prisoner and later we may be able to make an exchange for some of our men held by them. That's a direct order. Understood?

There was an uncomfortable silence for a moment. Vasken's mouth held a hint of insolence. "Anything you say, SIR!" he said, bowing slightly with a mocking gesture.

Varoujan heaved an exasperated sigh. "You know better than to sir me, Vasken. This is a civilian army. All volunteers. There's no one here who does not want to be. I'm sure you're not here for the pay."

Vasken and Shakie laughed out loud. "Pay? What Pay? I haven't seen a ruble in months. Pay . . . some joke, Varoujan."

"Enough,!" Varoujan exclaimed bruskly. "Do you think you are both able to take charge of things here until I return from Yerevan?"

"Don't worry, Varoujan. My sister here and I will hold the Corridor, so relax and go," Vasken said, nodding his head in Shakie's direction.

"I'm not your sister," Shakie lashed out hotly. "I'm a fighter, as good a fighter as you are. The enemy has a bounty on my head . . . Varoujan's as well. There's none on yours I notice."

"Only because they haven't recognized the rage of a disillusioned communist patriot," Vasken replied cynically.

"Enough!" Varoujan commanded again. "No disagreements now, of all times. Look at this." He pointed to an area on the chart. "We're weak here. This could be an ideal place to infiltrate behind our lines."

"You're right," Vasken replied, "we're vulnerable there. We'll have to keep patrols in that area day and night."

"Vasken is right, Shakie agreed, studying the chart. "We'll put patrols out immediately and cover the area. We should mine some of the paths there too."

"Good idea, but remember . . . put it on the charts!"

Varoujan picked up his jacket from the table and looked around. "I have to find someone to drive me to the nearest pickup area. I'll hop a ride to Yerevan from there."

"Are you packed?" Shakie asked.

"Yes, everything I need is right here in this bag." Varoujan answered, picking up a small canvas handbag.

"Let me drive you, Varoujan," Vasken offered. "It shouldn't take too long, and I'll be back soon."

Varoujan looked thoughtful for a moment. "All right. Let's go."

The two men climbed the few steps leading out from the underground bunker, and headed for an truck that had been captured from the Azeris. Vasken hit the starter when they got in, then scrutinized the road ahead.

"Are you up to driving over these narrow mountain roads?"

Turning his head, Vasken threw Varoujan an amused smile.

"As my dear group-leader friend Rouben would put it, "No problem!"

"Rouben? Is he still with you? I thought he was wounded in that last encounter? He should still be in the hospital."

"Yeah . . . he had a shoulder wound but they patched it up at the medic station. He refuses to be evacuated. He feels he may be needed again so won't leave."

"Didn't you order him to leave?"

"What do you think this is, Varoujan, a regular army for Christ's sake? As you reminded me, everyone's a volunteer. What do you want me to do, shoot him?"

"No, but he should have had that shoulder taken care of before it gets worse," Varoujan responded calmly. It could become gangrenous."

"It's alright . . . I looked at it. I told him to check it often and change the bandage. It's a clean wound, the bullet went straight through. He'll survive."

Varoujan studied Vasken curiously. "What do you know about treating wounds . . . are you a doctor?"

Once again Vasken threw Varoujan an amused smile. "No, but my sister is. She's in Yerevan. I've picked up a few things from her."

Varoujan registered shocked surprise. "What? You've a sister who's a doctor in Yerevan? My God, Vasken, you're a mystery! I wasn't even aware you had a family, much less a family member here. You never speak of your past or personal life. But I respect that. I have no wish to probe." Varoujan stared straight ahead at the winding narrow road, which was now beginning to elevate sharply. Vasken downshifted gears, concentrating his attention on the precipitous curve ahead. The landscape was changing, the dense underbrush thinning out, becoming angular and sharp with steep ascending promontories.

Vasken's face was as brooding as the landscape. He shrugged indifferently. "My life's no mystery, Varoujan. It's simply a life of disillusionment and misinformation. A waste. There's nothing I want to look back on." He turned to look at Varoujan. "Actually, my life began when I joined your army, the KDF. I find fulfillment in the execution of my duties, especially when it comes to killing Turks and Azeris."

"You speak immoderately, my friend, and with considerable acrimony. Such hatred drives a man to recklessness and clouds his judgement. But . . . I do not reproach you. We are both soldiers fighting a common cause. You have proven your value to us in many ways, in friendship as well."

Vasken smiled. "Wouldn't you agree a certain recklessness must be required when a man calls himself a patriot or fights for a cause?" he asked.

"Perhaps. But that may become a two-edged sword. Recklessness spurred by hatred alone may soon prove an imposter, a corrupter of the soul. Hatred is a jealous god my friend. It leaves little room for anything else."

"Such as?"

"Nobility . . . honor, love for a good woman, children."

Vasken laughed cynically. "Have you never heard that the wrath of so-called honorable men is sometimes worse and more deadly charged than that of scoundrels?" Vasken asked. "As for the love of a good woman, Varoujan, it's too late for all that now. I missed your "high road" a long time ago, although oddly enough for a time I actually thought I was on it." He shrugged lightly. "What the hell, there's no turning back now. But at least I'm here now, doing my best for the Armenian people of Karabakh.

"Your words are caustic and self-deprecatory my friend. What strange twist of destiny brought you to such conclusions?"

Vasken's expression darkened. "It's a frightful thing for a man to discover his ideals and standards of excellence are fraudulent and hopelessly flawed, he said bitterly, "worse still, to find out I've been hoodwinked . . . deceived and mislead by a pack of lies!" Vasken hit the steering wheel with his clenched fist.

"Lies? What lies, my friend?" Varoujan questioned gently.

"Bolshevic, communist lies, that's what. Lies of a worker's paradise, the great utopia, a panacea for the world's inequalities! And I bought it, the whole fucking package! Marx, Lenin, Engle. I followed these charlatans of deception blindly from university days, thanks to my professors, till my eyes were opened. Abruptly opened I might add. I saw through those fucking hypocrites who pose as compassionate champions of the underpriviliged and patrons of the people, but in their hearts they loathe and despise these very people. They are tyrants and fascists who, in their grasp for power, use the universities, the media and stupid jerks like me. And they're joined in their dark conspiracy by corrupt politicans, who ultimately help them rob and control the people." Vasken's face was a mask of irony. Listening silently, Varoujan studied him quietly, understanding now the disillusionment and pain that colored Vasken's life, the bitterness that fed his cynicism and hatred.

Varoujan turned to Vasken, his coal-black eyes a mix of anxiety and concern. "Listen, my friend, do not blame yourself for following the bolshevic path. We have all made mistakes, myself included. All that is in the past and you have nothing to do with what happened in the past."

"I hurt a lot of people, Varoujan, my family, friends, gullible people back home in the States who would listen to me. I undermined their will with lies, intrigue, demonstrations, propaganda. It's not easy to undo or reverse that. Nor is it easy for me to . . . repent . . . is that the word? I'm not religious."

Varoujan sighed heavily. "There will always be lies and intrigue, Vasken, as long as there are corruptible and avaricious men. But time passes, and new situations and confrontations arise where a man who has seen the light may redeem himself and go forward. Whether or not you call it doing the right thing to rectify the past or repentance matters little. So let it be."

"Now you're beginning to sound like my sister, Varoujan," Vasken replied, laughing uneasily.

They drove the next few miles in silence. The truck careened around another turn and the road began its sharp descent down the mountainside to the valley below where a helicopter sat on a makeshift pad, its rotors turning in idle. A medical unit waited there also for the evacuation of critically wounded personnel. Vasken drove cautiously down the precipitous road, carefully avoiding boulders and rock slides along the way.

When they reached the helicopter site, Vasken drove up to the pad and stopped. Varoujan jumped out and walked over to the medics, to identify himself and find out where they were going.

"We're taking critically wounded patients to Yerevan where they can be treated properly. We've done all we can for them here," they informed him.

"I have to get to Yerevan myself, do you have room for me?" Varoujan asked. "My wife and family were taken there after they were badly hurt by the bombing and strafing in Stepanakert. It's urgent that I get there."

The medic talked to the pilot and they both looked critically at Varoujan, but observing his military rank, nodded their heads. Approaching Varoujan, the medic beckoned him to follow. "the pilot says we will be overloaded, but we can make it, so hop aboard if you want to go," he said.

Before boarding, Varoujan turned to Vasken and gripped his hand firmly. "Remember . . . hold the line at all cost. I know I can depend on you and Shakie."

Vasken tried to give Varoujan Karamine's name, but the rotors were already turning, the powerful sound drowning out his voice. Varoujan boarded quickly and fastened his belt. He peered through the window and waved to Vasken who returned a stiff salute in acknowledgement. Once aloft, he looked about him. He was deeply moved by the faces of the young soldiers who had been wounded in the last battle for the corridor. God, he thought desperately, they're all so young, the cream of our youth! Why can't those damn moslems leave us in peace. He unbuckled his belt and moved closer to one of them.

"How old are you, son?" he inquired gently.

The young soldier registered a faint smile when he recognized Varoujan's face, the commander whom he had seen many times on the front lines fighting beside his men. "Seventeen, sir," he whispered hoarsely. A sudden downdraft shook the helicopter. Varoujan grabbed the railing of the three-tiered stretcher holder. "Seventeen? You should be in school, not here wounded from battle. Where are you from and what's your name?"

"Sir," the soldier began . . .

"Please! don't sir me," Varoujan interrupted. This is a people's army. I just happen to be your commander because I understand tactics. No sirs and saluting. Understood?"

"Yes, si . . . commander. My name is Vigen Gragoryan from the village of Togh, the Hadrut region. I was going to school when they came and drove us out. They killed my father and struck my mother who protested, then they did things to her," he said with pain in his voice. "I'm here to avenge what they did to my village, my parents. I'll never forgive or forget. Death is their forgiveness." His young eyes burned with defiance. "Do you have a cigarette?" he asked.

"Aren't you a little young to be smoking," Varoujan teased, taking a cigarette out of his pocket and lighting it. He placed the cigarette between the lips of the young soldier. "It's not good for your health to smoke."

The young soldier coughed a little as he inhaled deeply. "Yea, but I'd rather the smoke than the Azeri."

"Where were you wounded? Here at the Corridor?

"Yes. When they had that counter offensive trying to take it back. It was frightening, all those soldiers, tanks, and artillery. Believe me, I was scared."

"Fear is a good thing. It makes you think of what you're doing and then, you can react better."

"Well I can't quite remember how I reacted, but when I was picked up later, I was told I was great, and that I had killed about eight of the enemy. We held them back . . . " the boy's face grimaced in pain just before he passed out.

Varoujan made his way toward the corp men in charge of evacuation. "Don't you have any morphine for that young soldier?" he asked, pointing toward Vigen.

The corp men shook his head sadly. "No, there's not a damn thing I can do to eleviate his pain. I see it all the time and it rips me up. Let me tell you something, I'd rather be out there in the front than here."

"Why don't you inform your superior officer of your wish?"

"I have, many times. He'll have none of it. I was a medical student and have some small knowledge of medicine, which, he tells me, is crucially needed, so here I am, trying to do my best. It's not much, but I try to make them as comfortable as possible."

"Well, that's all we can expect of anyone," said Varoujan, patting his shoulder lightly, as he moved about the craft, talking to each one, while holding tightly to support himself against the up and downdrafts of the flight.

Varoujan felt the engine RPM slow down, and as he peered out the window he could see the city of Yerevan in the distance. Late afternoon light fell greyly on the city defining its perimeters and ancient spires in monolithic tones. He felt his spirits sink as an unexplainable heaviness gripped him.

The craft circled the outskirts of the city and headed for the air field where ambulances were waiting. It hovered over its pad and slowly descended until the wheels touched the tarmac, and the engines were brought to idle. Varoujan jumped out as the ambulances backed toward the copter, then he opened the doors of the copter and helped, until all of the wounded were put into ambulances.

"I want to go to the hospitals with you," Varoujan said, anxiously, "my wife and children were brought in days ago, and I want to find them and see how they are. How can I find out which hospital they're in?"

The driver pointed to a shed. "Over there, they have all the names of people who have been brought in, and they keep track of them. Go ask them, and I'll wait for you and take you there."

Varoujan was back in five minutes. "They're in Yerevan Mercy."

"Good, that will be our first stop. Most of the wounded here, will be dropped off at Mercy," the driver replied, gesturing toward the rear of the ambulance. "All of the hospitals are overflowing with patients. I don't know where they'll put everyone. I've even seen them in hallways."

Varoujan sat with the driver and the ambulance made its way down the streets and boulevards of Yerevan. He lit a cigarette and offered one to the driver who took it eagerly.

When they arrived at Yerevan Mercy Hospital, the driver backed into the load ramp and stopped the engine. Both Varoujan and the driver jumped out and headed for the rear of the ambulance and opened the doors. Hospital attendants joined quickly to assist them in the unloading of the wounded patients.

"My wife and children were brought in a few days ago from Stepanakert. Where can I find them? Who do I see to find out where they are?" Varoujan inquired nervously.

The attendant pointed to the receiving entrance where a middle-aged woman sat at a desk logging in patients. She was writing down pertinent information—name, extent of their wounds, where they were from, and in what battle they had been wounded.

"My wife and two children were brought in here two or three days ago. Can you tell me where they are now?" Varoujan asked tensely.

The woman looked at him thoughtfully, noting his rank and uniform. "Are you from Karabakh? What is your name?"

"My name is Varoujan Torossian. My wife's name is Azniv. Yes, I have just come in from Karabakh."

"Ah yes, I remember them," the woman answered as she scanned the book. "Your wife . . . " she began but stopped short as she looked at the register again.

"What about my wife?" Varoujan demanded sharply.

She looked at the book again. "Your wife . . . Look, you'll have to speak with Doctor Bagdasarian. Let me page her for you," she answered evasively, picking up the telephone and keying for the public address system. "Doctor Bagdasarian, pick up the telephone."

Varoujan stepped to one side, while the woman at the desk continued with the next patient. After a few minutes, the telephone rang on the desk. "Azniv Torossian's husband is down here, doctor, and wishes to see his wife. Yes, Doctor."

Varoujan watched the woman's face closely for some small clue of what was happening, but her expression remained stoic.

"Doctor Bagdasarian will be right down, Commander." she said, replacing the telephone on the receiver.

"Why can't you simply tell me where they are?" Varoujan said impatiently.

"These are the doctor's cases, and she has all the information," the woman said, avoiding his eyes, and continuing with her work.

Varoujan was uneasy. The aprehensiveness he felt all day overwhelmed him now and constricted his breath. His mouth felt dry, and his heart beat more rapidly. The minutes dragged. It seemed to him he had been waiting hours. He was about to return to the front desk when he saw a woman in a white coat with a stethescope around her neck. She spoke a few words to the person at the front desk, then quickly walked over to Varoujan.

"Hello, Commander Torossian. I am Doctor Bagdasarian," she announced, warmly extending her hand.

Karamine felt a sharp stab of pain in her heart when she looked into Varoujan's anxious face. His black eyes, reminded her of his children, and she noted the dark coloring of his skin, which marked him as someone who had spent long hours in wind and weather. He shook her hand firmly, but his eyes were piercing and serious; they betrayed his effort to smile and appear relaxed. How am I to tell him his wife was buried yesterday, Karamine asked herself, there is no easy way, I have to give it to him straight. She took a deep breath.

"Look . . . let's go to my office . . . then we'll see your children, Arax and Sabu," she said, touching his arm gently and directing him toward her office."

"No, I wish to see my wife," he demanded impatiently. "I've travelled all day with men dying everywhere around me. I'm anxious to see my family now."

Karamine closed the door to her office and motioned Varoujan to a seat. "Can I get you some coffee, or something to eat?" she questioned.

Varoujan fixed his fiery glance on Karamine's face. She's trying to tell me something, he thought. The dark premonitions he'd felt all day clutched him tighter now, preparing him for a final blow.

Karamine stood up and paced behind her desk. "Your son and daughter are fine, commander. They were operated on, but are recovering well. They were taken to my apartment and are there now with a competant nanny to care for them. They're comfortable and will remain there until they recover fully. Your wife . . . " Karamine began but hesitated.

"Yes . . . ?"

"Your wife, Commander, did not survive her wounds. By the time the helicopter got her she had lost a great deal of blood . . . I'm so terribly sorry, commander. We did everything we could to save her."

Varoujan's first reaction was shocking disbelief. It was some minutes before he spoke. "No . . . no, not Azniv," he denied passionately. His dark face flushed with hatred. "those butchers from hell . . . those curs of Belial! Hell itself would spit them out. They should be wiped off the face of the earth!" Varoujan covered his face with his hands. A thousand images of his wife washed over him like a tidal wave, tearing him apart in riptides of emotion. "Azniv . . . Azniv," he sobbed brokenly.

Karamine walked over to him and placed her hand lightly on his shoulder. She felt helpless and inadequate. After a few minutes, she returned to her desk and opened a drawer. She took out a bottle of vodka, then went to the lavatory to get some glasses.

"Here, take this," she said, pouring out a generous portion of vodka. She poured a smaller drink for herself. "It has its merits in time of stress,"

Varoujan took the drink. "Forgive me," he said, looking directly at Karamine, and trying to pull together some sense of composure. "My wife . . . it's difficult. She understood me as no one else ever has. She was beautiful, and strong, perhaps too strong. I begged her to leave Stepanakert when the trouble began. Can you tell me where she is buried?"

"Yes, I will take you there," Karamine answered softly.

"The children . . . how are they taking it?" Varoujan inquired.

"It was difficult at first, as you may imagine, but, they are adjusting well. They were there at the burial, along with some of our staff members. We found a priest to say a few words which I think she would have wanted. We tried to reach you, but it was impossible."

"Thank you for all you've done for us. I'm grateful you had the priest. She would have liked that. At the front, we have to bury them right where they fall. It's hard to get them back to their families. A few words are said, by me or my officers. I understand how difficult it is to get in contact with anyone in combat. And we have been into it deeply the past few weeks."

"My brother is fighting with the KDF," Karamine said. "I wonder if you might have come across him somewhere. His name is Vasken, . . . "

"Not Vasken Casparian!" Varoujan interupted abruptly. "Yes, yes of course! He mentioned his sister was a doctor in Yerevan, and there is certainly a family resemblance."

"You have met him then?"

"Met him? He and Shakie Tamarian are my first officers! They are ferocious fighters, the best I have. I respect them highly. So . . . you are Vasken's sister," he said, studying her intently. "We've just come through a bitter battle for the Lachin Corridor, and we've secured it."

Karamine smiled and refilled Varoujan's glass. "Commander, I'm happy and relieved to have some news of my brother . . . and to know he's under your command. He's inclined to be a little reckless at times. I worry about him."

"Vasken's his own man and can take care of himself, Doctor."

"Please call me Karamine. Look, I'm sure you're anxious to see your children . . . excuse me a moment," she said, turning to telephone and keying Andreas.

"When Andreas comes down, I'm suggesting that you stay at my apartment with your children during your visit," she said, facing him again. It's only a small apartment, but comfortable, and you'll be able to be with your children without distractions. There's food in the refrigerator, whatever we manage to get these days with the blockade, but nanny will make you whatever you need. I will make other arrangements."

Varoujan raised his hand. "No, no, I must protest. I cannot put you to so much trouble. You have already shown great forebearance and thoughtfulness to us. I will not put you out of your home."

Karamine laughed gently. "It will be settled in a minute, you'll see." There was a soft knock at the door and Andreas entered Karamine's office.

"Commander Torossian, this is Andreas Sassoni, one of our top nurses here at Mercy Hospital. Andreas, this is Azniv Torossian's husband, Arax and Sabu's father."

Andreas' face expressed concern when Karamine introduced her. She turned quickly to Karamine.

"It's all right, Andreas, he knows, I've told him," Karamine said softly.

"Doctor Bagdasarian did all she could," Andreas said, turning to Varoujan.

Varoujan's face became grave and aloof. "I fully understand, please . . . I understand. She told me all that is needed."

"Andreas, Commander Torossian will be here for a few days and will be staying in my apartment with the children. Is it okay if I stay with you and Alex during that time?" Karamine asked.

Andreas flashed a beaming smile. "Of course. We'd be delighted to have you. Alex will love it."

"You see? It's all settled, you have no choice but to submit."

Varoujan smiled wearily. He was too tired and drained by the day's events to protest further. He listened silently to Karamine's voice when she spoke to Andreas, making arrangements, and leaving orders. He felt he was in a dream world filled with strangers where there were no answers or meaning to anything; his only reality was numbing pain. Somewhere in the distance he heard Karamine's voice.

"Andreas will you cover for me and inform the staff I have left for the day. I want to take Commander Torossian to the cemetry, and then to the apartment."

"Certainly, and I'll call home and tell Nanny to set an extra place for dinner. We will all dine together tonight."

"I'll bring whatever leftovers I have, Andreas, and I believe I still have that bottle of wine Dr. Levon gave me."

"Good. I'll expect you then about five thirty."

Karamine turned to Varoujan who remained silent, lost in his own thoughts. "I'll just get out of this coat and get my jacket, then we'll go to the cemetry. After that we'll go to Andreas' apartment and see your children. We'll have dinner there and later you can return to my apartment with them."

Varoujan nodded listlessly and followed Karamine out to the hospital parking lot and toward a small vintage car.

"It's not much, but it's efficient and gets me where I want to go. I don't have to wait for a bus or trolly in the morning and . . . it's gas-efficient," Karamine said, laughing lightly and staring hard at Varoujan. His face remained expressionless, as though he had not heard a word she said. Just keep talking, she thought silently—he'll respond, sooner or later. She slipped behind the wheel and started the engine, then pulled out of the parking lot.

"Do you know your way around Yerevan?" she asked pointedly.

Varoujan shrugged indifferently. "Yes, I know my way around some parts of the city. I've been here a few times, but have been tied up in meetings so didn't have time to get around much."

Karamine shifted gears and made a turn on Sayat Nova Boulevard. They passed statues of old heros long past—Sayat Nova and Komitas, striking and impressive in their militant postures. From the car window

Varoujan gazed thoughtfully at the scenes, passing and changing quickly from view.

"What happened to all those stately old trees that used to line the boulevard? I see only stumps there now." he inquired dully.

"Sad isn't it? Unfortunately, they were cut down for fuel," Karamine explained, relieved that Varoujan had registered some sort of interest, and had come somewhat out of his despair. "Like everything else because of the blockade, fuel was in short supply."

She made a right turn to a narrow street and they drove the next few miles in silence. It was still early autumn, but the days already seemed to grow shorter. Crimson light fell swiftly behind the mountain skyline, and people hurried along the streets, or waited in solemn lines for buses.

"Forgive me, Doctor Karamine, but I am curious . . . " Varoujan said after a silence, "why are my children in your house?"

"Well, when your wife and children were first brought to the hospital, I looked at your wife's medical tag. When I did so, she took my arm, and held it tightly. She begged me to take care of her children, and not to worry about her. I believe she knew she would not survive and wanted to be certain the children were attended to. She made me promise to care for them before releasing my arm, and I've carried those words, along with my promise to her in my heart."

For the first time, Varoujan turned to study Karamine curiously. For what reason is she doing all this, he wondered, after all, she's a stranger and from another country. Why should she make such a binding promise, especially when she must surely witness hundreds of such cases daily. She's also a professional woman with a career, and married as well, if that ring on her left hand means anything.

"Varoujan attempted to smile. "Well, I am here now, Doctor, and I will take them off your hands. They should not be a problem to you. You are a busy professional."

"Excuse me, Commander, but I do not give my word lightly, and I promised your wife to see to her children. You will be returning to the front, and then what? For the time being, they are well cared for, and safe. Andreas is a nurse and has a son also. She has a competant woman there to take care of him, and now, this nanny takes care of all three children. You'll see. It's important you have peace of mind about this, as you don't need the additional burden of responsibility while you are fighting a war. And remember . . . you are fighting for the welfare of your children!"

Varoujan managed a smile. "You are quite a remarkable woman. How will I ever be able to repay you for this kindness to me and my family?"

"Simple. Just keep my brother sober and alive," Karamine replied.

"That I earnestly promise, to the best of my strength and ability." Varoujan pledged.

"Good. Then it's settled. Well, here we are, this is the entrance to the cemetry," she said, slowing down the car and stopping. "I'll take you to the site, then I'll leave you alone. I'll wait for you here."

"No, it's not necessary for you to leave . . . please," he said gently.

Karamine guided him past many freshly dug graves with only markers to identify the deceased. She stopped by a mound with a simple, wooden marker, and gently touched Varoujan's arm. "This is it," she said softly.

Karamine stepped back a few paces when Varoujan sank to his knees and covered his face with his hands. She heard him moan brokenly, then softly speak his wife's name. Karamine felt sharp pain for this valiant hero, who was proud in his virility and power to command, strong in his convictions of honor and truth, and so deadly fierce in battle. Love exalts a man, inspiring him to go beyond the limits set by ordinary standards, she thought, yet, at the same time love can wound, deeply. It's truly the source of our greatest vulnerability and pain. She studied him from a short distance away; A random flash of setting sunlight filled the small cemetry, touched his gaunt profile and part of the grave, then suddenly, was gone, leaving a chill and spectral stillness behind. A cool wind blew lightly from some distant vineyard, bringing with it the sweet scent of ripening grapes. The weight and heaviness of Varoujan's soul however, was obvious to Karamine. She longed to comfort him, but she understood the emptiness of words in the presence of desolation and pain. She also knew that at this moment he could feel nothing, he could only endure. God give him peace and comfort, she prayed silently.

After a short time, Varoujan stood up. His face was expressionless, drained by exhaustion and grief. He stood for a few moments, staring vaguely into space, before bending down to take a handful of soil. He looked at it for a moment, then to his wife's grave. "This is Armenian soil, my love, he said. "I know how much you love Karabakh. When we defeat those Azeris I will return you to your homeland, and let you rest there in peace in the surroundings you loved, the fields, valleys and streams. You will be home again, this I promise." He turned around to look fully into Karamine's face.

"She was everything that gave meaning to my life . . . " His voice broke, and a thin furrowed line ran deeply across his forehead. "She didn't even say farewell to me. How could she leave me like this? Forgive me, Doctor, but I am in great sorrow."

Karamine placed her hand gently on his arm. "Forgive? she whispered, "there's nothing to forgive."

Varoujan shivered. "I think it's time to take me to my children," he said, running fingers nervouly through his short-cropped hair before replacing his cap.

"Of course," Karamine replied, turning to walk toward the cemetry entrance.

In the car Varoujan was silent. Lost in the churning of his own thoughts and emotions, he was not aware that they had arrived at Andreas' apartment until Karamine pulled up and stopped.

"Here we are," she announced, "Let me run upstairs and get the children, and we can leave for my apartment immediately. Then you can have some private time with them before we return for dinner."

Varoujan smiled, but his smile held a touch of irony. "It will be good to see the children," he said, getting out of the car and leaning against it. He lit up a cigarette, and watched impatiently as Karamine disappeared into the building.

She came out shortly with the two children, Arax and Sabu. Varoujan's heart sank when he saw Sabu on crutches struggling to reach him. Arax moved slowly as well, but their enthusiasm and eager shouts of joy when seeing their father, overpowered his alarm. He ran to them, clasping both of them in his arms. Tears streamed down their cheeks when they described their mother's death, and both children told the story together, in one breath, pausing only to take short gasps between sentences. "Wait . . . wait . . . " Varoujan said, laughing, and holding up his hand. "One at a time. We have all evening to talk. Why don't we get in the car, and let our good friend, the doctor, take us to her home. We can talk on the way."

Once again Varoujan's emotions were assailed by a sense of profound loss and desolation as he watched his young son struggle to get into the car. Sabu was the more solemn of the two children. His eyes darted nervously about, and his small mouth was set defiantly.

"How soon do you think I can join you at the front, *Hyrig*? I want to grow up fast and go fight those Azeris who killed my mother," he said, his voice trembling defensively.

Varoujan took his son by the shoulders, and held him a few feet away. "My son, I hope by the time you are of age, this war will be finished. That's what I fight for now. I have no wish to see war in your life, nor have you experience the hardship and suffering of war. The Azeri will come to their senses and recognize the independence of Karabakh. Once there is peace, you will see our country flourish beyond all dreams. Don't hold this hatred and revenge in your heart, son. It is a poison that destroys all hope and reason for the future of our people. You are young and have a lifetime ahead of you. Let the love you've always had in your heart survive . . . and strangely . . . forgiveness."

Sabu stared seriously at his father for a long time, then thoughtfully, settled into the back seat of the car. Karamine was touched and mildly surprised by Varoujan's advice to his son concerning love and forgiveness. Forgiveness of one's enemies was somehow unexpected from this warrior who had so recently engaged in fierce fighting, and had experienced a devastating personal loss. He is an enigma, she thought. I wonder what his life and philosophy was all about before the KDF and all this struggle began.

"Here we are," she announced, pulling the brake and bringing the car to a stop before a two story building. It's only a short distance, and I've walked it often when the weather is fine.

Varoujan jumped out and quickly opened the back seat door to help Sabu out. Karamine took Arax's small hand in hers and they entered the building. When they reached her apartment, Karamine entered first then flicked on the electric switch.

"The power is on, thank God," she remarked, "I'm never sure when it will be out." Inside, Varoujan noted the small living-dining room, the tiny kitchen with a gas stove and diminutive refrigerator. There were also two bedrooms, which seemed to him more like closets. Still, it's better than what most people have, he reasoned.

"You seem to be well situated," he remarked, looking around.

"Here's the bathroom," Karamine said, opening a door. "If anyone wishes to use it, please do so now. I want to wash and pick up a few items to take to Andreas."

When both children shook their heads, Karamine went quickly into the small bathroom and packed a few cosmetics, then to one of the bedrooms, and put a few garments in a small overnight bag. Returning to the kitchen, she opened the refrigerator to take stock of items to bring to Andreas for dinner, and check supplies needed by Varoujan and his children.

"Here, Arax, take this plate of cold lamb and these vegetables and cover them with this," Karamine said, passing Arax a platter and a clean piece of cloth. "Everyone take something. You can leave your bag in my room, commander. I'll just need these few items."

"Is Hyrig going to stay here with us? Arax questioned in a small, piping voice.

"Just for a day or so, *Anush*. Now, please . . . thank our kind Doctor Karamine for allowing us to use her home.

"Thank you Doctor Karamine," Arax said, smiling politely.

Sabu nodded gratuitously.

"It makes me very happy to do so, Arax," Karamine replied, hugging Arax close to her. "Well, I think we've got everything. Shall we be on our way?"

Karamine led them out of the apartment and down to the car. She removed her apartment key from the key ring and gave it to Varoujan, then, started the car.

Varoujan sighed and closed his eyes. He was aware only of a dull and throbbing ache; Now the shock and disbelief of Azniv's death were gone, replaced by overwhelming sense of weariness. They drove the short distance to Andreas home in silence.

29

Varoujan Torossian was back at headquarters after two more peaceful, relaxing days with his children. The last visit with them was his third, since their mother had been killed, and he was comforted knowing they were healing well and becoming adjusted. The sharp edge of his sorrow was dulled somewhat by the memory of his children's laughter, the love and hope in their eyes. It's all Karamine's doing, he thought warmly—she's been like a mother to the children, and a god-send to me. What would I have done without her? She's a remarkable woman—what kind of man must her husband be to allow a woman of her caliber to remain here—so far away and for so long a time? I don't understand. He's either a fool, or a weakling. I would never permit it. Perhaps he doesn't hold her in high regard, and for that, I think he must be a fool.

Down in the bunker, he and his men knew the road below was the lifeline for supplies from Goris, Armenia, and they held it with fire and tenacity. Varoujan spread the topography maps out on his table and scrutinized them in detail, leaving nothing to chance. He was shrewdly aware that there was no such thing as an impregnable position. His intent was to make an Azeri offensive so costly that the enemy would be forced to break and retreat before their mission was accomplished.

He concentrated on the maps now, running his fingers over their defense perimeters, the general terrain and any possible approach the enemy might use. If they come through these areas, they will pay a heavy price, he reasoned to himself, they will be caught between the mined areas and the crossfire of our automatic weapons. Their best approach would be with heavy equipment down the main road here—he hit the charts on the table with a loud thump. Yes! That's the strategy I'd use if I were ordered to take the pass, and damn it, that's what they will do. And soon. They'll hit us with everything they've got—tanks, artillery and man power. It will be costly, but in war there's no other alternative. He rubbed his chin reflectively. Well—we're ready for them. We're already dug in, so let them come. They won't know what hit them. He studied the map again. The only time those butchers from hell will leave us alone is when they know they can't intimidate us, he thought bitterly. Unfortunately, we can only have peace through strength, so we must be strong always. Never again will we be deceived and tricked into giving up our arms—by them or any other international organization. Even in peacetime, we shall maintain a citizen's army that will be ready for any intrusion on our sacred soil. History has proven again and again to us, that the Turk or Azeri's word is not worth the paper it's printed on.

He pushed away from the table and stretched his arms above his head. Then, he picked up a box and pulled out the bottle of vodka Karamine had given him on his last visit. He poured himself a drink. Images of the past few days drifted back to his mind, and his senses whirled in a flurry of confusion. Again, he found his thoughts were of Karamine—playing games with his children their response and love for her—the deep sense of security she had restored to them. Then he thought of Azniv, and the old emptiness and pain returned.

He was interrupted suddenly by Vasken, who stepped down into the bunker. "Did you get that last report from Shakie's position?" he asked nervously.

"No, I had the transceiver tuned low and was looking over the maps. What's up?"

Vasken quickly turned up the transceiver and placed a call.

"This is HQ BLUE, This is HQ BLUE . . . Shakie, come in, Shakie come in."

"HQ Blue, this is Shakie at the perimeter, do you read me?"

"Loud and Clear," said Varoujan taking over.

"HQ BLUE . . . Azeri troop movements have been reported by the scouts at the point. They are heading down the pass with tanks, artillery and a large contingent of troops. It looks like a big counter-offensive. Three lead tanks with armored vehicles pulling artillery pieces moving slowly up the road were reported. We are dug in and waiting for them to come to the first strike position. Over."

"Will you be able to hold them?" Varoujan questioned sharply.

There was a brief pause. "We'll do what has to be done. We have a couple of Bazookas and have made up molotov cocktails as a greeting for the tanks. Don't worry commander . . . we'll hold no matter what. I have to go. Over and out."

"Shakie! If you need reinforcements, call immediately. I'll send Vasken down with his men and equipment."

"Understand HQ BLUE, understand."

Shakie Tamarian placed the transceiver down and turned quickly to her second in command, Souren, a young man in his early twenties.

"Quick, Souren, get the bazookas in position. We've got to get the first tank. That will stop the column dead. Then we will pepper the troops and keep them busy until the other two are knocked out. Those tanks must be stopped! If they're not, they will push their way through our lines and our losses will be heavy. Try at first to simply disable them; that way we can retrieve and refurbish them at the Stepanakert deport. Then, we'll use those tanks ourselves against the Azeri."

"Good," Souren responded.

"But remember, don't lose lives to disable. Destroy them if you have to, but don't sacrifice our men, understood?"

"Understood."

"All right. Now let's go to the perimeter and watch them come to us," said Shakie vehemently, picking up her rifle.

They moved out of the enclosure, and along with the radio man carrying the transceiver, the three headed toward the vital road leading to Armenia. At a strategic observation point high above the road, they stopped and lay flat in the thick shrubbery where they were well camouflaged.

"Do you have the plastic bombs with the time detonator? We may need it," Shakie asked Souren.

"Yes, I have two of them. You're not going to try that stunt again are you?" he asked, watching her closely.

Shakie smiled grimly. "If the bazookas and cocktails don't do it, we have no alternative. Those tanks must be stopped! You know what will happen to our men if they're not . . . they'll be slaughtered. I simply will not allow that to happen." Shakie placed her hand on the young soldier's arm. "Don't worry, Souren, I pulled it off before, and it will be easier this time. You just keep an eye on me and cover my movements if I have to move down."

"You were lucky last time, why push your luck."

"Don't worry, it will be all right. Anyway, the bazookas should knock them out. If not . . . " she raised her hand and gestured.

"You're our leader here. Who would take over if anything happened to you?" Souren argued.

Shakie Tamarian ignored his question; all of her attention was drawn to the road below as she intently focused her binoculars in that direction.

"Quick . . . Souren . . . get down there and move our men closer to the point to get a better shot at those tanks," she ordered, pushing Souren off hastily, "and wait for my signal."

When Souren left, Shakie quickly pointed her binoculars in the direction of the boulder landslide, they had built. The rockslide was held in place by timbers, and perched on top of a bluff, ready to be released on the road below.

"Do you think we have enough rocks and boulders up there to stop the tanks from retreating?" she asked the radiomen.

"More than enough to stop their retreat. Some of the road will be wiped out when those boulders and rocks come crashing down. I hope we'll get some of the troops too. No, they won't be able to retreat with those tanks . . . they'll be ours one way or another."

Souren scrambled back from his mission, nodded to Shakie, then lay down in the shrubbery with them and waited in silence. Through the binoculars, Shakie swept her gaze over the whole scene. Everything was in place, molotov cocktails strategically ready to hurl on the advancing tanks, other personnel dug in deep with automatic weapons, mortars and grenades—waiting. Shakie Tamarian let her binoculars drop and sighed. She looked at the young men around her and wondered heavily how many of them would survive this battle. They are all young enough to be my sons, she thought, and they should be in university learning to build, not destroy.

"Listen! Did you hear that?" Souren touched Shakie on the shoulder. They were immediately alert and concentrating, hardly daring to breathe.

In the distance, the unmistakable drone of heavy Azeri tank motors drifted on the quiet air, gaining momentum and resonance as they drew closer.

"Yes, it's the tanks," Shakie confirmed, checking her automatic weapon, making sure it was in firing position. She picked up the small microphone the radioman carried.

"HQ BLUE, HQ BLUE, come in, this is Shakie."

"Shakie, this is HQ BLUE. I read."

"We can hear the engines of the Azeri tanks approaching. We will engage momentarily. Keep in touch in case we need reinforcements."

"We will be monitoring this wave length for you. Keep your radioman in touch with us constantly. Let us know if you need help. We are ready.

"Understand, out."

Shakie placed the mike back on its receiver and turned to the radioman. God, she said to herself, he's just a boy—I want him to be safe. "Stay out of sight and out of the line of fire, and be ready to relay any messages we may need to send to headquarters," she shouted to him. "It will be imperative for us to let them know exactly how we are doing. Do you understand?"

"Yes . . . yes, I understand!"

"Good," she nodded her head.

Looking once more through the binoculars, Shakie saw the first tank, then the second and third, followed by armored vehicles filled with troops. Behind them, foot soldiers, ready for combat, marched in two columns on each side of the road. A wave of apprehension swept over her when she observed the strength of the enemy marching toward her men. It's going to be a bloody battle, she thought, but, we will persevere.

The Azeri tanks moved closer in range to the boulder slide and bazookas, the armored vehicles following a distance behind, assured of protection from the tanks.

Shakie motioned to the men at the rock slide to release the boulders onto the enemy and the road, then raised her arms to give the firing signal. The trap was set.

Bazookas blasted. The first missile struck the lead tank, unfortunately hitting the impregnable side of the turret. The other shot glanced uselessly off the side, exploding, and creating little damage. But a thundering avalanche of rocks and boulders tumbled and crashed their way down the mountainside toward the road and vehicles below.

The immediate effect was startling. Armored vehicles with Azeri soldiers aboard were smashed and pushed off the road into a deep ravine. Over and over they tumbled, exploding finally in a burst of fire and smoke. Molotov cocktails, hurled vigorously at the tanks, engulfed them in flames, forcing the Azeri crew to rapidly evacuate from the hatch on top of the turrets. Smoke poured from the hatches, as men scrambled and shoved their way out, coughing, burning and crying. Frantically, they pushed out of both exits in a mad effort to escape the flames, increasing now in ferocity. Some soldiers rolled on the ground, ripping off their tunics in an attempt to free themselves from their burning clothing. Away from the protection of the tanks, they were perfect targets for Shakie's men, who mercilessly, cut them down with blasts of automatic weapons. Their bodies tumbled down the steep ravine on the side of the road, where they lay motionless at the bottom.

From her position, Shakie saw the failure of the first bazooka attack on the lead tank. Now the tank advanced steadily with machine guns and cannons aimed and firing at every target in sight. She watched in horror as the tank's turret swung toward the bazookas and fired, destroying her men and equipment in a violent explosion. The tank's turret and cannon swung to the second bazooka's position, firing and destroying it, killing all.

Shakie gasped furiously. "Damn, damn . . . Give me those plastic bombs with the timers," she ordered, turning to Souren.

"No . . . no . . . you can't! It's suicidal! We need you,"

"Give me those bombs," she demanded sternly, looking toward the destroyed bazooka position. "Give them to me!"

Silently, Souren handed her the bombs. Shakie set the timer for twelve seconds, then proceeded moving cautiously down the bluff.

"Good luck, Commander," Souren called out to her.

Shakie nodded and continued easing herself down the embankment. At the bottom of the bluff, she moved warily toward the advancing tank, inching her way along to it's lower blind side. In one swift and experienced move, Shakie was able to leap in front of the slow moving tank, lie flat on her back and allow the unit to pass over her. With lightning speed while on the bottom, she attached both plastic bombs to the vulnerable underbelly of the tank and triggered them. When the tank passed over her, she took cover by rolling and tumbling down the embankment on the side of the road. The explosion of the plastic bombs that followed, raised the tank off the ground for an instant, blowing off its threads. It stopped dead in its tracks. Smoke poured out of the vents and flames shot up, burning furiously. The turret hatch flew open, as the crew pushing and clawing tried desperately to escape, only to be cut down rapidly with gunfire from the defenders. When the last one came out of the tank, he did so with his hands up in a gesture of surrender. He was picked up quickly, disarmed and put in the rear cover, where he was held prisoner.

When the young KDF soldier pulled off the prisoner's headgear, he was surprised to see the prisoner had blond hair and blue eyes. He attempted to question him in broken Turkish sentences.

"You're lucky that Vasken's not in charge of this battle today. You'd never be allowed to surrender. You Russian? You sure as hell aren't Azeri. Just what nationality are you?"

The prisoner looked at the soldier blankly, then shrugged his shoulders, not understanding a word. The KDF soldier pushed him roughly to the rear.

Shakie looked in Souren's direction and gave a "thumbs up" signal. She was quickly alarmed, however, when she spotted hundreds of Azeri soldiers pouring over the rock slide, fanning out and shooting at her men. Her heart sank when she realized how totally outnumbered they were. There's just too many for our men to handle, she thought desperately We've got to have reinforcements if we are to hold our position. She scrambled back to Souren under a hail of bullets, only to see him struck down by enemy fire. She ran quickly to him, and lifted him in her arms, but his open eyes and lifeless body expressed clearly to her that another comrade had fallen.

"Get HQ BLUE!" she called to the radioman. "Tell them to send reinforcements. We're being overrun."

"HQ BLUE . . . HQ BLUE come in. We're being overrun. we're being overrun . . . HQ BLUE . . . "

"Shakie, we hear you! We hear you!"

"Get your men down here fast. We're being overrun and will be wiped out. There's too many of them for us to handle, do you read?" Shakie called desperately.

"We read. We read. Retreat to the secondary positions and hold as long as you can Shakie, at all costs."

"I understand, Varoujan, I understand. Will do. Out."

Shakie placed the mike on the receiver and signaled to her men to retreat to the secondary position. Suddenly, she was violently thrust back against a rock boulder by a sharp bullet to the chest. She fell to her knees, then to the ground. Desperately, she tried to get up. Her chest burned as though a hot poker had pierced her, and the blood gushing from the wound quickly sapped her strength. The young radioman who had seen her fall rushed to her side immediately and tried to lift her.

"No . . . it's no use" she gasped weakly. Retreat . . . go, and tell them to hold until Vasken comes. Go!"

Once more the young radioman attempted to lift his leader. "I'll take you with me . . . "

"No" . . . Shakie ordered, coughing and spitting blood, "it's no use. I'm finished. One thing . . . don't let them take me alive," she said desperately, clutching the young soldier's sleeve. "You know what they do to women when they capture them, especially me . . . bounty on my head. They've been after me a long time. You know what you have to do. Shoot me!"

The young soldier looked at his dying leader in horror. "Never!" he protested, turning quickly to fire at several enemy soldiers who were almost on top of them.

"Please . . . you've got to," Shakie Tamarian pleaded.

"I can't do it, Commander. I can't," the young soldier protested passionately, firing his weapon once more at approaching Azeri soldiers.

With painful effort Shakie raised herself on one elbow. "Would you leave me to the Azeri if I were your own mother?" she questioned, with all of her remaining strength.

The young soldier grimaced, and bit his lips. Then with tears in his eyes, he lifted his weapon and fired once. Shakie Tamarian, their courageous and beloved leader fell back, and was dead.

Bullets screamed all about him now. The radioman lifted his automatic weapon again, and emptied the magazine on the oncoming enemy, dropping many of them. Through a hail of gunfire he retreated quickly to the secondary position and notified the men of the death of their leaders, Shakie and Souren. The word passed quickly through the perimeter making the defenders more determined than ever to hold on and not give one inch to the enemy. The Azeris moved fast however, trying to overrun the KDF position, and kept advancing.

The KDF volunteers opened up with artillery and mortar at blank range. The whole area was saturated with the smell of gun powder and cries of the dead and dying. In spite of their heavy losses, the Azeris kept inching closer to the secondary positions.

Suddenly, a stream of trucks drew up to the rear and scores of KDF reinforcements jumped out and took up positions along the line to hold the enemy at bay. Varoujan and Vasken vaulted quickly out of the first truck, seizing their weapons and running to the lead position where they took over command. They saw the radioman and called him over while continuing their rapid fire at the enemy. The boy was distraught and shaking. Vasken pulled him roughly by the collar.

"What the hell's wrong with you! Scared of dying? Where's Shakie and Souren?"

"Leave the boy alone, Vasken," Varoujan interjected. "Where are they, Son, we need to talk to them fast.

"Souren was killed with a bullet in his neck," he answered shakily, and Shakie . . . " he hesitated and tried to stop the tears that spilled down his face.

"What about Shakie . . . " Varoujan said gently.

"She was shot . . . in the chest . . . " the boy shook his head. "I didn't want to leave her . . . she ordered me to retreat."

"What! And you left her there? You fucking coward!" Why the hell didn't you get her out?" Vasken shouted angrily, grasping the young soldier by the front of his jacket.

"Vasken . . . leave the boy alone," Varoujan interjected once again. "What happened, Son."

"She knew she couldn't make it, and wouldn't let me take her out. She ordered me to shoot her. *Der Vormier (God have mercy on me)*" He covered his face with his hands. "I couldn't do it, and then she said . . . would you leave me if I were your mother? All I could think of then was what those Turks had done to my mother when they drove us out of our homes. I don't even remember firing the weapon. But, I killed her then," He sobbed, shaking his head and covering his face with his hands. "I killed my commander. *Der Vormier.*"

"You did the right thing, son," Varoujan said, placing an arm around the distraught soldier. There was nothing else you could have done under the circumstance, and it took courage."

"Sorry I was hard on you," Vasken added, hitting him lightly on the leg, before turning to Varoujan. "Now we've lost two of our best in this god-forsaken place."

"God-forsaken?" said Varoujan angrily, turning to Vasken. What do you mean? This is the lifeline we need for Karabakh. From here, we spread north and south taking everything in our way, until all of Karabakh is connected to Armenia. That is what you and I and the rest of the KDF are going to do. It's our purpose for being here."

Varoujan reached for his binoculars and scanned the landscape. "Looks like the Azeris have retreated out of sight behind that rockslide," he announced. "They're probably doing it because of our reinforcements."

"Do you think they'll try again?" Vasken questioned, while peering over the top of the embankment to see for himself.

"Oh yes, I'm certain of it," Varoujan answered. They have to take this pass and they know it. Perhaps they just want a respite to pick up their dead and wounded. We could use one ourselves. I wonder how many we lost."

The shooting and killing died down. An unnatural and heavy silence permeated the atmosphere. The air was filled with the smell of smoke, ashes, burning tanks and men. Cautiously, Varoujan and Vasken peered over their positions, always on guard for the enemy. The enemy had retreated. With their fingers on the trigger of their weapons, Varoujan and Vasken stood up and began to inspect the area. A yellowish haze settled over the landscape and the smell of death was everywhere. Varoujan motioned to his men to follow.

"Be on guard against another offensive," he warned, "but let's pick up the bodies of our dead and wounded while we can. Let's see also how many men we lost. Were there any prisoners?"

"Here's one," one of the soldiers called, while pointing to an Azeri lying on the ground. Both his hands and feet were bound.

"Untie him," Varoujan ordered briskly.

Vasken frisked him thoroughly for concealed weapons.

"He doesn't look like an Azeri," the soldier said. I thought perhaps he was Russian and tried to speak to him in Russian, but he's not that either." The soldier shoved the prisoner forward.

"Get your damn filthy hands off me, you son of a bitch," the prisoner shouted, in clear english.

Vasken's face registered shocked surprise. "Who are you and where are you from, you bastard? What the hell are you doing fighting with the Azeri?" he snarled in English, grabbing the prisoner by his coat collar, groining him hard with his knee and bringing him to his knees. He pulled the collar tighter and drew his gun pointing the barrel to the prisoner's head. "Talk, or I'll blow your fucking brains out. Talk and tell me why you're in this country killing Armenians,"

Varoujan stepped in and grabbed Vasken's pistol hand, then gestured for him to put it down. "No more violence, Vasken. Get all the information from him, find out his name, what he's doing here and for what purpose . . . but no more violence. Remember the Geneva Treaty about prisoners of war."

"You can take that treaty and jam it!" Vasken said belligerently. The Azeri are not abiding by it, why should we?"

"Because, Vasken, I am asking you to," Varoujan said firmly.

Vasken's face was a mask of cynicism, as he glared at Varoujan. Reluctantly, he turned to the prisoner, then asked one of the soldiers to get him a pencil and pad of paper.

"Your name and where are you from?" Vasken asked in a demanding voice.

"My name is Jack Hawkins. I'm an American and I'm from Alabama."

Vasken turned to Varoujan, and handed him the pencil and pad. "Here, you write and I'll interpret. His name is Jack Hawkins and he's from the States."

"How did you get here and why are you fighting us?"

"A group of us came to work for the America Company. They are interested in the Caspian Sea oil and development and research. The company wants to invest in the drilling for new oil throughout the area, and they want to make sure the country they are investing in . . . Azerbaijan . . . is stable. This war with Karabakh sure doesn't make for stability. It's draining their resources and creating turmoil in the country. The company was approached by the Azeris to help alleviate the problem by helping the Azerbaijani in their war effort, and the company obliged. We train officers and men to fight, in return for the company's investments for oil in the Caspian Sea. We've been here doing this for months."

Vasken's face darkened as his anger exploded. He reached for his pistol and cocked it at the prisoner's head. But before he could fire it, Varoujan struck down his hand, and the pistol fired aimlessly. Varoujan held his hand in a steel grip that surprised Vasken.

Vasken turned to the prisoner. "You're nothing but a fucking mercenary! You kill for money, you son of a bitch! Blood money!" Vasken shouted irately in english. He turned to Varoujan and translated the prisoner's words; still, Varoujan would not allow him to kill the prisoner.

"What makes you any better than me, and what are you doing here anyway?" the prisoner asked, glaring at Vasken, "You're killing Azerbaijani . . . for money, no doubt."

Vasken stared menacingly at the prisoner. "I am of Armenian extraction," he said, hitting his chest with his fist, "I was born in Boston, but, am Armenian through and through. I am fighting for my people, something you could never understand. Fighting for money? Hah! What a laugh! I haven't seen a ruble in ages. I'm here to help my people secure their lands from these bastard Azeri Turks who've been slaughtering our people for centuries. You, you son of a bitch, you're here for glory and money. What were you, a green beret? You enjoy killing?"

"I didn't understand what the situation was," the prisoner answered, "We were told the Armenians were the invaders."

"Read your history and learn something. This is all Armenian country and the invaders are you and the fucking Azeri. You, you bastard are on the side that loves to kill women, children and defenseless old people. Read history for Christ's sake instead of Playboy. This Commander of mine just saved your miserable ass this day. Remember that. I hope we don't regret it." Vasken continued to glare threatenly, at the prisoner, his hawk-like glance carefully scrutinizing the prisoner's entire appearance.

"Open your tunic," Vasken ordered abruptly, walking up to the prisoner and ripping open the buttons. "Just as I thought, Here, Varoujan, do you know what this is?" Vasken asked, pointing to a heavy black garment under the prisoner's tunic.

Varoujan shook his head. "This, my dear Commander is a light bullet-proof vest. No damn wonder we have to shoot these Azeri a number of times before we can kill the bastards. They're issued bullet-proof vests! Damn it . . . the sons of bitches! Get it off" he shouted, ripping at the prisoner's tunic and throwing him on the ground, "Get the Goddamn thing off!" When the prisoner handed the vest to him, Vasken fingered the label inside. "See that, MADE IN THE U.S.A." he shouted in anger. "We're now fighting Americans as well as Afghan mercenaries. they're all wearing American made bullet-proof vests. Who the hell else are we fighting?" he roared.

"Would you believe Russian mercenaries," Varoujan answered.

"Why don't you let me blow his head off?" Vasken yelled hotly.

"No, Vasken, he's too valuable a prisoner. We'll show the world how the Azeris are recruiting mercenaries from around the world, and especially the United States to fight us. Of course, they'll deny it, but this time we have a prisoner to prove our case properly. No, they won't be able to deny it. We also have his statement to back us up. This prisoner is a valuable part of our war for liberation and freedom. You will see. Our newly established government in Stepanakert will use this perfectly. They'll advise the United States of American involvement, and our captured prisoner's statement will back our premise. We'll show them the American military hardware we've captured as further proof of their undeclared war against us."

Vasken considered Varoujan's words thoughtfully. "Yes, I guess you're right, Varoujan, but I'm fed up with these bastards fighting for money, against us. I'd like to kill every one of them, march them through town and blow their heads off in a public square," Vasken said bitterly.

"That's just what the Azeri's would want us to do. Can't you see through that?" Varoujan replied calmly. "They and their cohorts would broadcast over the airwaves of the world, that those "barbaric Armenians" are killing defenseless prisoners. No, Vasken, as our own propaganda for justice, peace and relief, we'll use this prisoner and others against the Azeri instead. It's a better weapon. We'll get more mileage with the truth."

Vasken's face changed and he calmed down. "You're damn clever, Varoujan. I guess that's why you are our leader, and we mere followers," Vasken said in a surprisingly conciliatory tone. "Someone has to rein in the hot heads like myself. Of course, you are right."

Varoujan hit Vasken lightly on the shoulder and smiled, then turned to a soldier on his left. "Get the prisoner away to a prisoner internment," he ordered, before turning once more in Vasken's direction. "Vasken, get the men back to the perimeter, and dig in again. I believe the Azeri will try another counter-offensive and want the men to meet them on the outer perimeter. Hopefully this time we will not have to retreat. Where did Shakie and Souren fall?"

"I don't know. Let me get the radioman." Vasken walked toward the spot he had last seen him. The radioman was sitting in the same place they had left him; Vasken noted the young soldier was deep in thought staring vacantly into space.

"You were the radioman with Shakie and Souren, right?"

The soldier nodded silently.

"Where did they get it, we want to recover their bodies."

The soldier pointed to a knoll and underbrush, where he had been with them. "I killed my commander," he said tearfully, "I shot and killed her."

Vasken shook the boy gently. "Look, you had no choice, man. Would you have wanted them to take her while she was still alive? Can you imagine what they would have done to her before she died? I would have done the same thing."

The young soldier looked sorrowfully at Vasken. "You would?"

"Damn right. It was a brave thing you did, and she appreciated it, believe me."

Vasken's words seemed to comfort the soldier. They headed out toward the spot where his comrades had fallen. On the way Vasken glanced about the killing field where men were picking up the dead and wounded. Will this misery ever end, and is peace really possible, he wondered dismally.

"We'll bury them where they fell," he said to Varoujan, motioning with a spade he had picked up.

"Yes," Varoujan said softly. "They would want that."

Approaching the knoll they came across the torn bodies of Shakie and Souren. Souren was face down. They paused a few moments in silent tribute to the two valiant soldiers who had died for the freedom of their people. Varoujan rolled both on their backs, and straightened them out, folding their arms and closing their eyes for the last time.

Because of the rocky terrain, the task of digging a grave deep enough for both bodies was difficult. Although they took turns with the digging, Varoujan and Vasken found the task more time consuming than anticipated; They were grateful, however, the harsh mountain with its thick frosts had not quite settled in. The ground was flinty but still soft, and when the job was completed, they buried their comrades; Varoujan gave the soil on the mound a final pat with the spade. Brushing dirt from his trousers, he stood up then and raised his eyes toward heaven.

"Lord God," he began solemnly, "we commit the bodies of Shakie Tamarian, a valiant and courageous woman, and Souren Kouomjan, a young boy who heeded the call of his people in their dire need, to your loving care. They died in battle, but they were committed to peace. Receive them now into your kingdom, where honor and righteousness prevail, where all tears will be wiped away. May they live there in the peace and love they fought and died for on earth . . . "

Vasken remained silent, acutely watching Varoujan. A hell of a lot of good God has done for them, or us, he thought cynically.

A sudden eruption of gunfire, heavy artillery and motor blasts interrupted Varoujan's eulogy. With lightening speed, both men picked up their weapons and headed back to the men.

"Quick, get to your positions," Varoujan ordered sharply, waving them on. Clutching their weapons, the men dug in deeply into the earth, protecting themselves from bomb fragmentations exploding all around them. Vasken ran to the outer perimeter point where his men met the enemy in their counter drive. Here the enemy strongly attempted to push the KDF from their entrenched positions.

"Stay back and run the show from there," Vasken shouted at Varoujan who had come forward to observe what was happening. "I'll take care of things here. You're needed back there, now more than ever, since we've lost two of our best leaders."

Vasken and his men met the first wave of attack with heavy automatic fire and grenades. The Azeri persisted in their counter offensive however, climbing steadily over the rock slide and heading straight for the lines of defense. They threw everything they had in a last desperate effort to break through and destroy the corridor held by the KDF. Vasken's position was the most vulnerable, being the first point of defense. The other positions were holding firm, with streams of automatic gun fire, mortar and grenade attacks.

"Fix bayonets, fix bayonets," Vasken shouted loudly, when he saw they were in grave danger of being overrun by enemy forces. He pulled his short bayonet from its sheath, and slipped it into the muzzle of his weapon. The rest of his men did the same. Looks like we're going to do some hand to hand fighting here, he thought to himself. He nodded again to the men, and raised his thumb up in a gesture that they were ready.

The next wave of Azeris came hard and fast. Fighting furiously, they attacked all positions held by the KDF. In the lead position, Vasken and his men sustained the heaviest assaults, but, managed to hurl the enemy back in disarray. When they attacked again, Vasken stood up and emptied his magazine, spraying the oncoming enemy, while his men fired automatically. Suddenly, Vasken's magazine jammed. Yanking the cocking pin, he realized his magazine was empty, but quickly, he pulled another from his bandelier and slipped it into his weapon.

Suddenly, like a bolt of lightening, Vasken felt his whole chest burn as he was hit with rapid fire. Searing pain engulfed him, and blood gushed out of the wound, spilling freely over his hands. He had been hit in the shoulder, with a straight trajectory through the chest. His head spun; Everything around him blurred. His ears rang and his chest felt as though it was on fire. Trying to clear his lungs and catch a breath of air, he choked on his own blood. He stumbled and fell. Through the smoke and murky haze of battle, Vasken's eyes detected the vague outline of someone with a shining rod bearing down on him. The figure was poised to strike. The light was fading fast, but from somewhere in the distant past this scene was familiar to Vasken. The nightmares! he thought, the bloody nightmares! So this is what that was all about—my end, my bloody end! Well, I'll take the bastard with me. Vasken reached for his pistol and fired point blank at the oncoming figure. Although Vasken's bullet struck him squarely, the attacker continued his advance toward him, brutally thrusting his bayonet through Vasken's body, pinning him to the ground with his weapon and body weight. One of the KDF soldiers rushed to Vasken's assistance, pulling the dead Azeri up from Vasken's body, and making sure the Azeri was dead. He lifted Vasken slightly, hardly daring to move him.

"How're we doin'?" Vasken choked weakly, coughing up more blood, "looks pretty bad for me . . . "

"We're holding on, and the Azeris are retreating. How are you doing?" the soldier replied, cursing his own helplessness to do anything for Vasken.

Vasken stared blankly at the sky, as he fought for more air. "Shit . . . it's all been a lousy lie . . . lies lies lies," he panted weakly. Vasken's mouth slackened, and his dark eyes rolled back as the heavy breath of death was released from him. His body sank back, releasing him from this world.

From the other position, Varoujan was relieved to see the Azeris leave. In their final retreat, they had abandoned equipment, supplies and ammunition, as the KDF pursued them back toward Azerbaijan. The corridor was now secure, and the expansion of their positions would begin immediately—first to the northern mountains of Karabakh, then south, linking once and for all, Karabakh and Armenia on the western side of the country. Karabakh would never again be an island, surrounded on all sides by Azeri territory and forces.

Varoujan began his search over the battle field to count their casualties. "Evacuate the wounded immediately to the medical area in the rear and have them flown out," he ordered. "Get the names of the dead and bury them as soon as possible. I will notify the families personally, as I've always done. Strip the Azeri of their American bullet-proof vests, weapons, grenades and any other paraphernalia of war. Especially food! Then leave them. We'll wait and see if the bastards will want to pick up their dead and wounded. They could come under a flag of truce, so keep your eyes open for them. I want a body count of the Azeri to send a report back to Stepanakert headquarters."

One of the soldiers walked over to him to report Vasken's death. Varoujan shook his head sadly. How will I be able to tell Karamine her brother was killed in battle, he wondered. Somehow I never believed such a thing could happen to him. He seemed so invincible, but then, what are we gods? And this is war." The soldier guided him to the place where Vasken fell. Varoujan knelt beside him and touched his shoulder gently. "You weren't supposed to get yourself killed, my foolish comrade. How am I going to explain this to your sister when I promised to look after you. But, you were always high-spirited and did things your way."

One of the KDF soldiers carrying a spade approached Varoujan.

"Will I dig a grave for him here, Commander?"

Varoujan sighed heavily. "No, I'll do it myself. Vasken was more than a soldier, he was my friend, and it would be my honor to bury him here, where he fell."

When Vasken was buried, Varoujan paused momentarily, holding the spade upright as though it were a staff. For the second time that day, he raised his eyes to heaven and spoke a prayer.

"Receive this valiant soldier into your kingdom, Lord God, this patriot who came halfway around the world to fight for his people. Let his sins be washed clean by this baptism of blood, and forgive him his trespasses and transgressions, for he was deceived. Judge him kindly, and lead him into your truth, light and peace of your kingdom. Amen."

Varoujan stood up and turned to the soldier who stood by silently, waiting for instructions. With heavy heart, he scanned the casualty strewn perimeter; an early winter-grey sky added to the somberness; Varoujan shivered in the chill air, then joined his men in the grim task of picking up their wounded and dead.

30

Karamine reached for her glasses and strained to see the time on the small clock beside her bed. She felt she'd hardly slept. Grey morning light struggled to penetrate thin spaces between the shutter slats on her window, and heavy, drumming rain confirmed another damp and chilly day. Yerevan was engulfed by fog and drizzle for over a week, and Karamine felt the effect not so much in her body as in her spirit. She found herself longing for the buoyancy of sunlight, blue skies and clear winter air. Will this fog and rain ever lift, she wondered despondently, it seems like years since I've seen the sun. She sank back on her pillow allowing her eyes to drift randomly over the tiny bedroom. She shuddered slightly. How bare and meager it really is, she thought dully, recalling her spacious bedroom back in Boston—the ivory walls, gold-silk drapes, thick luxurious carpet. And Lance. What about Lance? These past ten months have been a lifetime without him. Yet the reality of my life here affirms my very reason for being. I love the children, Sabu and Arax, and my work at the hospital. It's everything I've ever wanted. But why do I feel so little joy, she wondered, and why do I seem engulfed by apprehension and dread, especially this week. Perhaps Lance is right. I am working too hard, and I worry too much, usually about Vasken. When I think about the disillusionment and despair of his life, the bleakness of his spirit, my heart breaks. Keep him safe, God, she prayed silently, I know he's not a believer, and, somewhere, he's gotten off the path and lost his way. But, I know it was You who helped me influence him that terrible night he wanted to end his life. Now, I call again, for Your help Lord. Protect Vasken as he directs his energies into a worthy cause, and help him understand the light of Your truth.

Karamine glanced at the clock again. Six-thirty, and the children were still sleeping. She had promised to spend the whole day with them, since it was her first day off in weeks. She smiled slightly when she thought about Arax and Sabu—they've brought me so much joy. In this short time I've grown to love them deeply—they're uplifting after a difficult day at the hospital, and I look forward to their enthusiasm and affection. They're like my own children. How can I ever leave them? The thought filled her with emptiness. They're so happy when their father manages to get away for a few days and visit with them, and, I have to admit—even to myself—I look forward to his visits also. She closed her eyes. The memory of Varoujan's resonant voice expressing himself tenderly to his children, or reading poetry to them in rich, flowing Armenian, moved her deeply, and had commanded her attention from the start. He's not like anyone I've ever known, she thought uneasily, but what does that mean? Am I becoming too fond of him? Do I enjoy being with him too much? There's no mistaking Varoujan's attraction for me. It's in his eyes and smile each time he sees me with the children. I tell myself it's only gratitude, but I know it's more. I feel a bond between us, a thread that spins beyond reason, as though somehow I've known him forever. Armenian heroes ride with him on phantom horses, each time he laughs, or tells a story; we seem caught up in some ancient drama, where time stands still, and here and now is the only reality. She turned restlessly in bed. I'm getting carried away, she said, aloud. Lance and I have been apart too long, that's all. I love Lance deeply; How could I possibly be attracted to someone else, no matter how dashing. Varoujan is different from Lance—he has the strength of steel and the mysterious aura of the unknowable. He's the stuff of legends, a commanding warrior. It's only natural I should admire him. Both men have tremendous strengths—Lance is vital, dedicated and scrupulous in his integrity. He's been more than understanding about my work here, although lately, I'm sensing a certain resentment and obstinacy, even a hint of antagonism in our last telephone conversation. Her senses whirled chaotically. Ah, Lance, she whispered to herself, I've made it difficult for you; I wish it could be different—I wish I was able to simply turn my back and leave, but how can I until I know I've done everything possible to help here. I long for the comfort and security of your arms around me. I will come home to you soon my love, I promise.

The muffled sound of children's voices, teasing and pushing each other in a friendly way, disrupted Karamine's thoughts. Ah Hah—they're awake, she thought. She slipped out of bed and put on her warm slippers and robe. I'd better get up and start breakfast, she thought, walking into the small kitchen. On the way, she stopped by the children's bedroom and stood in the doorway. She watched their activity with an amused smile for several minutes before they were aware of her presence.

"Well . . . I see you two are awake and lively this morning. Why don't you get up and wash before breakfast. We have a long day planned."

Arax and Sabu bounded out of bed and before Karamine could stop them they dashed toward her with childish laughter and threw their arms around her.

"You belong to us today," Sabu said with boyish enthusiasm.

"*Aiou, aiou,* (yes, yes)" Arax joined in.

"Okay, okay, after breakfast we'll decide what we're going to do today," Karamine said laughingly.

Between mouthfuls of milk, toast and tea, they decided on the day's activities. Because of the rain, their original plan of making a picnic had to be cancelled. Instead, it was decided they would visit the Children's Art Museum, where Arax and Sabu would view works by Armenian artists.

That afternoon at the museum, the children were amazed by the works of the young artists, and asked many questions regarding style and technique. Next, they drove in Karamine's small car to Republic Square to visit the National Art Gallery and the Museum of Armenia, where they discovered their historic past. They were astonished to see that for thousands of years, their country had been invaded over and over, yet to the present day, had managed to survive, and preserve their Armenian heritage. In minute detail, Karamine explained their turbulent past to them, and how they had become independent at last by the fall of the soviet union. Afterward, when the rain and drizzle had let up a bit, they sat on a bench in one of the parks, and ate lunch they had brought along. From their continuing questions, it was obvious to Karamine the day's events had made a deep impression on their minds and hearts. The time passed quickly, and when they arrived back at Karamine's apartment it was supper time.

After supper, Karamine smiled as she sipped her coffee and watched the two children on the floor, drawing in the sketch pads she had bought them.

"What are you drawing, Sabu?" she questioned.

"A picture of Hyrig," he answered, holding up the pad.

"Hmm, its good, and it does have a similarity. The boots and fur hat make him look like one of those old fadayes we saw today in the museum.

"Hyrig is my fadaye. He's my hero. When I'm old enough I want to be a soldier like him, and fight for our country."

"What are you drawing, Arax?"

"I don't know. I don't want to be an artist anyway. I want to be a doctor like you," she answered, placing her hand gently on Karamine's knee.

"You will, Arax, you will, I know it," Karamine replied, gently caressing the child's hair.

"I want to join my father and fight those Azeris. I want to free our people from them and the Turks. I wish I could do it now." said Sabu resolutely.

"Come here, Sabu," said Karamine, holding out both of her arms. "There's more to life than fighting, Sabu. There's peace and love. True, your father has to fight right now, there were no other choices. But, there will come a time of peace, when Armenia will need visionaries like you in the field of science. Armenia will also need engineers to build tunnels and bridges, explore for minerals, discover oil and gas. There will be many things to do, once peace is achieved, Sabu, things that will make our country great and prosperous. The world will be open for you, once this struggle is over and won. Just keep studying and learning, and being the best person you can be." She hugged him tightly.

A sharp knock startled them. Karamine hesitated for a moment, then slowly walked to the door and opened it. She was surprised to see Varoujan, muddied and weary, standing in the doorway. His clothes looked as though he had slept in them for weeks. Karamine felt a sudden shock of fear and apprehension. Why had he come unannounced this way, she wondered. It's not his usual pattern. She studied him with sharp concentration. His face seemed thinner, his dark eyes dulled, devoid of all but pain and weariness.

"Varoujan . . . come in! What are you doing here at this time?"

Varoujan smiled slightly as he greeted her, but did not have time to answer her questions. The children, surprised and overjoyed by their father's unexpected visit, rushed to him, embracing him enthusiastically. Varoujan caught them both in his arms and swept them off their feet. "Hyrig, Hyrig . . . you've come to see us, we missed you," they echoed in unison. "Look, we were out to the museum today, and we've made some drawings, this one's you," Sabu said, excitedly holding up his pad.

"Very good, Son," Varoujan responded warmly.

"This is mine, Hyrig," Arax chimed.

Varoujan glanced briefly at his children's efforts, but he looked quickly beyond them to Karamine in a way that filled her with uneasiness.

"Very good *anushigus*," (sweet one) Varoujan commented, "How do you like staying here with Doctor Karamine?"

"Doctor Karamine is our aunt now, Hyrig, she told us we could call her aunty."

Varoujan smiled gently. She's more than an aunt, she's a saint."

"How about you, son, are you happy here?"

Sabu looked to the floor and slightly scuffed his feet. "It's alright, I guess, I like Karamine and call her aunty, too, but . . . I miss being with you, Hyrig."

Varoujan looked sadly at his son. He also felt the pain of separation from his children. He dropped down to one knee and placed his hand lightly on Sabu's shoulder. "My son, I love you and want to be with you as much as I can, but . . . there's the war. You understand don't you? You're the man around here, and I depend on you to take care of the women while I'm gone, as we Armenian men have always done."

"Right," Sabu agreed reluctantly, nodding his head.

Slowly, Varoujan turned to face Karamine. "I only have a day or two, then I'll have to return as soon as possible. All hell is breaking now that we've taken Azeri land and connected Karabakh to Armenia. They're trying to get it back and the fighting is heavy and fierce."

"You look tired, Varoujan. Can I fix you something to eat? We've just finished supper, but there's enough left for another meal."

"Yes, that would be welcome. We don't get many hot meals these days, indeed, we're fortunate to get any food at all. I'll wash up first."

"Good, I'll make some hot tea, and after you clean up perhaps Sabu can tell you about our visit to the museums today.

Karamine was quiet while she heated water for tea, and warmed the leftovers; She felt a weight of uncertainty, and wondered again why Varoujan had come, especially now, when the time seemed critical. His appearance disturbed her, and the depths of his black eyes held a potential of dread. She waited anxiously while he finished the meal, and chatted lightly with his children about the day's activities.

"With all your work at the hospital . . . the long hours, you do not rest on your day off Karamine? You take my children on an outing?" he asked, entering the small kitchen and looking at her with deep affection.

Karamine laughed. "It was a treat for me, a break from the routine of my daily life here. The children are a tonic, Varoujan, they force me to go out and enjoy the city. Instead of returning home each evening to an empty room, there are two vibrant children to greet me. No, Varoujan, they're a blessing. I enjoy every minute with them."

Varoujan studied her intently; he felt a deepening warmth for this woman who had accepted his children, and gave them love in their time of trauma. His own loss had been softened by her tender caring, and when they were together, he forgot the pain and stresses of his life; Karamine gave him new incentives for living. Again and again he had struggled to reject his feelings for her, but she lingered in his thoughts, and filled him with urgent longings and desire. For this he despised himself. He had known both grief and passion, but guilt was something new. He longed to take her in his arms now, to protect her from the grim message he had come to deliver—the news of her brother's death. How can I tell her, he wondered dismally, and when shall I tell her. The longer I wait, the more difficult it becomes.

After Varoujan had eaten his meal, he and Karamine were entertained by the children's spirited behavior and manifold questions until Karamine suggested it was bedtime.

"You've had your fun for the day, now why don't you go in and get ready for bed. When you're ready, your father will come and tuck you in," Karamine directed. "In the meantime, I'll gather a few things to take to Andreas. I'll spend the night with her."

'No, Karamine, I can't let you do this," Varoujan insisted heatedly. I'll find a room somewhere, even at the barracks."

"We've been over this before, Varoujan. It's important you stay close to your children. They see you so infrequently. Andrea has extra space, and will love to have the company. It's settled. You look as though you need a good night's rest. How are things going in Karabakh anyway? And how's that brother of mine?" Karamine asked directly.

Surprised by the directness of her question, Varoujan gasped audibly. A painful shadow crossed his face. He forced himself to look at her. "Karamine . . . " he began haltingly, as though confused, "that is why I'm here. You could have learned through other lines of communication, but I wanted to be the one to tell you. Your brother . . . Vasken, was killed in that last battle for the Lachin Pass."

The color drained from Karamine's face, and she stared at Varoujan unable to utter a sound. She felt as though she had just been struck by a crushing blow to her solar plexus. Spinning physical weakness followed. Only Varoujan's strong arms prevented her from falling and passing out. He held her tenderly, stroking her hair and murmuring words of comfort. Karamine was unaware of anything except an isolating numbness engulfing her like a shattering wave of dark.

"Hyrig please come and say good night," the children called out, noisily breaking the silence.

"Yes, Varoujan, please . . . say good night," Karamine whispered mechanically. "You promised them."

"Of course, let me settle them, and I'll be right back," he answered gently, releasing her.

In the children's bedroom, Varoujan tucked the blanket securely around Arax. "You're as pretty as your mother, *anushigus*, he said tenderly, kissing her gently on the cheek. "I know you miss her, as I do. Sleep well, and remember I love you." He stepped over to his son's bed and touched him lightly on the shoulder. "Good night, son. I hope all this fighting will be over by the time you're a grown man. You can be whatever you want to be, an engineer, a builder. Your skills will be needed in the new Armenia."

"Yes, Hyrig, Aunt Karamine told me that before."

Varoujan looked tenderly at his son "I'm proud of you, Son, . . . and I love you. I'll see you tomorrow."

When he left the children, Varoujan returned to find Karamine packing a small suitcase in the bedroom. Her face was ashen, the pain of losing her only brother evident in every motion of her body.

"Where are you going, Karamine?" he asked quietly, standing in the doorway..

"Andreas," she answered simply.

"No," Varoujan answered firmly, placing both of his hands on her shoulders. "I insist and I insist again, I cannot allow this, Karamine. I will not put you out of your own place. I will make other arrangements."

"Please, Varoujan . . . don't argue. Stay here with the children. You have so little time with them. I'm comfortable with Andreas . . . I'm . . . " Karamine's voice broke and she began to weep uncontrollably.

Varoujan put his arms around her and held her closely. Karamine felt the strength of his body, and released the flow of her emotions to the comfort of his embrace. The rivers of tension, stress, anxiety, loneliness of the past months ebbed gently, easing the pain and crushing sense of weariness. Why struggle, she thought bleakly, it's useless. There's too much death and pain everywhere. I can't deal with it any more. For once, let me forget, block it all out and yield—yes, simply yield to life— to love—and to my own need for solace and consolation.

Varoujan held her closer, murmuring words of love and comfort. He tipped her face toward him gently, and kissed her tenderly on the lips.

"Karamine, *Hokiss* (my life, my soul) my sweet Karamine. I am no stranger to pain, and if I could but spare you this torment, I would. You must know how deeply I care for you, my love, I would give my life for you. Gladly." His hand caressed her hair and back, sliding effortlessly to her hips and thigh, then upward to rest gently on her breast. Karamine felt a desperate yearning. She opened her mouth to speak, but no words came. All of her training, reasoning and logic, all the defenses and fortitude provided by faith and belief systems now seemed like distant echoes, nebulous and unclear. Nothing before in her whole life experience had prepared her for this, the unrestrained compelling force of her emotions, her fierce need to respond. She was emptied of all else but desire. Karamine put her arms around Varoujan's neck and felt the quickening pulsebeat in his throat. Responding to his touch, she returned his kisses with fire. The room was silent, except for the uneven sounds of their breathing.

But as quickly as the moment came, it passed, and Karamine felt a sudden chill. She broke away, abruptly. "What am I doing? this is madness," she gasped. "I'm married, Varoujan, I have a husband!"

Varoujan took a step backward. His dark eyes filled with hurt, anger and surprise. "Words, Karamine, preposterous unbelievable words, without meaning or point! Husband? Marriage? Bah! What kind of man allows a woman he loves to leave him for so long, and to go so far away? I would never allow such a thing and neither would he if he really loved you. This you call a marriage? This is no marriage." Varoujan gripped Karamine and pulled her to him recklessly. "No, Karamine, you belong here, with me. We belong together, don't you see? You care for me, you share the love, passion and dedication of our people. The blood of our martyrs runs in your veins, and your spirit is the flame and fire of Armenia itself. This is your true home, not America. Once this war is over, we can build a life together as a family, you and I and the children, who love you as I do. We'll work together, with the rest of our people, to build Karabakh into a prosperous nation . . . and we'll give back to our country it's original name, Artsakh . . . "

Karamine pushed away from him and covered her face with her hands. When she spoke, her voice was barely audible. "Yes, Varoujan, everything you say is true. I do care for you deeply, more than I've ever admitted even to myself. I love the children, and Armenia. But you're wrong about my marriage, and my husband. It's because he loves me he allows me such freedom to be the best I can be. I know it's difficult for you to understand, things are so different here. Circumstances do not allow the luxury of following one's ideals, or the pursuing of a career, the freedom to grow within the boundaries of a marriage. I don't expect you to understand. But I know you understand loyalty and integrity, and the price we must sometimes pay to honor those principles. My husband loves me deeply, and I love him. My work here all these months, despite what you think, has been difficult for him, but he values and trusts me enough to know my motives are not based on vanity or caprice. You and the children will always be part of me, Varoujan. You've given me so much, I know I could not have survived or endured the suffering and loneliness here if it weren't for you. Yes . . . I care for you deeply. I've never known anyone quite like you, Varoujan, and I'll never forget you, but . . . my dearest Varoujan, it can never be, between us. Karamine shook her head and touched his face tenderly.

Varoujan's gaze was fixed on Karamine's face, his eyes filled with sadness and unfulfilled yearning. Reluctantly, he covered her hand with his, then dropped it.

"My country is worth more to me than riches or fame, yes even life itself, Karamine, but, without you to share my life the fire does not burn so brightly, *anushigus*. You are Armenia. The flame you carry within your soul is the light of our exalted heroines of the past. Though the forces of death and hell have been pitted against that light for centuries, the fire of our people can never be extinguished. I'll fight for you, Karamine. Like the warriors of old, I'll never give an inch . . . "

"Stop . . . please stop, Varoujan. Don't make it more difficult." Karamine's voice faltered, the weariness and numbing pain she felt, weighed on her heart like a heavy stone. She sighed deeply, releasing in that sigh the undertow of complex emotions swirling within her. "Varoujan, you will always be part of me; another time, another place, we might have had a life together, but it was not meant to be. I shall never forget you, Varoujan, or the blessing and honor you've given me today by asking me to marry you. You are the hero of my childhood dreams, that dauntless conqueror in the legends of our people. I'll hold you forever in my heart. But . . . I must go . . . "

Varoujan shook his head, his dark eyes flashing determination. He placed his hands on her shoulders. "No, I am not convinced, Karamine. Destiny is not so capricious as to bring us together this way for naught . . . "

"I can see you don't understand, Varoujan, and I cannot speak about it further, at least not tonight. I must go, and you are exhausted as well. Take a hot shower and get some sleep. The children will be happy to see you here in the morning."

"I refuse to put you out of your bedroom. I will take that shower, however, and then, I will sleep here, on the sofa. You need rest, and your own bed. I can sleep anywhere. Please, Karamine . . . it would make me happy to know that for this one time, we share the same roof."

Karamine smiled warmly "How can I argue, Varoujan? You're impossible, and I am so tired. Let me get you some towels and bedding, first, then I'll say good night."

Alone in her bedroom, Karamine buried her head in the pillow to muffle sounds of her bitter weeping. Hours later, a numbed and somber calmness descended, then Karamine fell into deep, but troubled sleep.

31

Varoujan closed his eyes and tried to sleep. The rain had stopped, and moonlight flooded the small room with intermittent bursts of light. Somewhere in the distance, he heard the raspy sound of rising wind, and the repetitive knocking of a loose shutter, echoing hollowly in the night. He turned restlessly. It was as though all the furies of hell gripped him in a relentless hold, forcing him to live again the nightmare scenes of battle, the agonizing trauma of death and dying. Images of his fallen comrades, and shadows of unknown volunteers, mere boys at most, floated before his eyes in an endless parade. He had loved them all and only wished he could pray for their souls, but somehow, he could not. A never-ending weariness consumed him, depleting his mind and body of all else but the awesome task ahead—securing the Pass linking the isolated land mass of Karabakh to Armenia. Will there ever be an end to disharmony—the frightful clamoring of people on earth, especially Turks and Azeris who thrive on savagery and useless bloodshed, he thought bitterly. There must be an end to it somewhere, or for what purpose were we created? God is in truth, remote and unknowable, if indeed, He exists at all. He sends little comfort when our hearts bleed with torment, and our lives are ripped apart. He smiled ironically to himself and thought of Vasken. Vasken of the arrogant face and manner, Vasken who had scoffed at piety, claiming "it was birthed in ignorance and servitude." Perhaps he was right, but I hope he has found peace at last from a lifetime of confusion, and most profound suffering.

Karamine had loved her brother, though she had never understood him. Her grief was real, and Varoujan felt a pang of guilt when he remembered her reaction to the news of Vasken's death. How could I have

320

been so selfish, thrusting my own desires forward at a moment she was most vulnerable, he wondered. He made a fist and struck his head. But then, there's no time for anything, for love or tender words, indeed there's hardly time for life itself, he reasoned. Karamine's tenderness invades me; she's taken hold of me, my thoughts, my dreams, my heart. All the women I have ever known before, yes, even Azniv, my late wife, fade as shadows before Karamine's brightness and grace. A tremor of longing washed over him as he recalled her embrace and passionate response to his kisses. For that moment, she was mine, he thought to himself, and he smiled in his remembering. She's too rare a treasure to give up lightly. No matter what she says, her husband, Lance, must be a fool, a weak-minded *"esh"* (ass), who doesn't deserve her. Well I can wait. This war won't last forever, then we shall see. In the meantime, let me sleep—I need to rest. He sighed deeply, then turned impatiently on the narrow sofa, to get into a comfortable position. The room was still in darkness, but the first grey light of dawn was dimly visible between spaces of the window shade. He closed his eyes then drifted off into restless sleep.

It seemed to Varoujan he had barely slept, when he was rudely awakened by the sound of heavy knocking. He glanced at his watch, and saw that he had slept a couple of hours. The knocking was insistent. "Karamine, open the door, it's me . . . Lance!" a voice called loudly.

Varoujan jolted. Quickly, he switched on the light, then slipped into his tunic, before moving to open the door. When Lance saw Varoujan, he barged in, pushing impatiently past him. Lance seemed puzzled at first glance, and surprised by Varoujan's presence, then his eyes darted quickly about the room as if to assure himself he had the right address. But his expression changed swiftly when Karamine appeared in the doorway of her bedroom. His blue eyes flashed with disbelief and outrage.

Lance lunged toward Varoujan, as though propelled by an explosive force. Taking Varoujan completely by surprise, he seized the collar of his tunic and smashed him violently against the wall, sending a lamp crashing to the floor.

"Lance . . . my God, what are you doing?" Karamine shrieked, frantically running toward them. "What are you doing here at this time of day anyway, and what do you think you're doing?" "My God, Lance!" Karamine tried to make Lance release his hold, but Lance ignored her, holding Varoujan against the wall in a steel grip, forcing his elbow against his throat, choking him in a deadly grasp.

Awakened by the noise and angry voices, Sabu and Arax rushed into the room. Panic-stricken when seeing a stranger hold his father by the throat, Sabu hurled himself at Lance, punching him furiously on the back. *"Vertzoor aghdod tzerkared, Hyrig"* (get your dirty hands off my father) he shouted.

Lance released Varoujan at once. But his eyes darted rapidly from Karamine in her dressing robe, the children and then to Varoujan, whose vivid black eyes were filled with surprise and rage.

"So this is the story, huh?" said Lance, his voice shaking with anger, as he turned to Karamine. "This is the reason why you refuse to come back home to America . . . why should you? You have everything you've ever wanted here . . . a whole family, a couple of kids, your work . . . why the hell should you come home. It's obvious to me you've made this your home. You have a whole new life here, even the kids you've always wanted . . . and a husband to boot! Great!"

"You're an even bigger fool than I imagined," Varoujan shouted angrily, taking a step toward Lance.

"Wait . . . please Varoujan," Karamine said, holding up her hand toward Varoujan, before turning to face Lance.

"If you've finished jumping to conclusions, Lance, perhaps you might take a moment out to listen to the truth and let me explain . . . "

"Explain? What is there to explain? It's all quite evident to me. Yes, your friend here is right, I am a fool, a damn fool. I should have realized what the situation was a long time ago. But love is blind as they say. I should have known you had some attraction other than your work when you made so many excuses to remain here, despite my loneliness, my pleadings, and my need for you to return." Lance's face was livid with pain and accusations.

"Your words are reckless and untrue. Your wife has done nothing wrong," Varoujan interjected, in a heated tone, taking a step toward Lance.

Lance wheeled toward him, and both men faced each other belligerently.

"Back off, pal, and stay out of this; this is something strictly between my wife and me," Lance said menacingly.

Karamine covered he face with her hands. This is a nightmare, she thought, the whole thing's a bad dream. She was crushed and shocked by Lance's vilification and slanderous accusations, the unexpectedness of his arrival, and his complete lack of trust in her. She dropped her hands, revealing her face, which was drawn and expressionless. There were dark circles beneath her eyes, and the lids were swollen slightly from too much weeping and lack of sleep. She gazed at Lance dispassionately, and at that moment wondered if she ever truly knew him.

"So . . . you burst in here without warning, you see a set a circumstances you know nothing about, and immediately, you judge and condemn. My God, Lance!" Karamine's lips were white and trembling, but she spoke the words calmly. "You were the one who taught me to 'check my premises.' "And, weren't you also the one who always claimed that 'to assume leads to doom.' She shook her head sadly. "For your information, this is Commander Varoujan Torossian, of the Karabakh Defence Force," she said, turning to Varoujan. He's been through some of the worst combat of the war these past few days, but he made the supreme effort to come here last night to tell me personally, that Vasken was killed in that battle. These are his children. Their mother was badly wounded in Karabakh, and the children were also wounded. I promised their mother before she died that I would take care of them, and that's what I've done. I wrote you about it . . . "

Lance's face changed suddenly, and his voice faltered. The news struck him like a thunderbolt. "Vasken . . . was killed? He stared at Karamine and for the first time noticed how pale and drawn she looked. She was thinner, and her eyes expressed a sadness he had not seen before. "I'm sorry, Karamine," he said quietly, "I know how much you loved and cared for him."

Varoujan remained silent, but kept his dark eyes fixed narrowly on Lance. After a few moments, he noticed the children, huddling nervously in the doorway; he walked toward them, then gently led them back into the bedroom, closing the door behind him.

"Forgive me, Karamine," Lance said in a barely audible voice, "I've missed you so much, and there are times when I'm afraid I'm losing you. I think I went a little crazy, when I came here and found another man comfortably installed in your living quarters. I had so looked forward to our being together, I just didn't expect it. I wasn't thinking straight . . . can you understand that and forgive me?"

Karamine stared silently at Lance for several long moments, then closed her eyes. She was deeply tired. The day's events had drained her of all emotion; she felt nothing now except a dull and nameless anguish. She opened her eyes and forced a response.

"I'm trying to understand, Lance, and yes . . . of course I forgive you. But when will you learn to curb that impulsive nature, and your temper . . . your accusations hurt deeply; you embarrassed me in front of Commander Torossian and you terrified his children. Did you intend to kill him?" What are you doing here at this time of day anyway?"

"I'll make it up to you, Karamine, I promise, and I'll apologize to Commander Torossian. But before going into the reasons for my being here, tell me about Vasken," he said with concern. "What about his body? I could take him back in the military plane and he could be buried in your parents plot, if you wish."

Karamine smiled wearily."No, no, Varoujan buried him where he fell, and that's what he would have wanted for his end. To be buried in the land he was fighting for, like our ancestors. No, he's finally at peace now, Lance. I've never told you, but he had changed completely. He was a different person from the Vasken you knew."

Lance dropped into the chair and stared quizzically at Karamine. "Different?"

"Yes, since coming to Armenia he had become completely disillusioned with communism. Seeing it in action here destroyed ever vestige of his socialist, collectivist thinking, once and for all. But, as with any man who believes passionately in a cause all of his life, then discovers that cause has betrayed him, it destroyed him. He wanted to end his life. Only by the grace of God was I able to prevent him from blowing his head off." She covered her face with her hands recalling the event.

Lance looked at Karamine but felt helpless. The silence in the room weighed heavily, intensifying his sense of self-reproach.He reached out to her and put his arms around her awkwardly. Karamine felt thin and limp in his arms. I've got to bring her back with me, he thought desperately. Karamine has suffered, more than I realized, and that's been the problem. We've been apart too long. We're losing sight of each other's needs and problems. I haven't been here for her, and today, my lack of understanding has only compounded our differences. Damn!

"Why didn't you tell me about it, Karamine? I know there was no love lost between Vasken and myself, but, because of my love for you, I care about everything that concerns you. Don't you know that?"

Karamine attempted a smile. Lance's voice stirred old memories and she realized sharply how much she'd actually missed her husband's support and love.

"I'm glad to see you, Lance, what are you doing here, and how long do you have?" Karamine asked softly, sitting down on the sofa and folding the blanket.

"Well, it wasn't planned, it all happened fast, and before I knew it I was on a plane heading for Armenia. You must be aware of what's happening politically and militarily here in Karabakh and Armenia."

"No, I don't know much about it, Lance. I'm in my small world here at the hospital, where we treat the people coming in from the fighting in Karabakh. That keeps me pretty busy, and the rest of the time I'm too tired to read up on the politics here. I just wish the war would end, that's all."

"Well, that's the point, Karamine. We were making headway in the congress and state department dealing with the aggression of the Azeris into Karabakh, and the displacing of the people there, but now, the KDF has taken Azeri territory and some of our supporters and backers in Washington feel the KDF have become the aggressors. Ted and I are having trouble convincing them otherwise. That's really why I'm here. I need the real story, information to take back home to prove the KDF is not the aggressor, that they only want independence and peace. I need some reassurances the fighting and aggression will not continue. Some have indicated they feel the KDF will push to Baku and take all of Azerabaijan."

"I know very little about that situation, Lance, so I'm not the one to talk with, but, let me call Varoujan. He's in the middle of it, so he can fill you in and give you a candid report."

Lance was silent a moment, trying to control a cold stab of resentment at the sound of Varoujan's name. "If you wish," he said reluctantly.

Karamine walked to the door of the children's room and knocked gently. "Varoujan . . . will you come out for a moment?" she called softly.

Varoujan opened the door and stepped cautiously into the room. His eyes no longer reflected anger and hostility, but were pools of black ice as he fixed his gaze coldly on Lance.

Lance regarded Varoujan stoically. He's a man of some stature and power, handsome too in a rugged sort of way, he noted; he commands attention. No matter what Karamine says, there's a danger here—he could be a threat to me—and our marriage.

"Varoujan, this is my husband, Lance Bagdasarian.He's here from Washington, representing the Congress of the United States. He needs some information on what's happening in Karabakh and the political situation in Armenia. I told him you'd be able to answer his questions better than I."

"Please . . . before we start," Lance began quickly, stepping forward and extending his hand, "I want to apologize to you, and your children, Commander Torossian, I'm sorry I attacked you, and terrified your children. I was completely out of line. Please accept my sincere regrets for my inappropriate actions."

Varoujan drew his eyebrows together and bowed stiffly. He took Lance's hand reluctantly. "It's forgotten," he said in a clipped voice. He studied Lance's six-foot frame, observing the casual, but expensive, fleece-lined nylon sport jacket. This American-Armenian cuts a fine figure with his sandy hair and handsome blue eyes, he thought contemptuously, but he's an egotistical, hot-head who fancies himself a patriot. Bah! What does he know of us? He stands here in his fashionable, high-polished boots and thinks he understands the men and boys whose only footwear is mud-caked and polished by the blood of their youth. How could he understand? He doesn't even understand his own wife, but for her sake, at least let me be civil. "How may I help you?" Varoujan inquired politely.

Lance took a small tape recorder form his pocket. "Sit down and let me record what you say," he said, making a motion toward the sofa. "First of all, Commander, can you tell me why the KDF did not stay within the perimeters of Karabakh and defend their positions there? Why have you expanded into Azeri territory? There are those back in Washington who view this action unfavorably, and now see the KDF as the aggressors, no different from the Azeris. This makes it difficult to recruit help for your cause."

Varoujan stared directly at Lance, but could not conceal the disdain in his voice. "I know it's difficult for you to understand, but apparently you and your friends in America don't realize that we voted for the independent state of Karabakh. Unfortunately, it is surrounded by Azeri territories, and they are squeezing the life out of us. The differences are irreconcilable. With nothing but threats and hostility all around us, we had no other choice but to break through the Lachin Pass to Armenia, and also to take Azeri towns which are being used as supply depots. I'll be damned if we'll return any of our land. Karabakh has always been part of Armenia and its people for thousands of years until Stalin annexed it to the Azeris in 1921. He did it to punish our people for not embracing the soviet Russian tongue and culture. He also did it to placate the muslim provinces of the soviet union. Ninety-eight percent of the people in Karabakh, however, are Armenian. We're now in the process of expanding that vital connection, the Lachin Pass, north and south, so once and for all we will have Armenia as a border on our west, and not be totally surrounded by hostile Azeris. As for the other territories we've taken on the eastern front, Agdam, Mirbashir and Fizuli . . . well that's another story. The Azeri have been using them as a staging area for supplies, in order to come in and kill our people." Varoujan shrugged. "Why shouldn't we defend ourselves, take and destroy their supplies when we are able? They wanted this fight, and we're retaliating, two-fold. Yes, we've captured those points and all their weapons and supplies and we intend to hold them as long as this war continues. We will need specific physical guarantees before we ever give back any territory. Treaties mean nothing to these people as we've learned from past history. You of all people should know this."

Lance remained silent, fixing his blue eyes intently on Varoujan. "This is a dangerous and delicate situation. How am I to justify and explain this recalcitrant action to Washington? There are members of congress and the state department who want you to return those lands back to the Azeri, so peace can be negotiated between both sides."

Varoujan hit the table with his fist, and stood up. His eyes blazed with fury. "Peace you say? Never, never! Those lands have been taken with Armenian blood! We in Karabakh don't give a damn what your congress or state department wants. You are thousands of miles away, in another world. Where were you when they were killing and butchering our people? Huh? What did you do?" His voice rose heatedly and the fury increased in his eyes. "Not a damn thing, and now you dare to tell us to give up what we have fought hard and died for? Don't tell us what we are and are not to do in Karabakh. Before there's any talk of our giving back hard won territory, instruct the Turks to return Anatola, Western Armenia and Mt. Ararat back to our people. Those Azeris are nothing but Turks, yes, that's what they are . . . butchering Turks!"

Karamine who listened to the conversation while dressing, came out of her bedroom and sat at the table. She felt the furious hostility between both men. "Please," she interjected, "we're all on the same side here. We'll accomplish nothing if this suspicion and accusation continues." She turned to Varoujan and placed her hand gently on his arm. "Varoujan, I know it's difficult for you to understand, especially now, when you've just been through hell, but Lance is here to help."

Lance bit his lip and tried to hold his reaction in check as he watched Karamine's hand rest lightly on Varoujan's arm. He felt a strong tide of dislike and resentment rise within him, toward this Armenian patriot who had obviously won his wife's friendship and trust.

"Yes, I understand your position, Commander," Lance remarked calmly, "I have read Armenian history and I agree with your premise totally." But the decision to give aid here is not mine. Try to understand my position. I must justify what you say and do to the congress, state department and even the president. We need their support if our people in Karabakh are to survive."

Varoujan glared at Lance, and tried to temper his response. "That, sir, is your problem. You can tell them there will be no peace unless the free and independent State of Karabakh is there to negotiate for that peace face to face with the Azeri. Karabakh is an independent republic now. As I said, we have a voted constitution and duly elected parliament and president. They will look to the needs of our people. Yes, and one thing more . . . Karabakh takes no orders from Armenia or any other nation, such as America. We don't need some party, thousands of miles away, selling us down the river, as they did in 1918. Tell that to your American congress and people."

Lance remained silent for a long time, nervously drumming an abstract tune with his fingers on the table. "What about this president of Armenia? Does he believe in democracy, a free market and all that entails?" he asked, in an insinuating voice.

Varoujan gestured with irritated impatience. "You and your people are so naive when it comes to this part of the world. Armenia's president was formerly a lieutenant in the KGB, and in his day, has banished many Armenians to the gulogs of Siberia. What more could you expect from an authoritarian person like that. It is authority no different from the days of the soviet empire. Remember . . . you still have the remnants of the old regime . . . the bureaucracy who do not want to lose power. This president is no exception. You'll see, gradually, he will silence the press and human rights organizations, and then will accuse the opposition parties, such as ours, the Armenian Revolutionary Federation, with fabricated charges in order to outlaw or silence them. What does he know of freedom? The ARF has been fighting for freedom ever since its conception decades ago. We've known for some time that this president's main objective is to get the ARF. He understands their strength among the people, and he knows it is the strongest opposition he has. If he can destroy them in Armenia, the rest of the opposition will crumble. He'll have to destroy it both in Armenia and the Diaspora, however. This surprises you, does it not?" Varoujan questioned, noting Lance's puzzled expression.

Lance shook his head. "I don't understand. Doesn't he have a constitution he has to follow?"

Varoujan laughed cynically. "It is the old bolshevic constitution. They were supposed to rewrite a new one, and have it voted upon, but who knows if it will ever transpire. The old bureaucrats are entrenched, and it is obvious the president and his cohorts don't want to relinquish the power they have by holding free and open elections. They know they would not win."

"They?" Who is the they?" Lance inquired.

"The president and his fellow henchmen in Yerevan . . . old bureaucrats . . . KGB, Secret Police, the police itself. They want to hold on to their power over the people. As I said before and want you to understand, elections are supposed to be held soon, but, they want to destroy all opposition, especially the ARF before the elections take place. Don't be surprised if they completely outlaw the opposition parties and the ARF before the elections. All they need to do is to have the parliament pass a resolution and declare them a subversive group, then have the courts agree. They control it all. Who is to stop them? They have the votes and the guns to enforce what they want, and believe me, they will. They will rewrite the constitution and you know who that will favor."

Lance was dismayed and taken aback. He was shocked to learn that after so many years of fighting for freedom, Armenians were now fighting each other again. "But the Armenian people are free now after all these years. Why can't they get together and do things in a democratic manner? I just don't understand," he cried, shaking his head and heaving a sigh of exasperation.

Varoujan smiled bitterly. "One thing we have learned from history . . . freedom is never achieved without bloodshed. Look at your America. How did it gain its independence and freedom? Bloodshed. French revolution and the Russian revolution, same thing. Although Armenia has had her blood shed through oppression and tyranny, she has never experienced bloodshed for freedom within her own country, among her own people. So . . . you see, this is the ghastly consequence."

Lance sat back in his chair and stared at Varoujan with disbelief. "What are you implying?" he exclaimed. "Revolution? Is that your answer, Commander? Armenian killing Armenian? I find this difficult to accept."

Varoujan paced restlessly. "I report only the truth of the political situation in Armenia. Accept it or not, it remains the truth. What is your answer Congressman?"

Lance raised his hands and let them fall in a gesture of helplessness. He turned off the recorder. "I have no answer, from the conditions you state." He shook his head. "Look, let me get back to Washington. I'll see if we can put pressure on the president of Armenia and the parliament. We'll try to get a guarantee that all opposition parties have access to radio and television, and that no party is banned or outlawed prior to elections for whatever reason. I'll get information to the proper departments and alert them to the situation here. They can then check to see what is being done to the opposition parties and particularly the ARF. We must be able to reach the president of Armenia and inform him that all monetary funds and supplies will end, if he does not assure the people free and open elections. We in Washington wish to see a peaceful transaction from an authoritarian rule to a democratic parliamentary system. We will want our representatives, or some international group to monitor the election to make sure there's no coercion or intimidation of the voters at the polls. We want to see a proper, open election. I'll demand that before we allow any more aid to Armenia."

Varoujan listened patiently. "And, if all your efforts fail, what then?" he said, slowly and deliberately.

There was silence in the room. Deep within, Lance felt a sting. He remembered his grandfather, Sahag, heard his voice thunder, and felt again the old fire and conflict in his veins. He knew the answer his grandfather would give—*Aroun Ge Hoisi Azadoution Hammar* (Blood flows always for the cause of freedom). He looked at Varoujan "Revolution?" he said somberly.

"No . . . no," Karamine interrupted quickly. "I don't even want to hear the word, it's not the answer! Our people have suffered enough! Everything will be straightened out and the elections will be fair to all sides. The president of Armenia promised that to the people, and I can't believe he would go back on his word."

Lance caressed Karamine's shoulder, and spoke to her in a comforting tone. "No one wants to see that happen, Karamine. When I get back I'll contact Ted and we'll do everything in our power to make the campaigns and election free of any fraud here in Armenia. We'll make sure the old soviet constitution is discarded and a new constitution implemented. Look . . . you certainly don't believe we want everything we've dreamed of for our people smashed by a handful of power-hungry men, do you?"

Watching Lance's tender touch and tone to his wife, Varoujan flinched slightly. "If there's nothing more you wish to know, I'll see to my children," he said, uncomfortably.

"I believe I have enough information, Commander," Lance replied. "If I need more I'll contact you again. Thank you. I'll get back to Washington and see what can be done to eleviate the problems we discussed today. We'll put a lot of pressure on the president of Armenia and his men there. Don't forget . . . many Armenians in America think he's great, and have been pouring a lot of money into the coffers of Armenia. They don't have the insights that you, living here and in Karabakh have, consequently they don't know the truth of what's happening."

"Yes, I understand how that could be. I wonder if the president of Armenia is keeping good records of all the money he receives from abroad. What about a Swiss bank account? Check on that as well if you can. Now, if you'll excuse me, I'll see to my children."

"Again, thank you for your help," said Lance. The two men eyed each other silently, then Varoujan walked to the small bedroom, entered and closed the door behind him.

"When do you have to leave?" Karamine asked when they were alone.

"Tomorrow late. There will be no other plane to get me back if I miss that one."

"So soon? That gives us very little time," Karamine said softly.

"Look, the car is waiting outside. Dress comfortably and come back to the hotel with me. We can spend the day together."

"You have a hotel room?" Karamine asked in a surprised voice. "Weren't you planning to see me?"

"That's something they do automatically, whether I use it or not, it's there for my use," Lance replied. "You know, Karamine, I've been at meetings since I arrived, trying to make head or tail of what's going on here in Armenia. That short conversation with Comander Torossian has filled in many doubts I've had about this president and the way he's been operating the secret police. The commander has verified my concerns of what's been happening here under the guise of democracy. It's appalling. Ted and I have received information from many sources. All our efforts to describe Armenia as a democracy are being destroyed. The Turkish Lobby is portraying the Armenians in Karabakh as the aggressors. I needed solid data to fight back, and that's why I'm here, to verify these sources. Ted wanted to come, but there was some pressing legislation, and they needed his vote." Lance pulled her into his arms. "So, here I am in Armenia again, asking my wife the same question . . . will you come home with me tomorrow? Just a simple yes or no."

Karamine took a deep breath. "Lance, how can I drop my work without a moment's notice, and just leave the hospital? They are so under staffed as it is. Please, give me a little more time to finish up here, and help them train some new people . . . "

"So, the answer is no. That's all I wanted to know," Lance interrupted irritably.

"Don't make it so cold," Karamine replied, in a hurt voice. "Aren't you interested in my reasons?"

"What difference does it make, the answer is still no."

"The difference is I would like to give you a reason for the delay and hope you would understand."

"Look, Karamine . . . we've been over it every time I'm here and whenever we talk on the phone. I understand your reasons, but, I'm getting damn frustrated about your constant concern here, while being back in the USA with me seems to be of no concern to you whatsoever. Perhaps I'm selfish, but I'd like to think I have some priority among your concerns."

Karamine shook her head in denial. "Surely I don't have to prove that fact to you after all this time, do I?"

Lance turned his glance from Karamine, then looked back at her dispiritedly. "All I'm saying is that somehow I feel empty and defeated inside when I think of us, and I don't know why. Karamine . . . it's been almost a year, we're living in two different worlds. How long can we go on this way? How do you think I feel when I see you wearing yourself out, looking so thin and pale each time I come here?"

Karamine touched him affectionately. "Lance . . . you're always here with me, and I long for the day when we can finally pick up our lives again, as they were. But, I have to finish the work I've begun here. I know it's been difficult, but all I ask is that you are patient just a little while longer. Please?"

Lance sighed and held her close. "Do I have a choice?" he whispered sadly.

"Look, let's just forget everything and enjoy being together today. I'll call the hospital and take the day off, then we'll go into the city. We'll have dinner tonight at one of the new restaurants that opened, and later we'll go to your hotel and relax. Okay?"

Lance smiled slightly and held her. He was not completely reassured. "Come on then, get dressed and we'll be off. The car is outside."

Karamine disappeared into the bedroom and dialed the hospital. Lance heard her muffled words of explanation, and instruction; he felt suddenly like an intruder in an alien world. How long can we go on like this he wondered dismally.

Karamine came out shortly afterward, dressed in comfortable jacket and slacks. She paused to knock gently on the door of the children's bedroom.

"Varoujan . . . children . . . I'm leaving now. The place is yours until tomorrow." She smiled at Lance as he guided her outside where a chauffered car waited. They climbed into the back seat, and drove away for their short rendezvous.

32

Lance's return from Armenia to Washington was tedious. Non-stop all the way, there was only one stop-over in Belgrade for refueling. Already he was beginning to feel the effect of jet-lag as time zones merged one into another. He knew it would take a few days to get his body back to a normal rhythm, but he had committed himself to the task ahead with dedicated zeal.

The long flight back gave him plenty of time for reflection. Despite all his efforts to the contrary, the memory of finding Varoujan in Karamine's house early in the morning, persisted and unnerved him. Of course I trust her, he told himself over and over, yet, tormenting thoughts continued to plague him. Why the hell couldn't she have come back with me, he thought resentfully. Her excuse of short notice and finishing a job before leaving with good conscience seems pretty weak to me. True, she promised to wind things up and return as soon as possible, but, I've heard all that so many times before, how can I believe she really means it this time. He closed his eyes. Their time together had been happy in spite of everything. They talked at length about home and family, all of their activities together. Their accommodations at the hotel reserved by the Armenian Government were luxurious, especially the available supply of hot running water, which Karamine utilized to the maximum. Lance felt a rush of emotion as he recalled Karamine coming out of the bath, shining clean and beautiful, as he had always pictured her. He had held her tenderly in his arms and made love, and they had stayed awake most of the night talking and reassuring each other of their love and reunion back home in America. The terrible hours of doubt and torment had ceased then, and they were in love again with all the enthusiasm and fire of their youth. But now, returning home without her, his loneliness and doubts returned. He felt a wall between them, nameless and obscure. Is it only in my mind, he asked, or is it indeed, the truth.

Lance's thoughts were still in turmoil when he landed at Washington Airport the next day. They continued after he had returned to his town house to get some rest. After a restless night, he got up early the following day and resolved to put his emotions behind him. Arriving at this office before any of his staff he sorted through the stacks of papers, bills and legislation piled high on his desk. He forced himself to concentrate on his report of findings, to the committee, the state department and executive branch, for their input and decision on the Armenian situation.

Everett Mason, his close, right-hand assistant was the first to enter his office and greet him.

"Morning, sir, how was your trip to Armenia?"

"Good morning, Everett . . . " Lance replied, glancing up from the papers on his desk, "it was fruitful, but most of the news from there is disheartening, to say the least." He tossed a paper in the out basket. "Things are ominous in Armenia, Everett. I talked to some interesting people there, and have a pretty clear picture of what's going on. Look, Everett, I have to get hold of Ted as soon as possible. I'd like to give him the information before seeing anyone about it. Will you try to get him at his office this morning and have him call me as soon as possible? I have to get this complete report ready for the committee and State Dept. so try to get him fast, will you."

"Do you want anything? Coffee? Breakfast?" Everett inquired.

"Breakfast would be great, Everett," Lance replied, realizing he hadn't eaten anything. Order a ham and cheese sandwich . . . and lots of coffee. I need to keep my strength up this morning to get through this pile of work today."

"I'll see if I can get Congressman Sohigian first," said Everett, leaving Lance's office and closing the door.

A few moments later, the telephone buzzed on Lance's desk.

"Ted? Yeh . . . I'm back . . . yesterday. You'd think I'd been away a month instead of a few days from the look of the paperwork on my desk. I'll have to go over what came in, besides making a complete report on Armenia."

"How was the trip? Did you get the information we were looking for?" Ted questioned, eagerly.

"Yeah, I got it, and it's not good, Ted. It's more desperate than we thought. Things are going from bad to worse since Armenia got its independence. The interim government seems to have a hold on the country; it's trying to control the opposition. It's a long story. We'll have to get together and see what can be done here on our end. As I said, I'll have to make out my report today and give the committee my findings tomorrow at the latest."

"Why don't you come by the house for dinner tonight. We'll relax and go over your report together, Lance."

"Sounds good, Ted. I'd like your input about some statements made by a commander of the KDF I met over there. His remarks were depressing, to say the least. Doesn't look good for our people, Ted, doesn't look good at all."

"Save it for tonight, Lance. Did you see Karamine? How is she? Tatiana is always asking when she's coming back."

There was a short pause. "Well, that's another story, Ted. Perhaps Tatiana can give me a woman's perspective on it, because I'm completely confused," Lance said in a dejected tone.

"You don't sound like yourself. Get your ass over here tonight, and Tatiana and I will cheer you up. Have no fear, Tatiana always knows." He laughed.

"Well, Ted, you know I appreciate you and Tatiana. Don't know what I would have done here in Washington if it weren't for both of you."

Ted laughed affectionately. "Hey . . . don't go soft on me, Senator, or I'll let you have it with both barrels next time at martial arts. In the meantime, get off the phone and quit feeling sorry for yourself. Finish the report, so you can bring it along with you this evening."

"Right. What time, Ted?"

"The usual . . . six thirtyish."

"See you then."

Lance placed the receiver back, and turned his chair around to look out the window. Hearing Ted's voice with its note of optimism and support boosted his spirits, and he felt somewhat more reassured about everything in general. He turned on the computer in his office and keyed in the operative formula to begin a new document—Armenia/Karabakh Report.

He was concentrating on the format of his material when Everett entered with his breakfast, cleared a corner of his desk and set it down.

"Eat it while it's hot, Sir." Everett instructed.

"Right, Everett," Lance replied, turning from the computer. "Smells good. I'm hungrier than I thought." He took a healthy bite from the sandwich, then a mouthful of coffee. "As soon as I get it on a disc, give it to Sandy to have printed out right away. I need to take it with me when I leave tonight. Congressman Sohigian and I will go over it together, and add any conclusions we come to before I see any of the departments involved. I don't want to be disturbed the rest of the day."

"Got it, Sir." Everett said, leaving the office and closing the door behind him.

Lance worked on the report most of the day, leaving the office only to take a short lunch break at the Senate Restaurant. He returned to his office and continued on until four thirty when Everett passed him the final draft.

"Good, Everett," Lance said, reading the report carefully. He was astonished by the logic of his own insights and thinking.

"If there's nothing else, Everett, I'm leaving now. I'll be at Ted's tonight. You have the number if anything drastic comes up." Lance said, placing the report in a folder and putting it carefully into a briefcase.

"Yes, Sir."

Lance glanced up at Everett thoughtfully. "Everett . . . will you please stop SIR-ING me? We are not in the service."

"What am I to call you?" Everett replied helplessly.

"Lance would help."

"That's a little personal."

"How about plain, senator? No, I guess that's a little too formal," Lance said with a smile as he slipped into his jacket. "We'll think of something. In the meantime, good night, and thanks to you and everyone who helped get this report out so quickly. Good job." He left the office, and walked toward the parking lot.

The day was warm with a fresh breeze, and the rich blue tint of sky was broken only by cumulus clouds. When he reached his small car, Lance decided to put the top down and enjoy the early spring air, and his drive to Ted's home, despite the hazards of driving on the heavily traveled Washington Beltway. Pulling out of the parking field, he smiled when he felt the bracing wind against his face. It's the tonic I need, he thought to himself, and he felt more invigorated physically and mentally than he had all day. Karamine would enjoy this, he reflected glumly; God, will she ever come back? As much as she tells me she misses me and our life together, I can't get past the feeling she's being drawn deeper and deeper into Armenia and its people. Then there's that Varoujan! The man's no fool. I'm damn sure he cares for Karamine, loves her in fact, especially when she's taking care of his children. I'd do the same if I were in his place. What about her? She must have some feeling for him—the way she spoke his name and touched him. Lance drew his eyebrows together in a brooding frown. I don't believe Karamine realizes it herself, but they have some sort of special bond that I'm not even part of, in fact I feel like an outsider, completely. He was the one who brought her the news of Vasken, supported and comforted her through it, then too, she loves and shares the affection of his children. How the hell can I compete with that? "Karamine", he spoke her name out loud, "don't leave me. I don't think I could bear it." He made a turn off at Ted's Beltway exit, then took a few side roads to the Sohigian home. I have to stop these tormenting doubts, he told himself. I'll drive myself crazy if I don't.

Lance turned in to the driveway of Ted's home. Ted's children, Vartan and Alexis playing in the yard, ran to greet him enthusiastically when they saw him.

"Uncle Lance, you're back! Daddy told us you had gone to Armenia. What was it like? I wish I could go," Vartan exclaimed excitedly.

The commotion brought Ted and Tatiana to the door, and they greeted Lance warmly.

"Come in, Lance. It's good to see you. Ted said you were back. Did you see Karamine?" Tatiana questioned.

"Give him some time to come in and get settled, Tatiana," Ted commented with a smile.

Lance laughed. "Karamine is well, Tatiana. She still feels she needs more time there."

"Children, go on with your game outside. I'll call you in when dinner is ready," Tatiana said, turning to Vartan and Alexis. "Come in, Lance," she said, leading the way to the living room.

"How about a beverage before dinner?" Ted questioned.

"Great. I could stand a good shot of scotch and water about now," Lance replied.

"I'll have a glass of chardonnay, Ted, there's some open in the refrigerator," Tatiana added.

When Ted went in to the kitchen, Tatiana observed Lance keenly. Perhaps it's only jet-lag, she thought, but, Lance looks a little haggard and dejected to me. "So," she began, "Ted tells me things don't look good for our people in Armenia, there's problems with the new President?"

Lance sighed heavily. "I'm afraid so, Tatiana. The situation is bad there. We'll discuss the report later."

"And how does Karamine feel about it all?" Tatiana probed. "When does she expect to come home?"

Lanced shrugged and closed his eyes. "Tatiana . . . I can't honestly tell you when Karamine will come home, if indeed she ever does." He said despondently.

Tatiana gasped with puzzled surprise. "What do you mean, Lance, if she ever does?"

Lance shrugged again, then turned his eyes directly toward Tatiana. "Just that. Karamine seems to be caught up in this whole Armenian cause . . . it's her desideratum, the fulfillment of her heart's aspiration, her life's dream, what more can I say? I don't know, I'm confused, except I feel I'm losing her."

"No, Impossible!" Tatiana protested in a loud voice. "Karamine loves you, Lance, I'm sure you must have misunderstood her motives for staying there longer. She loves you," she repeated.

Lance raised his hands in a gesture of despair. "Look, Tatiana, it's been almost a year. I asked her to come home with me this time, but she said she felt it was not the right time to leave. I don't think it will ever be the right time, frankly."

"Perhaps she has loose ends to finish up, Lance. Trust her a little longer. You know Karamine. She'd never leave a job unfinished."

"I worry about more than just loose ends," Lance said grimly. "When I walked in on her early in the morning, there was a man in her house . . . "

"A man in Karamine's house? For God's sake, what are you saying, Lance?" Ted cried with alarm, when he came back with a tray.

"Well . . . she had a good reason for it, and he had spent the night on the sofa, but, the whole incident has been pretty damn upsetting for me. It was an ugly scene, and of course, I come off as the bad guy, the villain."

"Why, what happened, Lance?" Ted asked in a concerned voice.

Lance shook his head, and smiled a little. "Well, I lost my cool, made a complete fool of myself. I slammed him against the wall, knocked over a lamp waking his two children, and Karamine. They all came running into the room, and his young son attacked me on his dad's behalf. It was a nightmare. Karamine was indignant, angry, embarrassed. She explained to me what he was doing there, then I felt like a first-class jerk. Her brother Vasken was killed in that battle for the Lachin Pass. It seems that Varoujan . . . that's his name, is a commander in the Karabakh Defence Force, and Vasken was under his command at the time. Apparently, he had just come in that day from the battlefront to give Karamine the news that her brother was killed. Also, Karamine is taking care of this commander's children. They were wounded when Karabakh was attacked, and were brought into Karamine's hospital, a long with their mother who died later of her wounds. To make along story short, Karamine promised their mother before she died that she would take care of the children, so, now . . . they live with her." He gestured with his hands.

"Didn't you know any of this before you walked in?" Ted questioned. "Didn't Karamine ever mention it to you?"

Lance laughed a little. "Well, Ted, telephone communications are difficult over there. It takes weeks before a letter comes through, and the few times we've spoken on the telephone has been short and not too clear. All of which doesn't help. Yes, I think she mentioned those two children, but I didn't expect to walk into a domestic setup. It looked like a real family scenario. No wonder I blew my stack."

Tatiana who had been listening with concentrated attention stood up and placed her hand on Lance's shoulder. "Listen to me, Lance, don't be so hard on yourself. Anyone would have done the same. At least the commander knows Karamine has a real husband, not some phantom living in a far-off land . . . in case he had any ideas. And he did sleep on the sofa! You saw the evidence of that yourself."

"Yes, circumstances can be damaging at times, Lance, if we don't know all the facts. I understand your reaction, but I also know Karamine, and I know she loves you," Ted commented sincerely.

"I know Karamine too, Ted, and she's always been an idealist, a romantic. You have to see this commander . . . he's the stuff of heroes, of legends. He's Antranig, Sabu and Dro all rolled up into one. Karamine has always loved those old stories of Armenian heroes, fadayees fighting in the mountains and rescuing our people from the Turkish hordes. I just have a gut feeling this guy ranks high in her esteem and admiration, more than she herself may even realize. Hell . . . she's taking care of his children, how can I fight that?"

"There's nothing to fight, Lance. I believe you're making too much of this," said Ted, firmly, "You've exaggerated the whole thing in your mind until you've lost all perspective in the situation. There's no duplicity in Karamine. She's a dedicated doctor and scientist on a mission to a cause she's believed in all her life. She's always loved children, and she loves you. Trust her."

"It's only natural Karamine admires this commander," Tatiana interjected, "but, it's not love, not the love she has for you, Lance. She's not about to throw away everything you both have together for some unstable illusion."

Lance stared thoughtfully at the glass in his hands. Then he raised it to Tatiana and Ted. "You're probably both right, and I am overreacting," he said. "Without Karamine I'm inclined to go off the deep end. Thanks, friends for letting me sound-off. I appreciate your input and patience. It helps. Oh . . . by the way, I almost forgot . . . the report, here it is . . . " Lance reached for his briefcase and pulled out a folder, then handed it to Ted.

Ted went over the report carefully, while Lance and Tatiana talked in detail about her children, and their plans for the summer. Tatiana wanted to return to Wisconsin, and their respective families, but Ted wanted to visit Europe. In the end, they had compromised and had agreed to take the children to Europe for a few weeks, as a broadening experience for them, then spend the rest of the time with their families.

"Have Karamine's parents been notified of their son's death? And, do they wish to bring the body back to America?" Tatiana inquired.

"Yes, I called them as soon as I got back," Lance replied. "I called my parents, too. Everyone feels comfortable with the idea of his burial where he fell. We all agree, it's what he would have wanted."

"How are your parents, Lance? I hope you'll bring them out to meet us if they come to Washington."

Lance smiled. "Well, they're pretty much settled down in Florida. They live in a retirement community, and have everything they need right there. It's on a golf course, and near a marina, so they keep active."

"This is alarming," said Ted, rising out his chair and placing the report on a table. He paced nervously. "How could such a thing happen in Armenia, and what's going on with the people in charge of the country?" he queried angrily. "Don't they know and understand how long our people have fought to become independent? What are they planning, a dictatorship with no opposition, for God's sake? I thought they were going to have a democracy, with a constitution, fashioned after the United States." Ted shook his head in disbelief. "It's difficult for me to accept the facts in this report, Lance. Are you sure you got the information from the right sources? How trustworthy are they?"

"I'd never rely on one source of information, Ted. I checked many; as for trustworthiness, who can guarantee how far any man will go in speech or action to further the aims of his own convictions and power. I took what I could get, and I tried to get as many opinions as possible. I've met with the president, parliamentarians, also the opposition parties, and the Armenian Revolutionary Federation. I've interviewed business people and ordinary workers, and believe me, there's a lot of dissatisfaction, anger and disappointment about the manner the administration of Armenia is taking its damn old time to formulate a democratic constitution and re-election of the parliament. The people are looking forward to a free market economy, and are ready to start up small businesses if the government releases them. No, Ted, believe me, I've looked into this thoroughly. But listen . . . it gets worse. I didn't want to mention this, and I don't want to put it in my report because it won't show our people in a good light as far as our own state department and administration are concerned, but, I'm sad to say there's been assassinations going on in the country."

"What?" cried Ted, aghast by the information he was hearing.

Lance shook his head wearily. "It's true. The president of the independent state of Karabakh and his Aid were murdered, and now, this president of Armenia is trying to place the blame on the Armenian Revolutionary Federation. Both slain men were members of that organization, and were held in high regard. They had come to Armenia to discuss Karabakh's independence, and the president's support for an independent state. It's obvious that Karabakh is a thorn in this president's side, since he also caters to the Turks for economic help as well. It's typical behavior of the old soviet KGB. Blame the opposition for something they themselves have done . . . divide then subjugate."

"What you are describing here is nothing more than the first steps toward a totalitarian state. When you see the media and the newspapers of the opposition being controlled, what's the next step? Outlaw the opposition?" Ted's face flushed slightly with outrage and indignation.

"Exactly. From what the commander told me that is precisely what the president is trying to do. He's planning to outlaw the ARF (Armenian Revolutionary Federation). When I met with him, I felt a distinct antagonism from him toward the ARF. Couldn't put my finger on the reason for it, though."

"The ARF has been the mainstay of the Armenian people for the last hundred years," Ted blurted, loudly. "The tri-colored flag they fly over the capital of Yerevan has been the ARF flag since the first republic in 1920. Where the Hell does he come off outlawing them? What's his reasoning?"

"Simple. He's afraid of losing power. From what I've heard over there, the people are for the ARF, and that will demonstrate in a fair and open election; there's no way he can win in an open election, and he knows it. My feeling is, he'll rig the election at the polls and it can happen. Remember Stalin and his famous quote? 'Let the people vote, just as long as we count the ballots, we'll win.'"

Ted threw up his arms and sighed helplessly. "So what's the alternative? Civil war? Armenian killing Armenian?"

"No . . . dear God, no!" Tatiana exclaimed, rising up from her chair and facing both men. "I can't accept this! I can't believe after all this time, when we're finally free and have an independent nation, that we'll plunge into a civil war. It's unthinkable! Surely there are some levelheads there to stop such a radical action from happening to our people." She stared in dismay from Ted to Lance. "Both of you are in a position to find a better way. There must be something you can do."

Ted's expression was disturbed, and Lance remained silent. "What if everything we try to do fails, Tatiana, what then?" Ted asked gently. "What if they are able to steal the election through whatever means? Should the people submit? Tyranny is tyranny, whether it's Turk, Soviets or one of our own. No, the Armenian people and the people of the diaspora cannot hide their heads in the sand and allow these people to seize power and subjugate the people again. Something will have to be done and done fast."

"But what?" Tatiana cried in despair.

"For one thing, we'll alert the state department, the administration and our committees in the house and senate as to the situation. We could inform them, that any foreign aid Armenia receives, will hinge on their commitment to free elections and a new democratic constitution the people can vote on. That could be a first step," Lance said.

"That's right," Ted added, "we could also say that all opposition parties will have amnesty, and be allowed to enter the political arena without intimidation or coercion by the government. If these simple measures are not met, humanitarian aid to Armenia will cease, and there will not be new laws condemning Turkey and Azerbaijan for their blockade of Armenia. That should shake up the President of Armenia and his cohorts." He turned to his wife. "Yes, there are a few pressures we can apply to those leaders in Armenia to release their stranglehold on the people."

"But won't the people suffer if humanitarian aid is cut off to them?" Tatiana asked.

"You have to understand, Tatiana", Ted explained, "it can't be helped. We have to force their hand or all will be lost."

"Yes," Lance pointed out, "in order to necessitate the establishment of a full democratic republic with a solid constitution, we'll have to do these things. We can't stand by and let a hand full of power-hungry bureaucrats subject the rest of the country. No, these are only some of the first steps to be applied. Also, through the banking committee, we can hold back the cash flow from the diaspora if we wish, but, this would be a last resort."

"But how will the people survive?" Tatiana asked sadly.

"They will survive," Ted answered calmly. "they have in the past and they will in the future. It will be difficult, but they will do it."

"Will those steps be taken before the elections?" Tatiana asked, apprehensively.

"We'll do everything possible to get it through on time, Tatiana," Lance assured her, "we've outlined our choices, that's all we can do from here in Washington."

Tatiana and Ted did not comment. Vartan and Alexis intruded boisterously, bursting into the room and demanding dinner.

Tatiana laughed. "They bring you down to basics fast. Okay, let's go, everything's been ready for some time. Get cleaned up children. Shall we go in to the dining room?" she said, turning to Lance.

At the table, Tatiana bowed her head and began to pray fervently. "Bless us O Lord, and these Thy gifts which we are receiving in the name of Jesus Christ. We thank you Lord, for your guidance and protection of Armenia in its independence. We ask You to bind the evil and destruction trying to seize power there, and I thank You also for giving Ted, and Senator Bagdasarian the wisdom, power and strength to take the necessary steps in preventing bloodshed, and to bring about a peaceful solution to our beloved Armenia."

33

Rouben Talatian cupped his hands as he lit the last of the American cigarettes Vasken had given him on his final trip to Yerevan. He inhaled deeply and watched the smoke spirals dissipate in the sleety wind now bearing down sharply along the precipitous Omar Mountain Pass. It had been several months since he had joined Varoujan and his men in the mountains of northern Karabakh, and already he had tasted the chastening life of a partisan soldier, who followed his leader without question. They had approached Omar earlier that day, forging waist-deep through an icy stream in freezing currents, then bounding head-long up a slope under a hail of bullets. Varoujan as always, took the lead, urging his men forward, inching their way up the mountain, de-termined to push the Azeris out. The threat from this area to Karabakh was serious, Varoujan had informed them. It was vital they take it, then hold the position; Varoujan was convinced it could be done with a handful of men.

Rouben had joined Varoujan shortly after hearing of Vasken's death. He had served Vasken faithfully as his guide in Yerevan and had been responsible for his trip to Karabakh where Vasken had met mem-bers of the KDF. He had learned to like and trust Vasken, and when months passed without any word from him, Rouben searched out Karamine who had informed him that her brother had been killed. Rouben, already disillusioned and upset by the internal politics of the newly independent Republic of Armenia, was deeply depressed by the loss of his friend. Almost at once, he made up his mind to join Varou-jan's group fighting in the mountains of northern Karabakh.

Winter still lingered in the mountains. The temperatures dropped to sub-zero temperatures at night, and most of the rocky terrain was still shrouded in untrodden snow. Rouben and the men were dressed in white to camouflage their activities and whereabouts. They had just re-captured Omar as the Azeris moved into Kelbajar, which is one of the gateways to Karabakh. With only a handful of men they secured their position there, and were holding well against any counter attacks. The residue of battle was everywhere—helmets and rifles stuck halfway in snow, ammunition abandoned, and the acrid stench of exploded shells. In every direction, lay dead bodies of Azeri soldiers who had tried to re-treat, but became disoriented, falling prey to KDF guns. But, Varoujan took no chances. He had already alerted his men, and placed them at strategic points around the perimeter of their position. They were now holding the high ground and were dug in deep. It would take a huge of-fensive to dislodge his men from their position, and Varoujan doubted the Azeris were willing to pay such a price.

Rouben made his way to a sheltered rock and snow enclosure where Varoujan sat huddled, trying to conserve his body heat in the freezing temperatures. "Great weather we're having up here, Rouben," he said jokingly, glancing up from the chart he was studying.

"Well, at least it's not snowing again," Rouben replied. "God, it's cold up here. I could go for a good stiff drink of vodka. Did you have a good visit with your children the last time you were in Yerevan?"

Varoujan smiled. "Yes, they were in good spirits and were happy to see me, as usual. Sabu wants to grow up fast, and come up here to fight by my side." Varoujan shook his head sadly. "Why does war seem so fascinating to young boys? Were you . . . or myself that way? I can't seem to remember. No, I always wanted to build, not destroy. If they could only see the horrors of war I doubt they would want any part of it," he commented, looking around at the carnage.

"Well, they should be in good spirits staying with Vasken's sister, Doctor Karamine. She's like a second mother to them, Rouben replied. She looked tired and worn out the last time I saw her, though. I know she's still grieving about her brother's death. I don't know why she wants to stay here, she should go back to America and be with her husband."

Varoujan looked at Rouben sharply. "Back to America? No, Rouben. She belongs here. She's more Armenian than any of us. Hell . . . she IS Armenia and everything it stands for . . . love, dedication and concern. No, Rouben, Karamine belongs here." he said firmly. He stood up quickly, as though anxious to change the subject, then pulled out his binoculars and carefully, scanned the landscape.

"Now that we have taken this position, Rouben, what I want is to hunt down the remaining Azeris who escaped from this last encounter. We have to. They will be hard-pressed and weak, and their morale will be at a low point, which is to our advantage. Let's clean them all out before they join up with other Azeris and come against us in a counter offensive. Get five men and we will start immediately," he ordered briskly. "Rouben . . . pick the toughest five."

"Yes, I understand, Commander." Rouben answered.

Varoujan called his second in command and informed him what he was planning to do.

"This is a simple job, Commander, we won't need you. You're our Commander, the men trust and respect you, they'll follow you anywhere. I don't want anything to happen to you. Please, Commander . . . let me go instead," he pleaded.

"Look, Onig, if need be, you can command as well as I," Varoujan said, placing his hand on Onig's shoulder. "No one is indispensible, least of all me. You are a good commander. You know the positions and orders. I've relied on your advice and counsel and always felt your arguments and premises were sound. We need men like you to lead, not just for second in command."

"We're ready to move," Rouben announced, returning with five men.

"Good," said Varoujan, slipping into his combat vest, then checking his automatic rifle, and patting his chest to feel the clips of ammunitions and hand grenades. "Ready men, let's go."

Varoujan led them to the perimeter of their defenses where they looked for tracks of the retreating Azeris in the fresh snow. The men pulled their scarves closer about their heads to ward off the biting wind, which struck them keenly, like cold steel. The men carried new assault rifles as well as fresh supplies of food, taken from dead Azeris. The food was a prize, since most of the men had existed on nothing but melted ice for days. Varoujan thought of the Azeri soldiers they were trailing and would have to kill. When the leaders of Baku, capital of Azerbaijan, realize that all we want is the independent state Stalin stole from us, then there will be real peace, he thought glumly. Most of the captured Azeri soldiers he had interrogated felt this whole area belonged to the Armenians anyway, and admitted, the only reason they were there, was that they had been drafted and sent out. At times, Varoujan had felt sorry for those reluctant soldiers, but, he thought resolutely, they have killed our people, as well as those I've loved—Azniv, my wife—Shakie, Souren, and Vasken. I must be relentless in my pursuit, and merciless in purpose.

They continued following the tracks through frozen terrain, plains and valleys. Occasionally, they came across a fallen Azeri who had been obviously overcome by the intense bitter cold of the mountain. They searched him for any information he may have carried, relieved him of his rifle, and continued on, leaving him to wolves. Eventually, Varoujan stopped at a point where he could see the valley below. "There they are," he shouted to his men, while scanning the landscape with his binoculars.

"Yes, I can see them down there against the snow," one of the men shouted.

"There's about fifteen of them," Varoujan announced, "they're fully armed, but, not in fighting condition." He looked back toward his men. "We will be outnumbered, there's fifteen of them" he confirmed.

"No problem," said Rouben with bravado.

"We can take them," one of the other men added, "that's why we're here, isn't it?"

Varoujan looked at each of his men and smiled affectionately. "You're absolutely right . . . that is why we're here. Let's move out and get them."

They moved slowly down into the valley and spread out in battle formation. They closed in on the enemy slowly, positioning themselves so the enemy did not have an advantage.

As soon as the KDF soldiers were spotted, the Azeris open fired with their rifles, not realizing Varoujan and his men were still out of range of their guns. Lacking a leader, panic set in quickly among the Azeri soldiers, and they emptied their magazines of ammunition without effect. Bullets, missing their mark, proved useless. With great deliberation, the men of the KDF crawled low on their bellies, making poor targets for the enemy fire. Exasperated, the Azeris finally stood up to get a better shot, making themselves vulnerable targets for Varoujan and his men.

Varoujan looked about at his men, checked their position, scanned the enemy again then gave the signal to fire the high powered assault rifles. The air was peppered with gunfire, forcing the Azeris to keep their heads down. Unfortunately for the Azeris, they had not dug in to wait for an attack, and had not anticipated the KDF would follow the survivors, once they had secured the mountain pass. Now, without a leader or plan, the Azeris fired haphazardly.

"Cover me," Varoujan shouted, as he crawled forward, while his men peppered the perimeter, forcing the Azeris to run for cover. Slowly, Varoujan moved in closer to the enemy, digging deeply into the snow for support, then with a quick overhand motion, he lobbed a hand grenade into the enemy camp, blowing up whatever cover they had and killing many of them. The rest fled in panic, but were cut down by short bursts of KDF assault rifles.

The fire-fight was over in a matter of minutes. Varoujan signaled his men to hold their fire, then listening intently, he raised his head to observe any activity in the enemy camp. To all appearances, everything was calm. Varoujan stood up and carefully scanned the area, then crouching low, and with rifle in hand he slowly advanced toward the position; He signaled his men to hold back, indicating his intention to see if anyone was left alive in the camp. Everything was deadly calm. Varoujan looked about again, then signaled his men to advance. His keen eye however, did not catch the slight movement from an Azeri soldier lying prone in the deep snow; the soldier fingered his rifle and moved it into position—waited, then fired.

The short burst of gun fire struck Varoujan squarely in the chest. It whirled him around and cut him open. He tried to reach for his rifle, but was unable, and it fell helplessly out of his grip into the snow. Varoujan stood for a moment before falling down to one knee, then dropped, face down in the snow.

Rouben was the first to reach him. He spotted the Azeri soldier who raised his rifle again, but, Rouben was too quick for him and he emptied the remaining rounds of ammunition in the magazine of his rifle on him and all of the fallen soldiers, to make certain no one was still alive. He rushed to Varoujan's side. "Damn, damn . . . why did he have to check the perimeter himself? Why couldn't he have waited for us? He dropped his rifle in the snow and bent down to turn his commander over. Varoujan moaned slightly. Rouben placed him on his back and held him in his arms, as he waited for the other men to come along. His eyes filled with tears, when he saw the extent of Varoujan's wound. "Why couldn't it have been me?" he sobbed, desolately. "Why couldn't it have been me?"

Varoujan moved his mouth slightly. Rouben attempting to hear what his commander was saying, placed his ear close to Varoujan's mouth. Varoujan's breathing was difficult, but Rouben heard the words Varoujan willed to speak, "Karamine . . . " He pulled Rouben's arm in an attempt to get up. "The children . . . "Karamine . . . tell her . . . I love her. . . . " He fell back with a deep groan and gasp of death, releasing his clutch on Rouben's arm. Rouben held him tenderly, like a child, allowing his own tears to flow freely. The other men joined him, grouping in mutual grief around their leader. This was a man among men, a man they would mourn and venerate for generations.

"Get some long heavy branches," Rouben ordered. "We'll get the coats off those two Azeris, and run the poles through the sleeves to make a stretcher for our commander's body. Make sure the sleeves are on the inside and the coat zippered up. We'll bring his body back with us. He should have a proper burial in Yerevan, alongside his wife. We'll have to move fast. We want to get back to our position before dark."

The men worked swiftly to construct a makeshift stretcher. They placed Varoujan's body on it, then slowly, they made their way back to the position they had taken from the Azeris earlier that day. The trail was well marked by their own foot tracks, as well as those made by retreating Azeris. The men took turns carrying the body back, feeling honored to do so. Each man carried not only Varoujan's body, but a special memory of their leader.

Onig was first to greet the small entourage. His heart sank when he saw Varoujan, and he was ripped through by pangs of remorse. "You wouldn't listen to me, old friend, you refused to let me go, and damn it, you got yourself killed! he said out loud, placing a hand on Varoujan's shoulder. "Who is to lead us now?"

"You will be leader now, Onig," Rouben declared, "and if you're half the man he was, there will be no problem. We will follow you to hell and back."

"Onig wiped his eyes with the back of his hand. "You're right, Rouben. And . . . if I am to be commander, then you are second in command under me, understood?"

"If that is what you want, so be it," Rouben responded spiritedly.

"What do you think we should do with his body, Rouben?" Onig asked. "Bury him here in the mountains like the rest of our fallen comrades?"

"No, we should take him back to Yerevan and bury him alongside his wife if that is possible. That's what he would have wanted, and I'm sure that's what his children would want.

"Good. We'll do that as one last gesture to our beloved commander," Onig agreed. "Let me get headquarters on the radio and see whether they could send a helicopter to pick him up. Why don't you go with the chopper, Rouben. It might be better if one of us is there with the children when he's brought back. You were with him at the end, and they might appreciate knowing the details of how their father died, fighting for our cause. It would do you some good as well to get away from here for a few days."

"I was going to make that request myself, Onig." Rouben replied. "It would be an honor for me to escort the body back." He looked down at Varoujan's body on the stretcher. "He did give me a message, before he died, that I'd like to deliver in person.

Onig looked around at the terrain. "We'll have to find a fairly flat spot for that chopper to land for the pick up. It's rough trying to land a helicopter in these mountains. I'll instruct the men to clear away more of the brush over there." He pointed to a flattened area, then walked over to the men to give them instructions.

In the meantime, Rouben slipped out of his combat clothes and took off his white field battle dress. He packed some bare necessities, knowing the restrictions of weight in the choppers, and then joined Onig to watch for its arrival. When the helicopter arrived, it circled the small pad the men had cleared, then gingerly, let down and settled on the ground, with rotors idling. A medic stepped off and quickly approached Onig and Rouben.

"Where are your wounded?" he shouted over the noise of the engine and idle rotation of the rotor blades.

"It's the body of our commander, which will be escorted to Yerevan by Rouben, my second in command here." Onig shouted back.

"You mean to say you had us come here for only one dead body? Bury him in the field with the rest of our fallen men," the medic said irritably.

Onig took a threatening step toward him. "Listen, you. . . . " Rouben however stepped in between them, and faced the medic, nose to nose. "Headquarters have been informed of our request and this operation was cleared; so, just keep your comments to yourself and do your job. Let's get this body back and get out of here."

Rouben's manner and tone of voice left no room for argument, and the medic stepped back. Silently, he assisted the men in boarding Varoujan's body, and within fifteen minutes, the helicopter was ready to take off.

"Tell his children how loved and respected their father was. Tell them how much we'll miss him, and tell them we love them," Onig said, as Rouben prepared to board.

"I'll be back as soon as possible," Rouben promised, while shaking Onig's hand and climbing aboard.

Sitting by the window, Rouben watched Onig and the men on the ground grow smaller until they were no longer in sight. He got up from his seat then, and walked into the cabin where he saw other wounded men who were being evacuated.

"We'll stop at the staging area first, and pick up more wounded, then head for Armenia," the medic informed Rouben, later, when he sat down next to him. "While we're there we can put the commander into a proper coffin before taking him to Yerevan."

Rouben nodded, but remained silent, turning to look out the window as they passed over the grey and coiling mountain ranges below. Varoujan's last words came to him, and he reflected on them now, realizing for the first time the true import of the words . . . "Karamine . . . the children . . . I love her." He must have fallen in love with Dr. Karamine, he thought to himself, of course . . . it's natural, how can I blame him? She is a wonderful woman, and a real inspiration for any man. I wonder how she felt about him? I know she has a husband she loves, according to her late brother, Vasken. It will be more difficult to tell her about the commander than I thought, much less the children. What can I possibly say to console them? He leaned back in his seat and closed his eyes. Overcome by weariness he drifted into a brief sleep.

The helicopter arrived at the staging area, circled and slowly let down to the landing. The medic jumped out and alerted Rouben to help him with Varoujan's body. They slipped him out of the cabin door and took it to a spot where many rough wooden coffins were stacked. There were large crosses burned into the covering lid, and the medic informed Rouben, the coffins were made especially for the fallen soldiers of the KDF. Carefully, and with the help of several men, they placed Varoujan's body in one of them. Rouben watched as they placed on the lid and fastened it. Then slowly, he helped lift it back to the helicopter, set it in the cabin, and securely strap it in. Rouben continued to help loading the wounded aboard the helicopter, until they finally waved goodbye to the men on the ground and the chopper took off, heading for Yerevan.

During the trip, Rouben talked to all of the wounded men, giving them words of hope and encouragement. When they arrived in Yerevan, he went immediately to the dispatch office to explain what had to be done with Varoujan's body. He gave them the name of the cemetery where Varoujan's wife was buried and details of where the body was to be interred. The dispatch office assured Rouben they would take care of it; they asked him to have the family attend the burial at that time, as they had many other burials as well.

When the details were attended to, Rouben looked around for a ride to the hospital where Karamine worked. He called out to one of the ambulance drivers. "Are some of the wounded going to Yerevan Hospital? I need a ride."

Noticing Rouben's uniform, the driver pointed to a vehicle. "Get in, it will be my second stop," he answered.

Rouben got into the ambulance and again felt lost as to how he'd approach Karamine and the children on the subject of Varoujan's death. Usually glib with words, this was the first time he felt unsure of himself, apprehensive and awkward. This was also the first time he was ever involved in the stark reality of human emotion, or became a painful bearer of the message of death. Yes, this was going to be 'a problem', he thought, soberly.

When they arrived at Yerevan Hospital, the driver swung the ambulance around and backed up to the emergency entrance. He honked the horn loudly, and a couple of aids came running out. He opened the rear door, and the driver and aids began unloading the wounded, then processing them as to their immediate needs. Rouben went directly into the hospital and walked over to a nurse at the front desk. She glanced up quickly from the list of incoming casualties she was checking.

"Doctor Karamine Bagdasarian, where can I find her please?" Rouben inquired.

The nurse shook her head. "She's very busy now, as you can see," she gestured toward the new arrivals, "can I be of help to you, soldier?"

Rouben hesitated. "No, I have to see her personally. I have some bad news for her, and an urgent message only I can deliver."

The nurse studied him for a moment, and seemed to understood the gravity of the situation. "Look, let me call an aid to take you to her office." She picked up a telephone and left a message. "Please have Dr. Bagdasarian go to her office as soon as possible. There's a soldier there who says he has an urgent message for her. Thanks." She turned to Rouben. "As soon as she's through with her patient, she'll meet you in her office." She motioned to one of the aids passing by, "Take this soldier to Dr. Bagdasarian's office," she ordered.

"Thank you," said Rouben, awkwardly.

Following behind the aid, Rouben was hit with the full impact of the war. Wounded were everywhere, even the hallways overflowed with cots and beds. When they reached Karamine's office, the aid motioned to a chair and Rouben sat down to wait. He tried to gather his thoughts, but he was restless. He got up and walked around the office. He passed Karamine's desk which was piled high with medical data and reports of patients. He noticed a large photograph in a silver frame on her desk, and he picked it up. This must be her husband, he thought to himself. Certainly doesn't look Armenian. Then he saw a coffee pot. Walking toward it he touched the pot and saw it was hot; he found a cup, rinsed it out in the bathroom sink, then filled it. The coffee tasted wonderful. Since fighting in the mountains, he hadn't had anything like it for months. He sipped it slowly relishing every mouthful.

"Rouben . . . it's been quite a while," Karamine said, entering her office briskly. I thought you were in Karabakh. So . . . you're the soldier who wants to see me. I'm glad you helped yourself to the coffee. It's American coffee sent to me from the States.

Rouben smiled. "I didn't think you'd mind. I had to have it. It's good coffee. We don't have anything like this at the front, much less hot. I kind of made myself at home here," he said sheepishly, holding up the cup.

Karamine laughed. "I'm glad you did, Rouben. That's what it's there for. Everyone comes in here for American coffee. Now, sit down and tell me . . . what brings you here?" She sat down behind her desk and looked at him with an air of expectation.

Rouben leaned forward and put the coffee cup on her desk. "I really don't know how to tell you this, Dr. Karamine," he began.

"Well start at the beginning," Karamine encouraged. "When you joined up you were with Varoujan, as I had suggested, right?

"Yes." Rouben remained silent for a few moments as he tried to organize his thoughts.

Suddenly a cold fear gripped Karamine. "Something happen to him, Rouben?" she said apprehensively.

"Yes. He was killed on our last patrol hunting retreating Azeris," Rouben blurted.

"Oh God! No!" Karamine got out of her chair and faced the window. She gripped the sill so hard, her knuckles pressed heavily white through the delicate flesh. Anguish, rage and disbelief tore her heart wide open and her senses spun chaotically in a sea of profound desolation and loss. "Not Varoujan," she whispered inaudibly, "no God, not Varoujan." Every fiber of her being screamed denial. Rouben watched her helplessly, not knowing what to say. "I was with him at the end," he began hesitantly, "He...he gave me a message for you Doctor...."

"A message?" said Karamine, turning around to face him.

"Yes . . . he said, Karamine . . . the children . . . I love her."

Karamine covered her face with her hands, and uttered a strangled cry. "Oh Varoujan . . . Varoujan!" She reached into her pocket for a tissue, and wiped her eyes. "Forgive me, Rouben . . . this is difficult . . . oh my God! the children! How will I be able to tell them their father is gone? First their mother, and now, their father." She sighed deeply.

"We all loved the Commander, Doctor, any one of us would have died in his place," said Rouben proudly.

"Karamine reached out and touched Rouben's arm. "Yes, I know that, we all loved him, and his sacrifice must not be in vain. You said you were with him, Rouben? What happened?"

"Are you sure you want to know the details?" Rouben asked.

"Yes. the children will want to know, and difficult as it is, it's better we know everything." When she looked at his face, and realized how much pain he had endured, and was suffering still, Karamine smiled at Rouben gently. "It's all right, Rouben, I'm fine now," Karamine assured him, "It's been difficult for you as well. You've been a kind friend to all of us, coming here to bring us the terrible news. It can't have been easy for you."

Rouben shook his head, and bit his lip. "I really mean it when I say, I wish it had been me, Doctor. He was a great leader. Anyone would follow him to hell and back."

Once again, Karamine smiled gently at Rouben. "Tell me what happened. Did they bury him in the mountains where he fell?"

"No, that's another reason why I'm here," Rouben said. "We decided he should be brought back here to Yerevan to be buried with his wife. We thought that's what he would have wanted."

"You were right, that's exactly what he would have wished. Where is he now, in Yerevan?"

"Yes, at the airfield. He will be taken from there to the cemetery about two p.m. tomorrow. I gave them his wife's name, and they are taking care of all the arrangements." He stopped and looked anxiously at Karamine. "How will I be able to tell his children?" he asked.

"You won't have to tell them, Rouben. I'll tell them." She glanced down at her watch. "As soon as I make some rounds, and leave some instructions for the new wounded patients being brought in, I'll leave."

Rouben felt a weight lifted from him. "Thank you so much Doctor Karamine, I worried about how I'd tell the children."

"You needn't thank me, Rouben. I'm the logical one to tell them. I know them better, and they are staying with me. It will be easier coming from me. Now . . . tell me what happened at the end." She bit her lip and tried to fight back her tears.

Rouben related the incident of the retreating Azeris in detail, while Karamine listened stoically. The scene played out before her left her drained and numb, devoid of all emotion. She had accepted death as inevitable. She saw it every day at the hospital and had dealt with it—pain, suffering and death. But now, she reflected grimly, the ever burning question of why the senseless waste of vibrant life that took its toll on innocent children, and left them orphaned and without hope. She sighed again, and looked at Rouben. "Are you staying over, Rouben, or are you heading back to Karabakh?" she asked.

"No, I'm staying for the burial tomorrow, and will head back as soon as I can get a flight. they need every fighter back there.

"Where will you stay?"

"I have family here I haven't seen for awhile. I'll stay with them and let them know I'm still in one piece."

Karamine walked around her desk and embraced Rouben. "I'll see you at the cemetery tomorrow then, Rouben. Thank you, dear friend for all your kindness to us, for all you've done for Varoujan. I'll make sure the children know. Good luck, *Fadayee* (Mountain fighter.)"

When Rouben left her office, Karamine called Andreas and gave her the bad news. "I must go to the children, Andreas and give them the news today. They are burying Varoujan tomorrow."

"They brought his body back to Yerevan?" Andreas asked.

"Yes, he's to be placed next to his wife. The men felt that's what he would have wanted. Look Andreas . . . I'm leaving the hospital now. I'll pick up the children on the way home. I'll have to tell them what's happened and prepare them for tomorrow. Will you report to the other doctors and ask them to take my rounds. I'll be at the apartment if anything comes up, OK?"

"Oh Karamine . . . how will you ever be able to tell them?"

Karamine shook her head. "Andreas, I don't know. the good Lord will have to give me the words. I just don't know."

Karamine drove quickly to Andreas' apartment. She informed the girl taking care of the children that she was taking them home early. Sabu and Arax, glad to be out of their school work for the day, were in their usual high spirits, asking questions, and wondering why Karamine was picking them up earlier than usual. When they arrived home, Karamine took off her jacket, then the children's and hung them in a closet. Where to begin she thought anxiously, watching their faces, registering their innocent expressions.

"Come, you two, sit here on the floor in front of me," she began. I have something to tell you, and I need your complete attention.

The children obeyed without question. Karamine took a deep breath, paused, then took each of their hands in hers. "Do you remember when you first arrived here to live with me? Your mother had been wounded badly and we were not able to save her?"

"Yes, how could I forget that, Sabu said somberly. I remember the cemetery, and the priest saying words over her before they lowered her into the ground."

"I remember too," Arax added. "We never saw her again."

"Do you remember there at the cemetery they were burying other soldiers who had been killed fighting in Karabagh?"

"Yes, they were *Fadayees*, brave men fighting to free Karabakh from the butchering Turks," said Sabu, peering at Karamine suspiciously.

"Yes, they were brave men indeed," Karamine continued, "Heros really, so you understand that your father is also a great and noble leader who fought for the people of Karabakh . . . and you've always known he risked his life doing so. . . . "

"Hyrig has been killed!" Sabu interrupted loudly in a wrenching voice. "He's been killed, and that's what you're trying to tell us, isn't it."

Karamine gasped, and stared at the young boy before her. The passions and tragedies of life reflected in his black eyes belied his youth and inexperience. Now, his voice was filled with bitterness and rebellion.

Karamine's eyes filled with tears, and she nodded affirmatively, "Yes . . . yes, my *anushigus*," she said in a low voice, "thus, has it ever been . . . death is the fate of heros, and we who are left must pick up the torch and carry on."

"I knew it", Sabu cried defiantly. "I just knew it when you came home early and brought us home. Arax began to cry. Then she ran to Karamine and threw her arms around her. "What will happen to us now?" she sobbed. "We have no one to look after us any more."

"Stop crying Arax," Sabu ordered firmly. "You have me to care for you. I'll always take care of you."

Watching him, Karamine saw the struggle and agony in his eyes. A boy trying to be a man, she thought sadly. But now, no longer able to control the flood of emotions, Sabu began to weep.

"Come here, Sabu," said Karamine holding her arms out to him. She held both of them close to her, and all three remained for some time, comforting and reassuring each other.

"Sabu and I are orphans now. What will happen to us?" Arax asked, tearfully.

"You will stay with me, until we can find out if you have relatives," Karamine reassured her.

"I don't remember any relatives," Sabu answered tearfully.

"Well, we're not going to worry about that now. You're here with me, and here you'll stay." She held them both tightly.

"Did they bury Hyrig in the mountains, like the other *Fadayees*?" Sabu questioned.

"No, they brought him back to Yerevan, and he will be buried next to your mother . . . they'll do that tomorrow. If you want to see him before the interment, it's possible. We could all go together."

"Yes, we would like to see him," Sabu replied, wiping his eyes.

Karamine smiled gently. "Good. Then it's settled. Now listen, children, I don't want you to have another moment's concern about what's going to happen to you. I made a promise to your mother before she passed that I would take care of you, and I intend to keep that promise. I want you both to work hard at your schoolwork and do everything they would want you to. Both your mother and father are in a beautiful place of peace and light. They'll always be with you, watching over you. And remember . . . you'll have me . . . always".

34

The Karabakh Defence Force finally succeeded in pushing out the Azeris, from Kelbajar in the north, to the Lachin Pass in the south, thus accomplishing their goal of connecting the western front of Karabakh to Armenia. With heavy losses in men and equipment, the Azeris now realized a military win was impossible, and their only alternative for the return of territories lost in combat, including Karabakh, was through negotiations.

Talks were being held in Helsinki, regarding the resolution of conflict, by the Organization for Security and Cooperation (OSCE). The Organization was chaired by Russia and Finland, who attempted, desperately, to bring both sides of the conflict between the Azeris and Armenians of Karabakh to agreement. The Azeris, with the help of their Turkish allies, insisted on full return of all territories, including Karabakh. Naturally, these demands were unacceptable to the Armenians and the independent State of Karabakh, now renamed **Artsakh** which was its original Armenian name prior to the Stalin giveaway to Azerbaijan in 1923.

A fragile cease fire halted the fighting momentarily. The Azeris however, with the help of the Turks and Russians, were now endeavoring to force their terms through the OSCE. But, the independent State of Karabakh, or Artsakh, flatly refused to consider the terms, demanding that their independent state be recognized by all. 'Let the Azeri come to the table alone to negotiate with us, without the help of the Turks who have been our relentless enemy for centuries,' the KDF demanded, 'let the combatants come to a lasting agreement.' The Azeris and Turks however, viewed this suggestion with great disfavor, preferring Armenia to negotiate without representatives from the newly formed republic. The same representatives were blatantly refused a place at the negotiating table, infuriating the independent State of Artsakh who then declared they would push the war, if necessary, to the capital of Baku itself.

At the same time these talks and negotiations were taking place, the bureaucracy and executive branch of the government in Armenia were looking toward the coming elections, and the formulating of a new constitution. Because of their fear of the opposition, the ARF (Armenian Revolutionary Federation) in particular, the current power structure there, through control of the media, launched a campaign of false charges against the ARF, accusing them of murder and terrorism. The government had no evidence to back up their accusations however, so the people did not buy into the propaganda. The ARF had been popular for decades with Armenians as the mainstay of the Armenian cause, so the people voiced their protest, much to the frustration of the government in charge.

Foreign journalists in Armenia reported to their newspapers that the National Security Agency of the executive branch of the government were running roughshod over the people's rights. They described beatings, arrests and unsubstantiated charges against all opposition party members, and, people were denied the basic freedom of assembly. When various organizations attempted a demonstration in Republic Square they were immediately dispersed, or shot by the National Security Police. In the government's push to silence opposition parties before the elections, all radio, television and newspapers were taken over or shut down. Assassinations were the order of the day. ARF members, Hunchogs and other opposition party members were systematically thrown into jail without recourse or due process; defense lawyers were routinely denied their requests to see clients or evidence of charges filed against them. The whole country was in such turmoil, the people doubted they would ever hold free elections.

Karamine was relieved the fighting and killing had ceased, even momentarily, although the sporadic attacks by the Azeri on the territory of Armenia went unreported in the foreign press. She was aware of all the events taking place in Armenia, but the prospect of a people's revolt with an ensuing civil war was an unthinkable alternative to her. She had already suffered too many losses from war—Vasken, Varoujan, and now, the two children she cared about who were left alone and orphaned. Varoujan's children were on her mind constantly. Since the day of their father's burial when both children demonstrated unwavering and steadfast courage, unusual for their age, she sensed a hollowness and deep anxiety in them. They clung to her tenaciously, as though by holding fast it would enable them to block out a hostile world that terrorized and crushed them. More than ever now, Karamine felt a surging need to shelter and protect these children from the altered circumstances of their lives.

She pressed her hands hard against her eyes, in an effort to shut out the emotional turmoil of the past few months. It seemed to close in around her ever more deeply, obscuring the well-defined plan and structures of her life. Varoujan had touched her life briefly, as a thread of light runs through a colorless pattern; his love was a gift she would treasure, and the memory of him was fixed in her heart forever. The thought no longer tormented her; she was released at last from the flood of contradictory and conflicting thoughts that had troubled and filled her soul with pain the past few months. Over and over, with growing awareness and a sinking sense of guilt, she had asked herself the question—how is it possible to love two men, and to love them both with honor, significance and passion? Is this the argument of a cheating and deceitful heart? I love Lance, more than life, and I respect him. My love for him is not diminished by my love and admiration for Varoujan. But, I have to face the question—if Varoujan had lived, would I have made the choice to stay? Everything I've ever longed for is here—children, my work, the land. Love has many faces, she had argued, and ah yes, now at last, I understand how this can be. Varoujan is not like anyone I've ever known before, he's the hero of my youth, the patriot of our cause, the *fadayee* of my dreams. He charged into my life as the ideal I had cherished, and when he spoke, his words were blood and fire in my heart. To have been loved by such a man honors me, and adds dimension to my life. But now, I see it all as the phantom dream it is, beautiful, illusive and enshrined on the altar of a young girl's heart. Reality is not the dream; one day I'd awaken here, and cry for everything I'd given up at home. She smiled wistfully. I'm glad I've gone beyond regrets and guilt, she thought. Now, there's just this oddly strange, consoling sense of peace—and sadness.

She poured disinfectant soap through her hands, then rinsed it off in a small sink outside the operating room where she scrubbed up for the next patient. She was relieved there were no new casualties arriving daily from the fighting in Karabakh, and she prayed the cease fire would hold and a resolution found for the future of Karabakh. The glare of harsh hospital lights in the room heightened the weariness in her face and emphasized the deep circles around her eyes. She had little sleep since Varoujan's burial, and her concern for the future of Arax and Sabu troubled her deeply.

Shaking water from her hands, and holding them high in the air, she pushed through the double doors to the operating room where Andreas held out her rubber gloves. Slipping them on, she checked the fit, feel and condition of the gloves. Nodding to Andreas, she moved to the operation table, and studied the leg of the young soldier lying there, to determine the right procedure. Andreas tied on her surgical mask, then Karamine began the tedious operation. She had barely started when suddenly, there was a loud rumble outside the room. Glancing through the door window she was surprised to see two heavy-set men attempting to enter the operating room. Strange, she thought to herself. Their conversation was muffled, and a few moments later they disappeared. Karamine dismissed the incident, and went ahead with the operation.

The staff outside the operating room however, were in a state of shock. Two men had entered the hospital some moments earlier, demanding to see Doctor Karamine Bagdasarian. When told she was operating and could not be disturbed, they tried to force their way through, imperiously informing the staff they were the National Security Police. The hospital staff was shocked and intimidated when the two men accused Karamine of subversive activities against the government of Armenia. They adamantly denied she could be capable of such a charge, and were able to restrain the men from interrupting her in the process of operating. "The operation is a short one, why not wait in her office", one of the doctors suggested, leading the way to Karamine's office.

As soon as the doctor left Karamine's office, both men ransacked through the papers on her desk. They opened her desk drawers, and searched through folders. Suddenly, with an unpleasant smile, one of the men held up a sheet of paper with the letterhead, SENATE OF THE UNITED STATES. These were Karamine's personal letters from Lance, which she had kept to read again and again, whenever she was lonely. The letters were filled with concern for her safety, because of all the political upheaval taking place in Armenia. "I've tried repeatedly to get through to you by telephone," Lance had written, "but it's impossible, so I'm sending you this message, hand carried by courier through the American Embassy. Karamine, I beg you, leave the country before it's too late. All hell's going to break loose over there, and the country will be ripped apart by civil war. If that happens, you won't be able to get out, you'll be stranded." His letter went on to describe some of the information they were receiving at the State Department and the CIA. "Here in the senate, we feel the coming elections in Armenia will be rigged in favor of the present government. The situation there has reached the point where fair elections are simply impossible. I'm worried about you, my love. Please . . . get out now while you can, and come home. I love you and worry about you constantly."

The agent's eyes glittered malevolently. "Here it is, hard evidence the doctor is a plant of the American Central Intelligence Agency", he said, holding up the letter.

"Good." said the other one, taking it from him and placing it in his pocket. "Keep looking, we may find something else."

When Karamine entered her office and found two men rifling through her personal papers, she was furious. "By what right do you go through my desk and papers without my permission?" she said hotly.

One of the agents flashed his identification in her face. "By the authority of the Armenian government", he replied, in a venomous tone. "We are members of the National Security Agency", said the other one gruffly, watching her with fox-like eyes.

"I don't care who you are," Karamine replied indignantly, "how DARE you go through my personal papers and documents. Where are your search warrants?"

"Both men looked at her and laughed scornfully. "Search warrant? My dear Doctor, we are the search warrant, we are the Armenian government. We need no further authorization."

"You have a constitution, even though it's a communist one. It still clearly outlaws any activity such as this, and you know it," Karamine stated defiantly.

Both men continued to sneer. My dear Doctor, you don't seem to understand, we are the constitution and the power now, and you, Doctor, are a subversive". He flashed Lance's letter in her face. "We have all the evidence we need, here in this letter I am holding, with it's letterhead THE SENATE OF THE UNITED STATES. In it you are given information from the American State Department of what's been happening here in Armenia with the uprisings of the ungrateful people. You were requested to leave for fear of civil war. It's all quite clear. You Doctor, are a member of the American CIA. I charge you as a subversive agent of the United States, and I hereby place you under arrest".

Karamine was speechless with shock and alarm as both men advanced toward her, gripped her firmly by the arms, then led her away. In the hallway, the staff had gathered in confusion and concern regarding the events taking place. In passing, Karamine caught a glimpse of Andreas' strained face. She called out to her in a desperate voice.

"Andreas, quick . . . get in touch with the American Embassy, and Dro, . . . he's a member of the parliament now. Tell him they're arresting me as a subversive CIA member."

The two men hurried her out and pushed her into a waiting car before she could say any more. The black car took off quickly, speeding toward NSA Headquarters, and Karamine sank into the darkest despair she had ever known.

Andreas called the American Embassy immediately. The Embassy was reassuring, positively affirming that, "as the wife of a United States senator, Karamine had nothing to worry about. We will act immediately, and see that Dr. Bagdasarian is released at once," they informed her. She also called Karamine's friend, Dro Aspedyan, who had been the former Commutarian of Yerevan during the earthquake. When Armenia had been a free independent Republic, he had run for parliament, and had won, against the entrenched bureaucracy there. He admired and respected Karamine, applauding her work, and supporting her in every way, especially in obtaining medical supplies. His help was deeply appreciated by all the hospital staff as well as Karamine, who had come to regard him as a good friend.

When Andreas informed Dro of Karamine's arrest, and of the charges brought against her, he was outraged. He promised to drop everything and have her released immediately. "I'll go down to headquarters and tear the place apart if I have to," he vowed hotly.

When he hung up, Dro Aspedyan dialed the telephone again with deliberate intent. A deep line creased his forehead as he drew the grizzled thickness of his brow together. Leathery of face, and a strong, stubborn mouth, Dro was a man of firm convictions. As former Commutarian of Yerevan, he had maintained astute control of the city's legislature, warily keeping an eagle eye on the balance of power, the subtle shifts in public opinion, and the constant threat of subversive ideologies. Now as a member of parliament, Dro's main thrust was to build a republic form of democracy, despite opposition from autocrats attempting to seize the reins of government.

"Hello . . . Ms. Tamanian? It's Dro Aspedyan calling from Yerevan. I must speak to the President. It's urgent. Can you put me through?" he said in an authoritative tone.

"One moment, Mr. Aspedian, I'll see if he's free."

"How are you Dro? A pleasant surprise to hear from you my friend. What is this urgency?" the President of Armenia said in a conciliatory tone.

"Good afternoon, Mr. President. Thanks for taking my call. I'll come straight to the point. Have you been informed that the NSA has arrested Doctor Karamine Bagdasarian as an American CIA agent? This is the most shocking and offensive piece of foul play I've ever seen in all my days in government."

"What! No I have not been informed of this doing. I am outraged. Who ordered this atrocious action?" the President demanded in an agitated voice.

"I don't know, I just got word from someone at the hospital who said they took her by force. Of all people, Dr. Bagdasarian, who's given so much to the Armenian people."

"I want to know who organized this charade." the President insisted angrily, "they must be mad. I just had a long conversation with her the last time I visited the hospital. One thing I know for certain . . . she's no subversive. As an American, she's given more to the people of Armenia than could ever be expected. Bah! what imbeciles!"

"I believe this whole organization is out of control, Mr. President. This is not an isolated case. It's happening over and over, and it should be investigated. But right now, my concern is, what are you going to do about this situation, Mr. President?"

"Do . . . do?" he questioned angrily. "I'll have their miserable hides, that is what I am going to do! In the meantime, you get down there right away and have her released. If there's any problem, have them call this office. Make sure you give Doctor Bagdasarian my heart-felt apology. Tell her that agency will be severely reprimanded for the stupidity of their arrogance. Fools! There could be repercussions in Washington that might hurt our sensitive relations with America. Get her out Dro!"

Dro hung up and left his office. He summoned a car and ordered the driver to take him down to National Agency Headquarters.

Karamine and the two agents had just pulled in to the NSH head-quarters. The men hustled her roughly through the corridors of the building to an interrogation room. The room was small and window-less, heavy with the scent of stale tobacco, dust and grime. The only fur-niture was a battered desk, and a few hard metal chairs.

"Sit down, there," one of the men ordered, pushing her roughly to-ward a straight-backed chair. The agent settled himself behind the desk, and the other one turned on a bright glaring light, and flashed it in her face. This is a nightmare scene from an old vintage movie, she told her-self. It would be amusing if it wasn't so serious. The whole thing is pre-posterous. She covered her eyes from the hot, white light, and a numbing kind of calmness washed over her. Lord, protect and deliver me from this evil, she whispered to herself.

"Now, Doctor," the agent began, with an indiferent half –smile, "let us review the evidence."

"Evidence?" Karamine repeated stoically. "what kind of evidence can you possibly have against me? Your charges are ridiculous. I've been working at the hospital in Leninaken and Yerevan for most of my stay here. Anyone at the hospital can verify that. I've had little time for anything else, not even for my own interests."

The agent's face became menacing. "Look Doctor Bagdasarian, the charges against you ARE the evidence. That's all we really need. How-ever, we also know all about your brother's trip to meet with Colonel Sergei Ivanovich, who secured arms for the Karabakh Defence Force for a price, when the trouble began in Karabakh. Unfortunately, the Colonel escaped, but we managed to catch one of his subordinates, and he gave us quite a bit of information about your brother. Your brother was up to his ears in undercover work for the outlawed Armenian Revolutionary Federation. Do you deny this?"

Karamine maintained her frozen calm, but her face was ashen. "I have no information whatsoever about my brother's activities here, I've never even heard of Colonel Ivanovich until now. Undercover agent, my brother? Ridiculous! My brother was a patriot who fought and died in the mountains of Karabakh for the cause."

The agent's eyes darted suspiciously. "What about this letter I hold in my hand, and the letterhead **The Senate of the United States**. This letter is all the evidence we need. The writer here refers to the internal problems of Armenia, then goes on to quote the State Department and the CIA. Please, Doctor Bagdasarian, for your own sake, admit to the charges, and make things easier for yourself. We have no wish to hold you like this, but we do have ways to make you talk, if necessary."

"Don't threaten me," Karamine replied defiantly, "I'm a United States citizen, and for your information, both of you to whom I've not been introduced, that letter is from my husband who is a United States Senator from Massachussetts. As a Senator he uses the official letterhead from his office. With all the turmoil and unrest in this country, he is concerned for my safety, and wrote me to return, before something like this happens," she pointed about the room.

"He mentions the State Department and the CIA."

"Karamine shrugged her shoulders. "Naturally he mentions it. So what? He's in the business of government. He consults with the State Department for advice, and sees people regularly from the CIA."

They were interrupted by the sound of loud voices in the outer office, then the door to the interrogation room suddenly burst open with such force, it slammed against the back wall.

"By what right do you arrest Doctor Bagdasarian, an American citizen? Dro Aspedyan blasted, while storming into the room. "What are these charges of subversion against her, and where is your evidence?"

One of the agents came forward with Karamine's letter, and thrust it into Dro's hand. "Here is the evidence. It bears the United States Senate letterhead. In it the State Department and CIA make references to unrest and upheaval here in this country."

Dro read the letter impatiently, then shook his head. "Fools, you stupid fools. You call this evidence? A letter from a husband concerned with his wife's safety." Dro's stocky frame bustled with authority, and his black eyes glittered with rage. "How did you come by this?"

"It was in her desk."

"By what authority did you go though her personal desk? Did you have permission to do so and did you have a warrant?

"No . . . we didn't"

"You stupid imbeciles! Fools! Can't you people understand the days of the soviet union and of holding and torturing people are OVER. You two relics from an obsolete Politburo had better change your ways, or you'll find yourselves in jail, for a long, long time. And remember this. As long as I'm in parliament, there will be no more of these episodes taking place ever again. Do you understand?"

The Director of the National Security Agency entered the room, interrupting their response. "I just received an urgent call from the President," he began, casting a furtive glance toward Dro. "He's quite upset about the arrest of Doctor Bagdasarian, here. He demands you release her at once." He turned to Karamine who sat watching the proceedings silently. "I want to apologize to you, Doctor, for any abuse or inconvenience my men may have caused you. I hope you can find it within yourself to forgive our transgression." He bowed stiffly.

"Good," Dro answered triumphantly, taking Karamine gently by the arm. "Come on, Karamine, let's get out of this miserable place.

Before leaving, Dro Aspedyan turned and looked back at the two agents, then to the head of the NSP. "You have not heard the last of this," he said. I intend to have a committee look into this mess and see whether or not you have broken any laws. I also intend to investigate any other arrests your people here have made, check the methods and the evidence. Let me state further that these remnants of the old soviet bureaucratic thinking are going to change, if I have anything to do with it. The Armenian people deserve better." He left the headquarters with Karamine, and together they got into his waiting car.

"What were you two thinking of, arresting the wife of an American senator," the head of Security Police questioned in a sharp voice, after Karamine and Dro left. I was just on the telephone with the President of Armenia. He was outraged you would perpetrate such a blunder to an American of all people. He doesn't want the Americans affronted, or to suspect our plans for taking over the country. Pick on Ramgavars, Hunchogs, Tashnogs or any other opposition parties. Break them, destroy them, but keep away from persons like Dr. Bagdasarian. She has too many friends here and in the United States. Let's not antagonize or arouse the Americans yet. As for Dro", he rubbed his chin thoughtfully, "the man has become a thorn in our side". He'll have his day, and soon".

Outside in Dro's car, Karamine closed her eyes and leaned back against the cool comfort of the upholstery. She took a deep breath. It felt liberating after the strangling-stale air inside National Security Headquarters. Her senses reeled with disbelief and anger, and a seething sense of violation gripped her. She was pale as death.

"Where can I take you, Karamine?" Dro asked gently when he climbed into the car. "Do you wish to go back to the hospital, or to your apartment?"

Karamine glanced at her watch. "It's a bit late to go back to the hospital now, Dro, why don't you just take me home."

Dro Aspedyan gave the address to the driver, then turned to Karamine and held out his hand to her. His dark eyes were filled with pleading. "Karamine, my dear friend . . . how can we make restitution to you for this most distressing of indignities? I know I speak for my people, when I say we have taken you into our hearts, as one of our own, an angel of mercy in a land torn by conspiracy, suffering and death. You have been a true gift. Your efforts and contribution to the people will never be forgotten. But, because of your total involvement in the hospital and the plight of the sick and dying, you have been unaware, perhaps, of our political climate here. By clarifying the political situation I hope, sincerely, that you will come to understand a little of what happened today, and . . . forgive us?"

Karamine said nothing, but the shadow of a smile traced her mouth.

Dro continued. "The country is passing through some difficult times since our independence. True, there were elections, but, no one was prepared for such a turn of events. In our wildest dreams, not one of us believed we could ever secure our independence from the soviet union and when it happened, who was there to take over? No one but the old apparatus of the Communist Party, the entrenched bureaucracy. The people elected a president and parliament, not knowing that most of these people belong to the totalitarian soviet system". Dro shrugged his shoulders. "The president himself was an officer in the KGB. Most of the parliamentarians were hard core communists, with the exception of a few like myself". He smiled bitterly. "We felt, since they were Armenian, they would automatically welcome democracy and freedom. We were wrong." He shook his head sadly. "They are still adhering to the old communist ways that we, the new democratic thinkers are trying to change. That's why we need your help. The West must help us to throw off the oppression of seventy years of soviet domination."

"But Dro, it has been months since you've had that independence. What has been accomplished to halt these arrests, false charges and tortures? Nothing, as far as I can see, absolutely nothing. I've even heard rumors at the hospital that there have been assassinations," Karamine said glumly.

Dro held up his hand. "Don't say that, Karamine. Many of us from various parties have come together. We've formed committees and a coalition in parliament to fight these abuses of power, and believe me, Karamine, I intend to look into the matter of your arrest immediately. Armenia has had enough subjugation by tyrants. We don't need it from any of our own countrymen. I've made it clear to them that the old ways are over," Dro said firmly. "They had better get used to it, or they will find themselves charged with criminal behaviour. We will fight them with every ounce of our being. Karamine, we want you to remain here and help us in our fight for freedom. You belong here."

Karamine smiled joylessly and shook her head. "It will be a tough undertaking to wrest the power out of their hands, Dro. they have the power . . . they have the guns! What can you the defenceless people do against them?"

"Everything depends on the elections coming up next month. We can do it if we can awaken the people and excite them enough to get out and vote. The bureaucrats could be voted out and new fresh members voted into the parliament for a united Armenian people, both here and in the Diaspora. We never could have done anything without the Diaspora. We would have been lost. We need them and their influence even more now to secure a free future for our people. We need people like you, Karamine.

Karamine sighed with weariness. "Please, Dro . . . I've made up my mind. I want to go home to my husband, family and good friends. I'm tired physically, but, more so mentally and emotionally, from everything I see happening around me. My husband, Lance, has been keeping me informed as you read in that letter. He feels the present government will win the election and pass the new constitution, which will certainly give the executive branch of the government wide power. You know what that will mean. An autocratic government who will have the power to dismiss parliament, and you know what he'll do to any opposition. I fear for the people here, Dro, and the future of Armenia. I refuse to stay and be a witness to it".

Dro Aspedyan looked at Karamine long and thoughtfully. "Then, there is nothing more I can say or do that will convince you to remain?"

Karamine smiled wistfully and shook her head. "No . . . I must return. Dear Dro . . . take care of yourself, and be careful. You have enemies. I didn't like the way the head of the NSA looked at you.?

Dro laughed with thinly veiled cynicism. "Yes, we are old adversaries. Don't worry about me. I am always careful".

The car pulled up in front of Karamine's apartment. She turned to Dro and took his hand. "I'm grateful to you for acting so quickly on my behalf today, Dro. I'll never forget it, or all the kindness and support you've given me at the hospital. I know with leadership like yours, the country is in good hands. I won't worry about it".

Dro lifted her hand to his lips and kissed it lightly. I'll see you before you leave. Try to forget today's unfortunate episode."

"Of course, dear friend." Karamine stepped out and slammed the door shut. She watched the car move down her street, turn the corner, then disappear from sight. Her mood was still heavy as she fumbled for her house key, but before she could find it the door opened and Andreas embraced her with astonishment.

"Thank God! They let you go. Thank God!" Andreas gasped with relief. "What happened? We've all been frantic."

Karamine breathed a sigh of relief. "Oh Andreas! give me a minute and I'll give you the details."

"How about a hot cup of tea?" Andreas inquired walking toward the kitchen.

Karamine smiled warmly, and began removing her shoes. "Yes, that would be perfect, Andreas. It's just what I need to soothe my feathers. Where are the children?"

"Asleep. I haven't told them anything. Have your tea and tell me what happened and about your release. Did they attempt to torture you?"

"Don't be ridiculous, Andreas. They questioned me about a letter from Lance, written on senate stationery, and about Vasken, of course. I didn't know he was involved in getting arms for the fighters of Karabakh. I feel good about that, and proud of him and the way he changed, and fought for his people."

"Well some of the stories I've heard say they torture the prisoners, and some have died right there under their custody."

"I don't know . . . they didn't do anything to me except shine a hot, white light in my face during the interrogation. Perhaps if Dro hadn't intervened who knows what they might have done. All I know is I'm grateful to be home."

"I also notified the American Embassy. They were quite shaken up about it, and intended to take action immediately, but I guess Dro helped you first."

"Yes," Karamine said, reflectively sipping her tea. "I wonder what might have happened had I not had such good friends to intervene. I shudder to think of it."

"Forget that . . . you're here now, and safe."

"Safe?" Safe as they'll allow me! Andreas, I've made up my mind to go home, back where I belong. As I told Dro, I should have listened to my husband and left months ago. Things are getting worse here, and will continue right up to the elections next month, with the president controlling every phase of it. Election boards, procedures, voter registration. The government controls it all," she said despondently.

Andreas heart sank. "No, Karamine! Oh no! I always knew this day would come, but I denied it. In my heart I refused to believe that you would ever come to the point of departure from us. I know it was unreal of me, but . . . it's just that I love you," her eyes filled with tears, "and I loved your brother who saved me and brought me here, to Armenia. What would I have been without both of you? What would have happened to me, and my child? I've lost Vasken, now I'm going to lose you too."

Karamine put her arms around Andreas, and held her tight. "Andreas, you must know you will never lose me", she said softly. "We are sisters, and I will always be there for you, even though I'm miles away. Soon you'll be a doctor, and will take your place here. You'll work so hard you won't have time to think, and you'll love every minute of it".

"I'd be nothing if it weren't for you and all you've taught me," Andreas sobbed. "I'll be so lost without you, like a child without its mother."

"Come, Andreas, you're not a small child, you're a grown woman with a son to raise. You're a survivor, and you can overcome anything life may throw at you. You've overcome so much already."

"It's just that I love you, and I feel I'll never see you again if you leave. And . . . what about them?" Andreas said, nodding toward the bedroom. "You're to leave the children as well?"

Karamine covered her face with her hands, as though overcome by weariness, then, she looked up and shook her head. "The children! Andreas . . . what am I to do about the children? There's got to be a solution. I love them, but, you know Armenian children are not allowed to leave or be adopted out of the country. Something will have to be done before I leave, but, it won't change my mind. I'm going home, and that's final, Andreas." She nervously fingered the double-set of wedding-engagement rings on her hand. "I'm going to try and get through to Lance now," She walked to the telephone and dialed the operator, then looked at her watch. It's about seven in the morning there, so he should be home. She gave the instructions to the operator, who indicated she would call her back if and when she got through".

"If she's unable to get through, I'll go over to the American Embassy. They have a special direct line to Washington. I'll need to see them anyway to get my papers in order for my return".

Andreas watched her sadly. She knew Karamine was firm in her decision, and she also knew there was nothing she could say or do to change her mind.

After some minutes the telephone rang. "They're ringing the number now," she said turning to Andreas. "Oh Lance, pick up, pick up, please God, let him be there," she whispered anxiously, when she heard the telephone on the other end ring many times.

"Hello . . . hello" Lance's voice sounded distant.

"Thank God, Lance, It's me, Karamine. Can you hear me?"

"Karamine, yes I can hear you. I've been trying to get a call through to you for ages, but have been hitting a blank wall. Did you get my last communication? I sent it through the Embassy."

"Yes, I got it. Look, Lance, I don't want to waste time, so I won't go into detail, but I'm coming home. You were right . . . I should have left ages ago, before things turned sour for me."

"What do you mean before things turned sour for you?"

"Well, they arrested me, Lance."

"What!" Lance's voice exploded with outrage and fury. "They arrested you!" he exclaimed in disbelief, "how dare they arrest you, or lay a finger on you. On what grounds and by whose authority did they dare to arrest you, Karamine?"

"Lance it's all right, I'm free now. I don't want to go into detail, I just want you to know I'm coming home, as soon as I can. I've had it. The political situation here is not good, and things are going from bad to worse."

"But why arrest you, for God's sake, Karamine, it just doesn't make sense to me," Lance interrupted angrily.

"They said I was a subversive against the Republic of Armenia."

"What? You a subversive? What was their evidence?" Lance shouted in an exasperated voice.

"Well, when they searched my office they found that last letter from you . . . you wrote it on senate letterhead, remember? Anyway, you had a few references to the political situation here, also the CIA. Then there was Vasken. Apparently he was running guns and supplies to the Karabakh fighters, which was illegal at the time because Armenia was still under the Soviet Union. They said I was a spy, a member of the CIA working undercover," she laughed incredulously.

"Look, Karamine, I want you on the first plane out of there, understand? the FIRST plane."

"Yes, I do understand, Lance, and I want to come home. As I intimated, things are getting worse here in the political arena and, I too feel the elections next month will be a farce. The government controls everything and they are crushing whatever opposition they may have. I doubt. . . . "

The receiver was filled with a sudden crackling sound.

"Hello . . . hello. . . . "

There was no answer from Lance, but an operater broke in. "You've been cut off for security reasons," she explained mechanically. . . .

"Security reasons? You mean this call is being monitored?"

"All calls going out of the country are monitored for the security of our country."

"What did I say that threatened the nation's security?" Karamine said in a frustrated tone.

"You alluded to political conditions and the upcoming elections here."

"What's why I was cut off?"

"Yes"

Karamine pressed her fingernails into the palms of her hand in an effort to control herself. "Look, I'm Doctor Bagdasarian, and I demand you reconnect this call to my husband", she said with forced calmness.

"I'm sorry, that line is broken and we will not be able to help you," the operator informed her coldly.

"I don't believe this," Karamine said in an exasperated tone. She heard the buzz of the telephone as the operator hung up. "How dare they listen in to my private telephone conversation? How dare they?"

Andreas did not respond immediately. "Did they cut you off? At least you were able to get the message through that you were returning. Why did they cut you off?"

"You heard me. I mentioned the elections, and they cut me off. They were actually monitoring my call". Karamine shook her head in disgust.

The telephone rang. "Now who could that possibly be, and what more do they want," Karamine said impatiently.

"I'll get it," Andreas replied quickly, picking up the telephone.

Andreas stood with the telephone in her hand simply listening in silence for some time. Her face expressed shock, then grief. She turned her back toward Karamine who watched her curiously. "No . . . oh no . . . !" Andreas' voice was almost inaudible.

When she hung up she turned around slowly to face Karamine. "Who was that, Andreas," Karamine demanded, alarmed to see Andreas' eyes fill with tears.

When she did not respond immediately, Karamine held Andreas by the arms and shook her slightly. "Andreas . . . who was that," she demanded again, in a shaking voice.

"It's about Dro."

"Dro? What about Dro?"

"After he dropped you off, he returned to his apartment, A group of men were waiting for him. Karamine . . . they attacked both he and his driver, and beat them horribly."

Karamine did not respond, but was overcome by sudden physical weakness. She collapsed on the sofa, clutching the sides for support. She felt her breath come in short gasps, and her mouth became parched and dry. "How is he?" she managed to whisper.

Andreas covered her face with her hands. "Karamine . . . he's dead . . . he died on the way to the hospital".

Karamine closed her eyes. The ghastly, spinning shock of this latest outrage was too much to bear. She felt she was drowning in a dark sea, where each wave engulfed her more violently than the last, and kept pulling her down to a place of nameless terrors. Dear Dro, she thought, a kind and decent man who has been my good friend, and who had come to my rescue this very day. All he wanted was to serve his country and people. He fought to see Armenia a free and independent republic, and now, finally he gave his life for that cause. Oh God, is there nothing here but sorrow, pain and death?"

"Are you all right," Andreas asked apprehensively.

"Yes, I'm all right, Andreas." she said at last in a calm voice. "Today has truly been a day of infamy. Tomorrow I'll go to the American Embassy and make arrangements to leave as soon as possible. I can't take any more. If I hope to preserve my sanity, my marriage, my life itself, I have to get out now, while I'm still able."

Andreas did not reply but embraced Karamine silently, then quietly, she left her. When she closed the door, Andreas heard the sound of soft weeping.

35

$\mathbf{B}$ack in Washington, Lance was in high spirits. Karamine was coming home. At last! Her call through the American Embassy the day after his communication to her had been cut off, did much to relieve his concern regarding her safety. Her arrest as a subversive agent had infuriated as well as frustrated him, because he realized there was nothing he could have done for her. The thought filled him with a stab of fear. From the reports out of the State Department and the CIA, he knew things were getting bad, but to arrest an American senator's wife on such flimsy charges was extreme to say the least. They were treading on thin ice. He had been tempted to have all humanitarian aid cut off until the country had committed itself to a democratic constitution, with open and tamper-free elections. However, he had second thoughts about it. He wanted to give them a chance to continue, and to see if clean elections were possible. But, deep in his heart, Lance did not did not feel a democratic solution would evolve with the present government; He decided to wait and see.

At the present time, however, Karamine was his main concern. She sounded like her old self, he thought, her voice positive and filled with enthusiasm about her homecoming. He smiled happily to himself. It had been a long time since he felt such certitude about their relationship. For months he had been steeped in abysmal, overwhelming doubts regarding her love for him and their marriage. Since the incident with Varoujan, he had been deeply depressed. Again and again, Karamine had tried to reassure him of her love, but, the pressures of lonliness, distance, and work weighed heavily on his heart. He was haunted by doubts, and the specter of losing her. They were worlds apart now, with different goals and challenges. Their old world of sharing each others lives and dreams, family life, even friends seemed to have somehow crumbled away in the bustling tumult of their present and separate vocations.

But today, his agonizing doubts were lifted. For the first time in many months, Lance felt light-hearted and optimistic. Karamine had called again from the American Embassy, giving him the schedule of her return, and the flight numbers. She told him how much she was looking forward to seeing him, to coming home and picking up their lives again. Her mission in Armenia was finished. Everything she had set out to do was accomplished, and for this Lance was was relieved and comforted. She'll be content to live with me in Washington now, without the ambiguous pulls and interests that had always drawn her away, and strained our marriage, he had reasoned. Armenia and its people will always be close to both of us; some day perhaps, when war and political strife is over, when there is peace at last, we can go back together, he remembered promising her.

But today, his only thoughts were of Karamine's return. I'm like a kid on a first date, he thought with amusement, while planning their first evening at home. Everything was perfect—A team had cleaned and aired out the Boston apartment, and Lance had ordered her favorite meal—New England lobster bisque, ready to take out from the most famous sea-food restaurant in Boston; he'd bought champagne and fresh flowers, and a special gift; a 24 kt. gold seagull pin with a diamond eye—a reminder of their first date, when they sat on the rocky shores of Gloucester, watched the waves and threw the last of their picnic scraps to the seagulls. He looked at his watch. It was 1:05 Karamine was due in at 2:20 P.M. Better get on the road, he thought, remembering Boston traffic, especially the busy route leading to Logan Airport. It wouldn't do to get stuck in a traffic jam today of all days. He had rented a car the day before when he arrived in Boston from Washington, and now, he picked it up from the garage. The day was warm and Boston was in the full thrust of early summer. Sailboats dotted the Charles River, and people strolled or sat leisurely on benches in the Common. Lance was happier than he had been in months.

He entered the Callahan Tunnel along with other cars heading to the airport. The airport signs loomed up large and clear. He passed several terminals before he saw the sign marked International Arrivals, Customs. Parking the car in the airport parking lot, he walked quickly through the double doors into the terminal. Scanning the screen, he saw Karamine's flight from Armenia, via Germany was on schedule. Making a note of the arrival gate, he walked to the customs and showed them his U.S. Senate identification card. He had never used his senatorial privilege before, and he felt a slight pang of guilt about doing so now, but he was impatient to see Karamine. He wanted her cleared and out of this place and home as quickly as possible.

The Customs Inspector recognized the senator from Massachus-setts immediately. "Just wait here, Senator, we'll take care of every-thing," he said with a smile. "Can I just say, I voted for you in the last election. The media really gave you a hard time, but that television state-ment of yours," he shook his head in admiration, "that really convinced me I made the right choice. You're doing a fantastic job there in Wash-ington. Keep up the good work, Senator"

Lance beamed. Everything and everyone was with him today, he thought elatedly, as the agent took off. He put his hands in his pockets and strained to see if Karamine's plane had landed. The rope bar had been taken down, he noted happily, and a throng of people were ad-vancing toward Customs.

Suddenly he caught sight of Karamine's five-foot frame and the cus-toms official who guided her carefully along the outside of the crowd. Lance could hardly contain his joy. It seemed to him he had waited for this moment a lifetime. He waved enthusiastically and called her name. "Karamine, Karamine! Over here!" The customs man saw Lance and pointed toward him. Karamine's expression was full of anticipation and joy when she saw him, and Lance moved quickly toward her.

But he halted abruptly. His entire posture, action and facial expres-sion froze like a piece of ice-sculpture. He seemed glued to the floor. Karamine held two children by the hand! His steel-blue eyes focused on them with mixed confusion and exasperation. He continued to smile mechanically, but behind the smile he was angered and perturbed. Varoujan's children! Those two children are Varoujan's! What's going on! What in God's name is she doing with that man's children? A new fear quickened his heart.

Karamine saw the swift change in Lance's expression, and her heart sank. Her worst fears were confirmed. She knew immediately she'd made a mistake by not informing him she was bringing the children. But circumstances had made it impossible to contact him from Armenia, and then, things were so uncertain regarding the children, she didn't ac-tually get the clearance to take them until the last minute. The Armen-ian government, embarrassed by the incident of her arrest, and Dro's death, was anxious to soothe her feathers. With the intervention and help of the Armenian Prelacy, they rushed through the necessary adop-tion permits, even though this was a procedure in direct opposition to their policy of not allowing Armenian orphans to be taken out of the country. Events had moved swiftly and everything had been expedited to accomodate her wishes. Her attempts to reach Lance for his input had been simply impossible. She felt she'd have a better chance of calling him from Germany, but again, long-distance communications between planes from the airport took time, and she didn't have time to wait. Now, seeing Lance's face, she realized she should have tried harder. I should have let him know, somehow, someway, she thought, unhappily.

She dropped the children's hands and rushed to him. His embrace seemed listless and aloof. She noted the anger in his vivid blue eyes, but he kissed her warmly, despite the confusion and rage roaring through his mind. "You've brought back Varoujan's children?" he asked, guardedly.

"Lance. . . . " Karamine paused, trying to find the right words, "Lance, I'm so glad to see you, I've missed you more than you know. Please try to understand . . . I tried to get through to you, but, it was so difficult. In the end, I just gave up and relied on your love and understanding on my decision to bring the children home".

Lance stared at the children. Sabu stared back sullenly and Arax looked at him with a shy, hesitating glance. He turned back to Karamine. "But why was it necessary to bring them here, Karamine? I'm sorry, but I'm afraid I don't understand why you have the Commander's children" Lance said stubbornly, looking at them once more, then shaking his head.

"Look at me, Lance", Karamine pleaded, and please . . . please try to understand. The children are orphans. I just couldn't desert them. Their father was killed, and their mother before that. There were no other living relatives. How could I abandon them? I'd never forgive myself. On her deathbed, their mother pleaded with me to take care of them. I made a promise to her then, that I would. When their father was killed I tried to find other relatives, but there was no one. They've suffered so much loss. How could I burden them further by losing me as well? If I deserted them now, my concern for their welfare and whereabouts would plague me forever. I've cared for them since their mother died, and I've come to love them. Their youth and eagerness for life made the hardships of my stay there more tolerable. With so much death and dying all around me at the hospital, the children lifted my spirits and kept me from brooding when I came home at night. They've come to love me, Lance, and to depend on me. I'm their life now. But . . . if it's all too much for you to accept . . . the orphanage promised they would take them. Her eyes filled with tears.

In spite of himself, Lance managed a smile. He put his arms around Karamine and held her close. What am I to do, he thought helplessly. Karamine is my life too. What hurts and concerns her, concerns me as well. How could it be otherwise. In the long run, the only thing that matters is our love for each other and being together. I realize it all the more when I'm holding her like this. He turned to look at the children who had been observing him from a few paces away. He motioned them to come to him. They didn't respond. They looked toward Karamine who smiled, nodded her head then beckoned to them. Arax came first. Her dark eyes were filled with innocence, but reflected pain and sorrow beyond her years. A black fringe of lashes shadowed her cheeks. Lance softened. A true 'daughter of Armenia', he thought, as he bent down and patted her raven-black hair. Sabu hung back. This was the man who had attacked his father, and now, he closed his fists defiantly. "Sabu, come here," Karamine called to him. The boy's expression reflected both fear and agression. He put his arms around Karamine and hugged her. Lance knelt on one knee and touched his shoulder lightly. "Sabu," he said gently, staring directly into the boy's eyes, "I know you and I got off to a bad start, but, let's make a new start . . . you, me and your sister. I can't replace your dad, but, if you'll allow me, perhaps I can be the best friend you've ever had." Lance extended his hand. "Friends?" he questioned. The boy hesitated a moment, then looked to Karamine, and next to his sister. Both seemed to reassure him. He looked at Lance's outstretched hand, then trustingly, he nodded his head and took Lance's hand.

The airport scene swarmed with jostling crowds and loud flight announcements. "Look, let's get the luggage and get out of here," said Lance, looking around. I'll go get the car, and meet you all at the front entrance."

Karamine placed her arms protectively around the two children and led them toward the Baggage Claims. Her heart was lighter than it had been in years. Driving from the parking lot, Lance smiled to himself, and shook his head. Karamine really has a knack for making me do things I hadn't planned on, but in the end, it's usually for the best. Seeing the three of them waiting for him now at the front entrance, he was touched by Karamine's expression. Is it because I haven't seen her in such a long time, or does Karamine look younger and more beautiful than I've ever seen her, he wondered. She looks natural with those two children. He pulled up by the front entrance, and jumped out to open the trunk. When they packed the luggage, Lance slammed the door shut, then looked at all three. "Okay", he said with a smile, "Let's get the show on the road, LET'S GET THIS FAMILY HOME."

EPILOG

The situation in Nagorno-Karabakh has changed since the publication of this book. Both sides -- Karabakh Defence Forces and the Azeri government -- have agreed to a cease-fire which has lasted a number of years. The Azeri government however, refuses to negotiate a settlement with the newly formed **Republic of Karabakh**; instead, they demand complete capitulation of all territories lost in the war. Leaders in **Artsakh,** (which is the original Armenian name for the territory), are seeking face-to-face meetings with Azerbaijan, with no preconditions whatsoever. As of this date, the Azerbaijan government has refused, and a stale-mate involving any peace talk is the result.

To the present day, the Turkish government is firmly allied with Azerbaijan -- they continue to supply the Azeri with tanks, aircraft and arms, along with training of the Azerbaijan army. With measures such as the blockade of Armenia and refusal to negotiate with the Republic of Karabakh, the Turkish government is attempting to abolish all hope of the people of Artsakh for independence.

With help from the United States and Russia, an Organization For Security and Cooperation (*O.S.C.E.*), otherwise known as the *Minsk Group*, has been formed for the purpose of peace keeping and confidence building, in the area. For now, they have a cease fire, but nothing else has been accomplished by way of negotiating a lasting peace treaty. Unfortunately, American oil Company interests in the Caspian oil fields of Azerbaijan and Turkey have subverted the objectives of the *O.S.C.E.*

In Armenia itself, however, the situation has changed for the better. New elections were held and monitored by outside election organizations. Because of these outside election organizations, corruption and fraud have been drastically reduced. The newly elected President of the Armenian Republic is working hard with all political parties of Armenia, as well as with the Diaspora to create a spirit of harmony and cooperation. A new Constitution has been written, and for the purpose of improving the economy, free trade policies are encouraged with the west, and private business invited.

With the help of the Diaspora, Armenia and Artsakh are optimistic about the future, as they continue to look for a lasting peace with their neighbors.

GAROONG *(The Crane)*
Peter Khanbegian

In his first novel, *Peter Khanbegian* tells the story of his people -- the Armenians. The saga begins with two friends escaping a bloody massacre, and arriving in America the early part of the 1900's. Their story is traced through three generations, from Victorian Boston to the college campus of the sixties.

In a rare merge of fiction and history, this quick-paced saga grips the reader with its courageous men and bold-spirited women.

In its universal themes of love and hatred, revenge and forgiveness, the author gives us a compelling novel, as well as a fresh view of the struggle of a people overcoming odds to find freedom and identity in a new land.

Hard cover 465 p. 6x9   **$18.95**
Post & Handl.   **$ 2.50**
ISBN 1-878696-00-9
(Canadian orders, add exchange plus $2.95)

"**Garoong** offers an excellent addition to the not widely known but frequently covered subject of Armenian ethnicity in modern American literature."
                              AIM Magazine --*Dr. Fred Assadourian*

"Khanbegian's sweeping saga about three generations in an Armenian family, and their levels of conflict with each other, might be recorded as one of the greatest works in Armenian-American literature, next to Saroyan's *The Human Comedy.*"
                              Armenian Weekly --*E. G. Avedissan*

WRIGHT PUBLISHING HOUSE
Gofftown Falls Rd. Box 5913
Manchester NH 03108